CW00741869

JOHN DAVI

RUNNING
AS FAST AS I CAN

DON QUIXOTE PRESS
GREENVILLE, OH

2023 Don Quixote Press
Greenville, OH.
Copyright 2023
All rights reserved.

LIBRARY OF CONGRESS CATALOGING-IN-PUBLICATION DATA
Graham, John David
Running As Fast As I Can: a novel / John David Graham
Paperback ISBN 979-8-9889808-1-0
Hardcover ISBN 979-8-9889808-3-4
Ebook ISBN 979-8-9889808-0-3
Audiobook ISBN 979-8-9889808-2-7

Library of Congress Control Number: 2023919047

First Edition

www.johndavidgraham.com

I am haunted by memories. They come to me at night, in the solitude of my room. A long procession parading by me, taking me back to those times long gone, people long dead. A lifetime of pain and joy, love and loss. All that remain now are memories. Yet regret, like age, is inevitable. If only.... How many times have I said that all these years?

Daniel Robinson

CONTENTS

PROLOGUE

SALEM HILL, OHIO, 2016. I've been the solitary inhabitant of this bedroom for the past three decades, but I've never really been alone. The ghosts from my haunted past parade by every night, filling my mind and taking me back to times long gone, people now dead and places forgotten by others. Yet to me they are very much alive and with me still. A lifetime of love and loss, but all that remain now are memories.

I've been surprised how quickly I've aged since my diagnosis. My hair turned grey long ago, but it's gotten thin, hardly enough to comb now. And my skin is wrinkled from all the weight I've lost. Even climbing these old stairs, something I've done a thousand times, now requires me to stop at nearly every step just to catch my breath. My eyes are beginning to fail me, making driving difficult, especially in the dark when headlights glare too bright. I didn't tell the kids, but they know, and they worry, especially Jonathan. He said he's seen too many accidents caused by old people. *Old people?* I never thought that would mean me, but it does now, I guess.

Perhaps that is why I find myself welcoming my nocturnal visitors. The past seems more clear, even more comforting than the present.

"Dad, we need to get going or we'll miss our flight," Emma calls from the bottom of the stairs. I smile, but I don't get up from my chair.

1

Of all the kids, Emma is the most like her mother. She doesn't have her red hair. Her sister has that. But every time Emma walks in the room and looks at me, I see Kate. The tilt of her head, the look in her eyes, and especially the way she taps her foot when she's upset. Obviously she's upset now. But not with me, and not even because I'm moving in with her family. She's glad for that. But like I said, she's just like her mother. She's only trying to protect me.

"Just looking at a note," I answer and gently unfold a yellowed piece of paper. I doubt she heard me, but it doesn't matter. Emma knows what I'm doing. She's seen me do this too many times these past thirty years. Even when she was a little girl and I was still drowning in my grief, she found me sitting here reading this note, tears running down my cheek. She always crawled up on my lap and "hugged away the hurt," as she called it. That's when I first knew she had her mother's heart.

The kids told me to sell the house, especially after they were grown and married. "Move away from Salem Hill," they said. "Come live with us. The grandkids need you."

I thought about it a couple times, but then I remember how Kate looked at me when we first saw this neglected, broken, shell of a house. The sagging porch, the damaged windows, the leaking roof. She was tapping her foot before we even got in the door. But together, we slowly transformed this ruined building no one wanted into more than just a house.

It was a healing place when I bared my great shame to her. It was a refuge from the hatred and violence that surrounded us when that girl disappeared and everyone blamed me. Especially after that horrid night at the city council meeting, this house has been my sanctuary, where I always have Kate with me. But now that I know my end is near, this house doesn't have the same hold on me it once had.

"Dad," Emma calls a second time, but I don't answer. I just caress the locket I've worn all these years. She can wait a few more minutes. I'm not ready to leave all my memories behind...not yet. I need to look around this bedroom one more time. *I need to feel you lying next to me again, Kate. I need to remember how lost I was until you saved me.*

I need to remember all of it—from the beginning.

CHAPTER 1
A BROKEN WINGED BIRD CAN'T FLY

CLAIRTON, PENNSYLVANIA, 1960. I can still see that model airplane I built when I was twelve years old. I was delivering newspapers after school when I first saw it hanging in the window of Thompson's Hobby Shop. I nearly fell off my bike! *Is that what I think it is?* Slamming on my brakes, I ran up to the store and pressed my face against the glass. It was! An authentic P-40 Tomahawk fighter plane—just like the one Frankie and I saw John Wayne fly last Saturday at the Clairton Theater. A genuine Flying Tiger—and it's for sale!

I rode to Thompson's store the next day after school, and the day after that, and stood on the sidewalk, staring at that beautiful plane.

"You gotta see it, Frankie. I swear it's the same one the Duke flew when he shot down all those Japs." Frankie Denardo lived on the same block with me since we started first grade together at Walnut Avenue School.

"I think it *is* the same one. God, she's a beaut!" he muttered, staring through the window. "Look at all those decals... and those wings must be two feet wide. I never seen a model plane that big."

"Me neither, Frankie. And it's for sale. Can you believe it?"

"I bet it costs a hundred bucks."

"Naw. I checked and it's only nine dollars and ninety-nine cents."

Frankie stepped back from the window and grabbed his bike. "Don't matter 'cause you ain't got ten bucks..." He smirked. "...unless you plan to ask your old man to buy it for Christmas."

I shrugged, then jumped on my bike. "Yeh, right. I got a better chance asking you for the money."

Frankie dug into his pocket and pulled out two nickels. "Here you go, Robinson. Merry Christmas!" He shoved them into my coat pocket. "Besides, Mr. Thompson is probably gonna sell that plane to some rich kid from Clairton Heights anyway. So forget about it and go with me to the Clairton Theater. There's another John Wayne movie playing."

Sometimes Frankie could be a real pain. I *had* to get that plane... But how...?

Mr. Thompson is gonna sell that plane to some rich kid in Clairton Heights. That was all I thought about the whole week. Every day after school I rode by the store, just to be sure it was still in the window. By Saturday it was driving me crazy. *Maybe there's some sort of payment plan, 'cause of Christmas...* I biked to Mr. Thompson store, took a deep breath, and walked up to the counter.

Mr. Thompson saw me, but kept talking to his customer. Just then two kids wearing high school letter jackets came in. "I'll be right with you boys," he said, nodding toward them. One of them pointed toward my plane and said something.

God, I hoped they're not gonna buy it!

"That P-40 Tomahawk fighter plane..." I called out to Mr. Thompson, but he didn't even look at me.

Those high school kids both laughed. I bit my lip.

"Mr. Thompson," I called out, louder this time. "That P-40 Tomahawk fighter plane you got hanging in the window. It's still for sale. Right?" He stopped talking to his customer, barely looking my way. "You're too young for that model, kid. Besides, it's too expensive for you," he grumbled and turned away. Those boys laughed again, and my face went red as I walked quickly out of the store.

My plane was all I thought about that night, all day Sunday, and in every Monday class. As soon as the bell rang, I pedaled as fast as I could to Thompson's Hobby Shop again. "Thank God, it's still there!" Dropping my bike on the sidewalk, I ran into the store.

"Mr. Thompson! About that fighter plane..."

He groaned. "Look, kid. I told you that plane's too expensive for you. Don't waste my time."

I dug into my pocket and pulled out a piece of paper. "Look here!" I said, holding it in front of him. "I make sixty-five cents a week on my paper route. That's two-dollars and sixty cents a month. That means I can pay for it in four months."

He shook his head. "Cash only, kid. Come back when you got ten bucks."

"But..."

Before I could say another word, he was gone. I stood there, my face hot again, then turned around slowly and left. "I'll be back in March," I called out, more for me than him.

I rode past the store two, maybe three times a week. And I saved my newspaper money—sixty-five cents a week, every week through December... January... Frankie bugged me every Saturday to take in a movie, especially when he saw that John Wayne's newest movie about Davy Crocket was coming to the Clairton Theater. But I told him no way. February dragged by, and every night I counted my money. Almost there...

Finally, March came. About time!

Early Saturday morning, as soon as Mr. Thompson opened his store, I was standing at the counter, smiling ear to ear. "Remember me? I'm here to buy that P-40 Tomahawk fighter plane you got in the window." I announced, emptying my peanut butter jar of nickels, dimes and pennies all over his counter.

He looked down at my money, then at me. Slowly, a smile spread across his face. "It's got a working motor. You'll need some fuel to go with it. That's another seventy-nine cents."

Maybe he was impressed a kid like me saved all that money, like I was one of his regular customers or something. I glanced quickly at my plane in the window one more time, imagining it soaring through the air, then pulled out my last handful of coins, counting them out on the counter without saying a word.

Mr. Thompson scooped up my coins, dropped them all into the register, and slammed shut the drawer. Then he reached for a large box on the shelf behind him and set it in front of me with a THUD! I stared at it, stunned. "You got to put it together, son," he grunted. "But I gotta warn you, it's the most difficult model I sell. You sure you want to buy it?"

"No problem, Mr. Thompson." I reached for my new airplane. "More sure than anything in the whole world."

He started to walk away, then stopped. "One more thing. The box says it can fly, but I don't recommend a kid like you try that. If you can build it, just keep it on your dresser or something."

I nodded, but all I saw was my beautiful P-40 Tomahawk fighter plane flying higher and higher—with me at the controls, just like John Wayne!

Finally, it was all mine!

It wasn't easy putting it together, especially in the dim light of the 40-watt bulb hanging from my bedroom ceiling. And it didn't help that our old coal furnace never put out enough heat to reach my room. The cold air blowing through my cracked window stiffened my fingers, making it nearly impossible to cut all those hundred little balsa wood pieces. More than once I dropped one of them and had to grope frantically all over the floor in the dark. I swore at that bulb every time it flickered and I made the wrong cut.

"There's gotta be a better way..." I muttered, blowing on my fingers to keep them warm. "I got it!" I draped a blanket over the window to block the cold, then snuck out to the garage and switched out the 100-watt bulb above my dad's work bench. He was too drunk most of the time to ever use any of his tools anyway.

Now I could finally build my beautiful plane.

First, I fitted the balsa wood fuselage together, slowly cutting each piece, then gluing them together with a special hardener for extra strength. The wings took forever because the spars had to be cut perfect, then pinned to the guide sheet while I glued a dozen ribs between them. The silk paper skin was even harder because it kept tearing. Finally, I realized I needed to sand the balsa wood real smooth, like it said in the instructions. This time I didn't tear a single piece when I wrapped it over the fuselage and wings. I didn't know what *EZ Dope* was, but the instructions said to paint the skin with it, and the next morning the paper skin felt as hard as metal—and shiny, too.

Now it was finally ready for paint. I picked a camouflage color, then added the decals, and even a shark's mouth on the nose, exactly like John Wayne's plane. My P-40 Tomahawk fighter plane looked... perfect! I stepped back, smiling.

I don't recommend you fly it. More for display. But I bet it could...

I need to show it to someone. But who? My mother was in one of her moods again and wouldn't come out of her room. But my father was watching television, and from what I could tell, he wasn't drunk yet.

"What do you think?" I asked and held my new airplane in front of him.

He didn't look up, but just took a long drink from his beer and kept staring at the baseball game on the television.

"It's an authentic P-40 Tomahawk fighter plane. You know, a Flying Tiger, like the ones that flew in World War II. You were in the war, weren't you, Dad? Did you ever fly in one of these planes?"

He still didn't answer, or even look at me. "Fuckin' Pirates," was all he muttered before swilling another long drink from his bottle, then wiped his mouth with his sleeve.

"Mr. Thompson said it was too hard for someone my age, but I built it all myself. It wasn't easy to put the frame together, 'cause it's made of balsa wood and covered with a silk paper I brushed with special stuff to make it real hard. Want to see all the decals?" I turned it around slowly, making sure the authentic shark's mouth faced him. "It's not one of those cheap planes with rubber bands. This one's got a real motor, and it can fly maybe a hundred feet in the air. You guide it with wires that attach to the wings. But I'm gonna keep it on my dresser 'cause it's real special."

I wanted my father to say something about my plane. *Nice job. Looks like it was hard to build. I'm really proud of you, son.* But he didn't say anything while I stood in front of him, anxiously holding up my airplane like some sort of offering to the gods.

"Want to see how the motor works?" *Maybe he'll like that.*

After what seemed like forever, he slammed the bottle on the table, gave me that irritated look I saw so many times, and shouted, "You're blocking the fuckin' game!"

He didn't hit me, not like he sometimes did, but I felt my lip tremble and my eyes burn wet with tears, like he just punched me hard in the stomach. I quickly turned away and wiped my face. Without saying another word, I walked out of the room and went straight to the backyard. I set my new airplane on the ground, filled the tank with fuel and flicked the propeller several times until the motor screamed to life. Grabbing my father's Zippo lighter from my pocket, I flipped open the lid, hit the striker twice to get a steady flame and held it under the tail until the oil paint on the skin ignited. Then I launched my wonderful new plane into the air.

For a few wonderful seconds, my special P-40 Tomahawk fighter with all those authentic decals flew up and up, just like I always imagined. But when the flames engulfed the wings, it suddenly veered sharply to the right, then down and down in a death spiral until it crashed to the ground. I wanted to cry again as the acrid smoke from my beautiful burning plane drifted toward me, but this time I didn't shed a single tear. I never built another model airplane.

———

It was my sixteenth birthday when Frankie showed up at my door and said he was taking me to the Clairton Theater for a John Wayne double feature. His father worked in the mill and frequented anyone of a dozen Clairton bars, just like my old man. We were in a lot of classes together, and both of us had newspaper routes since the seventh grade. He was as close to a best friend as I ever had.

"Happy birthday, Daniel," he announced, holding up two tickets.

I wasn't expecting anything, even from Frankie. "Sure. Love to see the Duke," I said.

"You need to tell anyone where you're going? I mean 'cause it's your birthday?"

The old man was passed out on the couch again, and neither of my brothers cared much what I did today.

And Mum...she wouldn't even know I was gone. I saw the pattern too many times. The crying, the threats to hurt herself, the long periods of silence when she stayed hidden in her bedroom, praying in the dark, not seeing or hearing anyone. She was better when Grandma Emma was alive. I was maybe five or six, and Billy wasn't even born then. I didn't remember much about her, just that she had blue eyes like Mum and me. But what I did remember is Mum would take us to Grandma's house when the old man was on one of his benders. She always made this raspberry cake for us. We even picked the berries for her in the backyard, and that made us feel real special. God, I loved those visits. But when she died...Mum just wasn't the same after that. The neighbor kids all said she was crazy. I was too young to know what crazy meant the first time it happened. But after a half dozen trips to Woodville State Hospital over the past ten years, I understood all too well now.

"Nah. It'll be okay."

Four hours later, the Duke was all we talked about as we biked down Wilson Street. "How tall do you think John Wayne is, Frankie. Six-two?"

"Nah. Six-four. I read that in a magazine. That's why Maureen O'Hara was so crazy about him in that movie. Tall guys get all the girls."

"Yeh, Frankie. Maybe we'll both be as tall as the Duke by our senior year. Then we'll get all the girls. too."

"Yeh, maybe."

My brother Robert greeted us in the alley behind our house. "Hey, shit head. Where you two been?"

Frankie gave him the finger and nodded toward me. "See you tomorrow," and pedaled down the alley.

"Goddammit, woman! What the hell's wrong, you stupid bitch?" the old man screamed from the house, obviously really mad about something—or nothing. It didn't matter.

"What set him off this time?" I asked, dropping my bike by the fence.

"Who cares?" Robert glared at the house. He was the oldest and tried to protect me and my little brother Billy from the old man, but he was never strong enough. None of us were. He always got the brunt of the old man's anger for any reason, real or imagined. Like closing a door too hard. That was the worst thing we could do when he was drunk, except when it was something else. We never knew what it would be.

"Fuckin' bitch. Get outta the way!" the old man screamed again. I looked at Robert, but he ignored me, picking up a rock and throwing it hard at Mrs. Martini's cat in the alley. It squealed and scrambled up the maple tree beside her house. Mrs. Martini lived next door and complained about everything we did. She was sitting on her porch, as usual, and she yelled something. But he ignored her too.

"God, I can't stand living with him!" Robert shouted, then grabbed another rock and hurled it down the alley, this time even harder.

"That's it!" He looked at me like he realized something obvious. "He's just *him*."

I had no idea what he meant. He was always saying crazy stuff like that anyway, especially about the old man. Most of the time, I paid no attention to him.

"I'm going to Frankie's house." I grabbed my bike. But Robert caught my arm and jerked me back.

"You really don't get it, do you?" He nearly spit the words at me. "You still want to believe this is a normal family. Listen to Mum crying, for god's sake. Does that sound normal to you?"

I didn't need to hear him rant again about what a lousy family we had, not today, not ever, so I didn't answer. But he wouldn't let it go.

"You ever call him father? Or even Dad?" When I still didn't answer, he squeezed my arm. "I didn't think so."

I tried to pull away, but he squeezed harder. "Names like that mean we got a relationship, maybe even some affection for *him*. But I got no relationship, and I'll guarantee you, no affection. To me he's just *him*— some abusive stranger who happens to live in the house with us."

He pushed me back, grabbed another rock and threw it toward Mrs. Martini's house. "Brutto figlio di puttana bastardo!" she yelled at Robert, but he just muttered something about foreigners, gave her the finger and stomped down the alley.

———

After that, Robert tried to avoid the old man as best he could, at least until a week later when he planned a special date with a girl who lived fifteen miles away in Pittsburgh. He said he wanted to borrow the old man's new fire engine red '64 Chevy Impala SS coupe. We both knew he bought it that spring to impress a neighbor woman he had tried to seduce. He always treated that car better than us and Robert detested him all the more for it.

"You sure you wanna do that?" I asked. "Nobody drives that car except him." But Robert never listened to me. He walked into the living room where the old man was watching the Pirates game on television and finishing another beer. His eyes were glassy, a sure sign he was pretty drunk already.

"Can I use the car Saturday?" Robert tried to act like it was just a normal question, but his jaw clenched like it always did when he had to talk to the old man.

He ignored Robert.

"I got an important date Saturday and I need the car." The words stuck in his throat, and he swallowed hard. Sweat broke out on his forehead. "I'll put gas in it."

The old man took a long drink, mumbled something about "another goddamn losing season," and kept staring at the game. The Pirates hadn't had a winning season in four years and he was not happy about it. Robert looked toward Mum in the kitchen, as if asking her to somehow intercede. But we both knew she had no more influence over him than we did.

"William, he's a good driver and he needs the car Saturday night," she finally said with little enthusiasm. "Let him use it, will you?"

He mumbled something. "I think he said yes," Mum told Robert, then went back into her room and closed the door.

My brother spent most of Saturday afternoon nervously getting ready for his date. I was standing in front of the mirror pasting my hair with Brylcream, when he opened the bathroom door without knocking like he always did. "I need to take a shower."

He pushed by me and turned on the water. He did that a lot, though most of the time I ignored it. I figured it was because he was two years older and used to getting his way. Or maybe because he was shorter than me. He never said anything, but I know it bothered him a lot.

Yet he had a way of knowing how to get under my skin, then jabbing until I reacted. He knew I hated my hair—shit brown—that's what he called it. And that lousy cowlick didn't help. I'd been trying for an hour to get it to lay flat. But I hated my freckles even more, and he reminded me of them every chance he got. "While you're at it, try scrubbing off those face farts." he said, pulling back the curtain and stepping into the tub.

"Screw you, Robert." I shot back too quickly. But he just stuck his head around the shower curtain and smiled that same irritating way he always did when he knew he really got to me, and that made me even madder. All I could think to do was flush the toilet and walk out. Hearing him scream about getting scalded made me smile all the way to Frankie's house.

When I got back two hours later and found Robert standing in front of the mirror in our bedroom, I'd already forgotten what he said about my freckles. "Did the old man say anything to you about tonight?" I asked.

"You mean did I get any advice from *him* about my date? God, you still expect him to be a real father. Well, that ain't gonna happen—and you know it. Remember that airplane you built when you were a kid? All I expect is the car key! That's it." He looked in the mirror again, straightened his tie for the tenth time, glanced at me and muttered, "Wish me luck," and walked away.

"Okay. Leaving now. Can I have the key?" Robert asked when he saw the old man in the living room.

He didn't answer.

"I gotta go now. Can I have the key?"

The old man took a long, deliberate pull on his bottle and stared at the television. Pittsburgh was playing Cincinnati tonight and the Pirates' manager Danny Murtaugh was being interviewed about the game. The old man hated Cincinnati, especially this year because they were in second place and far ahead of the Pirates.

He ignored Robert.

"I'm gonna be late. I gotta go. Can I have the key?" Robert's jaw clenched and the blood vessels in his neck bulged.

"Goddamn Murtaugh," the old man muttered and grabbed a cigarette from the pack on the table, trying several times to light it. He mumbled something about his lighter, yanked open the drawer and fumbled through it until he found a match, then slowly lit his cigarette. His eyes narrowed as he took a long drag, then slumped back into his chair, grabbing his beer from the table, all while Robert stood in front of him and seethed.

We all learned early on never to cross the old man, especially when he was watching the Pirates game. All those years working in the mill had hardened his muscles, and his temper, to the level that we all knew to give him a wide berth, even when slouched drunk in his chair. Robert never talked about it, but I still remember that one time he changed the channel when the old man went back to the kitchen for another beer. He hit Robert so hard with his fist that it was two weeks before he could see out of his left eye. But now Robert looked ready to avenge every single abuse over the past eighteen years. His jaw clenched even tighter and his eyes bulged wide, all while his face turned crimson.

"You said I could have the car tonight," Robert screamed. "I made plans and now, dammit, I'm using the car!" Before the old man could say anything, Robert lunged for the key on the table and ran out the door.

"You little goddamn prick!" the old man muttered when his drunken haze finally cleared enough for him to realize what happened. He staggered to his feet and threw his bottle toward the door where it shattered against the wall, nearly hitting me in the head. I saw him angry lots of times, but not like this. I couldn't move. I stood there while he stumbled past me and out the door after Robert, who was now struggling to unlock the car door. The old man grabbed him, but Robert spun and knocked him to the ground, then jumped in the car, slamming the door shut and locking it.

The old man staggered to his feet and yanked the door handle so hard again and again I thought it would break. "Open this goddamn door or um gonna bust it open!"

Mum came out of her room and walked past me to the yard. I

followed her. "Can't you do something?" I asked, but she had that same frightened look I saw too many times. I didn't think she even heard me. She just whimpered like she always did when he got violent.

Robert tried frantically to get the key in the ignition, but he shook so much he dropped it twice. That only made the old man madder, and he beat on the window with his fist. "You little goddamn prick!" he shouted again and stumbled to the front of the car. Even in his drunken stupor, somehow he managed to unlatch the hood, yanking it open. Climbing now on the bumper, he grabbed for the coil wire. "I'll teach you to steal my fuckin' car!"

Billy came out of the house and stood behind Mum, shaking and holding onto her dress.

Robert finally got the key in the ignition and the engine roared to life. Slamming the transmission into reverse, he floored the accelerator and careened down the street with the old man still standing on the bumper, while desperately hanging onto the radiator. "Stop the fuckin' car!" he screamed.

Robert swerved left and right, nearly hitting several parked cars, until a half block down the street, the old man fell off the bumper, slammed onto the pavement and rolled over several times. My brother didn't seem to notice, or care, but kept going down the street in reverse with the hood still up. At the corner of Walnut Avenue, he finally stopped the car, got out, slammed the hood shut and drove off.

The old man didn't move for several minutes. Then slowly he stumbled to his feet and staggered back toward us. I froze. I didn't know what to do, so I just held my breath and prayed while Mum grabbed Billy. None of us moved, or even breathed as he limped by, into the house and slammed the door so hard the windows shook. I looked at Mum, still too scared to speak. She didn't say anything either, but slumped to the curb with a blank look on her face, like she wouldn't hear me anyway. Billy and I didn't know what to do, so we just sat down with her, staring at our house, hoping—praying the old man wouldn't come out again.

"You were right, Robert," I mumbled. "He's just *him*."

The three of us sat there for maybe an hour, not saying anything until Mum finally stood up. "He'll be passed out on the couch now," she said without even looking at us, like this was something normal, and walked back into the house. We followed, but she went into her bedroom and shut the door. Billy and I stared at each other for several minutes, then went to our room and laid on our beds in the dark, still too scared to speak.

Sometime past midnight, Robert climbed in the window and got into his bed without getting undressed. I had a hundred questions for him, but didn't say anything. I just stared at the ceiling, worried what would happen to us now. It must have been a couple hours later. I'm not sure when. It was still dark outside when Robert asked of no one in particular, like it was something he'd been thinking about all night, "Ever wonder why Mum married him?"

"I think she did it to get out of Coal Valley." he said before I could answer, like he was talking more to himself.

I knew she grew up there. That was the poor part of Clairton, downwind from the steel mill that covered a thousand acres along the Monongahela River. I hated going anywhere near that place because all the smoke made my lungs burn for days. She never talked about Coal Valley, and I never thought about it until now.

"Maybe," was all I said.

Near dawn Robert got up and left the room. I followed him because I was afraid there would be another fight. When he saw the old man still passed out on the couch surrounded by empty and broken bottles, he walked down the hall to the kitchen where he found Mum. She was sitting at the table with the same dirty dishes that had been left there for days, staring out the window like she did most of the time. On her lap was Grandma's old recipe book. I thought she had been looking through it again, like she always did when she was upset. It seemed to make her feel better.

"I'm glad you're up," he said. "I didn't want to leave without saying goodbye."

She didn't look up.

"I can't stay here. Not after last night."

"What do you mean?" she asked, but with little emotion, like she wasn't listening.

Robert nodded toward the living room. "I'm leaving. I've had enough of him. I gotta go."

"Where? What are you going to do?" She looked up at Robert now, like his words finally sunk in.

"Join the Army, so I can get as far away from him as I can. I just wanted to say good-bye before I left."

She started to cry softly, and he tried to hug her, but it was awkward and she didn't respond. Robert turned to me instead. Grabbing my hand, he shook it. "Take care of her for me," he said, nodding toward the old man. Then he opened the door and left.

Mum didn't say anything, but I knew what she was thinking. I saw that frightened look too many times. All of us were going to pay now for what Robert did. I wanted to leave too, but I was just sixteen, with two years left in high school. I couldn't join the Army. I had nowhere to go.

"Don't worry, Mum," was all I said, but I was scared too.

She didn't say anything, but just pulled Grandma's recipe book close to her.

CHAPTER 2
WE LIVE AS WE DREAM—ALONE

CLAIRTON, 1964. None of us mentioned Robert after he left. He was gone and we did what we had to do—avoid the old man and pray he wouldn't come after us now. I spent all my time with Frankie, mostly hanging out at the Clairton Park. The city had a great pool that only cost twenty-five cents, so we rode our bikes there, usually around eleven when it opened, and stayed until dark when it closed. On most days we just laid on our towels by the snack bar and stared at Annette Morowski in her new pink bikini. Frankie even tried a couple times to impress her by going off the high diving board, but all he could ever do was a stupid cannonball, and that impressed no one—especially Annette Morowski.

"You know, Frankie, you're wasting your time thinking you got a shot with Annette. She's way out of our league."

"I don't think so," Frankie took a big bite of his Zero bar. That was our favorite pool food. And Peppermint Patties—especially when both were frozen because they lasted even longer.

"Her old man is some sort of boss at the mill and she's from Clairton Heights. You think she even notices guys like us? Don't waste time killing yourself on the high dive for her."

"Screw you, Robinson, and get me a Coke. I'm going off one more time and I plan to celebrate when I get back."

One thing I always liked about Frankie was his confidence. He was only five-foot nothing and weighed maybe one-hundred and thirty pounds of pimpled skin and bones, but he acted like he was God's gift to women, even when those women—like Annette Morowski—didn't seem to notice or care.

———

"You wanna come back tomorrow?" he asked when we grabbed our bikes at the gate.

"Can't. It's Sunday. Going to church, but you're welcome to come with me."

"I'm Catholic."

"Yeah, right." I shook my head, kicked up the stand and started pedaling toward the street. "When was the last time you were in church?"

"Christmas...I think the old man was sober that day and he made us go."

"No way. That was two years ago, 'cause I remember your old man got in a fight outside the church and the cops had to come get him. Besides, Christmas doesn't count," I said as we coasted together down the hill from the park. "Even my old man went to church once on Christmas."

We pedaled on in silence for several blocks, but I was still thinking about it when we reached Walnut Avenue. "How about we go to the pool after church?" I finally said. "Besides, you'll like Pastor Duncan. Sometimes he takes a bunch of us to Isaly's for Klondike bars. What do you say?"

"Klondike bars? God, I love those. Maybe." Frankie pushed hard on his pedals and cut in front of me.

"You bike like an old lady!" he called out as he quickly disappeared in the shadows.

"Screw you, Denardo!" I hollered back and pedaled hard to catch up with him, but he was too far ahead and couldn't hear me.

God, I loved those days at the pool with Frankie.

———

Mum spent most of the summer in her room. I don't know if she missed Robert, or even thought about him. I just know she never mentioned his name. Billy was different, maybe because he was just ten and Robert always tried to keep the old man from hurting him too much. Now he was gone and Billy looked to me for help. He didn't come right out and say it, but it was the way he followed me around the house, always asking if he could come with me and Frankie to the pool.

"Here comes the cowboy again." That was Frankie's name for Billy because he always wore that stupid red checkered cowboy shirt Robert gave him for his tenth birthday.

"Wait for me, Daniel," Billy called from the yard, and ran to the alley where we were getting on our bikes.

"I'm not gonna carry him on my handlebars again. I nearly got killed when I tried that," Frankie complained. "Just leave him," he yelled, pedaling down the alley.

I didn't want to leave Billy alone at the house, but he was right. What was I supposed to do? I ignored him and pedaled after Frankie.

Billy cried a lot that summer.

———

It was sometime after school started in September and I was stuck at the house with Billy. For some reason he wasn't bothering me as much as he did all summer, so I let him hang out with me in the backyard until Frankie arrived. We weren't doing much when Mum came out of the house. She just looked at us and smiled. I noticed that because I hadn't seen her smile in a long time, and I remember thinking how pretty she was. I never thought of my mother as pretty before, but seeing her smile now made her pale blue eyes shine, like she was really happy, or at least what I thought happy would look like at our house.

"I'm glad you're playing with Billy," was all she said. But then the old man screamed something from inside the house and that familiar cloud of sadness engulfed her again. She turned away and walked back into the house. For just that briefest of moments we felt like a normal family. It felt good.

———

We didn't see much of the old man after Robert left. I figured he spent most of his time working at the mill all day and closing down the bars at night. All I knew for sure, he wasn't at the house and we didn't have to face him. That was, until sometime in January when he came home drunk out of his mind.

"Fuckin' bosses laid me off!" he yelled at Mum. She didn't say anything, but I saw that same worried look on her face every time he bought something we couldn't afford. She walked back into her room and shut the door.

He spent his time at home now, drinking whiskey and yelling at us —mostly at Billy. He was the weakest one because he still wanted *him* to be a real father. He still wanted us to be normal. I gave up on that delusion when Robert left.

"Get outta the front of the fuckin' television, you horse's ass!" That was his favorite name for Billy—horse's ass.

I was sitting at the kitchen table when I heard him. "Goddammit! I said move!" I turned and looked into the living room just when he threw a bottle at Billy, barely missing his head. It smashed into the screen of the brand new color television he bought on payments for himself two weeks ago. There was a loud *POP*, and the screen went blank.

"I told you get outta the fuckin' way. Now look what you done!" he shouted, grabbing Billy by the arm and throwing him hard against the wall. Billy started to cry, and that made the old man even madder. He jerked him up by his arm, this time much harder, making him bawl out in pain. Mum opened her bedroom door, and that's when we both heard it—*SNAP!* Billy screamed so loud I thought he was dying.

"Billy!" I yelled, jumping up from my chair just as Mum shouted at the old man like I never heard before. "Damn you, William!" She grabbed a lamp off the table and smashed it on his head. A thousand glass shards exploded across the room.

For a second, he stood there, too stunned to move, blood running from a gash on the back of his head. His face contorted with rage as he turned and lunged at Mum. He grabbed her hair, then yanked back her neck and slapped her hard in the face—once, twice, three times. She covered her head, but it didn't help.

He was going to kill her this time, and all the years of his abuse raged up in me. "Ahhhhhhhh!" I screamed, running across the room. With all my weight behind my shoulder, I slammed into him from behind. He fell hard against the wall and slumped to the floor gasping for breath.

"Grab Billy and get outta here!" I shouted. She tried to lift him, but his arm hung at a weird angle and he cried out again. I grabbed his other arm, we both lifted him off the floor. Somehow, the three of us ran across the yard to Mrs. Martini's house where I pounded on her door forever until she opened it. She looked at Mum's face, now red and swollen, then at Billy, who was still crying and holding his dangling arm. That's when the old man came out of the house, looked all around until he saw us, then stumbled across the yard screaming.

"Get in house quick," Mrs. Martini said, locking the door just as he reached the steps. "Goddamn you old bitch. Open the fuckin' door!" He beat on it again and again. All of us were petrified, but Mrs. Martini wasn't scared at all. She just shot her fist in the air toward him like I saw a lot of the Italian guys at school do, then jammed a chair against the doorknob and just sort of smiled at him through the window.

"Goddamn you!" he screamed even louder, but Mrs. Martini didn't flinch a bit. She just mumbled what I thought to be a long litany of Italian curses and grabbed the phone.

"I need police at 317 Elm Street right away. There is crazy man try to get in my house. Come quick!" Then she hung up the phone, crossed her arms over her chest and glared at the old man. "Zitto cane che abbaia. Chi ti credi di essere?" she muttered loud enough for me to hear. I didn't know what it meant, but I had a pretty good idea.

It seemed like it took hours, but it was probably only a couple minutes before two police cars pulled up in front of the house and found the old man still berserk on the porch. Two cops arrested him while another one came in the house and talked to Mum. It was pretty obvious what happened, so they said they had to take all three of us to the hospital.

I looked toward Mrs. Martini as the policeman led us out to his car. I wanted to tell her I was sorry for what my old man called her, for what Robert did to her cat, and for all the things I said about her too. But all I could manage was the only Italian word Frankie taught me.

"Grazie." I mumbled as I walked by her.

She nodded. "Prego." she answered softly.

———

The doctor said Mum was okay, just a black eye and some bruises, but Billy had to stay there for a couple days because his arm was broken.

Some people from the welfare office came to the hospital to see Billy. The man said his name was Mr. Rudnik and he kept looking at his watch. I figured his next stop was the bar across the street from the hospital, because I saw those same swollen red eyes and splotchy dry skin on too many drunks in my neighborhood. He asked Mum a lot of questions about our family, about the old man, and especially Billy, all while looking repeatedly at his watch. Mum didn't seem to notice, or care. She hadn't said much since the old man beat her, and it was obvious, at least to me, that she didn't want to talk to strangers, especially when Mr. Rudnik asked about Woodville. She turned away, staring out the window in silence.

"Daniel, is there anything you can tell us about your family?" he asked me now. I looked at Mum, hoping she could tell me what to say, but she ignored us.

"We're okay," I mumbled.

He looked at his watch again and sighed. He and the woman with him talked for a minute, then both left without saying another word to us.

———

Mum and I didn't talk about the welfare people, or anything else after we got home from the hospital, but it was all I thought about. Finally, after two days of silence I confronted her in the kitchen with that question Robert asked me months ago. "Why did you ever marry *him*?"

She didn't answer, but just stared out the window with that blank look I'd seen too many times. I wasn't even sure she heard me. Finally, she turned, and for just a minute her eyes seemed to clear and focus right on me. "My life growing up was hard," she said slowly. "But it was nothing compared to what your father had to live with. I guess I just felt sorry for him." Then she turned back toward the window, as if that somehow justified all the abuse we had to live with every day, like none of it ever happened.

I couldn't believe what I just heard! Everything in me wanted to scream, *You ruined our lives and nearly got Billy killed because you felt sorry for the old man!* But I didn't say anything. I just stared at her and shook as the full weight of her words sunk in. "That doesn't make it any easier living with *him*!" I spit the words at her now, then turned away and walked out of the room.

A week later those same welfare people came to our house.

"Mrs. Robinson, we don't think it's safe for Billy to stay here," Mr. Rudnik said. "Eventually your husband will be released from jail. That's why we talked to your sister, Mary Wojcik, in Pittsburgh. She's willing to take Billy."

Mum started to cry.

"It's not forever," the woman with him said. "Just until your situation is...more stable. We think it's best for everyone, especially Billy." She reached for my mother's hand to comfort her, but Mum just got up from her chair and walked into her bedroom. Billy was standing in the hall and heard the conversation. I thought he'd be upset, but he didn't cry at all. He just went to his room and filled a bag with some clothes, put on his red cowboy shirt and left with the welfare people. I saw the old man hitting Mum in the face again. I heard Billy scream as his arm snapped. I saw my beautiful fighter plane in ashes on the ground. Those welfare people were right. Billy couldn't live with the old man anymore. None of us could.

I thought about Billy a lot after that... especially all those times I left him alone so I could be with Frankie. What if I hadn't been there when the old man broke his arm? One time I even called Aunt Mary. If I could just talk with him, ask how he was doing... maybe I could even take him to the Clairton pool with me and Frankie. She said he wasn't home, but she would tell him I called. "He's made a couple friends in the neighborhood now," she said. That made me feel a little better.

Mum stayed in her room and I listened to my radio alone in my bedroom. Some nights I dreamed about picking raspberries again for Grandma Emma's cake. In March, somebody from the jail called and said the old man was getting released and they wanted to know if she could come get him. Mum didn't say anything, but just walked back to her room and shut the door. The next morning, an ambulance came and took her to Woodville.

I had nowhere to go. I shared space with people called family. We had the same address, ate at the same table, even had the same last name, but we were strangers. We all lived alone together.

CHAPTER 3
IN THE BELLY OF THE BEAST

CLAIRTON, 1965. The first thing I noticed was the house didn't smell of cigarettes and stale beer—and it was really clean. And the furniture all belonged together. None of it looked used or handed down from relatives like my house. Along the far wall, there was a cabinet filled with books and pictures, and even fancy little glass statues. I especially noticed an RCA color television in the living room with a radio and stereo record player built right into it, just like one I saw last year in the Sears furniture department in Pittsburgh. I couldn't remember what it cost, just that my mother said we could never afford one. But the carpet really caught my attention. It was thick and soft, nothing like the bare wood floors and worn rugs in my house. It covered everything from the living room to the hall and up the stairs.

The only thing out of place, and since this was the preacher's house, it wasn't really out of place, was the Bible on the kitchen table. It was open alongside a notepad and a cup of coffee. It was obvious he had been studying for his sermon. This house was nothing like where I lived, with dirty dishes left in the sink forever, or clothes thrown all over the furniture, or empty beer bottles and cigarette butts covering the living room table. This house looked like those places I'd only seen in magazines or on television, not where people like me lived.

Even though he was a little shorter than me, Pastor Carl Duncan seemed much taller, especially when I told him about Mum going to Woodville again. What would he say? I looked down at the floor—and waited. "Of course, you can stay with us, Daniel," he said. "Our boys are grown, so their bedroom is empty. And we won't charge you anything because you can help us around the house."

I didn't know what to say. But he just smiled, laying his hand gently on my shoulder. "Would you like to see your room?"

Did I hear him right? My own room? In my house, Billie slept in the bunk bed above me and was always whining about something every night, and Robert hogged the whole closet.

"Yes, sir. I sure would," I said, following him up the stairs. *I'm going to be okay now!*

I attended the Clairton Baptist Church with my mother all my life. When I was there, I left all the yelling and abuse behind. For a couple hours, I was with people who were polite to one another, who said nice things, who were actually interested in me.

One time when I got a B in my English class, nobody at home cared, but Mr. Murphy was really impressed. He was a deacon in the church for as long as I remembered, and I thought he was almost as important as Pastor Duncan. "I knew you were a smart boy," he said. No one ever called me smart before.

Mrs. Donnelly, my Sunday school teacher, got me thinking about being a preacher. "I bet you'd be real good at it. Good as Pastor Duncan." I didn't think much about it then, but after seeing how people in church treated him with so much respect, and especially now that I was living with him, I got the idea I might like to be a preacher someday too.

I didn't see Mrs. Duncan much. She worked a lot of hours at Donetelli's Pharmacy in Clairton, and Pastor Duncan seemed glad to have someone to talk with. Sometimes he asked about my family and why I left home. He asked about my mother too, but I didn't want to talk about Woodville, even with him. Mostly we talked about me. What classes do I have in school? What sports do I like? Did I have any girl-friends? Sometimes we watched television, but we never watched the Pirates games. I hated the Pirates.

He never said anything, but I worried how I was going to pay my rent. In June, right after school let out, I thought it was a good time to ask if he knew anywhere I could get a job for the summer.

"Hey, Pastor," I said when I found him working in the yard. Even though it was Saturday, his face was clean shaven. His hair was still dark with only a few speckles of grey, carefully parted on the left side. Normally he always wore a white shirt and tie, even around the house in the evenings. But today he was wearing khakis and a striped pullover shirt, like I had seen in Kadar's men's store downtown. His penny loafers glistened in the morning sun. I saw my old man slouched in his chair, unshaven and wearing a dirty, beer-stained T-shirt. *Thank you, God, for Pastor Duncan,* I prayed under my breath, like I did every day since I moved in with them. He stopped raking and smiled. "How does it feel to be out of school for the summer?"

"Really good...and that's what I wanted to talk about with you. Do you have a minute for a question?"

"Of course. What is it?"

"I was wondering...I mean..." The words caught in my throat. I swallowed hard. "I... ah... was wondering if you know any place where I could get a job for the summer? You know, to help pay my rent here." I felt my stomach come up in my throat. *What if I can't find a job? What if he tells me I have to go back home?*

He laid the rake against the house and put his hand on my shoulder. "I told you, Daniel, I wasn't going to charge you anything."

"I know, but I'd feel better if I could pay you something."

He handed me the rake and smiled again. "What if you help me with some projects I need done in the yard this summer? We'll call it even then."

"I'd love to help you, Pastor Duncan." I nearly shouted because I knew he *really* cared for me! Those three hours I spent raking grass clippings never felt so good.

Two days later Pastor Duncan handed me a package. "When we were working in the yard, you mentioned a model airplane you built when you were younger. I got the impression that was something you liked to do, so when I saw this model car at Thompson's Hobby Shop, I got it for you. Think of it like a welcoming gift from me and the wife."

He didn't come right out and say it, but what I heard was, *You can be part of our family. You can be normal.*

"Thanks, Pastor Duncan," I said, but I wanted to say so much more.

———

Summer humidity and mill smoke hung heavy in Clairton most days, but I didn't notice. Pastor Duncan and I just finished that new deck on the back of his house he'd been planning for a long time. It was hard work, but he said he could not have done it without my help. That was when I decided to tell him about my plans. "I want to be a pastor...like you."

He put his hand on my shoulder. "I know you'll be an excellent minister," he said, patting my back several times.

I remembered showing my old man that Tomahawk fighter plane I built. A thousand memories of my family now flooded over me. My heart beat fast, sweat beaded on my forehead and I struggled to breathe.

Pastor Duncan noticed. He took hold of my arm. "Are you okay?"

"Just the heat," I said, forcing all those memories out of my head. "But I'll be okay now."

He gently touched my forehead and let his hand rest there. His skin felt soft and smelled of Old Spice that he always wore, nothing like my old man's calloused and tobacco-stained hands that reeked of smoke and stale beer. He smiled. "No fever. Good. You had me worried for a minute."

"I'm okay now."

Laying both of his hands on my shoulders, he looked at me, his eyes filled with kindness. "I just want you to know that all of us in the church, and especially me, we couldn't be more proud of you, Daniel." He tussled my hair.

No one ever did that to me before, not even my mother. It was embarrassing...but in a good way. "I appreciate that, Pastor," I felt my face grow warm as I looked down at the floor for just a second, then up at him. "And I'm really glad to be here with you and Mrs. Duncan. More than I can ever tell you."

"We're glad to have you here. So how about you and I go to Isaly's and get a Klondike bar? To celebrate your good news."

I really am part of his family now. "I'd love that. I really would."

———

Mrs. Duncan was working late again, so Pastor made supper like he did most nights she wasn't home. This time he said he had another surprise and handed me a catalog for a college in Philadelphia. "I thought you might want to look at this. It's for the best Baptist school in the state, you know, to study for the ministry. And I can help you get accepted there, maybe even get a scholarship."

I knew I'd have to go to college to be a preacher, but I had no idea where to go, and especially how to pay for it, and that worried me— until now. I just stared at that catalog.

I read and reread it every night in my room all week. I even told Mr. Murphy about it on Sunday. "I always knew you would be a preacher someday, just like Pastor Duncan," He carefully pulled a twenty dollar bill from his wallet and pressed it gently into my hand. "To start your college fund."

That night, alone in my room, I thanked God, for giving me a new family, and especially for Pastor Duncan. I slept better than I had in a long time.

———

It was a hot Monday evening in early August. Mrs. Duncan had gone to visit her mother in Pittsburgh, like she did every Monday. I was sitting barefoot on the floor of my room, basking in the most luxurious carpet I ever felt, and thanking God again for giving me such a wonderful new home. I heard a knock on my door.

"It's me, Daniel. Can I talk with you?"

"Sure, Pastor. Come in." I set aside the college catalog I had been reading for the hundredth time.

"I wanted to tell you the church is real proud you'll be going to college when you graduate," he said as he walked toward me. "Mrs. Duncan and I are proud of you too."

He'd been saying that a lot to me. I liked hearing it.

"The deacons and I have been talking. Since you'll be studying for the ministry when you finish high school next year, we believe there should be some sort of dedication service for you."

I saw Pastor Duncan and the deacons do that a couple times when someone was going to Africa to be a missionary, but not college. "I'd like that. I really would. When do you want to do it?" I thought he meant next year when I was a senior, or maybe in the summer after I graduated.

"I thought we'd pray now. I could dedicate your school plans and your future ministry to the Lord."

"Are the deacons at the church?" I never heard of a dedication service on Monday.

Pastor Duncan moved closer and gently mussed my hair again, like he did that day in the yard. "You've been like a son to me since you've been living with us. Neither of my own two boys felt called to the ministry like you, so I thought you and I could have a private dedication. Not in the church with the deacons, but just the two of us in my office, so we can pray together like family."

I had no idea he felt that way. *Like a son to me.* Without hesitating, I grabbed my shoes and jumped up. "Yes, sir. I'd be proud to have you pray for me."

We walked across the parking lot to the church and went up the steps to the side door. He didn't turn on the light, but there was plenty of evening sun still coming through the windows. We walked down the hall to his office where he opened the door and turned on a small lamp in the room. I thought I heard him lock the door, but didn't pay much attention. All that mattered was how important I felt being here with such a godly man—someone who thought of me like one of his own sons! That's when I knew I wanted to be just like him. More. Than. Anything.

"Daniel, why don't you stand with me in front of the Bible on my desk and close your eyes while I pray for you?"

"Yes, sir," I said and bowed my head, like I saw others do. But I kept my eyes open, just a little. He raised his arms high above my head, closed his eyes and prayed solemnly, "Lord, Daniel wants to follow your call into the ministry. I want to commission him into your service."

He placed both his hands on the top of my head, holding me firmly. "Lord, I want to dedicate Daniel's thoughts to you."

No one ever prayed for me like this...like I was really special. Pastor Duncan now put his hands on my shoulders and pulled me closer. I smelled the Old Spice he always wore. Was that whiskey I smelled, too?

"Lord, I dedicate all Daniel's strength, so he wins souls for you."

He moved his hands down on my face and squeezed my cheeks. With one of his fingers, he parted my lips slightly. "Lord, I dedicate Daniel's words to you, so he'll always speak your truth."

It was... uncomfortable. Nobody ever touched my lips that way. But I was never part of a private dedication service. *Maybe this is normal.* But it didn't feel normal. I hoped he'd be done soon.

But he wasn't done.

He got down on his knees in front of me and put his hands on my waist. Moving them down along my thighs, then up again, he prayed, "Jesus, I want to dedicate Daniel's legs, so he will always follow you." He kept rubbing, slowly up and down again and again. My head throbbed. I wanted to tell him to stop, but I just stood there, terrified, and prayed for this dedication service to be over. *Please God. Make him stop!*

But he didn't stop.

"Lord, Daniel will have a family one day..." He now put his hands between my legs, rubbing first across, then up and down, slowly, firmly over my pants, and with his eyes still closed as he mouthed that prayer. "...and I want to dedicate his children to you."

My whole body tensed. I couldn't breathe. I couldn't move. My mind raced. *Maybe he didn't mean to touch me there. Maybe it was a mistake.* But he didn't move his hands away. He kept them there, between my legs, while praying again and again, "Yes, Jesus...Jesus...."

My heart beat so hard I knew it was going to come right out of my chest.

Pastor Duncan slowly pulled down my zipper and reached inside my pants.

No! I screamed, but no sound came out of me. I was paralyzed. I couldn't move. I couldn't speak. I couldn't stop him.

He kept rubbing and praying, "Jesus...Jesus..."

Rage rushed over me and my whole body cried out at this monster I once loved. "Noooo!" I grabbed both his hands and pushed him away as hard as I could. He stumbled back into his desk and fell to the floor.

He looked up at me as the color drained from his face, his eyes wide now, and for a second I saw fear flash across his face. "Oh my God. You don't think that I...?" He sounded so weak, so pathetic.

"I'm going to tell the deacons what you did." I spit out the words, quickly zipping my pants. The sight of him repulsed me.

"Daniel." His tone changed as he got up off the floor. His face too. The fear and desperation were gone. He sounded distant, cold, his voice coming from deep within him, more like the growl of a cornered dog. He was... someone I didn't know.

His eyes narrowed directly at me. "You go ahead and tell the church this little story you just made up. No one's going to believe you anyway... no one, not ever," he said slowly, as if measuring every word for maximum effect. "Think about it. You're some confused kid I pulled off the street, whose father did God knows what to him growing up. Now you want to accuse me of some evil thing I can't even imagine. I'm a pastor. Do you actually think they'll believe the wild stories of someone whose mother is at Woodville? They'll think you're crazy too." He turned toward the mirror on the wall, straightened his tie, then looked back at me, "I'm going to forget this little delusion of yours. And because I'm your pastor, I'm going to forgive you, Daniel."

Why have you done this to me? I screamed out, but my mouth made no sound. I stood there, mute, broken, and so frightened. My whole body shook. I couldn't stop. My stomach rushed up into my throat, and I felt I was going to vomit all over myself.

Get away from him! I shouted over and over in my head, but I couldn't move. Finally, I forced my legs to turn and stumbled toward the door. I fumbled with the latch for what felt like forever until it finally opened, slammed the door against the wall and ran down the darkened hall and out of the church. *I've got to get away from him! But where?* Panicked, I couldn't breathe. My head throbbed. My only thought was to run to my room. I quickly locked the door, then slid my dresser in front of it so he couldn't come in, even if he had a key.

That college catalog he gave me was on top of the dresser. I tore it into a thousand pieces. "Damn you!" I screamed over and over until I dropped to the floor exhausted, and just sat there in the dark, alone, feeling so ashamed, so dirty, and so afraid. I prayed over and over for Mrs. Duncan to come home soon.

I wept.

———

"Frankie? This is Daniel. Yeah, from Clairton." I only talked to Frankie DeNardo one time since he left Clairton six months ago. He called me to say he and his mother were living in Wheeling, but he never told me why they moved.

The phone shook in my hand. My mother was still in Woodville and I had nowhere else to go. Frankie was the only one I could call for help.

"I know it's been a long time since we talked, but I need your help. Can I stay with you for a while, just 'til I finish school? It's a long story, but I got nowhere to go. I've been staying at Pastor Duncan's house, but I gotta leave. I can't explain it now, but I can't stay there anymore."

He didn't say anything.

"I know it's asking a lot, but I really need your help."

I thought maybe Frankie hung up, but he finally answered. For some reason, he sounded different though. His voice shook, just a little. "Of course, you can stay with us. It's better here than Clairton. Believe me."

"Thanks, Frankie. I really appreciate it."

I was about to hang up when he said something strange. "You'll be safe here." Then the line went dead.

———

Even though we'd been best friends all those years growing up, neither of us talked about Clairton. It was sometime around Christmas when I got a letter from my mother saying she was out of Woodville and back at the Baptist Church. She said Pastor Duncan was telling everyone how hurt he was I left without even thanking him for all he did for me. All the rage I felt that night in his office flooded over me, like it was all happening again. I heard him praying, felt him rubbing. My heart beat so hard, I thought my chest would explode. The room spun around and around until I wanted to scream for it to stop. It was all I could do to just rip her letter in pieces, fall back onto the bed and stare out the window, looking at nothing, but seeing everything.

"You okay?" Frankie asked when he came into the room.

I couldn't answer.

"Daniel. Are you okay?" he asked again.

"Just reading a letter from my mother," I finally answered. "She wrote something about Pastor Duncan. That's all."

That was the first time I said that name out loud since I came to Frankie's house. He stopped and looked at me. His eyes glazed as his face contorted and turned deep red, the blood vessels bulging in his neck. He breathed hard.

"I hate that sonofabitch!" he spit out through his clenched teeth. "All his baptism instructions in his office. That's what he called it, like it was something normal."

Frankie looked at me, but his eyes were vacant, distant. "That's why we left town, you know. When I told my mother what he done to me, she threatened to call the cops. But Duncan didn't flinch a bit, like it was nothing, like we was nothing. He told her to go ahead and tell the cops 'cause no one would believe her anyway. He said my old man was a drunk and a whore chaser, and I was gonna be no better. So she moved us here right after that. She said Duncan was probably right. No one would ever believe me."

Frankie collapsed onto his bed and didn't move or say anything for several minutes. He just stared out the window, back in Clairton again, back in Pastor Duncan's office, too scared to say anything, but too angry to let it go.

"You know," he finally said, his voice flat, drained of any emotion now. "I used to love Klondike bars, but now I can't stand to even think about them."

I wanted to tell him I understood what he felt—about everything. I wanted to tell him what Pastor Duncan did to me. I wanted to help my friend. But I didn't say anything. We never mentioned his name again.

CHAPTER 4
LOST IN WONDERLAND

WHEELING, WEST VIRGINIA, 1966: "You thought about what you're doing after high school?" I asked Frankie. It was a dreary Saturday afternoon near the end of our senior year, with nothing to do. I was sprawled on my bed in our room, staring at the ceiling, listening to him talk endlessly about Annette Morowski and all the other girls he planned to date in our new school.

"Not much. Why?" he asked without even looking at me, like it wasn't really something he wanted to talk about.

"I've been thinking I might go to college somewhere." I looked in his direction for some reaction.

"You're kidding!" He shook his head. "Where are *you* gonna go to college?" He didn't seem that impressed with my prospects.

"I have no idea," I sighed. "...but I'm gonna talk to the school counselor. Maybe he can help." I thought adding that would make my new plan more impressive. It didn't.

"You apply for any scholarships?" Frankie asked, but he already knew the answer.

"Not with my grades. No use wasting my time."

Frankie grabbed the Sears catalog off the table between our beds and started flipping through the pages until he found the swimsuit section. "This one looks like Annette, doesn't she?"

I ignored him, but he didn't seem to notice or care. Finally, he dropped the catalog on the table and stood up. "I'm thirsty." He would clearly rather talk about Annette Morowski's bikini, or any girl's bikini for that matter, not some stupid idea about college. "You want a Coke?" he asked, walking out of the room without even waiting for an answer,

"I'm signing up for the Army," he announced when he came back into the room and tossed a can at me. "The recruiter promised I could go to Germany. Why don't you enlist with me?"

I shook my head. "No way. I gotta go to college somewhere." I said it more to convince me than Frankie. "If I don't, I'll end up in some mill just like my old man." I popped the top off my Coke, took a long drink, and ended the conversation with a loud belch. Then, almost as an afterthought, I added, "I just gotta find a way to pay for it."

———

As luck had it, there was a way after all, one I never expected. "I know I saw that catalog just last week." Mr. Gilbert made several deep hacking sounds that turned his face bright red, as he rummaged through an old wooden filing cabinet labeled 'Colleges' behind his cluttered desk. "It was a school somewhere near Lexington, I think." He pulled out several more files and thumbed through them quickly, then shoved them back into the cabinet in no apparent order.

"Don't worry about it," I turned to leave his office. Frankie told me I was wasting my time anyway.

"Wait, wait. Here it is!" Coughing hard again, Mr. Gilbert grabbed a small booklet from the back of the bottom drawer and dropped it on his desk in front of me. "Kentucky Methodist College." He smiled broadly, like this was the most exciting thing he did all day. I tried to look past his dark, tobacco-stained teeth and the wheezing sound he now made trying to catch his breath, focusing instead on the building on the cover of that booklet. It was the biggest and most beautiful house I ever saw, surrounded by fields of deep green grass where several horses grazed. It looked like a southern plantation, or what a plantation must look like. *Too expensive for someone like me!*

Mr. Gilbert must have known what I was thinking. "It's for poor kids in Appalachia who can't afford to go to a state school," he said. "I think they let you work off your tuition."

I knew I was poor, but I never thought I lived in Appalachia. Then again, who was I to argue with the Methodist Church and how they want to read a map?

―――――

I got the first sign my life was going to change for the better when the bus climbed out of Wheeling and crossed into Ohio. We drove through one farm town after another—Cambridge, New Concord, and finally as we crested a hill near Zanesville, the terrain seemed to relax and open up before me. Just then, the sun broke through the clouds and washed over the land that now exploded in every imaginable color. For miles around me, all I saw was tasseled corn stalks that looked taller than me, covering the fields in the deepest green I'd ever seen. And the sky! It was the brightest blue—clearer than I thought possible.

But it was the air filling the bus that really caught my attention. It was so wet, so alive, that all I could do was breathe it in until I thought my lungs would burst. I never felt anything so wonderful... so pure. It was like I was reborn with a second chance to start my life over. I took another slow, deep breath and closed my eyes, trying to etch this perfect moment in my memory forever. Right here, right now, on this Greyhound bus on Interstate 70 just west of Zanesville, Ohio, my old life with all the shit that I called home was now dead and gone. My new happy life had officially begun.

―――――

"Good morning class. My name is Professor Warner and we're going to start our discussion this semester with the epic poem *Beowulf*." I immediately glazed over with the words 'epic poem' in my first class at Kentucky Methodist College.

"Name's Daniel," I whispered to a boy sitting in the next row. He looked every bit as bored as me. "What do you think of the class?"

"Mike Peterson," he said, not even trying to hide a yawn, "and same as you. But I'll get through it if Warner doesn't put me to sleep for the next three months. Couple of us are going to lunch after class. Want to come?"

Peterson said he was from Kent, a small Ohio town that was nothing like Clairton. Mostly farmers who came to town to shop, go to church and meet with friends. Everybody knew every family for three generations. They all went to school together, married into families they grew up with. According to Peterson, nothing exciting ever happened there.

I liked him immediately, probably because his family, and even his whole life, seemed so normal—or at least what I thought normal should look like. But what I liked most was his confidence. He seemed so sure of himself. Not that I was jealous. I just wished I could be more like him. He never asked about my home, and I wasn't about to tell him anyway. I was pretty sure he wouldn't understand my old man's drunken tirades—or Woodville. No one at my new home needed to know.

My first afternoon class was Introduction to Psychology. I hadn't planned to take it, but I needed the credit to fill my schedule and it was the only course open. Dr. Smith began his lecture. "Let's suppose you know someone who hurts others, someone who doesn't show remorse. Would you say he had a personality disorder?"

I sat up in my chair, listening intently to every word Dr. Smith had to say about my old man.

"Let's also suppose you know someone who has difficulty concentrating, difficulty sleeping, perhaps withdrawn from social interactions. Would you say she is depressed, even mentally ill?"

"How about a whole family of sick people?" I mumbled half out loud. The girl in the next row turned and looked at me strange, but my eyes were fixed on Dr. Smith.

"So why study psychology?" he asked. "To answer a question all of us have asked ourselves at some time. 'Am I normal?' And that, students, is what we will address this semester."

I asked that question a hundred times in my life. Here in Psych 101, maybe now I might find the answer. *I'm gonna do real well in college*, I thought as I picked up my books and headed to my next class.

———

If optimism was all I needed, I would've had all A's my first year. Unfortunately, that wasn't the case. "Are you Dr. Samuels? They told me at the dean's office you could help me. I'm having a little trouble with some of my classes."

Actually, I was having *a lot* of trouble in *all* my classes. I felt like I was stumbling through them with my shoes on the wrong feet. What brought me to his office at the beginning of my sophomore year was a letter from the college dean—something about my "continued stay at Kentucky Methodist College is now at great risk."

Dr. David Samuels looked to be in his late forties or early fifties. He was thin and tall, well over six feet, giving him an awkward, gangly appearance. His suit was worn, the cuffs and collar threadbare from too many years of use, and baggy too, like he bought it when he was younger and much healthier. His tie was not much better. It was a slim, black clip-on, the type I hadn't seen since I wore one for my sixth-grade school picture. His hair was cut short, not at all like many of the other professors who wore their hair stylishly longer.

But he didn't seem to care about fashion. Evident by his office, his focus was books. Every shelf was stuffed with hundreds of books of all shapes and sizes, all of them were shoved and stacked in no apparent order. And there was something else really strange about this Samuels guy. His whole office was a mess—except for this one corner of his desk. That's where he had a cup filled with pencils—dozens of them, red, blue and yellow pencils in all sizes. But the really weird part was some of them had a huge eraser. *God! How's this guy going to help me get organized?* I thought as I quickly looked around his office.

"Have a seat. Just move those papers off the chair." Dr. Samuels barely looked up from something he was writing.

"I can't stay," I mumbled, struggling to find a reason to cancel my appointment. "I think I ate something for lunch that didn't agree with me. Can I reschedule?"

"No problem," he said, still writing in his notebook. "Just call my secretary when you feel better."

"Maybe next week," I promised with little enthusiasm, leaving the room.

The other two counselors I called were both booked all semester, so I asked around campus about this Samuels guy. Apparently, he grew up in India. Missionary family they said. He spent the next twenty years as a missionary himself until he came back to the States a couple years ago. His health or something, someone told me. Now he worked as a campus tutor and counselor. Easy to talk to, they all said, like he really understood what you were thinking. A little quirky, but willing to do whatever he could to help a student. I decided to give him another chance.

"Let's look at your schedule, Daniel," Dr. Samuels said when we finally met. "It looks pretty normal. Nothing too hard that I can see. American Lit, Western Civ, and Abnormal Psychology. Interesting. What do you think of that course?"

I wanted to say I relived too many fights with my old man and too many trips to Woodville every time I opened my textbook. "It's okay, I guess. Thinking about majoring in Psych."

"What was your grade in your intro course?"

"C."

"If you want to major in Psychology, you'll need to do better. But don't worry. I'm sure I can help you."

I got up to leave, but stopped. "I do have one question, Dr. Samuels. That cup on your desk. The one with all the pencils. I don't get it. I mean nobody uses a pencil in college, do they?"

He smiled like he expected that question, even wanted me to ask it. "Actually, Daniel, those pencils are the most important things I have in my office, maybe in my whole life."

I had no idea what he was talking about... and I was beginning to reconsider my decision to meet with him again.

"I've been counseling with people for twenty-five years, and do you know what every one of them wanted?"

I didn't answer. I still had no idea what he was talking about.

"A second chance. So that's what I try to offer people here. That cup is my reminder that life is written in pencil, so we get a lot of second chances. I really believe that, Daniel, and I hope you do, too."

I remembered what I felt a year ago on that bus near Zanesville. "Okay," I muttered. If he could help me get a second chance with the dean's office, I was all for it.

I met every week with Dr. Samuels, or Doc as he preferred to be called. We talked about my assignments, test schedules, and mainly my study habits. He strongly recommended—that was how he put it—that I study in the library, not the student union where everyone partied at night. Who knew? I didn't tell him, but until I got to college, I had never even been in a library before.

But he was right, and after a few weeks, my grades started to improve. By the end of the semester, I realized I actually enjoyed the solitude of the library, surrounded by thousands of books with new ideas and stories about people and places I never heard of before.

"I made a B in Abnormal Psych!" I called out when I saw Doc walking out of the college post office right after final exams. I didn't tell him all I ever did was write about my family.

"Congratulations, Daniel. I knew you could do it." He smiled broadly at me. "Have you picked your spring classes yet?"

"You know, the usual. Another English class. British Lit this time. *Espanol*, and a psych course that might be pretty good. Experimental Psych. It's just an intro course, but someone told me we get our own lab rats to work with. Might be fun."

"I heard that's an interesting class. I'm sure you'll do well."

"This semester we will primarily be studying BF Skinner and his theories on learning called operant conditioning." Everyone knew that Dr. Walter Martin was never one for small talk in class, or anywhere for that matter. He was head of the psychology department for as long as anyone remembered. He never married, and now well into his sixties, devoted all his time to his research. Rumor on campus had it he actually studied under Skinner. This particular class on research was supposed to be his favorite, so I wasn't surprised when he started to lecture before the bell rang.

"I hear we'll be doing experiments with rats." A transfer student at the front of the class interrupted Dr. Martin. "When do we start that?"

Most of us had the same question, but no one dared ask. This was not a good start for the new guy.

"You are Mr. Allen, I believe." Dr. Martin glared at his roll book. It was evident to everyone but Allen that he was irritated with his question. "Yes, we will be conducting learning experiments this semester."

"When will we be doing that, Dr. Martin?" Allen asked.

This new guy was obviously a slow learner. *We might want to use him in some learning experiment,* I wanted to quip, like I would have in my other classes. But I just bit my tongue and smiled.

"Mr. Allen." Dr. Martin barely hid his irritation. "According to your chart, you're new to our school, and clearly new to my classes, so I'll let your intrusion go this time. But I sincerely hope this will not become an ongoing distraction for us, will it Mr. Allen?"

No more questions from Allen this time. *I think we just saw a rat in a maze learn something new.* I smiled again.

"As I was saying," Dr. Martin continued with his lecture, "in our study of operant conditioning, we will primarily discuss how learning is achieved through a trial and error process. Much of our class will be devoted to lectures on learning theories and processes. But the rest of our time will be in the lab where..." his eyes narrowed ever so slightly in Allen's direction, "...we will conduct various learning experiments, primarily using rats in what is called a Skinner box. Does that answer your question, Mr. Allen?"

He didn't answer.

Well, how about that? Operant conditioning actually worked!

————

"Say, Peterson. There's a girl in our Spanish class. You know, the tall brunette who sits in the front. What's her name?"

"The Ice Queen? Why do you ask?"

"No reason. I saw her looking at me yesterday and I thought maybe I might check her out."

"Her name's Elizabeth Johnson. She was a year ahead of me in high school in Kent, but I don't know much about her. Just that she's pretty stuck on herself. I think she's dating some guy already. Why? You're not interested in her, are you?"

Not now anyway. "Just wanted to know her name, you know, to be polite."

"Good thing. Take my advice and don't go near her. They don't call her the Ice Queen for nothing. Ella es la reina de hielo. Tear your heart out. But your call. Just don't come crying to me. No vangas a llorando a mi." All his classes, even Spanish, came easy for Peterson. I thought he was showing off, since he studied half the time I did. Sometimes—and this was one of them, he *really* irritated me. But I needed his help with my classes, so I tolerated his little condescensions.

———

"We will be conducting our first experiment with lab rats today," Dr. Martin announced, again before the bell rang. "One will be assigned to each of you." Like everyone in the class, I was anxious to start these experiments. Like Allen, that was why all of us took the course in the first place.

"My assistant will give each of you your assigned lab rat. Anticipating the next question from some of you," he looked toward Allen, "yes, you may give him any name you choose. That is, as long as it's appropriate."

I just saw a new movie called 'Charly' that Doc recommended. It was about a guy everyone picked on because he was slow. His only friend was a lab rat. "Charly. That's what I'm going to call you," I said, gently stroking his soft white fur.

———

It was halfway through the term before I got up the nerve to actually talk with Elizabeth Johnson. I was walking to the library one afternoon when I saw her sitting alone on a bench outside of our Spanish class-room. I had no idea what to say, or even how to say it, so I walked by her several times, looking for a way to introduce myself.

I was about to give up and go on to the library when she looked up from her book and smiled. "Hi, Daniel. Would you like to sit down?"

"Okay." I tried my best to sound as confident as Peterson.

We talked about nothing much, just the usual things people say when they first meet.

"What's your major?"

"Teaching." she said.

"Home town?"

"Kent, near Akron."

"Family?"

"Two sisters and a brother." She said her sisters were married, but her younger brother was still at home. "He works at the GM assembly plant nearby. That's where my father has worked for nearly thirty years."

"Involved?"

"Yes, I'm dating someone right now. You might know him. Craig McMasters. He's on the basketball team."

"Sorry. Not much interested in basketball." I didn't even try to hide my disappointment. If Elizabeth noticed, she didn't say anything.

"She's not that serious about him. I can tell," I told Peterson that night in the dorm. I wasn't sure if I wanted to convince him or me. Either way, he wasn't impressed.

"No vangas a llorando a mi."

———

"In our lab experiment today we will observe the effect of both positive and negative reinforcement," Dr. Martin told the class. "Your Skinner boxes all have levers. When your rat presses it, he'll be rewarded with a pellet of food. This is what we call positive reinforcement."

"Charly doesn't look very hungry, Dr. Martin. What if he doesn't respond?"

"Quite a dilemma then, Mr. Robinson," Dr. Martin said loud enough for the class to hear as he came to my table. "So how do you motivate a rat to eat when he's not hungry? You use negative reinforcement. In this particular experiment, that would be a mild electric shock to encourage him."

Dr. Martin pressed a switch that sent a shock to the grid making Charly jump and run around the box. After several frantic circles, he bumped the lever in the center. That stopped the shock and dropped a food pellet into his tray. At first Charly ignored the pellet, but Dr. Martin shocked him several times and made him run in more circles, bumping the lever again and again. He did this repeatedly until Charly finally ate the food pellets.

"That, Mr. Robinson, is how negative reinforcement works," Dr. Martin announced to the class. "As you can see, it can be just as effective as positive reinforcement. Don't you agree, Mr. Robinson?"

I didn't answer. Charly seemed agitated, confused, even hurt by what Dr. Martin just did to him. I picked up Charly and stroked his fur until both of us calmed down.

———

Elizabeth and I spent a lot of afternoons together walking and talking, mostly on the college golf course, sometimes for several hours. We were walking along the third fairway, on a quiet hilltop overlooking the school, when we found a bench under a large oak tree. "Let's sit here and enjoy the breeze," I said. "It reminds me of my bus ride to school, when I felt so alive breathing in that fresh country air. Like I was reborn."

She smiled. "My daddy sometimes says the same thing when he's been working in the garden. He says it makes him feel alive again after being in the factory all week."

"Then this will be our special place." I smiled back at her.

We sat down as I stretched out my legs and leaned back, then turned toward her. "I know you said you wanted to teach school, but you never told me what age."

"Elementary school, of course. I think that age is so much more fun to work with than high school. Don't you?"

Neither age sounds like fun to me. But she was wearing that beige blouse I loved.... "I agree. Elementary teaching sounds great."

"I wasn't sure what I wanted to do when I first got to college, but then my sister Janet...I told you about her, didn't I? Well, when she had her first baby and I saw how happy she was, I just knew I wanted to have lots of kids too. So teaching elementary school makes sense, don't you think?"

I nodded, but I was more focused on how her long dark hair glistened in the afternoon sun, and when the breeze shifted, wafting the scent of her perfume my way, I thought I was as close to heaven as I'd ever been.

Two days later, near evening, Elizabeth met me coming out of the student union. "I've got a surprise for you," she said, "something I want you to see on the golf course."

"Now? It's too dark to see anything." I had no idea what she had in mind—but I didn't care. I was just glad to be with her.

"Do you see it?" she asked when we reached the hilltop on the third fairway. But it was a moonless night and I could barely see my hand in front of my face.

"See what? Where? I don't understand."

She laughed and gently lifted my chin. "Look up. What do you see now?"

"God," I muttered, staring now at the brilliant infinity of stars, high and bright in the deep blackness of the sky that stretched across the entire landscape. "I never knew something this beautiful even existed."

"And there's more, Daniel," she said pointing toward the southern end of the vast expanse before us. "Can you see Leo? That's the constellation right below the Big Dipper? See that group of stars that look like a backward question mark? That's Leo. Can you see them?" She was almost giddy now as she pointed again at the sky.

"I'm not sure." I said. "I never saw the sky much in Clairton."

"Squint your eyes, like this," she said scrunching her face and biting her lip. "My daddy says that's how you can see the stars better when there's too much light on the ground."

I scrunched my face just like she showed me. "The most beautiful thing I've ever seen," I said, but I was looking at her. Not the stars.

"The best date I've had since I came to college," I bragged to Peterson back in the dorm.

He wasn't impressed. "You talk like you're a real couple, but the last I checked, she's still dating that jock."

I ignored him, but he persisted like he always did. "What is it about the Ice Queen that's got you so hooked?"

I asked that question a dozen times since I met her. *Is it her skin?* It's so smooth, all I want to do is hold her hands, touch her lips, caress her face tenderly. *Is it her hair?* It's the color of the dark night sky she showed me tonight, and when it rests on her shoulders so gently, it gave her a confident air that made me feel good just being with her. *Is it her eyes?* They're as dark as her hair, but deep, like shimmering pools drawing me toward her when I'm thirsty. But whenever I reached out, they seemed distant and pushed me back again. I didn't know what to tell him. The more I was with her, the more I wanted her. But the more I wanted her, the more I was reminded I couldn't have her, every time she mentioned Craig.

I didn't answer Peterson's question. I slammed the door and went out to the golf course to look at the night sky again—and remember our wonderful date tonight.

———

Everything changed a few weeks later when Elizabeth met me outside my dorm, crying so hard I barely understood what she was saying.

"It's-s...m-my...b-brother...R-Richard," she sobbed.

"What is it? Is he okay?" I never met her brother, or any of her family, but I felt like I knew them well. They were all we talked about on our walks together. He was the youngest in the family. Twenty years old. Single. He worked at the GM plant with her father. Good job I thought.

"Did he get hurt? An accident?" I asked, taking both her hands in mine. "Let's sit here."

As soon as we sat on the bench, she collapsed in my arms and sobbed. I pulled her close. "Just breathe, and tell me what it is." I tried to sound calm, but I was worried.

She took several slow breaths while I held her. "He's...g-going...to..."

Going to die? I pulled her closer, and she let her head rest on my shoulder. That seemed to help calm her. "Where is Richard going, Elizabeth?"

"V-Viet n-nam-m," she sobbed.

"I don't understand. Your brother isn't in the Army."

She looked up. "He's getting ...d-drafted."

I took her hand, squeezing it. "That doesn't mean he's going to Vietnam. I've got a friend who enlisted when I came to college, and he spent his time in Germany. The Army sends a lot of soldiers there. Maybe even more than Vietnam. Chances are good he'll go to Germany. If you want, I'll write my friend and see what he says."

She relaxed and breathed easier. "You really think Richard will be okay? I'm just so scared something will happen to him."

"I'm sure of it. Trust me." I pulled her close again.

"And you'll write your friend for me?"

"Of course, I will."

Elizabeth kissed me softly on my cheek. I wasn't prepared for that. My face felt suddenly hot. She reached into her pocket, pulling out a tissue and wiped her eyes. Then she leaned into me, gently kissing me again, this time on my lips. My heart beat so hard, I was sure she heard it.

"Daniel, I don't want to be alone right now. Can you spend some time with me?"

"Of course, I can. Whatever you need."

"I just need you to hold me, but not here. Can we go someplace where we can be alone? My friend Stephanie lives off campus. We can go to her apartment." She pulled me close and kissed me on the mouth again, this time passionately.

———

"Wow..." I couldn't help a long sigh as I fell back beside her. That... that was.. everything I imagined it would be! Snuggling warmly against my side, her head resting on my shoulder, Elizabeth murmured softly, her eyes half-closed. I let my eyes fall shut but I couldn't stop smiling. It happened so fast and... Now I just wanted to soak in this memory, in this bed with the love of my life, all day. Forever.

Ever since that first day in Spanish, I wanted this moment. I didn't know then what it would actually be like... like I was flying so high, so free, so alive! This was what I wanted—no, needed—all my life! Love, just pure, simple and complete love. What did that idiot Peterson know about love? About Elizabeth? I was hers, and she was mine. That's all that mattered!

"You're cute when you hum," Elizabeth opened an eye and grinned at me. "I can feel it through your body, you know?"

I chuckled. "I was? Wow, I had no idea." I couldn't remember when I was this happy. But who could blame me? Elizabeth Johnson loves me, Daniel Robinson!

"Eliza—" Just then, the Admin building tower clock chimed twelve times. Elizabeth wriggled back and sat up, stretching. "I've got a class." She leaned over and kissed me on the forehead. "When my mother called me about Richard this morning, I didn't know who to talk to. And then I saw you coming out of your dorm, just when I needed you. Thank you for being such a good friend, Daniel. I mean it."

Friend? After what we just did, you still think we're...? I nodded and forced a smile, but it didn't reach my eyes.

She didn't seem to notice. "See you after Spanish again?" she asked. "We can sit on our bench on the fairway, like we always do."

"Of course." My smile had already faded. I stared up at the cold white ceiling. She still loves me though. I know that!

———

Dr. Martin started his lecture again before the bell rang. "Previously, we have used both positive and negative reinforcement to motivate your rats. But if the reward and punishment have no correlation to their behavior, how will they respond to what is called a condition of learned helplessness?"

"Won't that confuse Charly?"

"Precisely Mr. Robinson. Our objective today is to see how your rat responds to an inconsistent environment."

I put Charly in the Skinner box, like I always did. He ran to the lever and pressed it, like he always did, but nothing happened. Charly pressed it again, this time with more urgency. A pellet dropped down and he quickly ate it. When he pressed it a third time, he was shocked. Charly jumped back and stared at the lever for several minutes. Then cautiously he pressed it another time, but again he was shocked. Squealing, he ran frantically around the box, like he didn't know what else to do.

"He collapsed," I told Dr. Martin when the experiment ended.

"Precisely, Mr. Robinson. When we induce helplessness by offering our rats a confused and conflicting learning experience, they realize they have no control over their environment, and they simply quit. In humans we call it a state of exhaustion. Do all of you understand that?"

Not if it means torturing Charly! I nodded, but I didn't like it. Not at all. I held Charly long after the class was over.

———

The semester ended and Elizabeth was going home for the summer. I wanted to tell her how I felt about her—about us. I wanted to come see her, and meet the family she talked so much about all year. I wanted us to be a couple.

I didn't care what Peterson said. All our walks together were real dates. We shared personal thoughts and feelings. We held hands. We kissed. We even made love once! We *were* a couple! It bothered me Elizabeth called that just being friends, especially when I saw her on campus with Craig. Her indifference to me at those times was maddening, but I never told her how I felt. If I make her choose, she might pick him. I could stand being called her friend, even if it hurt so bad every time... but after everything, I couldn't lose her. I. Just. Couldn't.

"See you in the fall," I said as I stood in front of her dorm and waved goodbye. I walked slowly back to the psych lab to be with Charly.

CHAPTER 5
LONGING FOR IMPOSSIBLE THINGS

WILSONVILLE, 1968: I thought summer would never end. There were no more than a hundred students on campus, and most of them were married and had no time or interest in me. I tried to keep busy with the algebra class I had to take and my job mowing lawns with the grounds crew. But I hated math in high school and after the first week I knew I wasn't going to like college math either. The evenings were the hardest, when I was alone in my dorm with no one and no sound, but the haunting whistle of the Norfolk Southern Railroad train passing through town. All my time was filled with thoughts of Elizabeth. *What's she doing now? Is she with Craig? Is she thinking of me?* The more I thought of her, the worse I felt. I tried to block all those nagging questions by reading some of the books Doc gave me, but I couldn't concentrate. I forced myself to read every page, sometimes even mouthing the words to fix my attention, but I remembered none of the stories. My thoughts, no matter how hard I tried, always turned back to Elizabeth. I even tried listening to some of those records Doc gave me. He said Beethoven helped concentration. But it didn't. All I heard was that whistle. *Maybe I should get on that train and just go wherever it takes me...away from this empty room.* Frustrated and exhausted, I always gave up and walked to the lab where I spent my time talking with Charly, and wishing the summer would end so I'd see her again.

———

"Hey Elizabeth. Just get on campus?" I called out when I saw her walking toward the cafeteria the first day of fall semester. I tried to sound calm, but it was all I could do to keep from kissing her right in front of everyone.

"No, I've been here for a couple days. Why?"

I just stood there, looking at her, stunned. "I thought you would've called me when you got on campus. That's all,"

"Craig came back to school early, so we made plans. But I can go for a walk with you tomorrow if you want to."

I didn't know what to say. A part of me wanted to wrap my arms around her, pull her close, and kiss her with all the desire growing in me all summer. But her indifference also repulsed me. I hated, despised and loved her, all at the same time. I had dreamed of this moment, counted the days until I would see her again, and now, after three agonizing months of separation, I was finally with her, but felt nothing but emptiness. In that moment, like a bird that crashed into a glass window and laid stunned, broken on the ground, I realized that no matter how many times I told myself we were a couple, nothing had changed since Clairton. I was still alone. This was not the happiness I dreamed it would be here in my new life. This was not the love I desperately wanted it to be.

"I can't go for a walk with you tomorrow—or any day," I blurted out without any explanation, then turned and walked back to my dorm as fast as I could. Yet with every step, I still hoped she would call me back and say she was sorry, say she loved me too. But she didn't say anything.

———

"Need some company, Charly?" I called out when I opened the door of the psych lab. "I sure know I do."

He scurried to the front of his cage and waited anxiously for me to open it. "You know she's still dating that Craig guy," I said, picking him up, then dropping to the floor with him on my lap, all while gently stroking his fur. "How could I be so stupid to think she would break up with him for someone like me? But we spent so much time together last semester... and we did make love. She calls that just being friends! Can you believe it? Friends don't act like you're really special, then ignore you when I've waited all summer just to see her again. What kind of friend does that, Charly?"

He tilted his ear toward me. I swore he was actually listening, so I gave him a food pellet. He quickly ate it, then scratched at my hand for another one. I dug into my pocket and gave him two more.

"Sometimes, Charly," I said, my thumb tracing a gentle circle on his soft fur, "I feel like I'm caught in one of Martin's damned mazes...just like you. I'm done running after her. I mean it!" He pressed his little head against the palm of my hand and rubbed gently. "Yeah...you know exactly what that feels like, don't you? Thanks, Charly, for listening, I mean. I needed to talk with someone."

We sat together in front of his cage all afternoon.

———

Most of the semester felt like a long sleepless night. I hardly remember any of it, just that I held to my vow to move on from Elizabeth. I ate in the cafeteria when she wasn't there. I walked to my classes a different way every day. I avoided the golf course where we spent so much time walking and talking that last semester. Even in the Spanish class we still shared, I made a point to come right at the opening bell and leave as soon as it ended. I didn't want to be tempted to talk with her. *Maybe Peterson's right. Maybe we never had a real relationship. But why do I feel so empty without her?*

"How are you doing today, Charly?" I asked when I turned on the light in the psych lab. He was curled up in the back of his cage, but squealed when he saw me and scurried to the front, clawing repeatedly at the door to greet me. I never told Dr. Martin, but over the past semester Charly and I had developed a way to talk to one another. Every time I came into the lab, I set food in front of his cage. At first it was just his usual pellets, but when I gave him a piece of my hamburger, he went crazy for it—especially when it was smothered in ketchup. Then I would open the door, pick him up and give him his food while gently stroking his fur. After a couple days he learned to let me hold him without the food. In time he felt safe enough to let me hold him for hours while we talked. Although I did most of the talking, he seemed to enjoy our conversations as much as me. Sometimes we talked about my classes, or even some of the girls on campus I thought about dating. Other times I read out loud one of the books Doc gave me, so we could both enjoy it.

I thought about showing Dr. Martin how much Charly had learned from me, proving that his damned electric shocks were a lousy way to motivate him, especially when a hamburger smothered in ketchup was available, but I didn't bother. *My conversations with Charly are just between us.*

"Tired of being cooped up? Me too." I said, unlatching the door and picking him up, gently stroking his white fur in my usual greeting. Doing that always seemed to calm both of us.

"How about we do something special? You know, it's nearly Christmas after all. Or I think it is. I've lost track of the days lately." School let out for winter break and only a handful of students were left on campus. There was no lawn work to do, so most of my time was spent in the lab with Charly. "What if I set up a little tree for us? We can have our own celebration. I've even got a little gift in mind for you." He stood on his hind feet and pawed his whiskers, looking bashful now, then sat back down on my lap and tilted his head at me. "What's that? You don't have anything for me? Hey, don't worry. I wasn't expecting anything. I'll be perfectly happy with your company. So what do you say, Charly? Christmas day? Noon?"

Charly stared at me for a minute, then dropped his head and nuzzled against my leg as I gently stroked his fur. "Don't know what to say, do you? And don't worry about thanking me. That's what friends are for, right?"

———

"Have you thought about doing some volunteer work this semester?" Doc asked. I hoped I'd feel better when classes started in January, but I didn't. Apparently, it showed.

"Me? I don't think so. I'm too busy this semester." I had plenty of free time, just like last semester, but working in some shelter, or whatever he had in mind, was the last thing I wanted to do.

"I'm helping a friend of mine this weekend. Ron Jenkins." He ignored my hesitation. "I may have told you about him. He was a pastor, but now he's got a rehabilitation house in Lexington, and we're doing some painting there Saturday.

Pastor? I don't think so.

"I was thinking you might like to help us. But if you're too busy, I understand."

I wasn't sure what to say now. I had spent hours in Doc's office talking about classes and books, but this was the first time he ever asked me to do anything personal with him. "You're gonna be there too? Maybe I can find some time. You know, just this once."

――――――

It wasn't much of a building. More like an old house that should've been condemned long ago. And the neighborhood wasn't much better.

"Come on in!" someone shouted when we knocked on the door. "I'm in the living room." Ron Jenkins looked more like a janitor than a pastor—and not a very good one. There was more paint on him than the walls. I thought he was about Doc's age, but not nearly as tall, maybe even shorter than me. But what I noticed most were his eyes. They were dark brown, but they seemed charged, even electric.

"I'm not much of a painter," he said, smiling as he wiped his hands to greet us. "Daniel, right? Doc told me all about you. I hope you're better at this than me."

I had no experience painting, but I was pretty sure I was at least as good as this guy. "I don't charge anything," I said, looking around the room at the mess he made.

"Good. Because that's all I can afford." Smiling, he handed me a brush. "And I'm glad you're here. I really could use some help."

I was surprised how much I enjoyed the work. I'd never done anything like this growing up because we could never please the old man. We learned to make ourselves scarce on those rare occasions when he worked around the house. But helping Ron felt different.

What I enjoyed most was listening to the two of them talk. "How many people do you think you'll be able to house here, Ron?" Doc asked.

"In theory, we can have a dozen men, but we may have to limit the number, at least for now."

"I don't understand." Doc stopped painting the door frame, turning toward him.

"Politics!" Ron slapped his brush hard against the wall, splattering paint in all directions.

"How so?"

"You remember what happened to you in India when you tried to open that school for street kids?"

Doc's face tightened as he slapped his brush hard against the door, splattering even more paint than Ron did. "Politics!"

"What do you mean?" I asked before I could stop myself, then turned away quickly, hoping they wouldn't notice my intrusion.

"It's okay, Daniel," Ron said, dipping his brush into the paint can. "It's no secret a lot of people don't like what I'm trying to do, even people in the churches. They complained to city hall, and now we might have to limit the number of guys staying here—if they even allow us to open up."

"I had no idea," was all I said, but I wanted to know more about this guy. *He's not like any pastor I ever met.* I felt my face suddenly hot as Pastor Duncan flashed through my mind. I slapped my brush hard against the wall, splattering paint all over my shirt. Both of them looked toward me, surprised. "Just covering a bad spot," I said, slapping it again. Harder.

Later, sometime around noon, when Doc went out to buy lunch, I was helping Ron clean the brushes before he got back. It was a good time to ask something I'd been wondering about all morning. "Doc told me you used to be a pastor. How'd you ever end up doing this?"

"Long story, but I'll give you the short version. You're right. I was a pastor. Something I thought I always wanted to do. You know, helping people. But after a couple years of it, I guess it wasn't what I thought it would be."

"What do you mean?"

"Don't get me wrong. I still believe in the church. I just think maybe we've lost our focus." He dipped a rag into a jar of thinner and wiped his hands, not even trying to clean all the paint from his arms and face.

"I don't understand."

He looked right at me, his dark eyes blazing now with excitement. "The way I see it, the church is supposed to be like an emergency room. You know, a place to help hurting people. But that means going into the street and getting dirty."

I'll bet that kind of sermon went over well with your church!

His face darkened, and he threw his rag on the floor. "Whenever I tried to do that, my church board kept telling me to spend my time with our members. We went over it again and again until I finally quit."

"Why didn't you just go to another church, you know, one that agreed with what you wanted to do?"

"I did. Two other churches actually. But it was always the same reaction. That's when I bought this place. I figured the only way I could really live what I believed was here, doing this. Does that answer your question?"

I nodded, but I had a hundred more questions now. I never met anyone like him, at least not a pastor. "How about I come back again… to help you? We can talk more."

I came back the next Saturday, and every Saturday into February, even when Doc wasn't there. I liked talking with Ron, especially about his plans for the house.

"Doc said you wanted to use this place for rehab. Do you mean alcohol?" I asked.

"That's what I thought at first. But the more I'm on the street talking with people, particularly kids, I think we'll need to focus on drug rehab."

"You mean LSD? I heard that's getting to be a real problem in places like San Francisco. I didn't know it was here too?"

"It's here. Believe me. But I don't think that's going to be the problem the media makes it out to be. I think it'll be heroin. That's what we need to prepare for."

"You're kidding? I thought heroin was mostly in places like New York or Detroit with, you know...."

"You mean black people? That's what everyone thinks, but addiction's color blind. Believe me."

I stopped painting, turning toward Ron. I never heard anything about addiction in my psych classes. "How can you help?" I asked. "No offense, but you don't have any counselors and not much of a house."

"You're right about that. But I care, and I think that's what addicts really need from us. I'm also taking classes at UK in drug rehabilitation counseling. Maybe I can't do much, but it's more than what I did stuck inside a church office. Maybe now, in this dilapidated old house in this neglected part of town no one even admits exists, just maybe I can make a difference with someone who's hurting. And isn't that what the church is all about?"

Pastor Duncan flashed through my mind again. I felt my heart race. "You would hope so, but I don't think that's always the case."

"I'm afraid you're right. But if I can make a difference with just a couple people..."

Since that first day when I met Ron, I thought a lot about what he said. Now, tired and covered in paint, working for nothing every Saturday, I realized why I liked being with him. When I was here, I forgot about Elizabeth. And when I really let myself, I even forgot Clairton. I felt better than I had since I started college—maybe ever. I liked feeling good.

"You know, Ron. I'm studying psychology. Maybe I can help with more than painting." I dipped my brush in the bucket again. "But don't worry, you can pay me the same as I'm getting now."

We both laughed.

"You just might have a future in this type of work, Daniel." He handed me another can of paint.

CHAPTER 6
THE FIRES OF SPRING

WILSONVILLE, 1969. It was Valentine's Day when I walked into my Spanish class. That's when I saw a note on my desk with familiar handwriting. Blood rushed to my face. *I miss our walks. I miss you*, was all it said, but it was enough to make my heart race with all the hunger I tried so hard to forget. It was madness to see her. Not now. Not ever. If I opened myself to her again, if I allowed my passion to come out, I knew she would consume me. But I couldn't help myself. My agony during our separation was too much. My only chance was to treat her coolly.

"See you after class," I said casually.

Elizabeth was waiting for me in the courtyard, nervously shifting from one foot to the other. "I'm not seeing Craig anymore." She reached out her hand for me.

Take my advice and don't go near her. They don't call her the Ice Queen for nothing. Tear your heart out. I hesitated. She noticed and dropped her hand, looked down at the ground, breathed in slowly, then looked up at me again, struggling to make eye contact. Elizabeth seemed so vulnerable standing in front of me. Those dark brown eyes that always pulled me to her, then pushed me back again and again, were now wet.

"I missed you too much, Daniel," she said, her voice shaking, just a little. "I miss our talks. I miss looking at the stars with you on the golf course. I miss all the things we shared."

Why should this time be any different?

Her lips trembled as she spoke. "What I'm trying to say is I'm sorry if I hurt you."

Everything in me wanted to pull her close. But I didn't say anything for a long minute.

"I want us to be a couple...please."

The wind shifted and a faint whiff of her perfume drifted toward me, tickling my memory of our beautiful lovemaking that glorious spring morning. I couldn't stop myself. I pulled her to me, kissing her full on the mouth, with all the passion, all the hunger that smoldered since I first saw her a year ago. *Now I know she loves me as much as I love her!*

———

We spent all our time together after that, studying in the library, eating in a quiet corner of the cafeteria, and especially walking together on the now snow-covered golf course. Even at night, when all we had to keep us warm was a blanket and each other, we discovered together Orion and Ursa, and even Taurus the Bull in the brilliant blackness above us. Elizabeth was taking an astronomy course this semester and she was really excited about it. I found the night sky calming and cleansing in ways I never imagined. This was our special time together, since I couldn't afford formal dates in Lexington. On these nights, holding each other in the dark, she told me all about her family and her plans to be a teacher. I said I was thinking about counseling, maybe even with addicts like Ron was doing in Lexington. "He offered me a job when I get my degree." I didn't mention it probably wouldn't pay enough to live on. That was a conversation for another day.

Sometimes we surprised each other with a little gift. "This reminded me of you." I handed her a card with a picture of a little girl hugging a puppy. "I remembered you said you loved your dog when you were little."

"It looks just like my Trixie!" She smiled, kissing me gently on the lips.

Elizabeth did little things for me too. Sometimes I'd find notes she hid in my books when I was studying for a test. Maybe all it said was *I'm thinking of you*. She knew how hard my classes were, and her notes made me study harder.

One time I drew a picture for her. It was more like a cartoon, but it had a little boy and girl holding hands and saying *It's been good growing old with you*. She thought it was funny, and talked about that picture for days.

The one thing I appreciated most about Elizabeth were her shoes. I was only about five foot nine, but always wished I was taller. When we started dating, if she wore heels to something formal like a concert on campus, they made her taller than me. I never said anything, but when I met her at the dorm for our date one Saturday, she showed up wearing her flats, even though they didn't match her new dress. I thought she never looked more beautiful.

The next Monday morning, when I opened my mailbox, I was surprised to find another note from her. *You have become a part of me that is missed when we are separated. I love so many things about you—your love of nature, your thoughtfulness. I love most of all how much you love me.*

I read and reread her note a dozen times. "You have become a part of me." I said that line aloud over and over again on the bench in front of the college post office. It was early March and still cold in Kentucky, but I felt warmer than I ever had. *You have become a part of me*, was all I thought about that whole week.

It was my turn to surprise Elizabeth now. "I can't believe we're having dinner at Shaker Village!" she squealed when I showed her our reservation. "All the girls in my dorm have been dying to go there since it opened last year."

"And that's not all." I slowly pulled another envelope from inside my coat and dangled it in front of her.

"The Inn, too!" She grabbed my face and kissed me several times. "Can we sit outside all night and watch the sky? I've wanted to go there since I got to college. My daddy said it's the best place in this whole part of Kentucky to see the stars because it's so isolated. Oh, Daniel, this is our best date ever." She kissed me again, then suddenly pulled back and tilted her head, "How did you ever get reservations? I mean, I heard it's terribly expensive."

"Let's just say I have friends in high places." I didn't tell her Peterson gave me the reservations because his girlfriend-of-the-month had to go out of town this weekend. I wanted to savor the moment.

"I can't wait for Saturday to come," she cooed, pulling me to her again. I took both her arms and held her in front of me, just memorizing everything about her—the dimple on her cheek, the way her eyes glistened when she was happy, even that little scar on her forehead from that bike accident when she was six years old. I reached up and softly caressed it, imprinting the feel of her warm, soft skin on my fingertips. Her breath felt so warm on my cheek as we held each other. *We really are a couple now!*

But everything and everyone else was a blur. I didn't know what to say to Doc when I ran into him in the cafeteria. "Sorry I missed our last appointment. Just been a really busy semester," I mumbled. The truth was I forgot about it completely—and both appointments before that.

"Are your classes going well, Daniel?"

"Great, Doc. Great. No problems there at all. Elizabeth and I are doing great too. Maybe we can get together next week."

"That would be fine. Just give me a call."

"I will. I promise."

He started walking to his office, but turned back toward me. "I almost forgot. Ron Jenkins called. He said he hasn't seen you lately. He wanted to know if you're okay."

"Like I said, I'm doing great. Tell Ron I'm real sorry about not getting back to help him. It's just my classes this semester. But after midterms, I'll give him a call. I promise."

———

"I've been looking for you all afternoon," Elizabeth announced when she found me in the library. "What's that book you're reading?"

"Something Peterson recommended by a guy named Jack Kerouac. Pretty interesting, actually."

A smile spread across her face. "I've heard of him. He wrote that book about traveling across the country."

"*On the Road.* Yeh, he talks a lot about the freedom being on the road, almost like it's a religious experience. I kind of felt that on the bus coming here two years ago. You want to read it when I done?"

"I'd like that," she said sitting down next to me. "And that's sort of why I was looking for you. Would you like to take a trip with me?"

"You've got me really curious now," I said, slapping the book shut. "But where? I mean, what are you talking about?

"I was wondering... something I've been thinking about..." She hesitated. "...if you'd like to go to Ohio with me and meet my family? Maybe for Easter?"

"Absolutely. I can borrow Peterson's car." I didn't even try to hide my excitement. *She really does love me!* I nearly shouted the words out loud.

Spring came early in Ohio, and now driving through all this farmland with Elizabeth, it was even more beautiful than I remembered. The fields were still brown, waiting for the crops to be planted, but the land seemed anxious to turn green again with new life. And now coming into Kent, it was all I imagined it would be. There were no filthy mills, no tenement houses, no empty stores or abandoned buildings, no people yelling obscenities out the windows. Instead, large painted clapboard houses lined every street, all wrapped with porches intended for sitting in the evenings, waving to neighbors, and where families would gather and watch their children play in the yard. *This is a place Elizabeth and I could live someday.*

"There's even a college here!" I pointed toward the sign by the road.

"Kent State. My parents wanted me to go there, but I'm glad I didn't now." She squeezed my hand.

I squeezed back, smiling.

"Daniel, these are my parents, Dennis and Mary Johnson. Mom and Dad, this is Daniel."

They both looked to be in their late forties or early fifties. Mr. Johnson was shorter than me, his hair thin and his stomach stretched his flannel shirt that hung slightly over his dirty jeans. He had probably been working in the yard when we arrived.

"Glad to meet you, Daniel," he said, shaking my hand firmly. I liked him immediately.

Mrs. Johnson, on the other hand, was tall and thin, and dressed more formally. I thought she had spent a lot of time getting ready for us to arrive. She nodded, smiling just enough to be polite. It was obvious Elizabeth favored her mother's side of the family.

She introduced me so naturally. And her parents welcomed me so easily. I wondered how my family would act. The old man would be drunk and tell everyone to get the hell out of the front of the television. My mother would probably just stare out the window and say nothing.

Mrs. Johnson led us into the living room, while I looked all around this strange and wonderful world Elizabeth came from. The house was old, like so many I saw coming into town. But it was a good old, well taken care of. Ornate rugs covering the hardwood floors were coordinated with the wallpaper in each room. And the furniture looked expensive too. I had only seen pictures of houses this beautiful in magazines in the library. Never in person. *I thought her father worked in a car factory. How can they afford this fancy house? Maybe he's a manager?* I got the impression the decorating was Mrs. Johnson's doing.

But it was the family photos on the mantle that really caught my attention. *So that's what her sisters and brother look like. Maybe I'll meet them today.*

"Where did you say you were from, Daniel?" Mrs. Johnson asked when we all sat down.

"Near Pittsburgh. A place called Clairton." This was not something I wanted to talk about with my new family. "But I haven't been there in a long time. I call Kentucky my home now."

"And your parents? Do they still live in Clairton?"

I felt my face grow hot. I wanted to say the old man was probably living in the back of some bar and my mother spent most of her time in Woodville, but they didn't want to know any of that. "They're both dead." I hadn't planned to say that, but it just came out. Elizabeth looked at me, surprised, even shocked. I turned back toward her parents.

"I'm sorry to hear that," Mrs. Johnson answered. There was a long pause in the conversation. None of us seemed to know what to say now.

Maybe I can tell Mr. Johnson that Elizabeth has been teaching me all about the constellations? Maybe I can tell him how beautiful the night sky was at Shaker Village, just like he told her it would be. Maybe we can talk about anything, but Clairton...

"Care to help me in the garage?" Mr. Johnson finally asked, standing up. "Gotta get the tiller ready for the garden. Early spring this year and Mary wants to get her plants in the ground as soon as possible."

I glanced at Elizabeth. "Think I'll go with your dad, if that's okay with you?" She nodded, glad to change the conversation, too.

I followed Mr. Johnson out of the house, but stopped on the back porch. Those questions about my family still upset me. "Mind if I get a drink of water?" I asked.

"No problem. There's a glass in the cabinet by the kitchen sink. Help yourself and I'll meet you in the garage."

I found the glass, filled it, and slowly took a long drink to calm my nerves. It didn't help. I was about to go back outside when I heard voices in the other room.

"Well?"

"Well what, Mother?"

"You know what I'm asking. Do you love him? Because it's apparent he loves you."

I held my breath.

"I don't know. I mean I'm not sure. That's why I wanted you and Daddy to meet him."

What do you mean you don't know? We've been sleeping together since February! I wanted to shout at her from the kitchen.

"Have you told him you love him?"

"Sort of."

"What does 'sort of' mean?"

"Well, I did write him this note and said I loved all these things about him. I didn't come right out and say I loved him, you know, enough to marry him. But I know that's what he's thinking. I'm just so confused. What should I do?"

Confused? My heart stopped. That word hung heavy in the air all around me.

"Elizabeth, we women have to be very practical when it comes to things of the heart. What sort of future would you have with Daniel?"

"He says he wants to be a counselor. I think with drug addicts."

"That's a fine thing, but it doesn't sound like it will provide much of a living?"

"What are you trying to say? You don't like Daniel?"

"Not at all. He seems like a nice boy. I'm just not convinced you should be planning your future with him. That's all."

Their words seemed to float past me in a fog of confusion—a language I couldn't understand.

"While we're on the subject of your future, you might want to give some thought to Jeffrey Baker. You know he's always been sweet on you. He just got back from the Army. He served in Vietnam and we're all really proud of him at the church. His mother said he's going to be an attorney."

"I didn't come here to talk about Jeffrey Baker, Mother. It's Daniel I care about."

I snapped back to attention.

"All I'm saying is Jeffrey's got a real future. Just something to keep in mind. That's all."

"If you don't stop talking about Jeffrey, we're going back to school right now!

I smiled.

"Your father and I both want the best for you. It might be with Daniel. We just want you to take your time and think about it. That's all."

"Mother, no more talk about Jeffrey. I mean it!"

Without making a sound, I gently set my glass in the sink, then quickly walked out to the garage to help Mr. Johnson with the tiller. My feet barely touched the ground. *She loves me!*

———

All I thought about the whole drive back to Kentucky was how Elizabeth stood up to her mother. I wanted to say something, especially about our plans together now, but then she'd know I'd been listening to their conversation. I tried a couple times at school, but I never had the right words. Finally, a week later, while walking and holding hands on the golf course, I just blurted it out.

"You graduate in a couple weeks and we need to talk about next year. You know, about us."

She didn't say anything.

"Elizabeth?"

"Sorry, I was just thinking about my mother. What did you say?"

"I said what do you think about us, you know, next year?"

Letting go of my hand, she stopped, her brow furrowed. "As much as we've talked, why didn't you tell me your parents were dead?" she asked. "I feel like you don't trust me, and that really hurts."

She looked so hurt, standing there. But I wasn't prepared for that question, and I definitely didn't want to talk about my family. Not now. Not ever.

"You know I love you, Elizabeth. It's just that I don't remember much about them. That's all." I hated lying to her, but I had no choice. I reached for her hand again, but there was little warmth in her response.

"Look at the time!" she said as the clock chimed in the Admin building tower across campus. "We both have a three o'clock class. We can talk about us tomorrow. I promise."

But we didn't talk about us the next day, or the day after that. A week passed and I hardly saw her. *Maybe I should tell her the truth. But will she understand?* Finally, a week before graduation, I saw her coming out of her dorm. "It's important, Elizabeth. We have to talk. There's something I need to tell you, but not here." I took her again to that bench under our favorite oak tree on the golf course.

"I need to tell you about..." A thousand memories of Clairton rushed over me, and the words caught in my throat. "...I mean, you graduate soon and we have to make plans for next year," I said instead. "I thought we were all set, about us I mean. But now I think you've changed your mind."

Elizabeth didn't say anything. She just stared at the ground for several minutes. Finally, she turned toward me with a distant look I hadn't seen in a long time. "Be patient with me. It's just that I don't have a job yet. That's all."

I squeezed her hand, but she didn't squeeze mine back.

I only saw her a couple times after that, and there was no chance to talk about anything serious. "I'm sorry, Daniel. I have to study for my last test. But I'll see you Friday night, like we've been planning. Okay?"

This was a graduation celebration we had been talking about all semester. I had borrowed Peterson's car, and his best tie because it looked good with my new sport coat. I bought it special for this occasion. But when she greeted me in her dorm lobby, I noticed she was wearing heels that made her taller than me, something she hadn't done since we started dating. Over dinner, I tried to talk about our plans together, but again she changed the subject. "Nothing serious now, Daniel. Let's just enjoy this restaurant together." she said, kissing me lightly on the lips.

I attended her graduation ceremony the next morning, but she didn't ask me to sit with her parents like I expected. Now she was going back to Ohio, and we still hadn't talked about our plans. I walked by her dorm several times, and I know her parents saw me, because they sort of smiled my way, but they didn't say anything. I waited until they walked back into the dorm, leaving Elizabeth alone by their car. Running across the street, I grabbed her arm. "We still haven't talked about next year—about us, and you're leaving today." I knew I sounded desperate, but I didn't care. I reached for her hand.

She took mine with little enthusiasm. "I'm sorry, Daniel. It's not a good time right now. You know, with all the rush to get back to Ohio before dark." She looked at her watch, then toward her mother, who was now walking to the car. "Why don't you come to my house sometime soon, maybe on a weekend? We can talk then. I promise." She kissed me quickly on my cheek, then climbed in the car. I waved to her as they drove off.

"Hey, Charly," I said when I turned on the light in the psych lab, but he didn't greet me like he usually did. He barely looked up. "Are you okay?" I asked, opening his door and reaching for him. "Sorry I haven't been here to see you in a while, but I've been busy with Elizabeth this semester." I saw her again, driving off with her parents, and leaving me standing alone on the sidewalk. "I just need someone to talk to. That's all." I closed my eyes and let the feel of his fur under my fingers now calm me.

———

One week led to another and then another, and soon May was gone and it was well into June before I finally forced myself to Doc Samuels' office.

"Elizabeth and I made plans for me to go to her house so we could talk about next year." I blurted out before I even sat down. "But there's always some delay...and it's been more than a month now!"

Doc leaned back in his chair. "Let me ask you this, Daniel. How many times has she called you?"

"We talk almost every night."

"I know you talk to her all the time, but how many times has she actually called you?"

I knew the answer, but I couldn't admit something I denied since she left campus. I stared out the window for several minutes. "She hasn't called me at all," I finally mumbled and slumped back in my chair. We both sat there, my words echoing in my head. *She hasn't called me at all.*

Finally, I stood. "I gotta go to work." It wasn't true, and Doc knew it, but I didn't care. I walked slowly back to my empty dorm room.

Lying on my bed in the dark, I stared at the ceiling, like I did most nights. *Ring-g-g-g!* I ran to the payphone in the hall. I always left my door open at night—just in case she called me.

"Hey, Daniel."

My heart beat faster hearing her voice again. "Hey, Elizabeth. Glad you called." I tried not to sound too excited,

"Can you come to my house this weekend?"

"Absolutely! No problem at all." I nearly screamed into the phone. "I don't have to work tomorrow, and I can borrow a car from one of the guys on the grounds crew. I already asked him about it." The words poured out of me in a flood of excitement. I caught my breath. "So then...great! I'll see you tomorrow morning."

"Good, see you then, Daniel."

She loves me!

Early the next morning, long before the sun was even up, I called Doc at his house, getting him out of bed. "Great news!" I shouted, even before he said a word. "Elizabeth called and I'm going to her house this morning. I'll tell you all about it when I get back." Then I slammed the phone down and ran out toward the parking lot.

———

Kent was even more beautiful than I remembered. *I'll bet she's waiting for me on her porch.* I remembered it wrapped around the whole front of the house. She said it was her favorite place, because her family always sat together there in the evenings. *We'll have a porch just like it someday when we're married!* I pulled in her driveway, jumped out of the car, ran up the steps two at a time, then knocking several times until Mrs. Johnson appeared.

"Hello, Daniel," she said politely. I wanted to give her a hug, like families do, but she didn't offer herself, and I didn't try.

"Elizabeth will be down in a minute." She walked back into the kitchen, leaving me waiting awkwardly in the hall.

"Daniel, I'm glad you made it safe." Elizabeth called from the top of the stairs. "Good trip?" She allowed me to kiss her hello when I reached for her, but it was not as warm as I thought it should be for lovers.

"Have you talked with your parents, I mean about us?" I tried not to sound anxious, but I couldn't help myself.

"Let's sit in the living room," she said, walking on ahead, without even offering her hand. A knot formed in my stomach as she motioned for me to sit in the chair, and not beside her on the couch.

"You know how worried I was about getting a teaching job. Well, I was offered one here in Kent. I start right after Labor Day." Her words seemed so... impersonal, like she was talking with just a friend—not lovers planning to get married!

"That's okay." I tried my best to sound positive. "I can do my grad work at Kent State, and you can keep teaching here." I wanted to sit next to her on the couch, take her hand, hold her in my arms. But...

"There's more, Daniel," she said. Her words hung heavy in the air. I held my breath...and waited. "We've had wonderful talks together, and you know I really like you, a lot..."

Oh God. My stomach came up into my throat.

"...but I've been dating a fellow from my church. His name is Jeffrey Baker. He was an Army lieutenant in Vietnam and now he's going to Kent State and then get a law degree, maybe at Case Western when he graduates. Anyway, I've had a lot of time to think, you know, about us. It's not you. It's me. I'm just not good enough for you. You deserve someone really special. That's all."

My head throbbed. My hands shook. The room reeled out of control. I wanted to put my hands over my ears, blocking out her words. But I just sat there, barely breathing.

"I really care for you, Daniel. I do, but..."

"Stop! Please don't say it." I know I sounded desperate. I didn't care. Standing, I took her hands in mine, then pulled her toward me. Everything in me wanted to hold her close until she realized she was wrong—about everything. But her dark eyes, those deep shimmering pools that always drew me to her, now seemed so distant. I stood there in silence for a minute, maybe more, just looking at her one last time. I let go of her hands, slowly walking out of the room. In the driveway, I turned and looked back as she closed the door on the life I could never have now. I drove back to Kentucky, back to college, back to my dorm room —alone again. Always alone.

———

"Charly. It's me," I called out, turning on the light in the psych lab. He didn't greet me at the front of his cage, but I wasn't surprised. Dr. Martin said he was getting old. "Charly?" I eased open his door. "Maybe he's sleeping?" He laid there.

"Are you okay?" I picked him up gently, but he didn't move in my hand for a minute... two minutes. His soft white fur felt so cold.

"Oh, Charly. No!" My eyes burned wet. I bit my lip hard. *How long has he been... like this? Why didn't someone check on him?* I felt my face flush hot as tears rolled down my cheeks. I didn't even bother wiping my eyes, but just stroked Charly tenderly, again and again. Slowly... I dropped to the floor and sat there with him on my lap...and remembered.

Charly. That's what I'm going to call you...

Look what I brought you. Hamburger! I heard him squeal again.

Listen how this book starts, Charly. It's by a guy named Salinger. I saw him again, tilting his head like he always did when I talked to him. Sometimes, I know he really understood what I said.

What if I set up a little Christmas tree for us? I've even got a little gift in mind for you.

Don't worry about thanking me. That's what friends are for, right?...

I held him late into the night.

I didn't call Doc the next day, or even go to work on Monday.

"Daniel, are you okay?" Doc called through the locked door of my room sometime on Tuesday, or it could have been Wednesday. I wasn't sure—and I didn't care.

I didn't answer him.

"It's me," he called again, this time louder. "The guys told me you haven't been to work for several days. Are you okay?"

I tried to ignore him, but he wouldn't go away. Finally, I staggered from my bed and opened the door, just a crack. "I'm sick,"

But he knew I was lying.

"Did you make your trip? I mean, did you see Elizabeth?"

I wanted to tell him what happened, that she dumped me for some other guy, that I felt so lost and alone, that I was dying inside. "Just sick. That's all."

"Can I come in? You look terrible. Anything I can do to help?"

"Not now. Like I said, I just caught a bug on my trip."

He ignored me, gently pushing open the door and walked into my darkened room. The shades were shut, the only light coming now from the open door. Walking past me, he pulled back both shades. Light flooded the room. "So how did it go with Elizabeth?" he asked again.

"She got a job," I mumbled, rubbing my eyes, trying to adjust to the first light I had seen since I got back to campus.

"That's good news, right? You were worried about that. Here in Lexington?"

"Ohio."

"Is there a school there so you can still study counseling?"

Slumping onto my bed, I swallowed hard, as the words caught in my throat. "She's seeing someone else." Tears welled up in me, filling my eyes. I turned away, staring out the window. I saw my whole life pass in front of me, every single miserable minute—all over again.

"You know, Doc..." my voice cracked. It hurt to say the words, but I couldn't stop them. "...sometimes I feel like Charly running down one maze after another. Everywhere I go, I get blocked.... and I'm so tired of running. Sometimes... I just want to roll over and quit."

Sliding his chair next to me, Doc sat down and laid his hand on my shoulder without a word. I turned back toward him, trying my best to sound confident now. "I'm still going to grad school and become a counselor, just like I planned. I'm okay, really."

He squeezed my shoulders, ever so gentle. "I think there's something else bothering you," he said. "What is it?"

I couldn't say the words. They were too hard.

"You can tell me."

"It's Charly. He died," I said, dropping my head onto my chest. "When I came back Saturday night, I found him. He had plenty of food and water and everything. Dr. Martin said he was getting old, but I think it was more than that, you know, cause I spent so much time with Elizabeth. I can't help thinking if I spent more time with him... then maybe he wouldn't have died."

I breathed a long sigh, looking up at Doc. "I know it sounds stupid, but when I found him dead, I sat on the floor of the lab and held him all night. I just couldn't let him go. Is there something wrong with me? I mean, crying over a lab rat. But I still can't stop thinking about him."

Doc gently patted my back. "I'm sorry that Charly died, Daniel. And no, there's nothing wrong with you. Charly was very special. But are you sure you're okay?"

"I'll be fine. Really," I said, stepping back and looking up at him. "I just need some time, you know, to think."

We both stood, then started for the door, when I stopped, looking at him again. "As weird as it sounds, I think Charly loved me more than Elizabeth ever did. God, I'm gonna miss him." Just admitting that, saying out loud how alone I felt all my life, it welled up then, this hot, sharp pain in my chest. I bit my lip to stop the tears, but it was too late. Dropping into Doc's arms, I wept. I wept for Charly, who died, for Elizabeth, who deserted me, for my father, who never loved me, for my mother, who was never there for me, and especially for Pastor Duncan, who crushed my soul.

"I just wish... that I had a normal family... like everyone else," I cried out between sobs, trying hard to catch my breath. "It would've made... my life... so much easier."

Doc held me, without saying a word.

CHAPTER 7
THE HELPLESS INSTRUMENTS
OF BLIND CHANCE

WILSONVILLE, 1969: I made it through the summer without Elizabeth by hiding in Doc's office reading every book on his shelves. Here was a refuge where I could escape my own world of rejection and loneliness. Here I travelled across millennia to times and places, where I met people I never dreamed existed, people like me who suffered through love and loss, yet not only survived, but conquered, and all with the turn of a page. Here, at least for a time, in this world of imagination, I found a respite from the real world that had always disappointed me so bitterly. Here, amidst all the stories on Doc's shelves, I found that I could be alone, yet no longer lonely, because a thousand new friends were always with me.

But I could never finish Hawthorne's *Scarlet Letter*. All I saw was Pastor Duncan, the one person I would never allow inside my sanctuary.

More than the books I devoured in Doc's office, just being with the only man who ever cared for me, helped ease my loneliness. Mostly we talked about what I was reading, but sometimes, when I felt strong enough, we talked about Elizabeth too...

It was never easy, though.

"I hate to say it, but there's a part of me that would take her back today if she called." The words caught as I turned and looked out the window at several couples walking by. I sighed. I only saw her. "Am I the only one who ever felt like this? I mean, is there something wrong with me, because I want someone who doesn't want me?"

"It might seem like that right now," Doc said, "but your situation is actually more common than you think. Trust me."

I kept staring out the window.

"Why do you think there are so many books written about lost love?" he asked now.

I still didn't answer him.

"School won't start for a couple days. Are you interested in reading about someone who felt the same way you do? It's called *Of Human Bondage*." He grabbed a book on his shelf.

"Maybe," I mumbled. "I got nothing else to do."

Three days later I was back in his office. "Hated it!" I tossed the book on his desk.

"How so?"

Grabbing a chair, I sat down hard. "I hated that guy Philip 'cause he was so weak. I've got no patience for weak people. My psych classes are full of them, always complaining how unfair life is. God, they make me sick sometimes!"

Doc tilted his head and rubbed his chin, like he always did when he knew he struck a nerve. "Let me ask you a question. Do you see me as weak?"

"Course not. You're the strongest person I know."

"What if I told you I have a severe deformity, just like Philip? Would that surprise you?"

I didn't answer. I wasn't sure what he meant.

"I've not told many people about this, especially here at the college..."

Sitting up in my chair, I leaned toward him.

"I think you know my parents were missionaries in India. But did you know I didn't live with them? Missionary kids were sent to boarding schools then. Believe me, they were something out of a Dickens novel. The headmaster, in particular, seemed to take great pleasure in humiliating all the Americans. He was especially brutal to me..." Sweat beaded on his forehead as he shifted in his chair. Pulling out a handkerchief, he wiped his face. "What made it even worse..." His words came slowly, staring past me now. "...it was all done in the name of God."

Doc took a deep breath. "Try explaining to a six-year-old boy your parents love God so much, they're going to abandon you in a hideous place for twelve years, just so they can help strangers in some remote village."

I stared at him, not blinking once, barely breathing.

"I still struggle with feelings of abandonment, like I'm running behind everyone else, like I can never catch up, no matter how hard I try. And what am I now, forty-eight? So I have a great deal of sympathy for weak people."

I had a thousand questions, but I couldn't ask one of them. I sat there in silence, with my eyes fixed on him, seeing him for the first time. This was... a special moment.

Doc cleared his throat, folding his handkerchief and stuffing it back in his pocket. Then he looked toward me. "Now about the book..." And just like that, our special moment was gone. "...didn't Philip walk away from Mildred and marry Sally? What are your thoughts about that?"

All I could think about was his boarding school, and that he trusted *me* with that very painful, personal story. I shook my head to remember what he just asked. "What? Oh, the book. To be honest, I was glad that Philip guy finally got some backbone. And I liked Sally. She was a simple girl, but she loved Philip completely. Not like that bitch Mildred. I'm glad the story ended that way."

"So you agree even broken people can find love?" He paused to let that sink in. "What I'm asking, Daniel, is do you think you'll find someone who loves you like Sally loved Philip?"

I wanted to believe he was right, but everything in my life said no. My face grew hot. Shifting in my chair, I looked down at the floor without answering him. Finally, I looked up. "I guess that's why I keep coming back to your office, isn't it? I want to believe what you're saying, but it's just so hard to..."

"To what, Daniel? Trust people?"

"I trust you. More than anyone. But there are some things..." I swallowed hard. "...some things I can't talk about. Even with you." That was as close as I ever came with Doc—or anyone—to open that dark part of my past.

"For what it's worth, whatever it is, I want you to know you're safe with me, like one of my own sons."

Like one of my own sons! That's what Pastor Duncan said to me when he... Suddenly I was back in Clairton, back in his office. I heard him praying, felt him rubbing all over me. *Think of something else, hurry!* I tried hard to push that memory out of my head, but now I was living it all over again. Fingers against my lips. Old Spice burning my nose...the room spun around... sounds were coming in from a distance.

"Are you okay, Daniel?"

My head felt warm and soaked. "I gotta go. I'm not feeling good right now." I ran to my dorm room, where I sat on the edge of my bed for several hours, in the dark. Finally, as the sun was rising, I buried my head in my hands. "God, if there is a God," I groaned. "I want to be different. Please God. Make me different. Make me normal."

But God was silent.

———

Fall semester started soon after that, and my classes kept me busy. I tried to be different. I even talked with Doc about my family. Just bits and pieces at first, but more than I ever told anyone. We talked about how the old man yelled at us one day, then said nothing for weeks, like we were invisible. We talked about how he embarrassed us with that neighbor woman, about his drunken tirades, and even that night he nearly killed Robert over the car he treated better than any of us.

"Where was your mother in all of this?" Doc asked. "Is she still with your father? You haven't mentioned her at all."

I tapped my fingers against my leg. I couldn't tell him she spent most of her time in Woodville. That's too... embarrassing. Am I going to be like her someday? Is that our family tradition? No one will ever know about that—ever. But the words just came out. I couldn't stop them. "She's in a mental hospital," I mumbled, slumping back in my chair.

"Am I going to end up just like her? Am I?" My voice no more than a whisper. "If I am, then there's no reason to go on."

My mother was crying again, holding Grandma Emma's recipe book. An ambulance siren wailed for her in the back of my mind, coming ever nearer. My chest was tight. My mouth dry, so dry. It was coming for me one day, too. I knew it.

Pulling his chair beside me, he put his hand on my arm, saying nothing. He just waited. Finally, slowly, I started breathing again. "For a while I blamed my mother for what we had to put up with from the old man," I said slowly now, measuring every word. "But her life growing up was a lot worse than mine... so I... forgive her for not being there for us. I don't even blame my old man, even though he really was a prick. Mostly I blame..."

The words caught in my throat. I couldn't say his name out loud. If Doc knew the truth, if he knew what Pastor Duncan did to me... I dropped my head onto my chest, staring at the floor in silence. Just breathing... in... out. That was all I could manage.

He leaned toward me, whispering. "Whatever happened to you, whatever has been choking you all these years, I want you to know, it wasn't your fault."

How could he know about Pastor Duncan? No one knows about that night...and no one ever will! I jerked my head up and looked right at him. "What are you talking about?" I asked, trying to sound calm. But I knew he heard the hitch in my voice. My heart raced.

He leaned even closer to me, then slowly, emphasizing every word, said again, "I want you to know, Daniel, it wasn't your fault."

My face heated. "I told you it was my mother's illness. That's all!" I snapped.

Again, he ignored me and gently put both his hands on my shoulders. "Daniel. I know we're not talking about your mother, or even your father. Whatever it was that someone did to you, probably someone in the church, someone very close to you, I want you to know it wasn't your fault."

My heart was like thunder in my chest. My pulse pounded in my ears. I wanted to run out of the room, but I couldn't move. "Dammit, Doc!" I jerked away from him, my jaw clenched. "I don't know what you're talking about!" Everything in me wanted him to stop asking about... But he didn't stop.

He put his hands back on my shoulders, his grip gentle, yet firm, leaned into me and looked right in my eyes. "I'll say it again. It wasn't your fault."

I shook, just a little at first, then more, until I couldn't stop. I was back in Pastor Duncan's office. I smelled his Old Spice...and the whiskey. I heard him praying, felt him rubbing. All the pain, all the rage, rushed over me again. My head throbbed. I felt my heart coming out of my chest. *I'm going to die!* Then I heard Doc's voice again. "It wasn't your fault." And again, "It wasn't your fault. I'm not going to stop saying it until you start believing it, Daniel."

Without even thinking, I repeated his words. "It wasn't my fault." I said each word carefully at first, intentionally, without emotion, wanting them to be true. I said them again. "It wasn't my fault." And again, this time with all those memories rushing over me. "It wasn't my fault! It wasn't my fault!"

I jumped up from my chair, walking quickly to the window. I looked back toward Clairton, back four years to that awful night when Pastor Duncan robbed my soul from me.

"It wasn't my fault, you sick bastard. It was all your fault!" I screamed as tears ran down my cheeks. "And I'm not going to let you ruin my life anymore!"

My words echoed off the walls until the only sound left was my heart pounding in my ears. Doc walked across the room and laid both his hands again on my shoulders. Without saying a word, he just held me. And in that moment, I knew... I really knew. It. Wasn't. My. Fault.

———

"Statistics is killing me," I complained again, this time after the fall midterm exams. "Another C, and I'm glad to get that. Believe me, you have no idea how much I hate math. It's not like I'll ever need it counseling."

Doc did his best to help me, but no matter how much I studied and memorized all the formulas, they never sunk in.

"How's your counseling course coming? Any better?"

"Probably get a B, but it won't be enough to bring up my Statistics grade. Truth is, I'm not sure I can put up with two more years of this stuff in grad school. I'm just burned out." This wasn't the first time I vented my frustrations with him. Grad school didn't make much sense anymore, not like it did when Elizabeth and I.... there was a sharp stab in the pit of my stomach just thinking about her again. *God, when will I ever be free of her?*

"So what are you thinking of doing when you graduate?" he asked. "I think you already know your degree in psychology won't open up a lot of job options."

I remembered something, an off-hand comment from Peterson a week ago. I was complaining about Elizabeth being so impressed that Jeffrey what's-his-name had been a lieutenant in the Army, like that was some big deal. "You oughta be a pilot! They get all the women," Peterson said. I agreed with him, but I was interested in just one woman.

"Martin told us that in his first class. But I just thought about something. It might sound crazy..." I hesitated, not sure how I wanted to say this. "...but what if...I joined the Air Force? You know, to be a pilot."

Doc sat up in his chair. He looked genuinely surprised.

"Think about it," I said, growing more animated now. "It's not like I'd be in the jungles of Vietnam. And if I still want to go to grad school afterward, the government will pay for it. What do you think? I mean about being a pilot?"

Doc leaned back and rocked slowly, mulling over what I just told him. "You know," he finally said, "that just might be a good option for you." We both sat there, not saying anything now for a minute. Then he leaned forward, opening his desk drawer. "I have a friend who retired from the military. If you want..." he hesitated, "...I can call him." It was more of a question than an offer, and until that moment, I didn't know the answer. Sure, I thought about it when I was tired of studying. But now....

———

May finally arrived and I was supposed to sign my papers for the Air Force right after I graduated, but the last thing on my mind was studying for final exams. All I could think about was Elizabeth. Two days ago, Peterson said he heard from someone back in Kent that she broke up with that Jeffrey guy.

"How about you and me taking a trip to Ohio?" I slammed shut my psych book... and waited.

He shook his head without even looking at me. "You really got it bad for the Ice Queen, don't you, Robinson?"

I hated it when he called her that, but I had gotten used to ignoring him. I just waited.

"Okay," he finally shrugged. "But the only day I've got free is Monday. We'd have to go up and back in one day."

"That's more than enough time for what I've got in mind."

I barely slept at all that night just imagining what Elizabeth would say when I told her my good news about the Air Force.

I've missed you so much, Daniel.

All I've been thinking is how wrong I was. Will you take me back?

A pilot! I'm so proud of you!

Yes, of course, I'll marry you!

Monday morning couldn't come soon enough for me.

———

After five hours taking turns driving through Ohio, I was relieved—and nervous—when I finally saw the sign. *Welcome to Kent. Home of Kent State University.*

When we pulled into her driveway and I saw her house again, I took several deep breaths, climbed out of the car and walked slowly toward her house. *It'll be different this time*, I told myself with every step.

I took a deep breath to calm my nerves, knocked several times on the door...and waited. I stood there forever, waiting for her. *Please God.* The door finally opened. "Mrs. Johnson. Hi. It's me, Daniel Robinson."

"Yes, Daniel, I remember you," she said, her face blank and her words flat, even cold. Not the sort of greeting I expected, especially since Elizabeth broke up with that guy. I was sure she'd be glad to see me.

"Sorry to drop in unexpected..." My voice cracked. "...but I had to make a trip nearby and I thought I'd say hello to Elizabeth."

Mrs. Johnson hesitated. "She's not here now," she finally said.

"When will she be back?" I tried to sound nonchalant.

"She's out of town all week. On her honeymoon in Florida with Jeffrey."

My knees buckled. I felt the air go out of me.

"When they get back, I'll tell them you stopped by. But it was nice seeing you again," she said and closed the door.

I stood there, too numb to move, but somehow forced myself to walk back to Peterson's car—and out of Elizabeth's life forever. I wanted to die.

"Married? God, Robinson, I'm sorry. I had no idea. Honest. I swear I heard from a girl here in Kent who knows Elizabeth. I know she told me they broke up. If I had any idea it wasn't true, I never would've brought you here. I'm really sorry, man. God, I feel awful."

Not half as bad as I feel! I turned away from him and looked up at her house one last time.

Peterson backed the car quickly out of the driveway, jammed it into gear, floored the accelerator and headed west out of town. We only drove a couple blocks when he suddenly slammed on the brakes, turning the car toward the curb. He smiled. "Listen, man. Don't let the Ice Queen ruin a perfectly good road trip. Think about it. We're a half mile from Kent State, with ten thousand girls all looking for guys like us. I know a couple of them—and I've got their phone numbers. You game? I mean, what've we got to lose?"

I just want to go back to my dorm, and back to Doc.

"Come on, man. This is your final semester of college. You gonna let the Ice Queen be the last thing you remember about Kent? It's a perfect spring day. For once in your life, Robinson, try to have some fun. It'll be like a graduation present. What do you say? You in?"

I didn't answer or even look at him. All I heard was Mrs. Johnson. *She's on her honeymoon with Jeffrey.*

Peterson took my silence as a yes and turned the car around and drove east on Main Street toward the university. We were going through the bar district downtown when we saw it. The sidewalks were filled with broken glass, debris and piles of rubbish. Every building on both sides of the street was damaged. Most of the windows were covered with plywood. Some buildings looked burned. Cops were everywhere.

"Look at that sign, Peterson!" I pointed toward an official looking poster on the front of a building. "Martial law! What the hell happened here?"

He only frowned.

We crossed the Cuyahoga River slowly, still staring all around, heading east toward the campus. "Don't worry about it," Peterson said. "Probably a party that got out of hand. Just look for Prentice Drive. There's got to be a phone in one of those buildings."

It was nearly noon. I expected to see the campus filled with students walking to class, not soldiers lined up everywhere. On the edge of the Commons we saw maybe a hundred of them climb out of huge Army trucks parked in front of a burning pile of rubble.

"That's the Ohio National Guard!" Peterson stared all around as he drove slowly down the street. "And I think that's the ROTC building they're guarding, or it *was* the ROTC building."

Dark, foul smoke drifted toward us from the huge smoldering pile of blackened beams, twisted metal and broken glass. It quickly surrounded us, and the car was soon filled with that acrid smell. Frantically rubbing my raw, burning eyes, I still couldn't see anything. And now my lungs were on fire! "God, Peterson, I can't breathe!" Coughing hard, he slammed on the brakes and rubbed his red eyes. "What the hell happened here?"

For once, I saw fear in his face... and that scared me. But I couldn't look away from that line of soldiers forming in front of us.

"Hey, what's going on?" Peterson called out the window to a student running by.

"We're protestin' the fuckin' war in Vietnam, man." He waved his arms, hollering back at us. Peterson jammed the car in gear and quickly caught up with him.

"What about the ROTC building?" he called again, this time much louder. "What happened to it?"

The protester stopped running, pointed at the smoking debris, and smiled. "We burned it down, man. The Army got no fuckin' business on our campus."

"But the National Guard...?"

"Fuck 'em! And fuck the war in Vietnam!" he shouted, running now toward a crowd forming on the Commons.

"I gotta see what's going on," Peterson said, his eyes wide with excitement. He quickly steered the car into a parking spot and jumped out.

I didn't know what to do, so I ran after him toward the Commons.

"God, Peterson! There must be a thousand people here!"

Suddenly a jeep drove from behind a line of soldiers, moving slowly across the Commons toward a large group of students. "You are ordered to disperse! You must leave the area immediately!" a soldier in the Jeep declared over a bullhorn.

No one moved. Instead they all chanted, "Pigs off campus!"

"You are ordered to disperse!" the soldier announced again.

The crowd moved forward and chanted even louder. "Pigs off campus!" Several protesters threw rocks.

Someone barked a command. Soldiers quickly formed several lines, then began marching right past Peterson and me.

"Did you see that?" I called over the noise.

"What?"

"Look at their uniforms. They've got their names covered. Why'd they do that?"

"Beats me. All I see is they got guns!"

"What's that mean?"

"It means they're expecting a war!" Peterson yelled back as we muscled our way through the crowd.

The protesters shouted louder, throwing more rocks.

Another command rang over the bullhorn, followed by several rounds of tear gas. Then screams burst from the crowd.

"What the hell's happening?" I called out, but Peterson didn't hear me. He pushed his way through the crowd, away from the gas now enveloping us. I ran to catch up with him, but the gas flooded my eyes. My throat burned, choking me.

"We gotta get away from these crazy hippies," I heard him yell from somewhere. "Follow me...."

But where? I couldn't see him in the crowd!

Rubbing my eyes, I thought I saw him for a second about twenty feet ahead of me, pointing toward a building at the top of the hill. I tried to call out, but my throat stung too much. All I could do was stumble after him.

"You are ordered to disperse!" the soldier in the Jeep barked again.

The protesters around me shoved forward, then flung more rocks. Some even grabbed the gas canisters and threw them back at the soldiers. Louder chanting rose from every direction. "PIGS OFF CAMPUS! PIGS OFF CAMPUS!"

The noise was deafening! Blinded by the gas, I tried to get away, but the crowd swept wildly around me. Suddenly, someone grabbed my arm, pulling me back. It was Peterson!

"I can't see—the gas!" I tried to tell him over the maddening noise, but my throat hurt too much.

"We gotta get outta here!" he shouted in my ear, leading me across the parking lot toward some building. The crowd surged around again. They pushed us left, then pulled us right, then pushed us left again. We couldn't move! Someone rammed into me from behind. I fell down, as the mob pressed in on me from all sides. Elbowing a guy in front of me, I clawed back to my feet. But I lost sight of Peterson again! *Where the hell is he?* I rubbed my eyes, frantically looking everywhere.

That's when I saw that kid, maybe ten feet in front of me. He didn't look any more than fifteen, but he was jumping up and down and screaming at the soldiers, "Pigs off campus! "Pigs off campus!" He was wearing a red cowboy shirt—the kind Billy always wore, and I froze. More people bumped into me from behind, knocking me left and right again. But I just stood there, transfixed by what I thought was my kid brother in the middle of all this madness.

Suddenly a gas canister hissed through the air and landed beside me. There were more screams! The crowd surged in from every direction. I was tossed back and forth in a wave of seething rage. *I can't see! I can't breathe! Please, God, get me away from all these crazy hippies...* but I couldn't take my eyes off that kid.

Without any warning, the soldiers suddenly turned, marching away from us. The crowd, pounded after them, sounding a victory chant, "Pigs off campus! Pigs off campus!" They shoved me forward, right next to that kid. He turned, saying something I couldn't hear. I stood there, staring at Billy.

"Wait for me, Daniel," he called from somewhere behind me. But I ignored him and pedaled after Frankie.

"I told you get outta the fuckin' way. Now look what you done!" The old man jerked him up by his arm and there was that god-awful sound when he broke it.

I saw him walking out the door with those two welfare people...wearing that stupid red cowboy shirt.

"Pigs off campus!" blasted in my ears again. I shook my head, looking up just as the soldiers reached the top of the hill. Suddenly, they pivoted toward us. *They're coming back. I have to run!* But I couldn't move in the crowd. *I'm trapped!*

The soldiers stood there for just a second. *Oh, God! They're pointing their rifles at us!* The wind shifted. Tear gas blew all around me again. Out of nowhere, a single shot screamed out! A god-awful silence followed for maybe two seconds, maybe a minute. It seemed like forever. That horrid sound hung in the air.

Then more shots—dozens of them—shattered the silence. Almost with one voice, the people around me cried out with this anguished wail. Everyone stampeded in all directions. Some got knocked down, others stepped on. A burly, bearded guy slammed into me with his shoulder. *I'm going to die!*

The gas cleared for a minute, as the crowd opened up around me. Dozens laying everywhere, screaming, crying...and some of them... weren't moving. I saw that kid again... just two feet away... on the ground with more blood around him than I ever thought possible. It ran from a gaping wound in his head, across the parking lot to the curb.

His face is gone! All that was left was a bloody, unrecognizable mass of flesh and bone and brains!

I couldn't think. I couldn't feel anything. I couldn't move. Someone grabbed my arm, spun me around and yanked me away from that sickening sight.

"Robinson, you okay? God, you got blood all over you! You hit?"

I couldn't answer. All I saw was Billy—no, not Billy! That kid in the cowboy shirt with his blood and brains splattered all over me.

"Robinson! For God's sake! We've got to get the hell out of here!" He yanked my arm again.

I shook my head. I had to wake up from this nightmare. "Peterson?"

"Run, dammit! Run!" He dragged me away from that horrid sight in front of me. We ran back to the car, through the terrified students, through the tear gas still clouding the air, through the bodies all over the Commons. Peterson slammed the car into gear, floored the gas pedal and careened through the parking lot. I had no words. What I saw, what I felt, how scared I was—there was no describing any of it. I'd been in hell, and I was never coming out again.

———

I need to see Doc! was my only thought when we got back on campus. I slammed the door of Peterson's car and ran to his office. It was nearly eight o'clock, but I hoped he was still there. He was the only one who could help me make sense of all the madness I'd just seen.

The light in his office was still on, so I didn't bother knocking. Doc looked up from his desk and stared at my shirt. "Daniel, you've got blood all over you! Are you okay?" He jumped up and hurried to me.

"Have you heard what happened at Kent State today?" I blurted out. "I was there!"

I tried to catch my breath. "The tear gas was so thick I can still taste it. What is it now—seven or eight hours later?"

"And the screams...." I could still hear them. "It was more like wailing. People were crying. Even some of the soldiers."

Just breathe.

"That's what I keep hearing in my head—even now—that wailing." I felt like I was talking from some faraway place. "The only way I can describe what I saw is *Dante's Inferno*. God, it was awful."

"Are you okay? The blood...?"

I looked down at my shirt, then back at Doc. "There was this kid..." I saw him again, jumping up and down in front of me, yelling at the soldiers. "He was wearing a stupid cowboy shirt. I can still see it. Red—and checkered. He didn't look more than fifteen. Same age as my little brother...and he was right next to me. I was talking to him... then I looked away, just for a second..."

I heard the shots scream by me again. "...then he was dead! They blew off his fuckin' head! For what?" I shouted.

I caught my breath. Doc tried to say something, but I raised my hand and cut him off. I had to keep talking.

"There were bodies everywhere. College kids, just like me. I could've been one of them."

Doc's eyes widened.

"If I was standing just a couple feet to the right. Instead of that kid, it would've been me laying in the parking lot with my head blown off. Why him, Doc? Why not me?"

All my emotions drained from me in one breath. I couldn't feel my legs. I fell back into the chair behind me, exhausted. I had to erase this day from my mind, but I knew I never would.

If I had just grabbed that kid before... Maybe he wouldn't have been killed.

If I had just grabbed Billy away from the old man before he broke his arm, maybe....

Doc pulled his chair alongside mine, taking my hand, like he did so many times when I was broken. "How can I help you?"

I closed my eyes. Those shots—and that wailing—rang through my head again. *Will they ever stop?* But I knew they never would. I didn't answer him for a long time. I didn't know what to say. "I really did try to believe in God," I finally mumbled, more to myself than him. "But I can't. Not after what I saw today." I looked up. "But I believe in hell. I've been there."

I stood, walking to the window, and looked at the psych building next door. "I can't go back to class tomorrow and spew out some irrelevant shit on my finals. For what? A grade that doesn't mean a damn thing anymore?"

"What are you saying?"

"I'm saying I quit. I'm done running!"

"What about everything you worked so hard for all these years?"

"None of it matters now. The game's rigged. Guys like me, we don't have a chance. Just like that kid, we can protest all we want. But in the end, we all get our fuckin' heads blown off."

"Are you sure? I mean, about leaving?"

"More sure than I've ever been about anything. Believe me. After what I saw today, I can't act like nothing happened. I can't."

"What about the Air Force? Your plans?"

"All that talk about serving my country. This afternoon I saw what it means.. and I'll never be part of that. Never!"

"What are you going to do? Where are you going?"

"I don't know. It doesn't matter. Nothing matters now."

Doc started to say something, but I stopped him. There was nothing he could say. I saw too much today. I turned away from him and looked out the window at the campus. A pale yellow moon was rising above the distant hill where I used to gaze at the sky with Elizabeth a lifetime ago.

"I've tried to be like everyone else here." My voice flattened now, completely drained. I felt... empty. "I tried to be normal. I did everything all of you asked me to do. I ran harder and longer than anyone else just to catch up. But look where it got me."

Doc got up from his chair and stood next to me. We both stared out the window.

"Will you keep in touch?" he asked.

"Of course, I will. I don't know when I'll see you again, but I'll never forget you. Never." I hugged him. "You're the only family I got," I said, hugging him again, harder. Then I turned and walked out the door.

"Vaya con Dios, Daniel," Doc called out.

I didn't look back. I couldn't.

CHAPTER 8
CALL ME ISHMAEL

CHICAGO, 1970. I didn't plan to go through Chicago. But I was going west, and the trucker who picked me up outside Lexington was going that way. According to my map, I could catch Interstate 80 and head west from there. The city looked easy to get through, so even when he dropped me off on the south side, I didn't think much about it. But which street went west? Most of the neighborhood signs were either turned, broken or non-existent. I spent the afternoon walking down one dead end street after another until near dark when I realized I was the only white person for miles in any direction. This part of Chicago was no place for a white kid from Kentucky Methodist College!

I was beginning to seriously regret leaving my safe dorm when an ancient pickup truck, so rusted I couldn't tell what color it was, slowed as it came toward me. *Am I getting a ride or getting shot?*

"You look like you're not from this neighborhood," the driver called out when he finally chugged to a stop in front of me and rolled down his window. "I'm going west. Want a ride?"

I threw my bag in the bed, hopped in the cab and slammed the door shut before that guy—the only white face I'd seen in six hours—could change his mind.

"Name's Freytag. Augie Freytag, from Mishawaka, Indiana, near

South Bend. That's where Notre Dame is. Both my boys went there. But not me. I'm just a farmer. Been milking cows for nearly seventy years now. You a farm boy? Sorry, what did you say your name was?"

It was obvious I wouldn't be getting any sleep riding with Augie Freytag. But I didn't care. It was better than being dead on some nameless Chicago street.

"Daniel Robinson. And no, I'm not a farm boy. But I do know my way around a John Deere mower. Worked on the grounds crew for three summers at college."

"What college?"

"Kentucky Methodist. Near Lexington. I'm hoping to see San Francisco."

"I can take you as far as Denver, Daniel," he said, shaking my hand. "That is, if you have a driver's license. I'll need you to take the wheel from time to time."

"Yes, sir. Be glad to drive. Truth is, I was a little nervous back there."

"God works in mysterious ways."

From what I could tell, Augie must have been seventy-five or more, but he didn't look it. Short, but solid and broad across the shoulders— and with a grip that nearly broke my hand. But it was his voice I noticed most. *Kind.* Like I imagined a grandfather would sound—if I ever had a grandfather. Right then, I knew I'd be safe with him, and I relaxed for the first time since leaving Doc's office.

Over the next one hundred and fifty miles across Illinois, Augie told me all about Mishawaka. He lived in the same house all of his life. The hardest time was the Great Depression when they had no cash income for nearly three years. "We had to live totally off the farm, just like my grandparents did when they moved here from Germany in 1857."

In great detail, he told me about every one of his four kids and how proud he was his boys graduated from Notre Dame, and his girls married college men too. He also talked forever about every imaginable detail of the dairy business, more than I ever knew or cared to know. But mostly he talked about his wife Marie. They were married forty-eight years. Then just six months ago, she was diagnosed with cancer and died soon after that.

"I'm sorry," he said somewhere near East Moline when he caught me dozing off. "I've had no one to talk with since she passed."

"No problem." I was more embarrassed that I might have offended my new friend. "Just been a long day. And I'm really sorry about your wife."

"Don't worry about it, son. Since Marie died, my kids say I do ramble on a bit when I get with people. So tell me about yourself. Family in Kentucky?"

Not a mean bone in this guy. I thought I could talk to Augie, at least about some things. Driving through Iowa and into Nebraska, between whatever sleep I could get, I told him how I put myself through college and how hard I had to study because I didn't learn much in high school. I told him about Elizabeth, and how it hurt me to lose her. I didn't tell him about Kent State. I wasn't sure how he'd react if he thought I was one of those hippies. "That's why I'm out here now. Just trying to clear my head of that girl."

The afternoon sun glared into the truck. Augie lifted his hat and wiped his forehead with his sleeve. This was the first time I noticed the severe tan line that ran across his face. His cheeks and neck were dark and leathered from a lifetime in the fields, but under that old, worn hat, his bald head was as smooth and white as a baby's bottom.

"I guess I'm doing the same thing as you, son. I'm traveling." He pulled his hat down, and without missing a beat, proceeded to tell me even more about his life in Mishawaka.

We drove on for another fifty miles or so until I got up the nerve to ask him something I'd been thinking about. "I don't mean to get too personal, Augie, but how are you able to handle Marie's death?"

"It's okay. I don't mind. It actually helps to talk about her." He smiled serenely.

"When Marie died, I realized there was more to life than just the farm. I sold the place last month and I'm heading to Denver so I can go down to Uruguay with the Peace Corps."

"Peace Corps?" I wasn't sure I heard him right.

"I know what you're thinking. The Peace Corps is for college kids like you. Not old farmers like me. That's what I thought. But then I heard they actually need old farmers to teach people how to make better use of their land. Turns out my seventy years milking cows was better than a degree from Notre Dame. So now I'm going to Uruguay. I guess that makes both of us wanderers, doesn't it, Daniel?"

I only had a couple hours sleep since leaving Chicago, but I was wide awake now. I never met anyone like Augie.

"Why Uruguay? I mean, why not travel to some place closer, like the Grand Canyon, or even San Francisco with me? I hear it's a great city."

"That's what my kids have been asking. I told them it's not just the traveling I need. It's what I do when I get there. I worked hard all my life. I made a good living at it too. Marie was always helping people, you know, poor people. I used to get mad at her every time she gave money to some stranger who would come to the door. I told her God helps those who help themselves. But she always said, 'Sometimes God needs our help.'"

He smiled again. "I didn't listen to her, so I guess the Peace Corps is my way of telling Marie she was right. That answer your question?"

"You remind me of someone I knew at college. A professor."

He laughed. "I'm no professor. I never even finished high school."

"Doesn't matter, Augie. You're a whole lot smarter than most people I've met. Trust me."

"We can thank Marie for that."

"Wish I'd met her. She sounds like a great woman." I rolled down my window to let more air into the cab. The wind felt good on my face. "Maybe I'll meet someone like her one day."

He gave me a meaningful look. "I hope so." Then he got real quiet for a long time, probably thinking of Marie again. I spent the time now staring out the window at the vast rolling miles of cornfields in every direction. The land seemed to ebb and flow with the wind, like an endless green ocean, broken only by an infrequent silo that served as a beacon guiding weary travelers home. Then as the sun began to drop low in the sky, far into the distance where it touched the land, a long thin line of deep purples and reds traced the horizon. It caught me unprepared, the beauty of this magnificent land that I never knew existed until today.

Just outside North Platte, Nebraska, at the only roadside diner we'd seen in hours, Augie broke the silence to announce he needed some coffee to make it to Denver by midnight. Someone in the diner said Glacier National Park was a great hiking spot. "Real peaceful," he called it, and that got me thinking I might like to go there.

"Where's your tent?" Augie asked when we climbed back into the truck. "And your sleeping bag?"

I just shrugged. "I guess I didn't think about it when I left school. But I'll figure out something when I get to Glacier Park."

Augie shook his head. "You'd never make it on the farm, son, but I've got an idea. See that 'Camping Equipment' sign down the road? Let's go see what they have."

I tried to argue, but it did no good. Before we left North Platte, I was the proud owner of a tent, back pack, sleeping bag, hiking boots and socks, and more trail mix than I could eat all month.

We said good-bye one-hundred and twenty miles later when the road turned south to Denver.

"I have something else for you." Augie handed me a little Kodak camera and several rolls of film. "To remember your trip. Not all memories are bad. Make some good memories on your journey, Daniel."

I didn't know what to say, so I just shook his hand several times. "I will, and don't be surprised if I come down to Uruguay and see you someday."

"I'd like that. And I hope you find what you're looking for."

"Me too, Augie. Me too."

———

Two days later, with lots of short rides and too much bad weather, Glacier National Park finally came into view. I enjoyed my time with Augie, but I needed solitude now. I hated to admit it, but I still thought of Elizabeth every time I closed my eyes. I had to be alone to find release from her memory, and everything else. My family. Kent State.

My first day walking the trails was exactly what I hoped for. At college I was always surrounded by people, forever in conversations about nothing that filled my time, but left me empty. But here in the wilderness, hiking the mountain trails, surrounded by the silence of the forest, with no sound but my own footsteps, I realized how much I loved solitude.

It was late in the afternoon of my second day, or it could have been my third day, I wasn't sure—and I didn't care. I only knew I was a lifetime away from Clairton and Elizabeth and Kent State. I set up my tent in a clearing high up in the mountains where there was a rock outcropping that overlooked the valley floor a thousand feet below. I thought I'd spend the next day sitting there reading, maybe even writing in that journal Doc gave me last year. He called it 'free therapy,' whatever that meant, but I never used it. Alone here in Glacier Park now, with no one and nothing but my own thoughts, it might be a good place to try writing something.

All that changed when a stranger stomped into my campsite near dark. "Mind if I camp here for the night?" The intruder threw his gear down on the far side of the clearing like he owned the place, not even waiting for me to answer!

A million damn acres and you have to camp right next to me! "Plenty of room." I lied, but I didn't even try to hide my irritation.

"Thanks." he answered without a hint of gratitude, oblivious to my frustration.

I yanked the tent flap shut. *I'm outta here right at daybreak—away from this asshole!.*

Sleep, if I could call it that, came in fits. The intruder called out to unseen people all night long, and every time I'd sit straight up in my tent. In the middle of the night, I'm not sure when, he screamed out, "They're coming! They're coming!" I had no idea what was happening, so I grabbed my hunting knife from my pack and held it close until dawn when I finally dozed off.

I don't know how long I slept, but sometime in the morning the aroma of real food over a fire tickled my nose. Opening one eye, then the other, my stomach grumbled as saliva ran down the corner of my mouth. I warily pulled open the tent flap.

"Got plenty." the intruder said without looking up from the pan he held over the fire.

I rubbed my eyes, not sure if I was still dreaming. "Is that beef stew?" I mumbled half out loud. I'd been eating nothing but dehydrated fruit and nuts that tasted no better than cardboard since I got to Glacier, but now I smelled real food!

"Just an MRE, but real stew." He poured some onto a plate and motioned me closer.

I wiped the drool away, jumped into my boots, and was at the fire with my spoon in hand before he changed his mind.

"Name's Saunders." he said.

"Daniel Robinson," I answered without missing a bite of my breakfast. "Just got out of college and headed west for a while. You know, to clear my head."

With each mouthwatering bite of his stew, it became more obvious that having a partner who could cook was not nearly as intrusive as I thought. "Where you from," I asked while he filled my plate again.

"A shit hole town near Pittsburgh called Kittanning." He spit out the words. "I guess I'm here to clear my head too."

What little I knew about that place wasn't good. Not much better than Clairton. But I didn't want to talk about either one of them, and definitely not here in Glacier Park. "Don't know anything about that area," I lied. "But you'll like it out here. As close to God's country as you can find."

He stared at his food without answering.

We hiked together for the next two days without saying much. I learned his name was Bobby. He might have been in the National Guard or something like that because his hair was barely long enough to tell what color it was. And he knew all about camping. A lot of guys in college talked about joining the guard to get out of Vietnam, especially if they had low draft numbers. But I didn't ask, and he didn't say. We might have been about the same age, but he seemed decades older. There was something about his eyes. They looked haunted, like he was seeing something else whenever he looked at me. Whatever it was, we didn't talk about it. Both of us were more focused on our own thoughts.

In the middle of the afternoon, I climbed out on a rock ledge we came across high up on the trail. From there I could see the entire valley that was at least a mile across, maybe two or three thousand feet deep. A cascading stream rushed freely from one end to the other, filled with snow melt from the upper elevations. Without a thought, I spread my arms wide, as if trying to pull in the entire scene in front of me, and take it with me forever. The smell of fresh pine needles filled my lungs as I took several deep, cleansing breaths, just like I did on that bus ride through Ohio nearly four years ago. In that moment, when it seemed the entire forest relaxed in front of me and I really listened, I thought I heard that stream calling me out of the mountains, on down the valley and west to the Pacific Ocean and my new life, wherever that would be. *This must be what heaven looks like!*

"You gotta see this," I called out to Bobby. He climbed up next to me, looked quickly at the valley and turned away, like it was nothing.

"When you've seen hell, it's hard to see anything else. Even here." He grabbed his pack and started up the trail toward the next ridge. Neither of us said anything after that.

Later that night we were sitting on the ground by our fire, just staring in silence at the soft glow of the flames. "When we were looking at that valley, you said something about seeing hell," I finally asked. "Were you talking about where you grew up?"

"Kittanning? No." he answered without looking up.

"Where then?"

For several minutes, Bobby didn't say anything, or even look at me. Then slowly he grabbed a cigarette pack from his bag, tapped it several times on his knee until one came out. He placed it carefully between his lips, lit it with a burning stick from the fire, took a long drag, and deliberately blew the smoke toward the fire. "Vietnam." He said it like a curse, still staring straight ahead.

"You were there? What was it like?" I caught myself. *Maybe he doesn't want to talk about it.* "Forget I asked. It's none of my business."

"It's okay," he muttered, still staring at the fire. He took another long pull on his cigarette, blew out the smoke slowly, then tossed the butt into the fire. Bobby now took another slow breath, as if weighing his words. "I signed up mostly to get out of that shit hole town I lived in. I knew if I stayed, I'd end up just like my old man, working all day and drinking all night. Then I'd get married to some girl who was just as trapped as me and wishing I'd left when I had the chance. The Army gave me the chance."

"Weren't you scared?"

"Not really. I was eighteen. I thought I'd save the country and come home a hero. But I lost that dream as soon as I got off the plane in Nam."

"What happened?"

"Got shot. That's what happened." he said, his voice flat, and his face numb.

"How? I mean, in battle?"

"Nothing heroic like that. I wish it was. Like I said, I just got off the plane and I was waiting outside the lieutenant's hooch for my orders. I heard some weird sound and someone yells, *Incoming!* I didn't know what the fuck to do, so I just stood there while all these mortars and shit started exploding everywhere."

"You're kidding me! What happened?" I couldn't believe what he was telling me so casually.

"I got hit in the ass with shrapnel and ended up in the hospital for the next month. What a way to start a fuckin' war."

"Did they send you home? I mean because you were wounded?"

"Fuck no. They just patched me up and ordered me back to my lieutenant. He sent me right out into the jungle on patrol. But that's another story."

Bobby rolled out his sleeping bag, climbing in with his back to me. It was obvious he was done talking, but I got the impression there was a lot more to his story than he was telling me. And his screams that again kept me awake most of the night confirmed my feelings.

The next morning, our stomachs full of what was apparently packaged Army food, we were warming our hands over the fire before we hit the trail. It seemed a good time to ask him about Vietnam. All I knew about it was what I saw on the news. Until now, I never actually talked with someone who was really there.

"You mentioned going on patrol. How was that, I mean, going into the jungle? Were you afraid?"

Bobby shook his head. "Scared shitless. We all were!"

As soon as I said it, I knew it was a stupid question. "Sorry. I just wanted to know what combat was like. You know, since I might be facing the draft. My number's pretty low." In spite of my vow in

Doc's office, I still had to deal with the draft. Maybe sooner than I hoped.

"It's okay, man," Bobby reached in his pocket for a cigarette. "I just haven't talked about Nam since I got back." He took a long drag and slowly blew the smoke toward the fire. "Combat's nothin' like you see in the movies. It's the scariest shit in the world. Believe me, there's nothing heroic, 'cause all you're thinking about is surviving another day." He took a deep pull on his cigarette. "It's the waiting that gets to you," he said slowly now. "That's what drives you nuts. Knowing you might get killed around the next turn in the trail. You don't see the VC, but you know they're out there. Even if they don't shoot you, you can step on one of their fuckin' booby traps. Either way you're dead. You just don't know when." He reached into his pocket, grabbed the last cigarette, lit it off his other one and threw the empty pack into the fire. "I seen a lot of guys go crazy worrying about staying alive. I learned on my first patrol to forget about coming home. Weird, ain't it? The only way to get through a war is to quit thinking about living."

Then, as if he was all talked out, without any explanation, he stood, flicked his cigarette into the fire, grabbed his gear and walked out of camp alone. I kicked dirt on the embers, but didn't follow, at least not too close. Whatever haunted him at night, it probably had something to do with Vietnam. We walked the rest of the day without saying much, just listening to the sounds of the forest—and the demons we both brought with us.

That night Bobby called out several times to unseen strangers in the dark. "Mitchell! Over there. In the bush!"

"Guerra, you hit?"

"Where the fuck are you, Washington? Goddammit, cover me!"

Sometime near dawn I finally forced myself to sleep until the falling snow woke me a couple hours later. Several inches layered the ground, and there looked to be even more at the higher elevations. We both thought it best to spend the day in camp, rest our feet and wait for the weather to clear. I was too tired to hike anymore anyway, and I thought it was a good time to read that book Doc gave me when I left. *Les Miserables*. He said it might help me understand second chances. I had no idea what he meant, but it was a thousand pages and too heavy to lug up and down every mountain in Glacier Park. Either I had to read it now or burn it for kindling. I was done carrying it.

Bobby spent most of the day staring at the fire and smoking one cigarette after another. It was sometime in the afternoon before he said anything, and it didn't make sense. Not at first anyway. "It's the kids that really scared me the most in Nam." He seemed to choose his words deliberately, as if he wanted to say this all day, but only now found the strength. "I mean there's so many of them all over the country, living in the streets, just surviving." He pulled another cigarette from his pocket and lit it. "Everyone told me not to help them. They said those kids could pick your pocket so quick you'd never know your money was gone. But I didn't care because they reminded me of my brothers and sisters back home." Taking a long drag while staring at the fire, he looked really tired even though we'd been resting all day. "There was this one kid I took in. You know, fed him and gave him a couple bucks every chance I got. I called him Joey 'cause I couldn't pronounce his name. The guys in my platoon all warned me not to trust him, but I didn't listen. I really liked Joey."

Bobby grabbed his knees and pulled his legs up close to his chest. He didn't say anything for several minutes, but just sat there, squeezing his legs and staring at the fire. "One day..." He hesitated, then swallowed. "...one day I saw that kid walk into our club. It was filled with our guys having a good time. He was carrying his shoeshine box, like he always did...." His face tensed and his dark eyes grew wide, seeing it all again. I wanted to ask if he was okay, but I just waited and didn't say anything. "...and then the club blew up!"

He shut his eyes, without a word, as if trying to force that awful scene from his mind. Then he shook, just a little at first, then hard, like he couldn't make it stop. After what seemed like an eternity, but was probably just a minute, he opened his eyes and looked toward the fire. "I got knocked to the ground..., but everyone in there...," he hesitated. "...a lot of the guys were from my platoon..." Bobby took a deep breath, still trying desperately to control himself. "...they all got killed!" He snarled the words, not much more than a whisper. But in the quiet of the forest, they screamed at me.

We both sat there now. Just breathing. The fire flickered, a log crackled.

"After that, I hated all the gooks." Raising his head, he looked toward me. "I wanted to kill 'em all...and I did...every time I went on patrol." His voice flat, even controlled, with no emotion now. I remembered all those John Wayne movies Frankie and I saw at the Clairton Theater. This was war and he was just a soldier doing his job. But this wasn't a movie, and Bobby wasn't John Wayne. "It's my last patrol I can't get out of my head." Looking down at the fire again, his voice cracked as he struggled with the words. "We were in this shit hole village where we knew the VC had been. We interrogated everyone, but no one would tell us shit. So finally my sergeant says, "Fuck 'em. Kill 'em all." So we did. We killed every fuckin' one of them."

He ripped open a fresh pack of cigarettes, pulled one out, but his hands shook too much to light it. I reached over and steadied his arm until he could light it, then draw in enough smoke to calm his nerves.

"Were they VC?" he asked no one in particular. "I don't know. And I didn't care. I just wanted to kill every gook I could for what they done to us." Then he looked up, his eyes pleading with me, "But they were nothing but old men and women...and kids...and babies...." He closed his eyes again, dropping his head onto his chest, limp, deflated, broken, as if admitting out loud what he had been holding inside was too much to bear. I watched him as his cigarette slowly burned against the flesh on his fingers. He didn't move.

"I know if there's a heaven, I ain't going there," he stammered, his eyes still closed. "I'm already in hell... and there ain't no way out." He dropped the last bit of that burning cigarette, staring now into the fire, and across the ocean to that place he never left.

I wanted to say something, anything, to help my new friend, but my mind was blank.

What would Doc say? I racked my brain, then I remembered what he did with me so many times. I moved over to Bobby's side of the fire and sat next to him. Silently, I put my hand on his shoulder and held him. His whole body shook again, this time harder, until finally he dropped his head into his hands, crying uncontrollably. I didn't say anything. I just kept my arm around him until he was calm.

"I'm okay," he muttered after several long minutes, "Thanks." Wiping his eyes with his sleeve, he stood up, then walked slowly to a clearing just outside our campsite. He sat there alone for an hour, maybe longer, staring at the distant mountains. Neither of us said anything the rest of the day. We just listened to the deafening silence of the forest.

In the morning the temperature was warm again, and we decided to move on. I was packing my gear when Bobby stopped and looked toward me. I thought he wanted to say something. "About yesterday..." He looked at the dying embers in the fire pit. I could barely hear him. He took a deep breath, as if gathering up all his strength. Then slowly, measuring every word, still staring at the coals, he said, "I came to Glacier to kill myself. I had it all planned. I was going to go back off trail as far as I could and swallow my gun. I couldn't take all the shit I was going through." He turned now, looking at me again. "But after talking with you, I thought about my family all night, especially my mother," his voice grew stronger with every word, "...and I think I need to go help her. You know, protect her from the old man." He cleared his throat. "So I'm heading back home..." He swallowed hard, then said, "I owe you my life...I mean it."

I didn't know what to say. There was nothing I could say. I remembered all those times in Doc's office—those times he helped me climb out of the jungle I called my home. I breathed my first prayer in a long time.

We hugged each other without a word, picked up our backpacks and walked down the trail in separate directions.

CHAPTER 9

BETTER TO SLEEP WITH A SOBER CANNIBAL THAN A DRUNK CHRISTIAN

SOMEWHERE IN MONTANA, 1970. I hiked out of Glacier Park, still feeling the euphoria of my last conversation with Bobby. *Take me two days with a couple good rides to reach San Francisco*, I promised myself and stuck out my thumb at a passing car.

With dusk falling ten hours later, standing in a cold drizzle that was quickly soaking through my jacket, I was about to give up for the day and roll out my sleeping bag in a nearby clearing, when I noticed a semi coming my way that seemed to be slowing.

Maybe this guy's going all the way to California. But at the last minute, just when I thought he was stopping, that asshole swerved his rig right at me and sped up! Without even thinking, I jumped into a ditch behind me. Suddenly my ankle was on fire and I fell over onto my side, nearly smashing my head into a rock. "Goddam hippie!" he yelled out his window, giving me the finger as he roared past. Too hurt and too scared to move, I laid there all night, convinced that trucker was coming back to get me. *I could disappear out here and nobody would ever know.* I didn't sleep, too scared to even close my eyes.

Heavy fog blanketed the ground sometime near dawn as I crawled out of my sleeping bag. My stomach growled, so I grabbed a hand full of trail mix from my pack. But that only reminded me of Bobby's cooking and my stomach growled again, this time even louder. That's when I heard grinding gears and a strained engine slowly making its way toward me, long before I actually saw it.

Maybe it's that trucker coming back for me? I thought about hiding in the ditch, just until I was sure, but I'd seen only a couple cars since I left the park. *I'm not getting stuck standing here for another day!* I had no choice, so I grabbed my pack and climbed back up the hill. My ankle was so swollen I had to loosen my shoelace. But that only made it worse, and every step felt like I was walking on glass shards. When I finally reached the road, the fog was so thick I couldn't see in either direction. That engine sound was rumbling closer, echoing back and forth in the valley. After what seemed like an hour, I finally saw something turn the bend and out of the fog less than a hundred feet down the road.

Thank God, it's not that trucker. But who—or what—is it? It looked like a school bus, or at least it had been one a long time ago. Now it was painted bumper to bumper in wild, exotic, even psychedelic colors— glowing orange, green, magenta, lavender, chlorine blue, and every florescent pastel imaginable. I just stood there dumbstruck, with my thumb outstretched, my senses frozen by the sight in front of me. The window slid open and a wave of smoke rolled out and drifted toward me —smoke that even with my four sheltered years at Kentucky Methodist College, I knew was marijuana.

Lots and lots of marijuana.

"Hop in, man," a voice called out from the haze.

I quickly weighed my options. *I can say no thanks, then stand in the middle of nowhere with my busted ankle for God knows how long until some other trucker tries to kill me because he thinks I'm a hippie freak.*

Or I can get in the dope bus with a real hippie freak.

I hobbled into the bus.

"My name's Mellow," the driver called out over the engine noise. He wore a bright paisley shirt that looked to be the same colors as the bus, and a brown leather vest and matching wide-brimmed hat with a large feather stuck in the band. The sun had not broken through the fog yet, I wondered how he could see anything through his dark sunglasses. But it was his mustache I noticed most. It ran down both sides of his mouth, hanging below his chin.

"That's Sunshine," he nodded toward someone in the haze behind him. "What's your name, man?"

"Daniel Robinson."

"Too formal, man," he said, pulling the door shut. "We'll call you Mountain Man, 'cause that's what you look like, a real fuckin' mountain man."

I rubbed the growth on my chin and glanced at the same dirty clothes I'd been wearing since I left Kentucky. *Maybe I am a mountain man now!*

"Just throw your shit in the living room by Sunshine." Mellow's barefoot partner sat cross-legged a dozen feet behind him on an old couch. She wore an ankle-length, flowered, bright yellow dress. A bandana held her long blonde hair back from her forehead, but it draped down over her ample braless breast.

"Hey," I grunted in her direction, dropping my pack, but she didn't respond. *Riding with these two freaks is better than getting killed by another trucker.* If I said that enough times, I might actually believe it.

"Want some weed, man?" Mellow handed me a joint, or I thought it was. I'd never actually seen one before.

"No, thanks." But now I had serious second thoughts about my decision. *First town we come to, I'm outta here!*

"That's cool, man." Mellow turned back and grabbed the stick to manipulate the transmission into first gear, but it wouldn't budge. "Shit!" He slammed it forward. "Fuckin' piece of shit!"

I looked around what Mellow called the living room. Even in the dim light and smoke-filled air, I could make out that couch where Sunshine perched, somehow bolted to the floor. A threadbare rug that looked even older than the bus was spread out in front of it, while a dozen *Grateful Dead* posters covered the windows. Behind the couch another filthy rug hung from the ceiling, alongside a doorway of sorts made of stringed beads that probably led to their bedroom.

"We're going to San Francisco. You ever been there?" Mellow called out, but I wasn't listening. My lungs struggled to adjust to what seemed to be more marijuana than oxygen, as I dug anxiously through my pack for a map. *There's gotta be a Greyhound going anywhere away from these two hippies!*

"What? No. Never been there," I mumbled. "How about you?"

"Lived there two years," Mellow yelled back, as he jammed the transmission through each gear until the bus finally reached full speed at thirty miles per hour. "Most beautiful city in the world."

Here it is! "Thank God," I unfolded the map on the bus floor.

"Where you from, Mountain Man?" Mellow yelled again over the engine noise.

"A college in Kentucky. Near Lexington," I quickly scanned the map. "Planned to join the Air Force. But I was at Kent State..." Suddenly I was back there again, screams echoing in my head. "That changed everything for me..."

I almost forgot that day while I hiked in Glacier. I was surprised how quickly it all came rushing back with just one question. I stuffed the map back in my pack and stared out the front window. I was there again...standing in that parking lot... hearing those shots... those screams. I saw the crowd running in every direction again... and that kid with the cowboy shirt. My heart thumped hard in my chest.

"Are you shittin' me?" Mellow hollered. "You were at fuckin' Kent State? No wonder you told the Air Force to fuck off. Way to go, man."

I desperately tried to block that memory from my head.

"Don't get the wrong impression," I finally said when I could breathe normal again. "I'm not that political. I was at Kent to see a girl. That's all. But she wasn't there and I just got caught up in a demonstration."

My thoughts flashed back to Elizabeth. I was on her porch again, with Mrs. Johnson, sounding so cold, telling me she was married, gone forever. *Time to change the subject.*

"Where are you from, Mellow? I mean, before you went to San Francisco?"

"Ohio. A little Catholic farming town called Minster. I was even an altar boy. And valedictorian of my class. I was Paul Atherton then. Voted most likely to succeed. You believe that shit!"

I wasn't sure what to believe, not since I got on this hippie bus with them.

"I got my degree in chemistry. Planning to take over my old man's pharmacy. But then I went on a graduation road trip to Frisco in '67 and kinda stayed. That's where I met Sunshine."

"So what do you do there? I mean, what kind of work do you do?"

"I'm sort of in the chemistry business. Just not in a pharmacy now, if you know what I mean."

I didn't.

"You sure you don't want a hit? Primo weed, man." Sunshine called out from behind me for the first time. She held out what I thought was another marijuana joint. "We grew it ourselves."

So that's what Mellow meant by 'chemistry business.' He's a dope pusher! "No thanks. I'm okay," I answered, reaching in my pack for the map again.

"What are you, a narc or something? Have a hit, man!" Sunshine demanded.

I wasn't sure what to make of her either. She looked like she should be in high school, not wandering the country in a dope bus. But there was something about her, something in her eyes, a sadness. She was also very pregnant.

"Let him be, Sunshine," Mellow hollered over the noise from the engine that sounded worse with each passing mile. "You really think the narcs are going to waste their time hitch-hiking in the middle of nowhere, Montana, just to bust a couple Prankster travelers? Don't pay any attention to her, man. With Vietnam and all, we've been in Canada for a while."

God, it's not the dope that's got them paranoid. Mellow's a draft dodger! "I'm not planning on going to Canada," I shouted back to him over the engine noise. "I just know I'm not putting on a uniform and do what I saw happen at Kent State.

"What's your draft number, man?"

"109."

"Then you'd better look real hard at Canada, 'cause there's no fuckin' way you're not getting drafted."

I hadn't given much thought to Vietnam, even when I was planning on the Air Force. But now.... *He's right. If I get drafted, I'll end up in Vietnam...just like Bobby.* I moved to the front of the bus, because I had a lot of questions for Mellow.

"So what's it like in Canada?" I asked, leaning in close so he could hear me. "Not that I'd actually go there. Just wondering. That's all."

"Canada's cool, man. They don't like this Vietnam shit any more than we do. But it turned out my number was never called anyway. You believe that shit? At least I was willing to make a stand for what I believed. Like you did when you told the Air Force to fuck off."

"It wasn't as dramatic as that," I said. "After what I saw at Kent State, I just knew I couldn't do it. So I left school. That's what I've been doing in Glacier. You know, getting that day out of my head."

I got uncomfortable talking about the Air Force and Kent State. They both reminded me of Elizabeth. I thought I was over her, but I could feel my stomach coming back up into my throat. I better change the subject again.

"So what's San Francisco like? I mean, is it as good as everyone says?"

"Better, man," he answered with genuine enthusiasm. "That's what I missed most when we were in Canada. But it's not just the city. Sure, it's a beautiful place, but it's the people that make it so great. I was there in the beginning, you know, when Leary and Kesey were there. Met them both."

"Who?"

"You never heard of Leary? Timothy Leary. God, Mountain Man, where did you go to school?"

"And Kesey's a famous writer. He wrote *Cuckoo's Nest*."

I gave him a blank stare.

"You're hopeless, man. What the hell did you do in college? Hide under your bed? They're only the guys who made LSD happen. They almost invented that shit."

"So that's what you meant when you said you were in the chemistry business—LSD!" Now I was really worried.

"Acid's not what you think. It's like a whole new religion. It's really beautiful, man. I mean it."

Mellow tried to drop the transmission down into third as we approached another hill. "Fuck!" he yelled, ramming the gear forward. "Like I was saying, I was raised Catholic, with all that guilt shit. But there's none of that in San Francisco. I mean everybody can just do his own thing there. Sure, all you hear about is the sex and the drugs. But that's only half of it. The best part is the spiritual stuff. Like friendship and community and sharing ideas. It's a place where helping people is more important than making money."

"Sounds like a really great city." I didn't want to admit it, but this Mellow guy was actually making sense. "I mean, the helping people part. They talked a lot about that at my college, but I only saw one guy who really lived it."

"Speaking of helping people, man, if you're interested in doing some acid, I got plenty." Mellow patted his vest pocket cheerfully. "My degree in chemistry was a good thing after all."

"No thanks. Drugs aren't my thing." That was it. I seriously had to get off this dope bus as soon as we found a town somewhere —anywhere!

With all their dope talk and my worries about getting busted, the conversation, and the miles that ancient bus could manage, passed hideously slow that first day. But the second day was better, and the third day was almost normal. There were no more offers to smoke, drop or shoot up anything legal or illegal. By the time we reached Utah, my attitude toward the bus, and my new friends, had changed, especially when we stopped at a small grocery store somewhere north of Salt Lake City.

"I know it's in here somewhere!" I frantically rifled through my backpack, pulling every item out onto the ground. Sleeping bag, socks, trail mix, knife, shirt, pants. *God! Where is it?*

Ten minutes later Mellow came out of the store and found me sitting by the bus. "You look like you lost your last friend, man."

"I can't find my wallet!" I didn't even try to hide my desperation. "I must have lost it when that trucker tried to kill me in Montana."

"Don't worry, man. I got you covered."

"That was all the money I had in the world! Without my wallet I'm screwed!"

"Don't worry about it." He handed me a $50 bill. "Like I said, helping people is more important than money."

I was so grateful I couldn't help myself. I hugged him. It seemed like the San Francisco thing to do.

As the miles passed driving west toward the Bonneville Salt Flats, Sunshine's attitude changed too. It was so noisy in the bus, we both spent most of the trip sitting in the back, as far from the engine as possible. That gave us plenty of time to talk, usually about nothing.

"What sign are you, Mountain Man," she asked. It was a casual question, the sort of thing you say when you're trying to strike up a conversation. But I had no idea what she was talking about.

"I don't know," I answered.

She looked surprised, even confused, like she never met anyone who actually said that to her. "When were you born?" she asked now, speaking each word deliberately.

"June. Why?"

Her eyes grew wide and her mouth opened just a little, as if surprised that even an ignorant waif from the intellectual wasteland of Kentucky didn't have even a basic grasp of such important spiritual matters. "June what?" she asked, but it was more of a demand, the sort of question a teacher would ask a student who was totally unprepared for class.

"June 25. Why?" I shot back at her, not even trying to hide my irritation. She was really getting on my nerves with all her stupid questions. "Does that make a difference?"

Her eyes rolled and she breathed a sigh, finally realizing the extent of my spiritual illiteracy, and the task now before her to lead me out of my deprivation. "God, Mountain Man. You don't know shit, do you?"

"Apparently not. So what sign am I?"

"Cancer, of course." She nodded just a little, but with an air of condescension, as if expecting me to show some gratitude for the enlightenment she just bestowed.

But I didn't care. "Ok. So what's that mean?"

She smiled, as if pleased for this opportunity, then took a quick breath and proceeded to share her wisdom. "Well, first of all, Cancer is full of contradictions. You're self-sufficient and don't need to depend on others."

"I put myself through college," I interrupted. I wasn't that impressed so far. "So what else do you know about me?"

"You like adventure. You're not afraid to try new things."

"Okay, I'm hitchin' alone across the country. Tell me something that's not so obvious." I closed my eyes and gave her an exaggerated yawn, but she ignored me.

"You're very loyal to your friends. That's because Cancer has deep emotions."

I tried not to show it, but I was listening now.

"Cancer is a nurturer. That means you'd probably be a good counselor or something like that."

I opened my eyes, looking at her. *How did she know that?*

"But Cancer is fragile and you need a lot of support, more than all the other signs. That means you can wallow in self-pity."

"That's where you're wrong." I snapped. I was done with the conversation, but Sunshine kept up with all her drivel.

"Cancer is the crab for a reason. A crab has a hard shell. Cancer people have a shell too. They really care, but they can't show it because they don't trust anybody."

The more she rambled on about all that astrology crap, the more she irritated me. "Anything else, or are you done?"

"Yes," she answered, completely oblivious to my annoyance. "Because Cancer has such strong feelings, you don't want to let go of the past. You know, old friends who have moved on. Like that girl you went to see at Kent State."

"Okay, that's enough of this shit," I snapped. "I've got a headache and I need to chill out for a while." I stood up and moved to the front of the bus next to Mellow, where it was too noisy for any conversation— particularly something stupid like astrology.

Sunshine just smiled.

———

We camped that night near the Bonneville Salt Flats. I sat alone about a hundred feet from the bus, still trying to forget all Sunshine's astrology crap, and just stared at the sky. There were no trees to block my view like there were in Glacier, and this was the first time since I left school, maybe the first time in my whole life, when I stopped and *really* looked at the sky without any distractions—like Elizabeth. The entire horizon, as far as I could see for what appeared to be a thousand miles in every direction, was a magnificent black void that was darker, purer, more fascinating nothingness—if there is such a thing—than anything I'd ever seen. I could feel that nothingness pull me in, as if I could somehow become one with that sky that was, in that moment, exactly how I imagined it was the day God created it.

And the stars! Every single one of them radiated a brilliant burst of light so intense, so dazzling, and so close. *There's Vega! Finally! God, I can almost reach up and grab it!* In that moment, all thoughts of Kent State, Elizabeth, and even Clairton, were forgotten. *This is why I came out here!*

I was basking in what felt like my own private display of all the glory of heaven when I heard Mellow's footsteps. "Mind if I sit with you?"

Absolutely I mind! But I remembered how he helped me when I lost my wallet. "Not at all," pointing toward the ground next to me.

"I can respect tokin' weed's not your thing, man," he said. It was obvious he'd been thinking about this for a long time.

"But acid's nothing like weed. Pot just helps me relax," he said holding up the fresh joint in his hand, "Dropping is more like a spiritual experience. Why do you think they call it *Instant Zen*? I mean, it's like seeing God."

After listening to Sunshine blather all day about astrology, I was in no mood to hear about the theology of LSD now. *Remember the wallet.* I took a slow, frustrated breath. "I'm listening."

He lit his joint, took a long, slow draw to fill his lungs, then held it for several seconds.

"I'm Catholic, man," he said, slowly breathing the smoke out through his nose. "All my life I was taught to fear God, and mostly fear the nuns. By the time I graduated from college, I lost my faith. But acid renewed it, man. It's like the deepest mystical experience I've ever had."

I couldn't tell if Mellow was serious, or if it was the weed talking. I didn't answer and Mellow didn't seem to notice or care.

"You're Protestant, aren't you, man? You know the Bible, right? You know that story about the Apostle Paul seeing a vision of God on the road to Damascus? Tell me he wasn't on something like LSD. I'm serious, man. Think about it. Here's this really uptight guy who was a religious expert. He spent all his time hassling people who didn't believe just like he did, right? Then he claims to see God and his whole life gets mellow. Now he loves everybody. That's exactly what LSD does, man. I had the same vision of God that changed my life, just like his. I mean it, man."

I wonder what Doc would say if he was here? I smiled thinking of the two of them discussing the spiritual benefits of LSD.

"Before I turned on, I was always uptight, just like my old man. That's why we never got along." Mellow pinched the end of his joint between his lips, then took one last slow draw. "But now I've got peace inside. Real peace." He laid back on the ground and smiled, as if that settled the discussion, at least for him.

I looked up at the stars again, hoping to recapture that celestial vision again, maybe even discover some deep universal truth hidden there that I could now share with Mellow. But all that came to me was both of them were the strangest people I ever met, yet I liked them. And for the life of me, I couldn't think why.

"I'll give you this, Mellow. You're a true believer," was all I could think to say. "If what you're telling me is true, then San Francisco is going to be a really beautiful place."

———

The next morning all three of us were up with the sun. The plan was to make it to Reno in two days, then just a couple more days to cross the Sierra Mountains, on to San Francisco. But as luck had it, with each passing mile the dope bus strained more and the gears screamed louder. Somewhere in the middle of the Nevada wastelands near Elko, it finally breathed its last.

"Shit!" Mellow yelled as he wrestled the now dead bus to the side of the road. "Don't worry," he called out to Sunshine, her face flushed by the afternoon heat and the growing discomfort in her belly. "You and Mountain Man sit under that tree while I look at the engine. Probably just a broken belt or something." Mellow yanked open the hood. I hoped he was right, but I wasn't optimistic. I never thought the dope bus would get this far.

"Shit! No broken belt," he yelled again and crawled under the bus to look at the engine from below. Sunshine and I were left to pass the time together while Mellow banged on the engine with no luck. "So when's your baby due?" I asked, while hanging a tarp from the tree to protect us both from the blistering sun. It did little good, but she didn't seem to mind. Nothing bothered her as long as Mellow was there to take care of her.

"I think in three months. I haven't been to a doctor yet, but I'm pretty sure he, or she, will be born in September sometime."

"Thought of a name yet?"

"I was thinking of calling him *Blue* 'cause that's my favorite color. And it'll even work if it's a girl."

"We're not namin' the kid *Blue!*" Mellow hollered from under the bus.

"He can be so straight sometimes. God, you'd think he was still living in Ohio." She turned toward the bus and yelled back. "Blue's my favorite color and I want to name our baby *Blue!*" That seemed to settle it for her, but I had a feeling she would name the baby whatever Mellow wanted.

"So what are you going to do in San Francisco? You're not planning to live in the bus, are you? I mean, because of the baby and all."

She looked at me the same way she did when I didn't know my sign. "Of course we're not going to live in the bus. We've got plenty of friends we can crash with until Mellow starts his lab again. We'll be fine once we get to San Francisco."

"What about the cops. I hear they really cracked down on LSD, even in San Francisco. What if he got arrested? What will you do?"

She shook her head slightly. "He won't get arrested. He's too smart for that," she said deliberately, like I was just a kid. That settled it for her. She trusted him completely for the past three years and there was no reason to stop now.

I just shrugged.

"It's the engine, man," Mellow said, crawling out from under the bus. Wiping the grease off his face and hands, he dropped down beside us under the tree. "Looks like it might be the head gasket or something. There's no way I can fix that, not without a mechanic. But I figure we can camp here for the night, then I'll hike into town in the morning and find someone."

"See, I told you, Mountain Man. He'll take care of us." And with that she climbed slowly back into the bus to prepare supper.

———

It was sometime after midnight. I wasn't sure exactly what time because I threw away my watch in Glacier Park. And neither of them had used a clock since they first got high three years ago. "We use Native American time," they told me that first day in Montana. Whatever time it was, I knew something was wrong with Sunshine. Something serious.

"Mountain Man, wake up!" Mellow called from the back of the bus. "She's bleeding. We gotta get help!"

"I'll go," I stumbled in the dark to find my boots.

"With your bum foot? No way, man. You stay here and take care of Sunshine while I hike into town." He grabbed his pack and was at the front of the bus before I could even answer. "With any luck, I'll be back in a couple hours. I just hope there's a hospital somewhere in this shit hole town." He kicked open the door, jumped out and disappeared into the night.

Taking care of Sunshine scared me to death, especially now—but I didn't tell him that, and definitely not Sunshine. "Whatever you need. You can count on me." That's what I told him, and I meant it, but I was worried.

Mellow was gone for hours and I was getting scared because Sunshine was groaning more. *Maybe if I talk to her, maybe that'll make her feel better.* It was all I could think to do.

"You know, you never told me where you're from, Sunshine." I could hear her breathing hard in the dark. I thought she was in pain. "And I don't even know your real name." I didn't know what else to say.

She didn't answer, not at first. Finally, between hard breaths, she said, "Cheryl Wilson." Pant...pant... "From Royal Oak. Near Detroit."

Keep her talking. "What took you to San Francisco? When was it, three years ago?"

Pant... pant... "My old man drank too much."

"Mine too. I don't blame you for leaving home."

Pant... pant... "He liked to beat me."

"Mine too."

She was silent for several minutes. I thought she wanted to say something...something difficult. "One time he... he did things to me... That's when I left." Then she was quiet again.

I was back in Pastor Duncan's office. I could feel him rubbing me...

"But when I got to San Francisco, I put all that shit behind me. That's why I'm Sunshine now. No asshole is goin' to hurt me again. Ever!"

I was the one breathing hard now. My head throbbed. "I hope San Francisco will be good for me too," I said, but for the first time, I understood Sunshine. Tough kid. Maybe if I had been more like her when Pastor Duncan....

I heard a siren in the distance, coming closer and closer until a car door slammed. Mellow ran into the bus, followed by a deputy sheriff. "How's she doing, man?" Mellow didn't try to hide the desperation in his voice.

"I can't tell. I just know we've got to get her to a hospital," I called out from the dark. I was worried too.

"There's one in town, kid," the deputy answered as he turned on his flashlight and made his way to Sunshine. "Help me get her in my car. It'll be quicker than waiting for an ambulance, and I don't think we have time."

Hearing that only scared Mellow more. "I'm going with her, Mountain Man. You stay here with the bus and I'll get back to you when I know something."

"Let me know as soon as you can if she's okay." I grabbed his arm as he climbed in the squad car. "I mean it, Mellow." I squeezed hard, just to make sure he heard me.

"I will, man. As soon as I know something."

———

The next two days were spent walking in circles around the dope bus, sitting under the tarp trying in vain to write something in that journal Doc gave me, staring down the road toward where I thought the town was, and praying to a God I hadn't talked to in a long time. They were two of the longest days in my life—when finally an old truck pulled to a stop in front of our campsite and Mellow climbed out. Without saying a word, he opened the cooler and took a long drink from the water jug. "This Nevada heat is killing me, man. How can people actually live here?"

"I don't give a damn about the heat!" I shouted. "How's Sunshine? I've been going crazy with worry."

"She's okay now. They got the bleeding stopped, and she didn't lose the baby. But the doctor said she needs lots of rest or the next time it might kill both of them. The bad news is the bus is dead. I talked to a mechanic, and he thinks the block's cracked. He said junk it."

"So what're you gonna do?"

Mellow took another long drink while I waited for him to answer.

"Well...?"

"She can't make the trip," he said, wiping his mouth with his sleeve. "Even if we get to San Francisco, we've got no place to stay 'til I can score with some of my old friends. But she can't survive that either. So I did something I swore I'd never do."

"What?"

"I called my old man. I hated to do it, you know, to ask him for help, 'cause we haven't talked since I left Ohio. Shit, we never talked much even when I lived at home. But I had no choice. Not with Sunshine and the baby's life on the line. There was no one else I could call."

I wondered how I would feel if I had to call my old man for help. I didn't know if I could do it, even for Sunshine and the baby. I stared right at him, hanging on every word.

"So what'd he say?" was all I could manage to respond.

"I knew he was going to tell me to fuck off, like he always did whenever he thought I was weak. *Tough it out like a man*, he'd always say. I thought sure as hell he was going to tell me that same shit again."

"Well, did he?" I nearly screamed the question.

"No, man. He told me to come home." Mellow's face contorted, still struggling to believe what his father said. "And that's not all. He told me he was sorry for all the shit he said to me. He said he wanted me to forgive him? Can you believe it?"

"What about Sunshine? Did you tell him about Sunshine and the baby?" I was almost as glad for the news as Mellow.

"Sure, I told him, and I thought he would tell me to leave her here. I swear to God I wasn't going to do that. But he didn't. He said we're all welcome to come home. Can you believe it?"

"So what are you gonna do? I mean, how are you gonna get to Ohio? Can Sunshine travel now?" I had a hundred questions for him.

"He's going to buy us both plane tickets. Turns out there's an airport in this shit hole. As soon as Sunshine is well enough, we're both going back to meet my family. You know, have the baby there where it's safe for both of them."

"Is she okay with that? I thought her heart was set on San Francisco?"

"Not really. She's been different with the baby. I noticed it right away, especially lately. The more pregnant she was, the less she liked living in the bus. She thinks Ohio will be good for our baby."

Almost as an afterthought, Mellow added, "And we're definitely not naming it *Blue!*"

We both laughed for a least a minute, like that was the funniest thing we ever heard. But the truth is, we were both just so happy she was okay. All I thought to do was grab Mellow and hug him. He hugged me back. Hard.

Three days later when Sunshine was released from the hospital, I stood in the airport in Elko, snapped a quick photo of my friends and waved a final goodbye. They were going back to Ohio to rebuild two broken lives together around their new baby—who would never be called Blue! And I was going west toward San Francisco to see the city that Mellow—who now called himself Paul again—said was as close to God as any place can be.

"I'll write you from San Francisco," I called out to them.

CHAPTER 10

STRANGER IN A STRANGE LAND

SAN FRANCISCO, 1970. It took nearly a week and a dozen rides to finally reach the Pacific Ocean. I didn't mind the time, or even those hot days in the Nevada desert, and the cold nights in the Sierra Mountains. But getting hassled by the cops in Sacramento scared me when they didn't believe my story about losing my driver's license in Montana. I thought I'd have to call Doc Samuels to somehow prove I'm not some Commie hippie radical intent on overthrowing the government. I didn't dare mention Kent State. None of that bothered me too much because I remembered my trip with Mellow and Sunshine and smiled.

God, I miss my friends already! But now I was finally standing across the bay from San Francisco. The wind blew off the water, filling the air with a pungent, salty smell of the bay. Seagulls flew overhead and dipped down to pick up bits of food the tourists left behind. I breathed in the fresh sea air until I thought my lungs would explode with excitement—just like Mellow promised. *A new life. That's what I've got here.* I reached in my pocket and squeezed the roll of $20 bills Mellow gave me at the airport in Elko. *San Francisco really is a place where helping people is more important than making money.*

I felt good—no, *reborn*—standing in the front of the ferry as we crossed the bay with the full force of the wind and water blowing in my face. Like I did in the mountains, I spread out my arms to absorb the entire scene in front of me. "I'm alive! I'm really alive!" I said too loud for several tourists nearby. They turned and stared, not sure what to make of this bearded traveler talking to himself. But I didn't care. I was happier than I'd ever been in my entire life!

There were so many places I wanted to see—Fisherman's Wharf, Golden Gate Bridge, maybe even Lombard Street. I saw that strange looking place in a magazine once and I promised myself I'd go there someday. I wanted to ride the cable cars too, but I had to find Mellow's friends first. I pulled out the note he gave me. 560 Nathan Street. Off Ashbury. He guaranteed I could crash there till I found my own place.

By early afternoon I finally reached the corner of Haight and Ashbury streets and noticed a sign pointing to Golden Gate Park. *That's where Mellow met Sunshine. Maybe I can meet some of their friends.* I was surprised there weren't more people partying in the park, like Mellow said. I walked around for a while, so at least I could tell him I'd been there. *It really is the most beautiful city in the world.* "You were right, Mellow," I said, looking all around me as I walked.

That's when I saw the girl—and my heart stopped! She was sitting on a bench overlooking a steep bluff that dropped down to the bay. Her dark hair blew freely in the wind as she leaned back. Her long legs were stretched out, so the afternoon sun highlighted every soft curve of her body—just like it did with Elizabeth...

My heart raced. There we were, together again, on our favorite bench on the golf course, my arm gently resting on her shoulder as we talked about our future together.

"God, when will I ever be free of that woman?" I said too loud. The girl must have heard me because she walked quickly out of the park. That embarrassed me, but I was more upset that even here, in the most beautiful city in the world, thoughts of Elizabeth still haunted me. *I need to find Mellow's friends so I can start my new life!* I grabbed my pack and walked out of the park.

"I'm looking for 560 Nathan," I said to a guy coming toward me. He ignored me and kept walking.

"Do you know where Nathan Street is?" I asked someone else, but he didn't even look at me.

"How do I get to Nathan Street? It's supposed to be just off Ashbury," I called to a woman pushing a cart. She was too busy having a very animated conversation with herself and didn't notice me.

As the fog started rolling in from the bay, I felt the damp, cold air press against my face. *Maybe I'll ask someone in that store for directions.*

"I'm looking for Nathan Street. It's supposed to be around here." The clerk glared at me.

"You buying anything?"

"I'm looking for 560 Nathan Street. A friend said I could stay there."

"Don't know nothin' about no Nathan Street. If you ain't buying nothin,' you gotta move on. You damn hippies are always stealing from me."

I started to complain, but caught a glimpse of myself in the corner mirror. *Maybe I need to wash off all this road dirt.* I quickly counted my roll of bills. "I can afford a motel for one night." I mumbled and grabbed my pack and walked out to the street. Two men followed me. Something about them made me nervous.

"You lookin' for Nathan Street?" one of them asked. He was a lot bigger than me, with long, matted hair held back with a filthy bandana. He kept looking over to his partner.

"Yeah. I am," I answered cautiously. "You know where it is?"

"Know it well. We'll take you there," the other one said. He was much smaller, even gaunt, under his tattered Army jacket and worn jeans. His eyes seemed too large against his sunken cheeks. They darted all around as he spoke, and there was something vacant about them. "Just follow us down that street over there, and then through an alley to Nathan Street. It's not very far." He nodded to his partner to follow.

What should I do? It was getting late, and I do need to meet Mellow's friends so I could start my new life right away. Mellow said helping people is all that matters here. *I'll be okay.* I walked after them down several dirty streets. A lot of discarded furniture and junk cluttered the sidewalks. And maybe a dozen or more people, even dirtier than these two guys, stared at us from the shadows as we passed. This was not the San Francisco Mellow described. There was something about this place—and my guides, that made me nervous.

"You sure this goes to Nathan Street?" I looked back over my shoulder toward the light on the corner.

"We're almost there," the little one said, darting a glance toward his friend. "Just through this alley."

I remembered those streets in Chicago. "I'm okay now, guys," I turned around and started to walk away as quickly as I could. But the big one grabbed me from behind.

"You ain't going nowhere!" he shouted. Almost on cue, the little one punched me in the face so hard I fell to the ground. My head exploded in pain! "Give us your fuckin' money or we'll kill you!" he yelled, kicking me in the stomach.

"Uhhhhhh....!" I vomited all over my coat. The big one grabbed my pack and yanked it open. I tried to stop him, but the little guy kicked me in my back and my head—again and again. My whole body screamed out! I couldn't breathe. I couldn't stop them. All I saw were black spots as one of them ripped open all my pockets, kicking me in the back one last time... Then they were gone.

Silence...just the sound of my heart hammering my ribs with each agonizing breath, and my head nearly bursting with every gasp for air... over and over.

I laid there in a pool of blood and vomit, afraid to move. I must have passed out because I never remembered much after that. All I knew was when I woke up, I thought I was going to die alone in this filthy, cold alley. *As close to heaven as any city can be.* Then I passed out again.

Sometime, probably in the middle of the night, I woke to hot breath on my face and a wet tongue scraping over my cheeks. Two dogs were licking my bloody face. *Where am I?* I tried to get up and push them away, but every part of my body shrieked. There was a dull ache around the back of my head, like a vice, my eyes had nearly swollen shut, my nose felt broken, and my ribs felt like knives tearing at my lungs with every breath. *Where's my stuff?* I reached for my backpack. *Gone!* Frantic now, I searched through my pockets. *My money's gone too!* I tried to call for help, but my lips were too swollen. All I could do was groan. *No money, no wallet, no ID. Everything's gone! I'm gonna die in this alley and no one will ever know.* I wanted to cry, but I couldn't. It hurt too much.

I slid in and out of consciousness all night. A couple times I tried to get up, to get help, but I could barely move. Sometime after dawn I forced myself to limp out of the alley and down the street, hoping, praying someone would help me. I stumbled down Haight Street where a lot of people walked by, some stared, some turned their heads, but all of them acted like they saw a dozen other broken, bloodied people hobbling down the street every day. No one cared. Somewhere in the confused fog in my mind, I remembered seeing a gas station nearby. *But where?* It was hard to think, but I forced myself to focus. *It's this way...maybe.*

When I finally stumbled into the wash room, I could hardly see, let alone recognize that person staring back at me. Both my eyes were blackened and nearly swollen shut. There were several large, filthy gashes on my face that still oozed, and my nose was twisted and bent out of shape. *Broken!* I screamed when I touched it, but no sound came out of my mouth. My lips were too caked in dried blood, too swollen. I tried to take off my jacket to check for bruises, but I couldn't even pull the zipper down. Both shoulders felt on fire. I was pretty sure I had a couple broken ribs too. *Please, God. Help me!*

"Can uh call poece?" I struggled to ask the guy standing behind the counter. My whole body throbbed with every word. My ribs howled in protest.

He stared at me.

"Can uh call poece?" I asked again, louder this time.

He pointed toward a sign on the wall. "Phone's for store business only."

"I got muhged. Rwohbed."

He pointed to a phone booth on the corner, then turned away to watch the baseball game on the little television on the corner shelf.

"Peese...."

"Goddamn Giants." He reached up and changed the channel instead.

I hobbled out the door and looked up and down the street. *Where can I go? What am I going to do?* Even if they could hear me, no one cared.

I walked for hours, going nowhere, until I couldn't walk any more. It had to be sometime in the afternoon when I found a church.

"I ca get hep here." My first tinge of hope welled since I met those two muggers.

I tried to open the front door. Locked! *Maybe there's another door somewhere.* I limped around the corner and found a sign. *Office: Official church business only.* But that door was locked too! At least there was a buzzer nearby. *Thank God!* I pushed it, but nothing happened. I pushed it again. Still nothing. This time I held it. If anyone was in that church, they had to know I *really* needed help.

"Can I help you?" a very irritated mechanical voice answered through the buzzer box.

"I nee hep." I said slowly. It still hurt to talk. "I wuz muhged las nigh. Money wuz stowen. Cun ou hep?"

"Are you a member?" asked the box.

"Not hewe. I jus got hewe and was rohbed las night. Los ewrythin. Hawen't eawen all day."

"I'm sorry. We only help our members," the box responded curtly, then clicked off.

I pushed the buzzer again. "Cun I use yu fon n caw home?"

The box didn't respond. It just clicked off.

I buzzed again, and then again. Finally, the box answered, this time not even pretending to be polite. "I said we only help our members! There are so many of *you people* asking for help. We can't help everyone. It's church policy. If you don't go away, I'll call the police."

The box clicked off.

I wanted to push the buzzer again, to tell her I wasn't some street bum. "Dam u! I jus nee hep!" I slapped it with my fist, then hobbled down the street, more hurt and lost than ever.

At Castro Street I turned south, away from the alley where I was beaten, and the church where I was beaten down. I didn't know where I was going. I just walked. I found myself somewhere on Market Street, near the Castro Theatre. I thought it must be dinner time because a lot of people were going into the restaurants. My stomach growled. When was the last time I ate?

Someone came out the back of one of those places and dropped something in a dumpster. My stomach growled again. That's garbage! I turned away. But my stomach grumbled, louder this time. Watching the door for several minutes, then looking carefully up and down the alley, I took a quick breath to steel my nerves. *Nobody will see me.* I walked slowly into the alley, still looking all around, just in case someone else came out of one of those buildings. Except for the street lights, the alley was dark, and there was a lot of water everywhere. Maybe someone hosed out the dumpsters to keep down the smell, but it didn't help much. The whole place reeked.

But the vomit and dried blood on me smelled worse, so I didn't really care. I just swished away the flies all around and flipped the lid back without making any noise. The single dim bulb above the door gave me just enough light. That's when I saw it. Laying right on top of some smashed cardboard was a genuine turkey, lettuce and tomato sandwich! Or at least half of it, still wrapped in a napkin, so it didn't actually touch any garbage. I swallowed it in two bites. Saliva filled my mouth, while my tears welled. I never in my whole life tasted anything better!

My stomach grumbled again as I lifted up the cardboard. *Is that a hamburger?* Carefully I brushed off some coffee grounds on top of it and devoured it just as quickly. After that, I didn't care, and just ate everything I found—a handful of cold french fries, a half-eaten piece of chocolate cake, and even a bruised apple and a couple of celery stalks that looked like they came right off the grocer's shelf. When I reached the bottom of the can, I found a half-eaten loaf of bread—but then the door clanged open again,

"Hey you. Get outta there!" someone yelled.

I jammed the bread into my pocket and quickly hobbled out of the alley toward a park I remembered passing earlier. "For later." I patted my pocket. I was talking to myself a lot now, just like all the other street people.

The next day was no better. No food. No help. No hope. *Maybe I can call Doc collect? Sure. That's what I'll do. Doc can send me some money for a motel. Then I can get a job and pay him back when I get my first paycheck.*

"Collect call for Dr. David Samuels," I heard the operator tell Margie, Doc's secretary. "Will you accept the charges?"

"I'm sorry. We're not allowed to accept collect calls," she said.

It's me. Don't hang up! I screamed out in my head. But before I could say anything, she spoke again. "Dr. Samuels isn't here. He's out of the country for another month." Then the line went dead.

I dropped the phone, slumping back against the glass door. *What am I gonna do?*

My legs felt like jello. I sat crumpled on the floor and wracked my brain, desperate to know what to do. *Maybe I can get a job somewhere. Yeah, that's what I'll do. Any job. It doesn't matter. Just till I can buy some real food, and maybe a place to sleep.*

I took several pained breaths, braced myself, and limped down the street, trying my best to look optimistic. There were a couple places with *Help Wanted* signs in the window, but everyone I talked to said they didn't need anyone. I walked down a dozen more streets and talked to what seemed like fifty people, but I got the same answer. Finally, exhausted, I asked some guy drinking from a paper bag, if he knew where I could find a job. "I'm real hungry."

"Don't need no job," he answered without bothering to look up. "Just ask for spare change. I get lots of money doing that."

But I'm not like you! I wanted to scream, but I didn't. I just walked away, even more determined to find a job. Two hours and a dozen more rejections later, and when it started to rain, I walked up to a guy coming toward me. The swelling in my mouth had gone down enough so I could speak, at least a little.

"I was mugged when I got in town. All my money was stolen. Can you spare any change?" He walked by without looking at me.

I asked another man.

"Get a job, you hippie!" he barked without even slowing down. *I'm not one of those people! I was going to be a counselor, but I got mugged.* I didn't say anything because it wouldn't make any difference.

———

I made it through the first week by learning what places were best for panhandling, and which restaurants didn't care if I scrounged through their garbage, as long as I was discrete. I learned to ignore the rancid smell of my filthy clothes. And I got used to being rousted by the cops every time I found a dry place to sleep. But I never got used to the way people treated me—like I didn't exist! I was just an irritation, an intrusion, not a real person. They just wanted me to go away.

I thought it was Saturday, but it was hard to keep track of the days. All I knew for sure was that I was exhausted, and desperate for just one decent night of sleep. The sun was setting, and the fog was coming in again. I shivered, like I did every night. Back in college I thought the fog romantic, especially when I was walking with Elizabeth, but here it was just cold. I wrapped an old plastic garbage bag around me and curled up on a bench in a dark corner of the park. I noticed someone walking by. I thought he was just a kid, but I couldn't be sure. He looked toward me. "I've got nothing for you to steal, so get out of here!" I yelled.

"I ain't gonna steal nothing, man. I just wanted to tell you it's not safe in the park after dark. I wouldn't stay here if I was you."

I didn't trust him, or anyone here in San Francisco. I was still mad at myself for going with those two guys into that alley. *If I'd been more careful, I'd be living in my own place now instead of sleeping on this filthy bench!* I must have said that a hundred times. But there was something about this kid. For some reason, he didn't scare me. But still... "I'm okay. Now go away!"

He started to leave, then stopped. "Listen, man, if you got nowhere to stay, there's a shelter down the hill on Pequod Street. I'm staying there and they got room."

I still didn't know if I could trust him, so I didn't answer.

"Just go down Haight ten blocks and turn left on Pequod," he said anyway. "Look for the sign that says *Mission*. Ask for Elijah. He runs the place. Tell him James sent you." He turned and walked away.

It rained most of the night, and even my plastic blanket didn't keep me dry. In the morning, soaked to the bone, cold and coughing a lot harder than I did last night, I decided to check out the place that kid said was nearby. Where was it? Pequod Street?

"Is this the Mission?" I asked a scraggly man standing in front of an old building. There was a line of people waiting to get in. He pointed up at the sign above the door. *Pequod Street Mission.*

"When do they open?"

"Eight for breakfast, but if you need a bed, you gotta come back after three. Just line up here."

"Thanks, man." I was surprised how good it felt to be treated like a human again. Except for that kid I met last night in the park, this was the first kind thing anyone said to me. When the door opened at precisely eight o'clock, I followed the other men into the Mission. The place looked like it was a church once, even a respectable one, but that day was long gone. It needed too many repairs that were never going to be done. No one seemed to care, or even notice.

Instead, everyone was more focused on the kitchen in the basement. This was probably the only meal most of these guys would get all day. But then the only thing I ate yesterday was that soup I bought when some couple gave me two dollars. I thought it was the best minestrone I ever had! Outside I didn't notice the acrid smell. But inside the Mission, with all these men standing so close together, the air was quickly clogged with a muddle of sweat, dirt, urine, putrid body odor, and what seemed like a great deal of alcohol. Only a heavy dose of cooking grease and smoke from the kitchen seemed to overcome it, eventually. Most of the men looked starved and no one seemed to care about the smell—including me.

I finished my second plate of eggs and rubbed my belly. The growling had stopped...for now anyway. For the first time since I arrived in San Francisco, I started to relax. Suddenly there was a loud crash of metal and breaking glass behind me. "Damned lousy drunk!" someone shouted. Some guy passed out and fell to the floor right on top of a mess of ham, eggs, bread, coffee, silverware and broken glass that splashed all over the aisle. Now everyone was shouting at him.

"Goddammit, Watson. Not again!"

"Somebody get Elijah, so I can finish my breakfast!"

There's gotta be someone to help him. But no one moved. They just shouted louder. "Is anybody going to help that guy?" I asked no one in particular.

"That's just Watson. He comes in here drunk every day," a grizzled man sitting next to me said dully, like it was a normal part of the breakfast routine. "You outta be glad he didn't piss himself or puke on the table like he done a couple times. He'll be okay. Just ignore him."

But I couldn't ignore him. I hadn't been on the street long enough to be that numb. Not yet anyway. I got up and went to Watson, lifted his head off the floor, grabbed a rag from a nearby table, and gently wiped the eggs and dirt off his weathered face. *No cuts I can see. No bruises. Just really drunk.* I pulled off his cap and tried to wipe the grime off his bald head, but it was obvious it would take a whole lot more than my rag. For a minute, something moved in his stringy beard. Lice? It was obvious he soiled himself, but judging from his clothes, it could have been a month ago and he wouldn't have known the difference. He smelled so rancid I was sure I was going to vomit my breakfast.

"He okay?" someone asked from behind me, but I didn't turn around. I held Watson and wiped the last of the mess off his face.

"He's alive, but I don't know for how long. I'm no doctor, but my guess is the booze will kill him, not the fall. Is there someone here who can help him?"

"That's the hard part about working here," that same person said. "Watching people kill themselves one drink or one needle at a time, and we can't stop 'em. Wish we could, but we can't. So we just try to give 'em what we can. Today for Watson it's some breakfast and a safe place to pass out."

I turned around to see who was talking to me.

"Name's Elijah," he said. "You interested in a job? I run the Mission and I could use some help. 'Specially someone like you who seems to care. Don't pay much, but includes a bed and meals."

Without hesitating, I agreed. I didn't even ask what job it was.

"I studied psychology. Will that help?"

"Not unless they gave you a broom with your degree. I need a janitor. But what I really need is someone who can do what you just did for Watson. You drink? God knows I don't need another drunk working for me."

"No sir."

"Good, then you're hired. At least I know you'll show up in the morning. Grab an apron. I need your help in the kitchen." And with that, Elijah turned and walked away.

"My name's Daniel Robinson," I called out. He never even asked, like it didn't matter.

CHAPTER 11
FAMILY IS WHERE YOU FIND IT

SAN FRANCISCO, 1970. I stayed with Watson for maybe twenty minutes until he woke up. "Are you okay?" I asked, but all he wanted to do was complain about somebody stealing his breakfast. I helped him back to his seat and got him another plate of food. But now, if I was going to work for Elijah, I needed to do *a lot* of scrubbing first. After what felt like a million miles and a lifetime of pain, that shower was more than just soap and water. It was a holy experience, a baptism of sorts, my new birth of freedom. Standing there, naked, in my new home, with my new job and a full stomach, as all the pain and street grime washed down the drain, something Doc said broke through the fog of my memory. He said change is natural. Fragile things break, and people come and go in our lives. *That's why I keep these pencils—as a reminder that we all can get another chance.*

And here in this neglected church-turned-homeless shelter in the underbelly of San Francisco, where a hundred broken men, like Watson, were given some breakfast and a safe place to pass out, I found the second chance I desperately needed.

I wasn't laying in an alley, hiding in an underpass, or sleeping on a park bench with one eye open, watching for cops or muggers to roust me. I made it all the way across the country and now I have a job and my own room. I felt... triumphant! *I did it. I really did it!*

I was walking toward the kitchen, thinking how good it felt to not be scared anymore, when I noticed someone familiar following me. He looked more gaunt, ashen, even sickly than he seemed in the dim light of the park last night, but I recognized him immediately—that kid who told me about the Mission! "James, isn't it? I hoped I'd run into you again. I want to thank you, you know, for telling me about this place. I wasn't doing too well on the street."

He was small, at least four inches shorter than me, and too thin, like so many kids I saw on the streets. His long brown hair was parted on the left side, hanging free and hiding half his face. His jeans hung loose and his flannel shirt was too big, making him look even smaller. He looked no more than fifteen.

"I hear Elijah hired you." He gave me a slight smile, but there was a sad, hangdog look about it that made me wonder what someone his age was doing in a shelter.

"He sure did," I said, "but I still don't know what my job is. It wasn't much of an interview. Then again, I didn't really care. I just needed a job."

"That's why all of us are here. We got nowhere else to go." He looked at me with a face that might appear as expressionless to anyone else, but there was something behind those sad eyes—was it pain? I wasn't sure. All I knew was he helped me when no one else would. "Don't worry about it," he said. "I hear you'll be helping me keep this place from falling down. Lousy work, lousy hours, and worse pay. But it's a lot better than the streets." There was also something familiar about him. *That kid at Kent State, but with sad eyes—like Sunshine.* I liked him immediately.

As we walked, James told me that Elijah had been running the Pequod Street Mission for as long as anyone remembered. No one really knew much about him, even his age. James said some of the men were sure he was just forty, but others were convinced he was at least seventy. No one really knew because he kept his head shaved, so even if his hair was grey, it didn't show. And his black skin hid most of the wrinkles and scars that came with living on the streets. "All I know is he always talks kind to everyone, no matter what they did, or how bad they smell. I guess you could say he's the only stable thing most of the guys here have."

"Mr. Robinson." Elijah met us in the kitchen. "James probably told you he needs help keeping this place clean." I noticed his voice sounded strained, even raspy. I thought it might be from living on the street... or maybe booze. "But more important," he said, "I want you to remember everyone here deserves respect, no matter who they are or what they done. It's more important than food and a bed. That's all you got to know here. You understand me?" Doc Samuels said he learned the same thing working on the streets in India, that dignity was sometimes more important than food or water, maybe even oxygen. I nodded, as Elijah turned and left the room—and that was the extent of my training.

———

"You done cleaning yet?" James asked when he found me later that afternoon in the shower room. "We gotta go to chapel. No chapel, no dinner. It's the rule here."

I couldn't help wondering again what brought him here. *He should be in a high school classroom, not mopping floors in a shelter.* "Elijah didn't tell me anything about that," I said, hanging my mop in the closet. "But it might be interesting."

"It won't be. Trust me. Rev. Jonah always preaches about sin. Sometimes I think that's all he believes in."

"You ever complain to Elijah?"

"Sure, but all he says is the Mission is run by some church and Rev. Jonah is their pastor. If we wanna eat here, we gotta go to chapel. He don't agree with it, but it's the rule. So just do what everyone else does, and get some sleep while he's preaching."

Rev. Jonah preached for the next thirty minutes, quoting one Bible verse after another, growing louder, more animated with every verse. I heard this sermon a hundred times at college. Not as emotional, and never this loud, but the same sermon. I tried to sleep through it like James said, but every time I closed my eyes, Rev. Jonah thundered out some new verse and pounded on his Bible. He woke up every one of us in the room. Finally, mercifully, I heard him say, "In conclusion…"

"Thank God," I mumbled too loud and James elbowed me, chuckling. But an old man in front of us, who smelled as bad as Watson, turned around. "Shut up or we'll never get no dinner!" I elbowed James even harder and laughed. It felt good to laugh again.

"If you'll repent," Rev. Jonah called out to the men, "and if you'll come to the altar and ask Jesus to forgive your sins, then you'll be saved." No one ever came forward to get saved when the preachers at college said that, so I was really surprised to see a half dozen men come to the altar.

"I don't get it," I whispered. "The sermon wasn't that good."

"Don't matter," James answered. "Everyone knows they can't go to dinner till enough people get saved. So we make sure there's plenty of saving going on at every service."

"Sounds hypocritical," I said and laughed again, "but smart."

———

I spent my first week at the Mission learning my new job. But it didn't take much training to mop floors, clean toilets or hose out a putrid dumpster in the alley—even if the smell did make nearly retch the first time I did it.

When Elijah had me help him fix a leak in the kitchen sink, I thought it was a good time to ask him something that had been bothering me all week. "I haven't seen Watson since my first day here. You know, the guy who passed out onto his food tray. Any idea where he is?"

"Believe me, I know who Watson is. And no, I ain't seen him either. My guess he's probably in jail again. He goes through cycles. He does good for a while, goes to meetings, even gets a job. Then he falls hard off the wagon, like you saw. He'll show up again. He always does."

"Isn't there something we can do? I mean, how can we just watch him kill himself and do nothing?"

"We're doing something." Elijah grabbed the wrench to tighten the drain pipe. "We're giving him a safe place to come when he needs it.

Beyond that, there's not much more we can do. Not till he's ready anyway.

"You sure about that, Elijah?"

He stopped working, looking at me from under the sink, hesitated, then said, "I don't talk about it much, least not with anybody here, but you been to college and I think you might understand. I was pretty deep in the bottle myself. Everyone tried to help me quit, just like Mr. Watson. But until I got ready, I wasn't listening. Not till I hit the bottom of the bottle anyway."

"But what if Watson's never ready? You know it'll kill him. Can't we stop him?"

Elijah shook his head. "All we can do is make it easier for him to want to stop. Show him we care. That's why the Mission's here. To show people a way out of the gutter."

"You mean Rev. Jonah's altar calls? I doubt they're doing much good."

"Don't be too hard on Rev. Jonah. In his own way, he really cares for these men. It's just that he's trying to scare people into believing. Like a lot of churches, that's all he knows. Truth is, it was God who got me out of the bottle. Not because someone preached at me. But someone was there waiting for me when I hit bottom. What you did for Mr. Watson is what I'm talking about. Seems to me you might make a pretty good preacher yourself someday."

I shook my head. "Forget it, Elijah. I've got no plans to be a preacher. Except for one of my college teachers, I haven't seen much in the church to attract me. I'm planning to be a counselor. I can do more good doing that."

"I think you'll be a good one too. But right now, we got a sink to fix."

I had all my work done by noon. That meant I was free to travel around San Francisco in the afternoons. I wanted to see all the places Mellow talked so much about. But I didn't want to risk going down another wrong alley again.

"I'll take you to my favorite place in the city," James offered.

"Sure. Where?" I asked.

"To see the *Painted Ladies*."

"What makes you think I want to go with you to the Tenderloin district? What do you think I am, some sort of pervert?"

"Not *those* painted ladies, and you *are* a pervert for even thinking I was asking that." He rolled his eyes and shook his head. "I'm talking about houses, not whores. The most beautiful houses in the city. Someday I'll be living in one of them. I just thought you might want to see what they look like. But if you don't want to go..."

"Sorry. I had no idea." I tried to sound apologetic, but I still didn't know what he was talking about. Then again, it was a beautiful June day —the sky had been clear all week, with temperatures around a perfect 75 degrees, and the wind from the bay was so wet, so alive, it reminded me of that morning when I found Elijah's Mission. I owe that place—and James—my life. And now everyday felt like another new beginning for me. "Okay. I'm game. Take me to meet your ladies."

We walked west to Steiner Street then north to Alamo Square to the park.

"What did I tell you? Beautiful, ain't they?"

"All I see are old houses."

"Of course, you idiot. But look how they're painted." His voice suddenly louder and his otherwise placid expression morphed into someone I never knew existed. His eyes wide, his pale skin now flush with emotion, James shook his head, then shot his arm in the air and pointed at one house after another as he embarked on a long, passionate lecture, tracing the history of every one of the houses on Steiner Street. They were what he called *Italianate style*. Originally, all the houses in the neighborhood were painted like this, he said. About fifty years ago they were getting pretty shabby, so everyone painted them gray because the Navy used so much of that paint on the ships in the harbor and it was really cheap."

The more he talked, the more animated he got. "Can you believe it?" he asked, his eyes wide and looking right at me. "They actually thought that made them look pretty! God, people can be so stupid sometimes."

Without missing a beat, James proceeded to describe, in loving detail, how a decade ago, some artist decided to use really bright colors to restore his own house. Everyone complained he was spoiling the neighborhood. But then a lot of other people started doing the same thing. "It's called the *colorist movement*," he said, now looking at me proudly, as if expecting some response reflecting my new enlightenment.

I stared blankly at him. *They're just old houses*! I also thought James sounded a lot like Sunshine when she tried to explain all the nuances of astrology. I tried to sound interested. "They're nice."

"Nice? That's all you can say? These are some of the most beautiful houses in the world! Where'd you say you came from? Kentucky? Did everyone live in log cabins there? Look at all those colors! All the intricate details, the columns, the corbels, the gable decorations. Just those spindles above the doors and windows alone are irreplaceable art. And that's just on the outside. My God, Daniel, all the work that went into making each house. Every one of them is a masterpiece of Victorian architecture at its finest!"

This was clearly a religious experience for James, but all I saw were old houses. "They're *very* nice?" I tried my best to sound sincere.

"I'm wasting my time talking to an idiot!" He turned and stomped back toward the Mission, reminding me more than ever of Sunshine.

In spite of my obvious lack of culture, James continued to take me on tours of the city. He even surprised me with a special gift. "Another Kodak camera—to replace the one you got stolen." I didn't know what to say. I never expected that, but I sure appreciated it, especially with all the sites he was showing me.

"Then let me get a picture of you standing in front of your ladies—now that I know they're not whores!"

We both laughed at that for days.

I thought a lot about Mellow and Sunshine on our city tours. I wondered how they were doing back in Ohio, and if their baby was born. *Did they name it Blue like Sunshine wanted*. I laughed again, just thinking about my friends. *I know they'd like James.*

It was a quiet afternoon in September when we were walking through Golden Gate Park, just enjoying the quiet, staring out at the bay and not saying much. We were somewhere near the bench where I saw that girl my first day in the city. I realized I hadn't thought about Elizabeth at all since I got to the Mission. San Francisco never looked more beautiful than it did at that moment. We walked on toward a stand of tall trees where we saw this skinny kid, just sitting on the ground, staring out toward the bay. I thought he was maybe fifteen or sixteen, and he reminded me a lot of James, except for his face. The only word I could think of was *old*, like he had been on the street for a long time and his face had somehow aged beyond the rest of his body. He was hunched over, his mouth dropped open, eyes half-closed with his head dropped against his chest, like he was sleeping, but...not really.

"Think he's okay?" I asked, but James didn't answer. He just stared at that boy.

"Don't bother," he mumbled. "He's on the nod. Nothing we can do."

I wanted to ask what he meant, but he had a frightened look on his face, and I let it go. "Let's go back to the Mission," was all he said, turning away and walking quickly out of the park.

James didn't say anything more the whole way back to the Mission. I had a feeling he was still wrestling with some of the demons hidden behind those sad eyes. *Maybe I should talk to him about it tonight*? But that didn't seem to be something he wanted to talk about, at least not now. I didn't see him much the rest of the week, but Elijah had both of us pretty busy and I kind of forgot about it, until Friday when I knew something was wrong. It was right at curfew and I was about to lock the doors, like I did every night.

"Mr. Robinson. You seen James?" Elijah stopped me as I walked past the kitchen where he was still working. I always wondered why Elijah never called James *Mister*, like he did everyone, including me. At first, I thought it was because James was younger than everyone else in the Mission. But I had a feeling it was more personal, maybe he saw him like family.

"He's always here at curfew...most times even early," Elijah furrowed his brow, biting his lip. I never saw him do that before. He threw his towel on the counter, checked his watch, then looked at me. "He don't like to be on the streets too late."

I locked the door. "I don't understand. Why?"

"He never told you?"

"Told me what?"

"Heroin. He's been clean since he got here, but an addict's got to be careful. Start hangin' in the old places with the old friends, and the old habits come back. Seen it happen too much. He's been acting strange lately. Real quiet. You notice it?"

"Sort of, but I'm not sure. I don't know what to look for. And we never talked about his past. I didn't even know he was an addict. Think he's okay?" I unlocked the door, looked up and down the street one more time for James. "Where is he?" I mumbled to no one in particular, then relocked the door, this time slowly, almost like a prayer.

"I don't know." Elijah sounded even more worried than me. "Hopefully he'll just show up with some damn excuse about missing the bus and I'll chew his ass good for not calling me. He'll be real sorry, and that'll be the end of it."

Neither of us believed it.

Two days later a couple cops Elijah knew brought James back to the shelter. He was filthy, and pretty groggy. He could barely keep his eyes open, his words slurred. But he was alive.

"We found him in an alley off Castro Street," they said. "Don't know how long he's been there. We thought about taking him to the precinct, but I recognized him from your place. Once a kid like this gets in the system, they don't ever come out the same. I thought he'd be better off with you." I heard Elijah's years on the streets, and especially now at the Mission, had given him a long list of contacts at the precinct. Everyone knew there were times, like now, when it was better to bend the law a little.

"Thanks, guys. I really appreciate this," Elijah said. "I owe you."

We took James upstairs to a side room off the dorm to go through withdrawal—something neither of us looked forward to.

"Can you stay with him tonight?"

"Not even a question," I said, pulling back the blanket on the bed.

"It's gonna be a tough night, especially for James. Pretty soon he'll start feeling like shit. Can you handle it?"

"Like I said, not a question."

"Then you'll need more sheets and towels 'cause he's going to be sweatin' something terrible. And a bed pan. When the diarrhea starts, he'll never make it to the toilet. It's going to be a long night."

Three days later when James finally kept a little soup on his stomach, we knew he got through the worst of it. But he was still shaking so much I had to wrap him in blankets, then hold him close until the fit passed. It was early on the fourth day when he was calm enough to talk. "I'm so sorry I let everyone down," was all he said again and again.

"You're gonna be okay now," I told him every time. "You had us worried. Even Rev. Jonah was here praying for you."

"I'm so sorry," he said again, and then cried. This time I didn't say anything. I just held him until he fell asleep.

Elijah constantly checked on both of us through it all. "You must be exhausted," he said when he found me asleep in that chair by James's bed.

"I am, I think. But I'm too numb, and too relieved to feel anything." I rubbed the sleep out of my eyes. "Do you think he's okay now? I mean, is the worst over?"

"Physically, yes. Mentally, I can't say. Heroin is some really bad shit. You don't just quit. Some people fight it forever, and James may be one of them people. We'll see. But you did good. I'm real proud of you."

I was so tired I could barely stand up, but hearing Elijah say that revived me.

Over the next several days, James slowly regained his strength. He was eating more, and even walking around the Mission. But still, we worried. "He's real vulnerable," Elijah warned. "He's clean, but I don't think he's over it yet. Just keep a close eye on him. That's all we can do now." Elijah suggested I get him out of the Mission to rebuild his strength—and his confidence. So we went touring again, like we did so many afternoons. A hundred questions ran through my mind on our first trip outside the Mission. *Why didn't I see this coming? What can I do different now?* I just knew I had to be more careful. Neither of us could afford to go through another overdose. Next time the cops may not find him.

I laid awake half the night thinking about that, until something Elijah said floated up. *It was God who got me out of the bottle. Not because someone preached at me. But someone was there waiting for me when I hit bottom.*

"Maybe I can just be there for him," I said and breathed a quick prayer.

In the morning when I checked on him, he was too weak to come to work, or even come to the kitchen, so I took him a plate of eggs, a slice of ham and a piece of bread. "Thought you might be hungry." I laid the tray on his bedside table, then slid a chair next to him. He smiled, just a little, and I sat down without a word. That's where I spent all morning.

I was surprised to find him up and dressed, even before the sun broke through the morning fog. "I think I need to get out of the Mission. You know, stretch my legs," was all he said. Elijah wasn't anywhere around, and I didn't want him to go out alone—not yet. "Great. Let me grab my coat and I'll go with you. I could use another tour of the city."

We rode the bus in silence, mostly staring at the city. Finally, when we reached Nob Hill, I asked him something I'd been thinking about all morning. "You know, James, you never told me what brought you to San Francisco. Other than those ugly houses you love so much, you don't talk about yourself at all."

"Not much to talk about," he muttered as we stepped off the bus.

"Okay. For starters, where'd you come from? I don't even know that."

He looked my way, but didn't say anything, not at first. I thought he was going to sidestep my question again, but then he seemed to let go of whatever he was wrestling with.

"Near Detroit. A little town called Lapeer," he said barely loud enough for me to hear.

"You're kidding? A friend of mine came from Detroit. She and her boyfriend are the reason I'm here now. I wish you'd told me that before." Now I *really* wanted to know all about him. "How'd you get here?"

"Greyhound."

"That's not what I meant, and you know it. Why'd you come here?"

"Same as everyone. I heard about all that was happening, and I decided to see it for myself."

"How old were you? I mean, you were still in high school, weren't you?"

"Yeah. Fifteen."

Billy flashed through my mind. *He would be sixteen now, just about the same age as James. I wonder if he's okay.* I drew in a quick breath. *Not the time or place for those memories.* "Weren't you scared? I mean, I nearly died on the streets when I got here, and I'm twenty-two. How'd you survive?"

He kept walking north on Hyde Street and didn't answer.

"I think you told me you've been here for two years. But you've only been at the Mission for what, six months? Where were you living all that time?"

His hair blew across his face, and he quickly brushed it back without answering. He looked so thin, so pale. *Just a kid... a sad, lost kid.*

"Here and there. No place in particular," he finally said. At the corner of California Street, he stopped and looked toward a huge church on the hill. "How about we go into Grace Cathedral? I like sitting in there sometimes. You know, like a reminder that maybe there is a God."

I wasn't sure what he was talking about, but whatever it was, I had a feeling it was a lot more than just heroin. "Sure," I said. "I think I need to remind myself of that sometimes too."

———

The next morning when I found Elijah in the kitchen, I asked him if he could tell me any more about James.

"I don't know much more than you do," he said. "Hand me that wrench, will you? Damned sink's leaking again. Why you asking?"

"You told me to keep an eye on him. You know, make sure he didn't get in trouble again. So I was asking him about where he came from and stuff like that. Did you know he came from Detroit, just like my friend Sunshine? He said he's been here two years. I know he's only been at the Mission for maybe six months. So I asked him where he lived before he got here. You know, just trying to make conversation. But he got real nervous, like he didn't want to talk about it. What do you think he's hiding?"

Elijah put down the wrench, slid out from under the sink and sat up. "How do you think a pretty boy like him gets by on the streets in this city?"

"I don't understand."

"Think about it. You seen all the hookers, haven't you? Well, it's not just women who sell themselves to get by. There's a lot of people who prefer pretty boys too. Especially in this part of town."

"You mean...?"

"That's exactly what I mean."

All I heard was Pastor Duncan. *Daniel, why don't you stand with me in front of the Bible and close your eyes while I pray for you... Please God. Make him stop!* Squeezing my eyes shut, I forced that memory out of my head. "How do you ever get past something like that?" I asked, more for me than James.

"You just do," Elijah said. "You got no choice, and I think James knows that. That's why he likes to sit in that church... to remind himself no matter what he done, he can still change stuff in his life."

"Maybe..." But that got me thinking about something Mellow said all the way from Montana. "The people I met coming here...they were here in '67. They said it was like being in heaven. Mellow called it a place where helping people was more important than making money. But all I've seen are dirty and dangerous streets filled with vacant people just trying to survive one more day. What happened?"

"Drugs." Elijah growled the word. "It started with LSD. But in no time, it was heroin, and nothing good comes with that shit. These streets eat up kids like James. Just to survive, they'll do whatever it takes. You saw that in the little time you was on the street. That's why I'm not judging James. When I was in the bottle, I did some things to get by I'm not proud of either."

"What can we do, Elijah?"

"We're doing it. He's here now, with you and me. All I care is he's willing to start over one more time. Church calls it grace. I call it survival."

"Does Rev. Jonah know? I mean, does he know what James did on the streets?"

"I doubt it, and I'm not telling him. He's really not a bad guy, but his understanding of forgiveness is pretty limited. So he don't ask, and I don't tell him most of the shit these guys done. He lets me do what I need to do to make a difference here. That's all that matters."

Elijah closed his toolbox. Our conversation was done for the day.

That night I laid awake again, staring at the ceiling, thinking about something I said to Ron Jenkins. *I'm studying psychology. Maybe I can help with more than painting.*

"Maybe is another word for hope." I closed my eyes and slept better than I had in a long time.

———

By November James seemed to be his old self again. Elijah and I both thought the worst was over. But late one Friday night, near curfew when I was locking up the Mission, I noticed James wasn't in. I was about to tell Elijah when there was a hard knock on the door. I opened it and saw those same two cops who found James that last time. I felt a knot in my stomach.

Elijah went outside to talk with them. I couldn't hear what they said, but I could see their faces. They looked serious. Elijah slumped against the door.

My heart stopped.

"It's James," he said, closing the door. "They found him again in that same alley off Castro Street."

"Is he okay?" But the ashen look on his face already told me the answer.

Even in the dim light of the hall, I could see him shake. He didn't have to tell me. I knew.

I felt the air go out of me. I was back in that alley, lying on the ground, beaten, struggling to breathe. But this felt worse... a lot worse. I grabbed a chair and fell into it. It was all I could do to just mutter. "How?"

"Overdose. They said it looked like he got a hotshot of heroin. The needle was still in his arm. Now they want me to go down to the morgue and identify his body. I done that too many times. God, I hate my job sometimes."

What can I say to Elijah? But I needed him to help me even more. We could barely look at each other. He left for the morgue without a word, and I went back to my room, collapsed onto the bed, then buried my face in my pillow. "Damn you, James!" I screamed over and over.

"Hey, shut up in there!" someone yelled at me through the wall.

"Yeah, shut up! We're trying to get some sleep in here!"

"FUCK BOTH OF YOU!" I grabbed my shoe and threw it against the wall as hard as I could, smashing a framed picture of James with his damned *Painted Ladies*.

"And damn you, James, for being so stupid... and...and weak...." The room was quiet, except for the sound of my tortured breathing.

"And damn me, too," I finally muttered. "cause I didn't see it coming..." I fell back onto my bed, exhausted, and just laid there in the dark—alone again. "I'm sorry I wasn't there for you, James," I whispered as the tears ran down my face.

———

I didn't see Elijah until the next afternoon. I found him on a ladder in the kitchen rewiring a light. "I need you to get that window fixed on the second floor before it rains again."

That's all you have to say? I need to talk about James, not fix a damned window! "How can you act like nothing happened!" I screamed.

Elijah kept working on the light and didn't even look at me. "You gotta let him go. We got a hundred other guys here who need us."

I couldn't stop myself. "How... how can you say that? I thought you actually cared for James!"

Elijah laid his pliers down, looking right at me. "You're right, Daniel." This was the first time he ever called me Daniel. "I didn't mean what I said. I'm just as sick as you are. But we can't change what happened."

I didn't say anything. I was still too mad at Elijah... and at me. *Why didn't I see this coming? What more could I have done for him... for Billy?*

Elijah climbed off the ladder and put his hand on my shoulder, like Doc Samuels did so many times. "I know you been blaming yourself all night, but this wasn't your fault. You hear me, Daniel?"

I gave him a dead stare.

"All that blaming don't do no good, but just eat you up with guilt. You did all you could for James. His death ain't your fault. You understand me?"

Elijah grabbed me by both arms and pulled me close. "I never told anyone about this. You gotta swear you'll never say nothing about what I'm gonna tell you."

I nodded, my eyes fixed on him while he took a deep breath.

"I wasn't much older than you." He spoke slowly, struggling to find the right words. "I had a job here in San Francisco, good job, 'specially for a black man with no college. I was married. Her name was Ellen. We had a son, Joey, after my father."

He took another breath.

"We was renting a little apartment across the bay in Oakland. Nothing fancy, but we were happy. We even had plans to buy a house someday. I was putting in a lot of hours at work, sometimes on weekends too. You know, saving for a house. Ellen complained I wasn't home enough. She said it was hard with me gone so much, but I didn't listen. I told her I had to do it for us, for our house. But one day—it was a Saturday. I remember like it was yesterday."

He squeezed my arms, shaking as he talked.

"I got a call at work from Ellen. She said she couldn't wake Joey from his nap. I told her to take him to the hospital right away, but it was too late. The doctors said there was nothing they could do. They said it happens sometimes with babies. They don't know why, but it just happens. Nobody blamed us... but I blamed me. If I hadn't worked that Saturday..."

His voice trailed off, as if he was living that day again. "And for what? A couple more bucks for a house that we'd never buy now?"

Elijah looked straight at me, but not seeing me. He looked drained, exhausted. He squeezed my arms even harder, holding onto me to finish his story. "Ellen and me... we tried to get over it, but we couldn't. We kept asking the same questions I know you been asking. Before long, we had nothing more to say to each other, until finally she left. I blamed myself for that too. That's when I started drinkin' hard."

He took another deep breath. I couldn't take my eyes off him, hanging on every word.

"After that I lost my job and ended up on the street. You know the rest of the story. You seen it every day with these guys. It took me twenty years to get here, with too much pain and a helluva lot of regret. So when I say you gotta let James go, I know what I'm talking about. If you don't, twenty years from now, you're gonna be talking to some other kid about not wasting his life like you did. You understand me, boy?"

I nodded, without saying a word. I knew he cared for James even more than I did...and I knew he cared for me too. I wrapped my arms around him, holding him close. We both held each other and cried for James. Then, after several minutes, I let loose of him, turned without a word and walked out of the Mission and up Steiner Street to James' *Painted Ladies*. I had to say goodbye to my friend. That's when I got my plan... or at least the seeds of my plan.

———

Over the next several days, I kept thinking about what James said, about how much he wanted to live in one of those houses. It was a crazy idea, and I didn't know if it could be done, but I had to try.

"Elijah, you've got contacts in city hall, don't you?"

"Some, but not much." His brow furrowed. "What do you have in mind? Don't tell me. I got a feeling I don't wanna know."

I ignored him. "I've been thinking about James. Not like before. But I was thinking how we might give him something he always wanted." I told Elijah about my plan.

"If we can get James' body out of the morgue, then have it cremated, we can take his ashes to Steiner Street where he can live forever, just like he always wanted.

He studied me, his eyes fixed, silent. "I know I ain't got the money, and I doubt you do," he finally said.

At least he heard me. That's all that mattered.

"How you gonna pay for cremation?"

I was ready for that question. "That's where you come in. With your connections, I know you can find somebody to pay for it."

Elijah's brow furrowed again and he shook his head. "I doubt it, but even if I could, and I ain't saying I can, but even if I could, there's no way city hall will ever let you bury James' ashes in those rich people's yard."

"Let me worry about that. You just get somebody to pay for the cremation, and I'll take care of the rest. We owe it to James."

"I ain't promising nothing." Elijah looked even more skeptical now. "I'll make a couple calls. But that's all I can do. You understand me?"

"That's all I'm asking."

I turned to leave, but Elijah took my arm. "For what it's worth. Even if it don't work, I gotta admire what you're doing. I know James would appreciate it."

"That's why I'm doing it. For James."

Two weeks later, early in the morning while the fog was still thick, and sure no one could see us, we walked to a hill in the center of Alamo Square. Memories rushed over me with every step. Our stifled laughter in the chapel, hanging onto the cable cars going through Chinatown, his god-awful descriptions of those houses. I heard his voice, right here with me... *There's a shelter down the hill on Pequod Street. Ask for Elijah. Tell him James sent you.* He gave me a home when I needed it... and now I was giving him one.

With a stiff wind blowing in from the bay and toward James' *Painted Ladies*, we scattered his ashes into the air, then stood there in silence, watching them drift toward those beautiful houses on Steiner Street he loved so much.

"Now he's home." I wiped my eyes, and walked back to the Mission.

———

I tried to act normal, but I kept thinking about what I said to Ron Jenkins. *I'm studying psychology. Maybe I can help with more than painting*—or being a janitor here. Maybe...

Elijah noticed. "You okay?" he asked, when he found me sitting in the kitchen.

"Yeah, fine. Why?"

"Don't disrespect me by telling me what you think I wanna hear. Now what's going on? Is it still James?" He slid a chair next to me and sat down.

"It's not James," I answered too quick, then caught myself. "That's not totally true. I'm okay with his death now. But I'm not really over it. I just can't go on acting like nothing happened... I've been thinking about something."

"What?" Elijah's eyes narrowed—and he waited...

"Nothing you need to worry about," I said, resting my hand on his shoulder. He relaxed a little.

"It's just that I'm thinking about going back to school. You know, to be a counselor. But for kids like James... to help people with addictions. I keep thinking if I'd known what was going on with him, then maybe..."

"This ain't guilt talking, is it?"

I took his arm and squeezed it. "I've been thinking about counseling for a long time, Elijah... for my own reasons. I kind of forgot about it for a while. But James got me thinking about it again. That's the truth. I mean it."

"I understand. I really do. And I think that's a great idea. You gonna go to school here? You could stay at the Mission."

"I thought about it, but I still have the draft hanging over my head back in Kentucky. I've got to take care of that first. But when I get it settled, then I'm going to get my counseling degree. I owe it to James."

"I'm gonna miss you around here, Daniel. You know that, don't you?"

"I'll miss you more than you know, Elijah."

We hugged each other, then we hugged again. I missed him already.

CHAPTER 12
NO BAD STUDENTS. JUST BAD TEACHERS

WILSONVILLE, 1970. Two weeks and a dozen rides later I was knocking on Doc's office door again.

"I think I'm ready to go back to school," I announced, walking in the room. A shocked smile spread across his face, before he jumped up from his chair and nearly ran across the room. We shared a silent hug for several long minutes. "I've only been gone for seven months, but it seems like seven years," I finally said, breaking loose from his grip.

Doc stepped back, still holding onto my arms. "Lazarus has risen," was all he managed to say, before hugging me again.

We stood there in more silence, savoring this moment. Finally, I slowly stepped back.

"I've got so much to tell you about all that happened, all the people I met—like Bobby." The words just poured out of me now. "I met him in Glacier Park in Montana. He'd been in Vietnam and he was thinking about killing himself because of all that he'd seen over there, but after some time with me, he decided not to. But it's not like I did anything special. I mean, I just tried to do what you did with me... you know, listen to him. And he said thanks to me, he was going back home now to help his mother because his old man was a lot like mine."

I took a quick breath. "Oh, I forgot to tell you about Augie. He's this old dairy farmer who picked me up in Chicago. He was going to Uruguay to work with the Peace Corp 'cause his wife just died, and this was his way of honoring her. Can you believe it? He gave me his Kodak camera and told me to make some good memories on my trip. It got stolen in San Francisco when I got mugged..."

Doc's eyes were wide as saucers now. His mouth dropped open.

"...but don't worry. I had my film cannisters hidden in my pocket, so I still have my pictures, and I can't wait to show all of them to you—especially Sunshine and Mellow. They're two hippies I rode with all the way through Utah."

I had to catch my breath, grabbed a chair nearby, and sank into it.

"I can see this is going to be a long story...." Doc said, dropping into his own chair, and offering a feigned sign of relief.

"Sorry, Doc. I just feel like I haven't seen you in a lifetime." I couldn't believe I was actually talking to him again. "So much has happened, and I want to tell you about everyone I met—especially James. Truth is, he's the reason I'm here today..." I slid my chair toward him. "...and he's probably the reason I'm still alive."

Doc leaned forward, eyes fixed on me as I talked slower now, sharing every detail about San Francisco, from my first day when I got robbed and nearly killed, about panhandling, what happened at that awful church, even about eating out of dumpsters and sleeping on the streets. "It was pretty scary for a while, believe me."

"That's when I met James. He found me sleeping on a bench in a bad part of the city. He told me about Elijah's mission where I got a place to stay for free, and even a job as a janitor. It was lousy work cleaning up after a hundred drunks every day, but I learned a lot from Elijah. Not so much about janitoring, but people."

I nodded toward him. "Elijah reminded me a lot of you, like when he said no matter what any of the men did, all he asked them to do was just start over one more time. That's how he defined grace."

"What about James?" Doc asked. "You said he saved your life. I'd like to hear about him." His hand cupped his chin as he waited.

I closed my eyes, taking a deep breath. "He was just seventeen..." and for the next hour I told him all about James, why he ran away from home, how boys like him are used on the streets, how he survived it all. I even told him how James taught me that everyone had to get saved in chapel every day, or Rev. Jonah wouldn't let us go to dinner. "We had to make sure there was plenty of saving going on at every service." We laughed at that.

But I kept the best part for last. "Did you ever hear of some old houses in San Francisco called the *Painted Ladies*?"

"Sure," he shrugged. "It's a whole neighborhood of restored Italianate style homes that are noted for their intricate architectural details, and especially their colorful exteriors. That whole area is considered to be a masterpiece of Victorian architecture at its finest. Why do you ask?"

I shook my head. I felt like I was listening to James all over again. "Well, I thought they were whores, not fancy houses. Can you believe it?" We laughed even harder now. Talking like this, about all those things we did together, it was almost like he was here with me again. Almost.

Then I was quiet. "There's more, Doc." The smile disappeared from my face. "James also taught me about heroin." My words caught. I looked down at the floor, then out the window at a student walking by. I turned back toward Doc and swallowed.

He held his breath... and waited....

"All the way to San Francisco, Mellow made it sound like drugs were no big deal. But he left the city before heroin hit the streets, and that's what James got hooked on. I thought he was over it... but he relapsed a couple times..."

I saw those two cops talking to Elijah... saw him slump against the door again. "...and that last time killed him." The air went out of me all over again.

Doc put his hand on my shoulder. "You know James' death wasn't your fault."

"I know, Doc. That's what Elijah told me, too. I just think he reminded me a lot of my kid brother Billy. They were about the same age. You remember Billy?"

He nodded.

"That's when I realized I still want to be a counselor. Not like what we talked about before, but for guys like James. You know, so I can help someone get a second chance...." I saw James' ashes drifting toward his beautiful *Painted Ladies...* and took a deep breath. "...before it's too late for them too."

"That's a wonderful goal, and I've always thought you'd be a really good counselor." Doc leaned back. "Any idea where you want to go to school?"

"Not really. I haven't thought that far ahead. I don't even know if I'm done with college yet, 'cause I left before finals." What would Doc say now? What *could* he say? That day in his office when I was so angry, so hurt, so confused...it seemed a lifetime ago...

"I've got good news about that." Smiling, Doc reached into his desk drawer and pulled out a large manilla envelope. "After you left, I checked with the dean's office, and you had enough credits to graduate, even without completing your final exams."

Did I hear him right? I didn't say anything.

"You got your degree, Daniel." He handed me the envelope. "Your diploma!"

A thousand memories rushed over me.

I gotta go to college somewhere. If I don't, I'll end up in some mill just like my old man.

This college is for poor kids in Appalachia who can't afford to go to a state school. I think they let you work off your tuition.

I made a B in Abnormal Psych, Doc!

I breathed out a deep sigh. "It's been a long journey, hasn't it?" I muttered. "I couldn't have made it without you, Doc. You know that, don't you?"

He smiled proudly.

We both sat there for several minutes, reflecting. "Daniel," Doc finally broke the silence, "Kentucky's got a good grad program. You can ask Ron Jenkins about it. That's where he's going. You know, for his drug counseling certification."

I sat up and cleared my throat. All the way from San Francisco I'd been planning what I was going to ask him, but now I couldn't find the right words. "That's where I need your help. I know what I said about the Air Force... and I meant it. But before I start grad school, I still have to deal with the draft now that I'm out of college. My number is only 109, and I'm pretty sure I'll get drafted if I ignore it. And that probably means Vietnam. To tell you the truth, after talking with Mellow, I was actually thinking about Canada. But then when James died...."

I swallowed. *God, I miss my friend.*

"...I realized I need to get my life back on track. I was hoping you knew of some place like Elijah's mission where I could do my draft commitment. I think it's called alternative service. But I want to work with kids. While I'm there, maybe I could get my counseling degree somewhere nearby. Crazy idea, huh?"

Doc stroked his chin. "Not that crazy actually. Just a lot of variables to contend with." He pulled out his address book from his desk drawer and quickly thumbed through it. "Here it is. I might know a place that could fit what you're thinking. It's called St. Augustine's Children's Village, near Cleveland. Sister Rose is the person we need to talk to. And if it works out with her, Case Western University is nearby. Let me give her a call and see what she says."

———

I never actually met a nun before. There were plenty of Catholics in Clairton, but I was never in one of their churches. I had no idea what to say to Sister Rose now. Her dark blue uniform, and her hat, or whatever it was called, made her seem unapproachable, even threatening, especially with those large wire-rimmed glasses magnifying her dark, intense eyes.

"Mr. Robinson?" she asked when I stepped into her office. I hesitated, then stumbled on the rug, grabbing the back of the chair to steady myself. Not a great start.

"Mr. Robinson?" she asked again. I just stared at her.

"Mr. Robinson, I take it you're either a deaf mute or you're not Catholic. Either way, I can assure you that you'll be fine here at St. Augustine's. We desperately need a man for our boys' cottage, so let me show you where you'll be living." She looked me up and down for several long seconds, as if she could see right through me with those glasses of hers. "And you'll need to get yourself a real coat. This is Cleveland. Not Kentucky."

Not someone to waste words on polite conversation.... But all I said was, "Looking forward to meeting the boys."

She arched an eyebrow. "I see you're not a deaf mute after all, Mr. Robinson."

I smiled, just a little. *I might actually get along with her... in spite of her being a nun.* "Your cottage is this way." She stood, walking briskly toward the door. "Follow me."

I didn't come to St. Augustine's totally unprepared. I did a little research, and apparently the Sisters of Charity were pretty radical. First, they moved from the city fifty years ago and built what they called a "children's village" on farmland far outside of the city. That upset most of the Cleveland Catholics, as well as all the Protestants in the village of Boston nearby. Second, they welcomed anyone, regardless of their faith, or lack of it, and that upset everyone. That is, until Cleveland disintegrated into an economic and social quagmire. Then everyone turned to St. Augustine's for help.

"That is Francis Cottage over there, Mr. Robinson." Sister Rose pointed toward a one-story, solid red brick building on the perimeter of a courtyard outside her office. There looked to be maybe a dozen more cottages, all identical, except for the names above each door. Benedict, Joseph, Anthony, Patrick and Thomas, surely the boys' cottages. On the other side of the courtyard must be the girls' buildings—Cecilia, Anne, Bernadette, Catherine, Elizabeth and Miriam. But it was the courtyard that caught my attention. It was more like a school playground, complete with swing sets and slides, and even a small basketball court. Although the temperature was in the thirties, much colder than San Francisco, the playground was crowded with kids of all ages, playing and laughing while several nuns looked on. The kids looked great, but the thought of working with all these nuns... *What have I gotten myself into?*

Sister Rose ignored my anxious look. "There are ten boys in Francis Cottage, Mr. Robinson," she said as we walked into my new home. There were two boys sitting at a table doing homework. Some others were watching television. Everyone sat up straight when they saw her.

"Hello, Sister," they all chimed in unison. But they ignored me.

She nodded at the boys, then looked back at me. "As you can see,

155

they're older. Some are nearly fourteen, but all of them are far behind where they should be in school. Considering the situations they came from, they've actually done remarkably well."

I wasn't sure why, especially with her being a nun, but for a second something in her eyes gave me the impression she looked on these boys a lot like Elijah did Watson. *At least she knew my name before she hired me.* I smiled at that thought.

She turned toward the door. "Let's go back outside, so we can talk more freely."

I followed quickly behind her.

"You've got a degree in psychology, don't you, Mr. Robinson?"

"Yes, Sister."

"This is probably our hardest cottage. Since July we've lost our last three house managers. That's why we desperately need a man here."

Her dark eyes focused on me. "I won't gloss over the situation, Mr. Robinson. These boys will push every button you've got. But they're only trying to see if you'll stay. Everyone in their lives has quit on them. That's why they're here. But we have to be different. Do you understand what I'm saying, Mr. Robinson?"

"You mean give them some breakfast and a safe place to pass out?"

Her eyes narrowed, and I immediately regretted saying it. "I'm sorry, Sister Rose. That was just something a friend of mine who ran a street mission once told me."

"Not exactly how I would phrase it, Mr. Robinson, but yes, we try to help them where they are, even when they may not seem to want our help. Sometimes that's all we can do.

"I think I understand, Sister."

"Good, because we here at St. Augustine's are the only real home some of these boys have ever known. Most of them have never had a man in their lives. At least, not a man who stayed. So to be quite blunt, that's why I hired you. You can't quit on them, at least not for the next two years, because of your commitment to the draft board."

Hearing all this, I wasn't sure I could live up to her expectations. "I think my degree will help me, Sister," I said, more for my benefit than hers.

"Actually, it's not your degree I'm interested in, Mr. Robinson. I did some checking when I saw your application. You didn't list any family. My guess is you might understand what these boys are feeling far better than you realize. So I pushed through your application. The boys won't be easy. Not at first, but I have a feeling you'll do very well here."

I hope she doesn't give me a broom now! I smiled thinking of Elijah again, but all I said this time was, "It's Daniel, Sister. Just call me Daniel, please."

"Daniel, it is then. Now why don't you go back into the cottage and introduce yourself to your boys."

"Wh—alone?"

"Of course."

I was hoping for something more. An introduction, maybe even some bit of advice. Something. Anything. But she just turned and strode back toward her office without another word. "Okay," I mumbled, watching her from the door of Francis Cottage—my new home.

———

I walked slowly into the living room. "Uh...I'm Daniel Robinson...the new house manager." One of the boys at the table glanced up. I nodded, and I thought he was going to say something, but he just turned back to his paper. No one else bothered to look at me. I stood there for a minute, wondering what to do now. But then Sister Rose's words came back. *These boys will push every button you've got.* "For what it's worth, guys. I'm glad to be here. And I'm looking forward to meeting all of you at dinner tonight." I waited, but no one said anything, so I just walked on into my bedroom.

Dinner, I soon learned, was brought to each cottage by the kitchen staff, but I was responsible for actually serving it to them. There were four small tables in the dining room, three on one side where the boys sat, leaving a single empty table on the other side of the room.

Everyone in their lives has quit on them. That's why they're here. But we have to be different.

"You know, I never did like eating alone," I said, looking around the room. "If you boys don't mind, I'd like to rearrange the tables. How about if we slide them all together? Family style."

157

Nobody moved. I noticed they all looked toward one boy. He was thin, but bigger than the others, possibly the oldest. And probably the leader in the cottage. He stared at me, as if trying to figure out what I was up to.

"Let's start with my table. Okay? And can you help me move it?" I looked toward him. "My name's Daniel. What's yours?"

He didn't speak or move at first, but I just stood there waiting. Finally, he got up and grabbed the other end of my table. "Daequan," he mumbled. I guessed him to be maybe thirteen or fourteen. He had a full afro haircut he obviously spent a lot of time combing. But what I noticed most were his eyes. They seemed distant, guarded—a lot like James when I met him in the park. *I wonder what brought him to St. Augustine's?*

I hoped for more conversation at dinner, but I wasn't really surprised by the silence, not after what Sister Rose told me. *We try to help them where they are, even when they may not seem to want our help.* My job description said nothing about this, but I had an idea. "Let me help you guys with the dishes." I started clearing the table. They all stared at me.

After a couple days of this, I thought the boys would open up to me, at least a bit. But Sister Rose was right. They pushed every one of my buttons—especially Daequan. And the other boys followed him.

"I need you to pick up your clothes." I didn't yell or threaten them or anything like that. Pick up your clothes and put them in your dresser. Just a simple request—but not for Daequan.

"We don't have to listen to you," he muttered, not moving. The other boys watched. I waited, looking right at him. *Be patient.* Finally, he got up, stuffed his clothes into his dresser, and slammed it shut.

The next time he did that, and then the third time, I was running out of patience. No matter what I asked him to do, I always got that same guarded look, and that same defiant attitude. What made it worse was the other boys did the same thing now.

"Anthony, you need to turn off the television and do your homework." His teacher told me she wanted him to practice his subtraction assignments every night. But he ignored me and kept staring at the television. "Anthony!" Still no response, so I turned it off. "No television for anyone until your homework is done!"

"No fair!" he screamed, quickly joined by the other boys in the room. "We don't have to listen to you!" I tried to remember what Sister Rose said about pushing my buttons, but it didn't help much. By the end of my first week I was constantly turning off the television and yelling at everyone to get their homework done, or clean their rooms, or whatever else I asked them to do—but it was never any use. I was exhausted. *What have I gotten myself into?*

I wanted to complain to Sister Rose, and a couple times I went to see her, but before I actually knocked on her door, I always remembered what she said about everyone quitting on them, and each time I walked back to my cottage willing to try again.

———

It was another dreary February Saturday. All the boys were watching television, like they did every weekend, when I got an idea.

"Anybody want to play baseball?" I asked.

No one answered. A couple boys eyed Daequan, who kept his eyes glued on the television.

"I found an indoor ballfield that's perfect for spring training." I held up a bat and ball. "Anyone up for some batting practice?"

Again, no one moved—except for the Antonelli brothers. Louis was twelve, and a year older than Michael, but I saw both of them going through a huge collection of baseball cards almost every night. "Indoor ballfield?" Louis asked. "No way." I remembered something I read in their file about their father getting killed in Vietnam three years ago, and their mother spending most of her time now at the state hospital.

"Absolutely, Louis. It's not heated, but it's warmer than the playground—and a lot better than watching *Roadrunner* cartoons all day. You game?"

Louis looked at Michael, then at Daequan, who didn't respond. No surprise there. He hesitated, then motioned for his brother to follow him.

St. Augustine's storage barn had a ceiling high enough to handle any pop flies the boys could hit, and more important, it had been empty since I arrived. I figured no one would mind if I laid out infield baselines. "What do you think, boys?" I said, sliding open the door. "We can't play a real game with just the three of us, but we can do some serious batting practice."

Louis swung and missed my first pitch, then missed again with the next two pitches. Finally, after missing it the fourth time, he slammed the bat on the ground. "I hate baseball!" he yelled.

Maybe if someone had played baseball with me when I was twelve... "You know, Louis, you've actually got a good swing. You just need to choke up on the bat."

He glared at me, but then his face softened. He bent over and grabbed the bat, this time gripping it two inches higher. It worked. He hit the next pitch off the rear wall of the barn, stood there motionless for just a second, then thrust his arms high in the air, like he saw the Cleveland Indians do each time they hit a home run too.

On Michael's turn to bat, he choked up without even being told.

Not a bad Saturday afternoon at the Cleveland Stadium for all three of us.

I thought things would go better now, at least with some of the boys, but another week in, nothing changed. If anything, it got worse. They still argued with me about everything. Even Michael and Louis didn't want to play baseball again, not after I saw Daequan talking to them that night.

The final straw was that damned radio that Daequan always blasted through the cottage. "Turn it down." I said for the hundredth time. I didn't yell. I wasn't rude. Okay, maybe I was a little irritated, but who wouldn't be if you had to listen to the Jackson Five blaring all night long?

"At least change the channel!" It was a reasonable compromise.

He glared up at me and grunted. "What do you want me to listen to? Your music?" It wasn't really a question. More of a line in the sand.

I yanked the cord out of the wall and stalked back to my room.

I was in Sister Rose's office the next morning. I hated going to her, but I didn't know what else to do. "Can't you do something with the boys? None of them will listen to me, especially Daequan. He's unteachable!"

She didn't reply, or even look up, but kept writing in her book, as if she didn't even know I was there.

"Sister?"

Finally, she looked over the top of her glasses, the way she did when she was too busy for conversation. "There are no bad students. Just bad teachers," was all she said, then started writing again.

What in the world does that mean? I stood there, waiting....

She glanced up again. "Is there anything else?" It was obvious our meeting was over, at least for Sister Rose.

"I guess not." I walked out of her office even more frustrated. Now I avoided her as best I could, but after another week of fights with the boys, when I saw her walking toward me in the hall, I was determined to get a straight answer. *No more of her fortune cookie advice this time!*

"Good morning, Daniel."

I've got a cottage filled with juvenile delinquents and that's all you've got to say? I wanted to scream, but held my tongue.

"Have a good day," she said without waiting for my response, walking on by without even a nod, like what I was going through didn't matter!

It just blurted out. "You're wrong, Sister," I called. "It's not going to be a good day. In fact, none of my days have been good... and I don't know what to do, especially with Daequan." I hoped she'd finally punish all of them. "None of the boys will listen to me because of him."

She stopped, turning toward me. "Maybe the problem isn't Daequan."

Oh God, not more of that no bad students crap again!

"What do you mean, Sister?" She was really irritating me now. "He's the one who never listens."

"That's my point, Daniel. I know he's not listening to you, but have you tried listening to him?"

"I'm not sure I understand." My jaw tensed. "All I'm asking him to do is normal family stuff, like make his bed and pick up his clothes."

"That's the problem, Daniel. None of these boys come from a

'normal family,' or at least how you define it. Especially Daequan. Have you read his file? Do you know what his family was like?"

"Sorry, Sister. I haven't had time. I've been so busy just keeping up with my schedule every day." I knew as soon as I said it, she'd never accept my excuse.

"That's why we insist our house managers live here. So you'll have time. I suggest you spend the afternoon reading Daequan's file and then come see me tomorrow and we'll discuss what you've learned."

"Yes, Sister," I said, but it was a waste of time.

Daequan Jefferson
Born: April 17, 1956
Mother: Charise Jefferson. Deceased
Father: Donald Riggs. Incarcerated since 1958.
Arrived at St. Augustine's: May 4, 1970.
Referring agency: Cuyahoga County Children's Services

Daequan is the oldest of four children. His mother Charise has been arrested five times for drug use and twice for prostitution. Daequan's father has been incarcerated since he was two years old. He is aware he is in prison, but has expressed no desire to contact him, nor has his father expressed any desire to contact Daequan.

All four children have been placed in foster care three times. All were returned to their mother when she completed drug treatment programs. Daequan has been involved with the juvenile court on four occasions, mostly for truancy. Eventually it was discovered he was leaving school to get the welfare check from the mail before his mother cashed it to buy drugs. Daequan was using it to buy food for his family. Once he was charged with unruly behavior when he ran away from home.

Daequan stated his mother's boyfriend Roland Peters was abusing him, but no charges were filed at that time. Mr. Peters was arrested in March of 1970 when school officials reported seeing numerous bruises on Daequan. Sexual abuse was also suspected. When confronted with this, Charise Jefferson initially denied anything happened. However, she eventually admitted "maybe he did it."

Two weeks later, on April 10, 1970, Daequan found his mother dead in her bedroom of an apparent drug overdose.

Recommendations:

Daequan needs a stable environment with authority figures who are strong enough to overcome his initial attitude and actions that will likely be disruptive.

It is strongly recommended he be referred to St. Augustine's Children's Village.

Janice T. Johnson,
Cuyahoga County Children's Services caseworker.

I was in Sister Rose's office first thing the next morning. "Tell me what I need to do."

She was already pointing at a chair in front of her desk before I even finished speaking. "It's actually quite simple. You complained he doesn't listen to you. Try listening to him. These children, especially ones like Daequan, they don't trust adults. So we have to earn their trust."

"I've tried to talk to them, Sister, but they don't listen."

"I'm sure you have, but have you actually listened to them? Believe me, it's the universal language. When you listen, *then* they'll know you care. Then, and only then, will they hear you."

Her gaze softened now as she waited for my response. A flood of memories rushed over me...

"Billy!" I yelled, just as Mum grabbed that lamp and smashed it on the old man's head. His face twisted with rage as he grabbed her hair, slapping her hard in the face again and again. She covered her head, but it didn't help. Nothing could help us now.

You go ahead and tell the church this little story you just made up. No one's going to believe you anyway...no one, not ever.

Show them we care. That's why the Mission's here. To show people a way out of the gutter.

"I'll do whatever it takes, Sister."

CHAPTER 13
LIGHT SHINES BEST IN DARKNESS

CLEVELAND, 1971. All the boys were required to attend Mass every Sunday. The sisters said it was part of the normal life they lacked in their own world. I had to attend too. But after too many Sundays doing my best to understand it, I was just as lost—and frustrated—as the first time I attended. This Sunday I happened to be sitting next to Daequan in the chapel, but he barely glanced at me. No threatening looks this time. Just the same cool disregard that seemed to be his default response lately.

I tried to focus on Father Ken's homily, but he droned on and on as always. "Dear God, please make this sermon end soon!" I muttered to no one in particular. But I guess it was loud enough for Daequan to hear, because he snickered. I thought of James and smiled. *I'll bet there would be a whole lot more saving going on if he was here. God, I miss my friend.*

After Mass I found Daequan in his room. "Is it just me, or are Father Ken's sermons really boring?"

"They're boring," he mumbled. It wasn't much, but it was the first civil thing I heard from him since I arrived.

"Need some help cleaning your room?"

"Maybe," was all he said, but to me it was volumes.

There wasn't much to clean, just some clothes on the floor and a blanket that needed folded. He had few possessions that I could see, but I did notice the picture on his dresser—a woman with four kids. No one was smiling. "Your family?" I asked.

He just nodded.

We had another brief, but more meaningful interaction about a week later. It was a cold and snowy March day, but this was my first night off in weeks. I planned to make the most of it by going to a movie. I never got around to buying that winter coat Sister Rose said I needed, and I was nearly frozen just walking to the parking lot. "Does spring ever come in this god-forsaken city?" I muttered, digging through my pockets. *Where are those damn keys?* Frantically, I searched a second time. Then I saw them—laying on the seat inside my locked car!

I yanked the door handle several times, hoping, praying I might have left it unlocked. I even tried the other door—just in case. It was locked too! "Damn! Damn! Damn!" I pounded on the roof of my car, then stood frozen to the bone for several minutes, not sure what to do now.

"I think I can help," someone behind me said. I turned around and saw Daequan with a metal coat hanger in his hand. I had no idea what he had in mind, but I was too cold and frustrated to say anything. I just watched, amazed, as he gingerly slipped the coat hanger above the driver's door window and down around the lock, yanked it up quickly —and just like that, the door was open!

"How'd you do that?" was all I could think to say.

He just shrugged.

I shook my head and smiled. "Forget I asked. Maybe it's better I don't know. But thanks. I mean it."

He nodded, then started walking slowly back to the cottage. I checked my watch. *Damn! I'm late for my movie.* Jumping in the car, I quickly started the engine, hesitated, then cranked down the window. "Hey, Daequan. When was the last time you went to a movie?"

———

I thought things would get better with the other boys now, especially since they all followed Daequan, but nothing really changed. *No bad students. Just bad teachers.* I reminded myself of Sister Rose's stupid saying a dozen times every day as I read through the boys' files. I had no idea what some of them had been through... until now.

Anthony Jackson apparently had a pretty normal family until his father got killed by some junkie who tried to rob him. When Anthony started missing too much school after that, the welfare people got involved.

Dennis Lorenzini was left in St. Michael's Church when he was six years old. His mother just disappeared. He was fostered out several times, but he always ran away. He's been at St. Augustine's for two years —the longest he has stayed anywhere.

Mikey and Jack Dugan were lookouts for some drug dealer in their neighborhood. The judge was going to send them both to juvie prison, but their public defender convinced him that St. Augustine's was their only chance.

And the stories went on and on. *No bad students. Just bad teachers.*

———

It was Friday night. Everyone was sitting in the living room, looking bored and complaining about nothing good on television, when I got an idea and went looking for Mr. Johanson. He was the maintenance man for St. Augustine's, and from what I could tell the one time I talked with him, the person to go to if I ever needed anything special for the boys. Twenty minutes later I cracked open the kitchen door of the cottage, carefully looked all around, quietly laid out two gallons of chocolate chip ice cream and a dozen huge chocolate cupcakes on the table. No one around.

"Is that chocolate?" Someone asked from behind me.

I turned and there was Anthony Jackson, his eyes as big as saucers. He stood there, staring. I knew he loved chocolate as much as me because I heard him talking with Dennis Lorenzini about how his father always took him to the ice cream store on the corner "before he got killed..."

"How...where...did you get that?" he finally asked.

"Let's just say I've got friends with keys to the storage room. So how about you help me scoop it out for everyone else? It'll be our surprise."

It was a good night for all of us—especially Anthony.

———

Unfortunately, my new connection with Daequan and some of the other boys didn't make Father Ken's sermons any more interesting. After another month of his dronings, I'd had enough. It wasn't fair I had to attend Mass when I wasn't even Catholic! "If I can only figure out a way to tell Sister Rose...." I muttered on my way back to the cottage.

As fate had it, she came out of her office just as I passed by her door. "Tell me what, Daniel?"

Somehow, all I could think of was Frankie Denardo on that 10-foot diving board. *Better ease into my cannonball with her.* "Sister, I just wanted you to know things are going better with the boys now, even Daequan."

"I've seen that" She looked at her watch, like she always did when a conversation didn't get right to the point.

"I have a question about today's Mass." My heart pounded. "You know none of the boys are Catholic."

She motioned me into her office. *Good sign.* I took a quick breath. "From what I can tell, most of the boys have never been in any church," I said, quickly walking after her.

"Do you have a question for me, Daniel?" Sister Rose was never one for small talk.

"I think it's safe to say they really don't understand the Mass."

"I'm sure they don't. But I'm still waiting for your question."

I stepped toward the edge of the diving board. "I think Father Ken is a great guy. But I'll be honest with you, the boys all think his sermons are really boring." *There I said it! Now what is she going to say?*

She pulled out her chair, then pointed toward the other one in front of her desk. "Is it just the boys, or should I assume your concern is more personal?" Her tone softened.

Maybe she isn't going to fire me after all! "I guess what I'm asking..." My heart wasn't beating so fast now. "...are all Catholic sermons as bad as Father Ken's?"

"Ah, the question at last," she said with feigned relief. "To be candid, most Catholic sermons are worse. Father Ken is considered by many in the church to be quite good. But I get the feeling there's more to your question than just Father Ken's homilies."

I took a quick breath to bolster my confidence. "Until I got here, I'd never been in a Catholic Church, and I had no idea what went on there. But I've got to tell you, Sister, I've been going to Mass with the boys for several months, and I still have absolutely no idea what it's all about. If I'm confused, I know the boys are too." Mentioning them might make my complaint less offensive.

"Again, Daniel, is there a question in all of this?"

Too late to back off this diving board now. I breathed a quick prayer and dove right into the pool headfirst. "Why is it so important for me to go to a Catholic service when I'm not Catholic?"

Sister Rose didn't say anything for a minute. She didn't even look mad. She just clasped her hands, as if gathering her thoughts. "Do you remember what I asked you to do with Daequan a month ago?" she finally asked.

"I'm not sure what you mean."

"Let me refresh your memory. I said you need to talk less and listen more if you really want to get through to him. Do you remember that?"

"Yes, I've been doing that, and it's helped. We're doing much better now." I didn't mention the car key incident.

"I know you are. But I want you to think of Mass like talking with Daequan. If you're not communicating, who's the one not listening?"

"I don't understand."

"It seems to me, a lot of churches do all the talking to God, but very little listening. If we really want to hear what God is telling us, don't you think we should be listening more?"

"Isn't that what the sermon's all about? I mean I'd listen a whole lot more if Father Ken was more interesting."

There was a long pause. She seemed to be weighing her next words. "Did you know I wasn't always Catholic, Daniel?"

"What? I'm sorry. What did you say, Sister?" I was caught completely off guard by the sudden and personal turn in the conversation.

"I said, did you know I wasn't always Catholic?"

"No," I answered cautiously.

"It's true," she said casually. "I converted when I married my husband."

Now I had absolutely no idea what to say. I felt like I was looking in her room and seeing her without her habit, like she was somehow... a normal person.

She ignored my frozen look. "I felt much the same way you do when I started attending Mass, I mean about the homilies. Believe me, they were worse then. But when my husband was killed in the war in Europe, the Church was the only thing keeping me from losing my sanity. All I remember was being too numb to talk, or even think. But do you know what happened?"

I was too numb myself to answer, mesmerized by what she was telling me. I could barely keep my mouth closed.

"I just listened to God. That was all I could do," she went on, ignoring my dumbstruck look. "That's when I saw, or more accurately, when I *felt* what Mass is really about. It's supposed to be a sacred place, a healing place where we bring all our hurts and pain and leave them for God to handle. That's what I did. And that, Daniel, is how I got here. By listening to God, not Father Ken."

My mind flashed back to that day in Doc's office when he told me about growing up in that horrid boarding school. *Maybe I can trust her too.* "I had no idea, Sister," I managed to say, but now I had a hundred questions. Mostly why was she telling me this?

She must have guessed my thoughts because her face was suddenly soft, almost welcoming. "Daniel, I believe you understand what these boys have been through better than a lot of our staff, and even some of the sisters." She leaned in, her eyes fixed on me. "There's nothing in your files, and forgive me if I'm wrong, but I get the impression you may have been in a similar situation growing up. You don't have to say anything. It's none of my business. But I believe if you can make it, which it certainly seems you have, then you can help these boys make it too."

I stared at her for several minutes. *If only James had come here when he ran away from home, then maybe...* Sister Rose sat there, waiting for my reply, without checking her watch even once.

"I'm planning to be a counselor," I finally admitted. "I was thinking about going to grad school when I got done here. But if you think it'll help me with the boys, and if it wouldn't interfere with my schedule..., maybe I could start taking a couple classes this summer."

She sat up straight with a slight smile. "It's interesting you should mention that. The board and I have been talking about starting a new counseling program here. Maybe we could work out something with you, Daniel."

Hearing that brought out the same feeling I had riding with Augie —that I was going down a road I'd never been before, seeing new places, and meeting new people...

Everything would get better now. My skin tingled! I felt...hope.

I couldn't help but smile. This was the best news I'd heard in a very long time—maybe ever. "One last thing, Sister." I stood to leave. "Could you talk with Father Ken? I still think his sermons are terrible."

"So do I, Daniel, but there are some things that neither I nor God can correct."

———

The summer started off quiet, so I used the time to plan some things I could do with the boys, things they never did before. Maybe hiking in the woods behind St. Augustine's, or biking to a pond I saw a couple miles away for some fishing. Andre Harris said something about fishing with his older brother once.

I might even have extra time for my new classes. But all that changed when Joey Martinelli arrived. Sister Rose said his parents had been killed in some sort of car accident. At first his grandparents took him in, but they were too old and too sick, and couldn't handle an eight-year-old boy, especially one who was struggling to understand why his mother and father both abandoned him. They sent him to St. Augustine's and promised to visit him every Sunday, but that only lasted two weeks.

Small for his age, Joey was the youngest boy in our cottage. He sat alone on the playground most days, and cried himself to sleep at night.

Some of the older boys, mostly Mikey and Jack Dugan, made fun of him for it. I told them about his parents getting killed, and that he really needed us to be his family now. But they just stared at me, like I was talking a different language or something. I couldn't watch over him every minute, but I didn't know what else to do... especially when I saw him sitting alone and crying. All I saw was Billy running after me as I rode my bike down the alley with Frankie.

"Not this time." I went to Sister Rose for help.

"Some of the older boys are calling him a crybaby, and that only makes him more of a target. I told them about Joey losing his parents. I thought that would make them want to help him." I felt my face warm. "But now they just ignore him—and I think that makes Joey feel even worse." *Wait for me, Daniel.* Billy called from my memories.

"But that's not what really worries me. The reason I'm here is because he's got this wall around him that I just can't get through. I don't know how to help him." I bit my lip and waited...

Sister Rose nodded solemnly. "The other sisters and I are well aware of Joey's struggles. And you're right. The problem is not really the other boys. It's Joey. He's gone through a terrible shock losing both his parents and he's still grieving."

"What else do you think I can do, Sister. I mean, we can't just let him sit alone and cry, can we?"

She removed her glasses, wiped them slowly, put them back on and met my eyes. "None of us know what to do, Daniel. We need to pray to St. Francis for a miracle."

I hadn't prayed, at least not a real prayer, in a long time, but I prayed hard every night for Joey.

A week later, I got my answer. At first, I didn't pay much attention to Daequan sitting on the playground bench with Joey. I thought they were just sitting together. Another day I saw them on the swings. Again, just sitting, not saying anything. But the next time I saw them, Daequan was pushing Joey's swing, and I heard him laugh. He didn't cry as much that week.

A couple nights later, I heard Joey calling for his mother again. I got out of bed and went to his room, same as usual, even though it wouldn't help much. *Another sleepless night!*

I was about to go in when I noticed the crying stopped. Instead, I heard someone singing. *Maybe Joey turned on his radio...*

"I see trees of green, red roses too,

I see them bloom for me and you,

And I think to myself what a wonderful world...."

I cracked open the door and slowly stuck my head in the room. There was Daequan, sitting on Joey's bed, rocking him gently. But there was no radio playing. It was Daequan singing to Joey!

"...The colors of the rainbow so pretty in the sky,

Are also on the faces of people going by,

I see friends shaking hands saying how do you do,

They're really saying I love you..."

I gently shut the door and walked quietly back to my room. *You were right, Sister. There are no bad students.* Laying in my bed, I thanked St. Francis for my miracle.

———

The rest of the summer was quiet. The Antonelli brothers wanted to play baseball every day because they were better than anyone else in the cottage. Instead, we spent a lot of time at that pond, where Andre caught the biggest fish every time. "My Mama taught me how to cook it perfect," he bragged. I was never a big fan of fish, but I thought it had more to do with his mother than it did dinner, so I let him try it. And truth was, he's not a bad cook after all. Daequan seemed to have the most fun of everyone, especially when he caught his first fish. I never saw anyone more excited over a stupid catfish too small to eat. But to Daequan, it was like catching Moby Dick!

Saturday nights were our special times. I convinced Sister Rose to let me take all the boys out for what I called "some quiet time to prepare for Sunday Mass." I didn't tell her we did most of our preparing at Pinkie's Pizza Parlor in town. Ten boys, fourteen pizzas, twenty-four bottles of Coca-Cola, and lots of loud music on the juke box. I had no idea a kid as small as Michael Antonelli—he couldn't be more than four-foot tall and seventy pounds soaking wet—could chug an entire bottle of coke in one gulp. But Louis dared him, and Daequan chimed in with a double-dog dare, so he had no choice. His stomach nearly popped three buttons on his shirt when he finally emptied that bottle. Even Daequan was impressed with what everyone called "the longest belch they ever heard."

We didn't sneak back into the cottage until well past midnight, but no one complained about Father Ken's homilies anymore. Everyone—including me—was so exhausted we kept nodding off during the Mass. Twice Sister Rose raised an eyebrow at me, but she never asked about our Saturday night 'prayer vigils'—and I never told her anything different.

It was a great summer with the boys. James would have loved it too.

September arrived too soon, and school was set to start again. I wasn't expecting any problems since all of them went to St. Augustine's parochial school. Except for Daequan. He was now fifteen and ready for high school. That meant he had to go to the public school in the village of Boston nearby. Sister Rose knew he was smart enough for the work, and I figured he was less hostile now. But neither of us was sure how well a white country school could handle their first black student from Cleveland.

It didn't take long to get the answer.

"Daniel, can you go to the high school?" Sister Rose asked the first day. "Apparently Daequan is in the principal's office and they're talking about expelling him."

"You're kidding me? I expected there might be some issues, but not the first day. What happened?"

"They said he was fighting. Apparently he punched another student."

"Who started it?"

"The principal said it was Daequan. Unprovoked, too. But I have my doubts. I've been hearing from some of the parents in the parish that the school wasn't too happy about taking one of our boys."

"Did they mean one of our *black* boys?"

Sister Rose snorted. It was apparent she already knew the answer. "My guess is there's a great deal of racial tension involved on both sides. I want to keep a low profile handling it. That's why I called you. They're sending him home, at least for the rest of the day. I want you to go to the school and tell the principal we'll take care of Daequan. And it might help to apologize for his behavior."

"What if it's not his fault?"

"Let me make it very simple for you. Daequan is black. He's from the city, and he's in St. Augustine's. It doesn't matter who started it. It's Daequan's fault for just being there today, at least in the eyes of the principal. So just tell him whatever you have to, so they don't expel him. Daequan has his first real chance with us, and I don't want him to lose it. Do you understand, Daniel?"

"Perfectly, Sister. I don't like it, but I understand." Sister Rose and I had developed a mutual understanding of sorts, like the relationship I had with Doc. I could speak honestly, no subjects off limits, but she would answer me honestly too.

When I parked the car in front of the school, I sensed the tension even before I shut off the engine. Not that I actually saw people staring at me from inside the building, but I could feel it—and I was a white guy. *If this is what Daequan felt, I don't blame him for popping somebody.*

"Daniel Robinson to see Principal Jackson," I said to the secretary in the school office.

"He's expecting you," she answered barely concealing her irritation with me. Or probably with St. Augustine's for sending a student who obviously didn't belong here.

————

Principal Jackson didn't stand when I entered his office, but just nodded toward a chair opposite his desk. He reminded me of Mr. Danko, my tenth-grade math teacher who always looked like he would rather be shouting plays to the football team he coached after school, instead of wasting time in a classroom wearing a choking necktie and a dress shirt two sizes too small. He took particular pleasure in humiliating those of us not on his team, as if we were not worthy of his time.

Principal Jackson glowered at me. "What was your name again?" he barked.

"Daniel Robinson...sir." I didn't mean to say "sir." It just slipped out, like I was back in Mr. Danko's class again. I swallowed.

"I want you to know, Robinson, that we don't think *Deekwon*..." He said it slowly, as if struggling with a foreign word. "...based on his actions, we just don't think he fits in here."

I wasn't sure what he expected me to say. *No problem. We'll just send him back to Cleveland, if that will make you feel better.* But I remembered Sister Rose's instructions and swallowed hard. "I'm very sorry he caused a problem at the school today... and I can assure you it won't happen again." I felt a knot in my stomach.

"I should expel him for what he did... for the good of the school. We can't have disruptive students coming in from outside the community." His face relaxed. "You people at St. Augustine's need to understand that *Deekwon* is better suited in a city school with his own kind."

What do you mean with his own kind? City kids...or black kids? I wanted to scream at this jerk. The knot in my stomach tightened. "I will..." *punch you in the face* "...certainly talk with Sister Rose about your concerns, sir." I bit my lip, swallowing hard again. "I know he doesn't... deserve it, but we would really appreciate it if you would give him another chance."

He sat there and stared at me in satisfaction, like Mr. Danko when he humiliated me with a question he knew I couldn't answer. "I believe in giving people a second chance," he finally said. "But I just won't tolerate any more violence from *Deekwon*. The next time he does something like this, there won't be any more second chances. You understand me, Robinson?"

"Yes, sir. And thank you."

He motioned toward the door.

What an asshole!

Daequan was waiting for me in the outer office. Neither of us said anything as we walked to the car and pulled out of the parking lot. After driving some miles in silence, I clicked on the car radio and scanned the dial until I found the Jackson Five playing, then turned up the volume so both of us could enjoy it together.

"You know, I really appreciate what you have been doing with Joey,"

I said as we neared St. Augustine's. "The other boys have started hanging out with him because of you."

Nothing. He kept staring straight ahead.

"I don't know what happened at the school today, and I don't need to know... unless you want to talk about it. Both of us know it was a racial thing. But what really matters is Andre and Terry will be going to this same high school next year, and they're going to face the same shit you did today. Do you understand what I'm saying?"

He nodded slowly.

"Daequan, both of these boys came from the same neighborhood as you. And you know Terry's story. It's no different than yours. Except you're a lot stronger than him. Without your help those crackers in that school will eat them both alive. I know you can do it. I saw what you did with Joey. You've got what it takes to make a difference with Terry and Andre, and the other boys too. They all look up to you." I paused, letting that sink in. "I also know it won't be easy. But for their sake..., are you willing to try?"

He just stared out the window for at least a mile. Finally, he turned toward me and said, "Okay, if it'll help Andre and Terry."

Both of us were silent the rest of the drive home.

———

Daequan's first semester at Boston High School progressed in fits and starts, but mostly fits. Some reports initially came in about his attitude, whatever that meant, but there was no more violence. I asked him a couple times how he was doing, and he would just grunt "okay," like he didn't want to talk about it.

But one night, sometime right after Halloween, he seemed quieter than usual. The other kids were all asleep when I found him in his room, staring at the ceiling. Even in the dim light from the hall, I could see he had been crying. I sat down on the side of his bed.

"How're you doing at school... and no bull shit this time. I don't deserve that. So what's really going on?"

For a second, I thought he was going to tell me the same thing, but he didn't. Instead he looked up at me, his eyes wet. "I found this in my locker today." He reached under his bed, grabbing a piece of rope that had been fashioned into a crude noose. "I didn't know what to do, so I just stuffed it in my coat so no one would see it."

What the—a noose? Everything in me wanted to protect him, hold him now, tell him he would be okay. "I'm sorry, Daequan. I really am." I didn't know what else to say. I took the noose outside, threw it in the garbage can and walked back to Daequan's room. I stayed quietly with him, until he fell asleep. *This kid doesn't have a chance.*

Sister Rose and I both knew it was only a matter of time before something happened. There were too many bigoted, frightened people in the community who felt just having Daequan in their school was a threat. We also knew he wasn't strong enough to take all the pressure on him. Eventually he would react, and then Principal Jackson would have the reason he needed to expel him, which was what he wanted to do since that first day. In December he got his chance.

This time Sister Rose and I both went to the school. She said nothing the whole drive from St. Augustine's, but I could tell she was really mad by the way she marched into the building, then glared at two teachers in the hall who were staring at us. We found Daequan waiting for us, standing at the office door.

"They said I didn't belong in their school," he fumed. "They said no niggers are allowed in Boston."

"Who said that, Daequan?" Sister Rose's voice was controlled. Too controlled.

"Donald Vinson and his friends. They cornered me in the boys' room."

"Did they actually say that, Daequan? It's important you tell me their exact words. Do you understand?"

"Yes, ma'am. That's exactly what they said."

"And what did you do?"

"I tried to remember what you and Daniel said about being an example. But when that white kid said my mother was nothing but a whore, I snapped." He punched his fist into his palm.

"What happened then?" she asked.

"When they saw blood coming from his face, the boys ran to the cafeteria and told everyone I started it."

"Is there anything else you want to tell me?"

His eyes filled with tears. "Just that I'm sorry, Sister. I didn't mean to hit him. But he didn't have no right saying that about my mother."

She nodded slowly, her eyes fixed on him. But they seemed... soft, like she saw him as one of her own family, yet hard, determined to protect him.

"You're right, Daequan." was all she said. She turned abruptly, motioning for me to follow her into Principal Jackson's office. I squeezed Daequan's shoulder lightly. "We'll talk more back at the cottage." I whispered as I walked past him.

"I warned you when you first enrolled that boy there'd be trouble," he said before we were barely in the room. "And I warned Robinson after that incident the first day, we can't allow our children to be put at risk from these people."

Sister Rose grabbed a chair and positioned herself directly in front of him. Her face was hard and cold now. "And who do you mean by 'these people,' Mr. Jackson? Surely you don't mean black people, I hope." Sister Rose had a way of using words as weapons, to chip away at someone, one question at a time, until they admitted what she already knew was the real story.

It was apparent this meeting was not going to be nearly as polite or apologetic as the last one. I only heard her use that tone once when she fired a staff member for calling one of the kids a *nigger*. She had no patience for ignorance, and even less when it came from people who should know better. Principal Jackson was certainly guilty on both counts. *There's blood in the water now!* I bit my lip to hide a smile.

"I simply meant disruptive people." he answered too quickly. His voice quivered.

"I know exactly what you meant, Mr. Jackson, so let's not mince words. I know you don't want Daequan here because he's black. Your staff knows you don't want him here, and your students know it as well. Most important, Daequan knows it. The fact that he's done as well as he has this semester is clear evidence he's not one of 'those disruptive people,' as you suggest. It's very clear this is a racial issue, starting with you and going on down to every level of your school."

"Sister Rose, I take offense at the very suggestion..."

"I'm sure you do, Principal Jackson." she interrupted. Her temples pulsed. It was obvious she wasn't giving him a chance to justify a blatant dereliction of his duty as an educator. She moved in for the kill.

"Principal Jackson, did you know I'm a member of the NAACP?"

Sweat beaded on his forehead.

"I know it may come as a surprise. I mean, a white Catholic nun in rural Ohio. But I joined a decade ago, during the civil rights protests. And I'm still quite active. Did you know that?"

He still didn't answer, but he shifted awkwardly in his chair and tugged at his tie.

"Let me put it this way. You and I both know Daequan was provoked today. I don't know all the details. But I can assure you my fine friends on the legal staff of the Cleveland branch of the NAACP will find all those details. And they'll even find out about all those racist comments you made in the lunch room, or on the golf course with your friends, or even at your church. They're very good at this sort of investigation, you know. And when they do find all you've been doing to break Daequan's spirit these past three months, I feel very confident you'll have trouble finding a job as custodian in any Ohio school. Do you understand what I'm saying, Principal Jackson?"

You really nailed the prick! I screamed to myself. But I kept my face carefully calm.

The color drained from him, and he only offerred a slight frightened nod when the full impact of what Sister Rose said finally sunk in.

"Just so there's no misunderstanding, I'm holding you personally responsible for Daequan's success this year. Do I make myself clear, Principal Jackson? If there's even the least hint of another racial incident such as this, I will have my friends with the NAACP, along with their friends on the Plain Dealer staff, all camped out in your office."

Sister Rose never raised her voice once, but I might have just witnessed a bloodier beating than what happened to me in San Francisco.

"I think we're done here today, Mr. Robinson." she said, then turned toward the principal again. "Unless you have something you wish to add?"

It seemed to take every ounce of strength he had left to breathe. He shook his sweaty head.

As soon as we got in the car, I blurted out the question I'd been dying to ask since I saw Principal Jackson nearly wet himself. "Sister, are you really a member of the NAACP?"

Without even hesitating, she said, "No, of course not."

"But were you part of the civil rights protests?"

Again, she said no in that same flat manner.

"Do you even know any NAACP attorneys?"

"Of course not, Daniel. I've spent my life running a children's home. Why would I have occasion to need an attorney?"

"But you said, I mean, you told Principal Jackson you'd bring all those people into his school if Daequan was bothered again, like you were best friends with all of them. Wasn't that a lie, Sister?"

She turned toward me, lowering her head just a little, looking over the top of her glasses now. "Lie is such a nasty word, Daniel. Let's just say I was focused on the greater good, shall we?"

"Not bad for a nun," I wrote Elijah that night. "I could've used her in that alley in San Francisco."

————

Daequan's school situation calmed considerably, and I was able to settle into my own routine. I liked my classes at Case Western. When I started the program, I thought I wanted to focus on addictions, like I told Doc. But after working with the boys this past year, and especially with that new program Sister Rose was talking about, I took a class in clinical mental health counseling this semester. My professor called it "pre-addictions counseling". I even told Sister Rose about it. "I should be nearly finished with my master's degree by the time I get done with my draft commitment... and you know, if you think I could help with your new program..."

"That is a discussion I'm sure we can have, Daniel." She seemed glad to hear that.

What I couldn't tell her..., the one thing I missed most... was someone to share all this with. I hadn't dated much after Elizabeth.

With the time I spent with the boys, and especially with my grad classes, I was too busy to even think about dating anyone. But there were times, usually when I was alone, and especially around the holidays, when I wished I was dating someone.

It was June. School was out for the boys and I was between semesters with my classes. I had time to myself now, time to think. That's when I realized tomorrow was my twenty-fourth birthday. I doubted anyone would know, or even care. I was feeling more alone than I had in a long time. *I need to get away from here for a while. Maybe go camping or something.*

Sister Rose had something else in mind. "I need you to work tomorrow with the boys."

"But Sister, I've got plans."

"I'm sorry, Daniel. I need you here." And with that she left the room, making me feel even more alone and depressed.

Late that night, long after the boys were in bed, I stood in the parking lot, leaning against my car, sipping a coke, and just staring up at the sky. I shook my head. I had been looking forward so much to getting out of here... for a break. Maybe meet some new friends. It had been so long since I talked with someone my own age.

There she was again. Those dark eyes that pulled me in so many times. That caramel smile. How many times did I share this sky with her all those nights on the golf course?

But you're married and I'm still all alone, Elizabeth....

———

The next afternoon the cottage was dark when I walked into the living room. I thought it strange because the boys should have been there. Suddenly the lights came on and everyone jumped out from hiding and shouted at the top of their lungs, "Happy Birthday!" I hardly recognized the room. It was covered with dozens of handmade pictures, signs and decorations, and the biggest, brightest one hung across the entire ceiling in huge red letters, *HAPPY 24TH BIRTHDAY, DANIEL*! Best of all, in the middle of the table was the most beautiful chocolate cake I'd ever seen in my life—and it was covered in candles! Joey Martinelli giggled as he lit every one of them. I was completely surprised—by everything, especially when I saw Sister Rose come into the room.

"You knew about this, didn't you?"

"I can't take any credit. It was all Daequan's idea."

"You're kidding me? How did he do it? I mean all the decorations, and especially the cake. How did he know chocolate's my favorite?"

"Anthony! Drop that fork!" I yelled as he made a quick stab at the cake. "And don't you be eyeballing it until I get a piece. You hear me?" He dropped the fork, reluctantly, but still kept staring at it, his mouth watering.

Sister Rose smiled, then looked back to me. "I think he had some help with those particular areas," she said. "I believe Ruth Ann Drabowski from Miriam Cottage may have given him some assistance. You know Ruth Ann, don't you, Daniel? Nice Catholic girl, about your age, and pretty too. It's a wonder someone hasn't married her yet."

"I know her, Sister, or at least I've seen her on the playground with her kids. Our boys played soccer with her girls a couple times. She seems nice enough, but I've never talked much with her."

But Sister Rose had my attention now. "You say she helped Daequan with the party?"

"Yes, she did. But you might want to thank her yourself. I think she would appreciate that."

"I just might do that, Sister. And thanks, for the advice, I mean."

CHAPTER 14

LIKE A BOAT WITH A TWISTED RUDDER, I KEEP COMING BACK TO THE SAME PLACE

CLEVELAND, 1972. I was looking forward to Christmas dinner at Ruthie's house.

"Daniel's got a girlfriend. Daniel's got a girlfriend," Joey giggled when he saw me coming out of my room wearing a new sport coat and red Christmas tie. He'd been saying that ever since he saw Ruthie and me two weeks ago holding hands in the parking lot.

"We're just friends," I said for the hundredth time, but it never stopped him, and the truth was, I didn't really mind hearing it. Ruthie and the whole Drabowski family accepted me as one of their own since we started dating six months ago. Maybe dating wasn't the right word. When I asked her out the first time, I suggested dinner and a movie. "Sounds boring just sitting there all night not saying anything to one another," she said. "But I know a better place to go. You'll love it. Trust me."

The Drabowski family—all eight of them—were sitting on the porch when I drove down the long dirt lane to their house on Saturday afternoon. As soon as I stepped out of the car, I caught a whiff of fresh hay mixed with a pungent measure of cow manure from the barn at the end of the lane. Ruthie and both her parents walked quickly out to the yard to greet me. "I'm glad to meet you, son." Mr. Drabowski wrapped his huge calloused hand around mine and shook it hard. "Do you know anything about farm equipment?"

"A little, sir," I winced a bit with his grip. "I used a John Deere mower every summer when I worked on the grounds crew in college."

He chuckled. "Good. 'Cause I could use your help on the farm."

"Daddy!" Ruthie protested. "Let him at least say hello to mother before you drag him off to the barn!"

"Sorry, Ruth Ann, but I thought Daniel would feel more comfortable there with me, instead of answering a hundred questions from your mother." He nodded to the woman standing beside him.

Mrs. Drabowski wiped her hands on her apron, reached for mine, and pressed it gently. "Just ignore him," she smiled warmly at me, pushing back a lock of brown hair that had fallen across her face. "Ruth Ann told us all about you, Daniel. And her brothers and sisters can't wait to meet you." She looked back toward the porch at the rest of the Drabowski family, who were leaning against the railing and giggling at me.

"Have it your way, Nancy." Mr. Drabowski gave me an obvious wink. "When you need a break, I'll meet you in the barn."

I had to glance down to force back a laugh. Thankfully Ruthie was too busy giving her father a mock scowl and didn't notice. I bit my lip, looking at Mr. Drabowski. "Glad to help you, sir, but give me a few minutes with the kids first." A low moo from the barn filled the air.

"Good. And it's Joe, son. Just call me Joe." He winked again and walked toward the barn, then opened a gate to a pen off to the side where twenty or more cows stood. It was probably milking time.

The Drabowski farm was everything I always pictured it to be—a large, two-story white frame house set amongst a stand of massive oak trees at the end of a long dirt lane that ran through a hundred acres of corn, already bright green and chest high. Behind the house towered two tall grain silos, and a huge dark red barn that looked recently painted. Several trucks and a tractor were parked in front of the barn. And from the pungent odor now drifting my way, there were hogs somewhere around too.

"Would you like to meet the rest of my family now, Daniel?" Ruthie reached for my hand.

"I'd love to," I smiled as we walked up the steps to her porch. But just for a second, I remembered walking onto Elizabeth's porch that last time. *She's married and gone!* I closed my eyes, shaking my head to force my thoughts back to Ruthie.

———

After that first date in July, I spent a couple hours every Saturday on the farm with the Drabowski family. In the beginning it was just in the afternoons, but without me even asking, Sister Rose arranged for one of the St. Augustine volunteers to help with the boys, so I could spend the entire day with my new family. If I wasn't working with Joe, I helped Ruthie take care of her five brothers and sisters.

"Andrew, Ruthie wants you and your brother to get your chores done before lunch."

"Okay" they both called as the screen door slammed.

"And tell your sisters they need to help get lunch ready."

"Okay, Daniel," they called again. I stood there for a few seconds watching them run toward the barn. *What are they, fourteen or fifteen years old? But they work as hard as any man. I wonder if I could bring some of my boys here some day?*

"I really appreciate your help," Ruthie said when I found her in the kitchen, stirring something on the stove. Mrs. Drabowski had gone to town with Joe and left us in charge of the house. She wiped her hands on her apron, and shifted a loose, dark brown strand of hair behind her ear, before she caught me staring at her. "What are you looking at, Daniel?"

"I was just thinking how much you look like your mother. That's all."

"So you're saying I look forty-two years old!" Her lower lip protruded, giving me a wounded puppy look. "You really know how to make a girl feel good, Daniel Robinson!"

I slid my arms around her waist and pulled her to me. "I meant it as a compliment." Ruthie's mother was what I pictured a farmer's wife to be—solid, but not heavy, yet strong enough to raise six kids and drive a tractor, all at the same time. She was a pretty woman, without making much fuss about her appearance. Whether it was her stained apron she constantly wore in the kitchen, or wading through barn muck to help Joe with the cows, her only focus was her family. It didn't matter if it was that penknife Andy couldn't find, or a sewing needle Mary wanted to fix her doll's torn dress, or even enough change for all the kids to get a candy bar at Woolworth's in town, she always had whatever they needed. Maybe that's why she was always humming to herself as she worked. She obviously loved what she was doing.

"Your mother's the prettiest mother I know, and I'm sure you'll look just like her when you're forty-two," I said.

Ruthie pressed her cheek against mine, her brown hair tickling my neck, and whispered in my ear. "How will you ever know unless you're with me, Daniel?" Her voice was almost a purr, husky and teasing, but then she quickly pushed me back. "Get out of my kitchen or I'll never have lunch ready on time."

"Now you really sound like your mother!" I hurried out of the room before she could react.

I thought a lot about Ruthie's family since we started dating. It was not so much that they didn't scream and fight like everyone I knew in Clairton. All of them seemed so content, even happy, like they were doing exactly what they wanted to do in life. It was obvious Joe loved his farm. More important, he loved his family, and they all loved one another. I never expected people to be this kind to me, and I felt good just being with them. "Like the family I never had." That's how I described them to Sister Rose.

But there was something that bothered me, too. They were not what I call 'curious people.' There were no books in the house, and the only magazine anyone read was the Ohio Farm Journal or the Catholic Telegraph. They had a television, but no one ever watched a news program. They didn't seem to care about the world or ideas outside their farm, their family or their church. Even though Ruthie was really good at her job, she wasn't interested in going to college. Simple people. That's what I thought...and I wasn't sure it was a compliment.

That was made very clear the one time I asked Ruthie about politics. The boys had been driving me nuts all day, complaining about every-thing, and I was desperate for some adult conversation with her. We were sitting together on the porch swing, holding hands and relaxing for the first time in days. "Do you think Nixon will get reelected?" I asked. "I mean, with all that stuff about Watergate?" That was all my classes had been discussing the whole week.

She offered a benign smile, like she always did when I mentioned anything other than St. Augustine's or the farm.

But I really wanted to know what she thought. "What about Nixon? Do you think he was involved like everyone says?"

She shrugged, sliding next to me and squeezing my arm. "I'm just glad to be with you, Daniel."

Sighing, I looked up at the dark sky and noticed the Big Dipper. *Can you see Leo?* Elizabeth's voice echoed in my memory. *That's the constellation right below the Big Dipper. Can you see it?* I forgot how much I missed those conversations.

I pushed that thought away. I really cared for Ruthie. She was the nicest person I ever met. She loved her kids in Miriam Cottage, and everyone at St. Augustine's said she's the best house manager there. And the way her brothers and sisters acted with her, it's obvious they all love each other. But...

———

"Are you sure you can make it in time for dinner?" Ruthie asked. "It's always been our tradition to go to Christmas Eve Mass. I was really hoping you could be with us."

"I'm planning on it. Sister Rose said all the boys will be with family or volunteers for the holiday, so the cottage will be empty. Besides, we're going to celebrate Christmas with them before they leave, so she told me not to worry about anything, and just have fun with your family." I always had the impression Sister Rose was pushing this romance to grow into something more serious. She never said a word, and I never asked, but I wasn't opposed to it either.

"Okay, remember, dinner's at six o'clock. But it's better if you come early. My brothers and sisters are a handful this time of year and I really need your help getting them ready."

This was my first Christmas with a real family, and I left St. Augustine's two hours early with my arms filled with presents. I clicked on the car radio, opened the window and turned up the volume. "Dashing through the snow in a one horse open sleigh..." I sang along as loud as I could the whole drive to the farm. *This is my best Christmas EVER!*

"Daniel's here, Ruth Ann!" the kids shouted nearly with one voice when they saw me coming up the porch steps. The front door slammed open, and all of them came running out to greet me—and inspect the presents I carried.

"What do you have for me?"

"Is that big one mine?"

"I'll help you carry some of them, Daniel."

They swarmed around me so fast I nearly dropped my presents all over the porch. "Ruthie! I'm gonna need your help out here. The kids are driving me crazy!"

She stuck her head out the door and smiled. "I warned you," was all she said, and turned back into the house.

The rest of the evening was a whirlwind of excitement, between decorating the tree, eating a huge Christmas Eve dinner, the kids running all through the house, and finally drinking eggnog with everyone in front of the fireplace, where all the stockings were hung across the mantle. There was even one with my name on it right next to Ruthie's. I was feeling so good I didn't even mind attending midnight Mass. Of course, sitting with her entire family, all while holding Ruthie's hand the whole time, made even Father Ken's homily enjoyable. A couple times she saw me looking up and down the pew at everyone and smiling. I couldn't help myself. I felt like I really was part of their family, especially when Mrs. Drabowski, or Nancy as she insisted I call her now, asked me to spend the night, so I could see the kids open their presents in the morning.

All of us gathered around the tree far too early for me, but the kids were up and begging to open all their presents. I wasn't worried about what I got for Andy and Paul. They'd been talking about that remote-controlled airplane for months. It was a lot better than the one I built as a kid, and maybe I was as excited as them when they opened it. Finding the right gifts for the girls was a lot harder because I never had any sisters. Ruthie said Mary would love an Easy Bake oven, because she was ten and liked to help her mother in the kitchen. And Janice needed another Barbie doll for "her family". Both girls said it was exactly what they wanted.

Little Michael was only two, so I had absolutely no idea what to get him. But Ruthie and I went shopping together at Kresge's and found a special toy that had all sorts of flashing lights and made a lot of noise. "He'll love this," she promised. He squealed with excitement when he turned it on!

Now it was my turn to open Ruthie's present. "All nine Beethoven symphonies! How'd you know... I mean, I've always wanted this! They must have cost a fortune. You shouldn't have done it, Ruthie." For the first time in our six months together, I was completely surprised by her.

"Do you remember our first date?" She laughed, clapping, really pleased with herself. "You told me about that teacher you had in college who introduced you to good music. What was his name, Doc something? You said you always wanted to build a collection of your own someday. Well, Daniel, I've been saving since then."

"So you're saying you knew on our first date we'd be spending Christmas together?"

"Of course. Women just know these things, don't we, Mother?"

I looked at Ruthie, then at Mrs. Drabowski, and finally to Mr. Drabowski, who just shrugged.

"I feel bad now. I had no idea on our first date I'd be sitting here today, so I didn't have six months to save for your present. It's not much, but I hope you like it." I handed her a large box wrapped with a gold ribbon.

Everyone stared anxiously as Ruthie carefully untied the ribbon and opened the box slowly. Inside she found another wrapped box. Mary and Janice both squealed and clapped their hands when they saw it. Inside that one was another, even smaller box. Now it was Ruthie who squealed. Carefully, she untied this ribbon, then handed it to her mother, who looked just as excited. That's when she found it! A necklace with our initials engraved on the back of a heart-shaped locket. There was a note attached to it. *Being with you these past six months has been the best time of my life. Daniel.*

A single tear ran down her cheek, then dropped onto the note.

"I wanted you to know how I feel. I was really nervous about it, but Sister Rose thought it was a good idea. Was it, Ruthie? I mean, is it okay?"

She cried, then hugged me, and cried some more. Now Mrs. Drabowski cried, and that set the tone for the rest of the day. That night, long after everyone else had gone to bed, we stood together on the porch. A cold wind blew in from the west as we held each other tight and stared at the stars, just listening to the night sounds in the afterglow of a perfect day. She nestled her cheek tenderly against mine and whispered ever so softly. "I love you, Daniel." She pressed her soft warm lips against mine.

I really cared for her... without any doubt! But did I love her? Holding her now in my arms at the end of a perfect day with her family, who was everything I never had. All my life I wanted a place to belong, someone to love me, someone to love back, to grow old together, surrounded by our children who love and need me. *I'll have all that now with Ruthie!* My arms slid around her waist. Hers draped around my neck. We held each other as her wet eyes glistened in the moonlight. *Tears of love for me.*

I brushed aside that long strand of hair that always fell across her face and the words just came out. "I love you too, Ruthie."

She melted in my arms and cried softly. "Thank you... for today," she cooed, then sighed, kissing me, lightly, then passionately. "Drive safe, Daniel...and I'll see you tomorrow..."

Her kiss was all I thought about driving back to St. Augustine's— when out of nowhere, another kiss flashed through my memory. I was standing in front of my Spanish classroom again. Those deep brown eyes pulled me toward her. *I missed you too much... I want us to be a couple.* I felt Elizabeth's lips press against mine, smelled her perfume again. All the hunger I thought long dead and gone, now flooded over me. My whole body was suddenly hot, my head pounding with desire for her!

I yanked the steering wheel to the right, slamming on the brakes. The car slid forever on the gravel berm until it finally lurched to a stop a couple feet into a frozen field. "Why, God!" I screamed, pounding the steering wheel again and again. "Why can't I get that woman out of my head, even on the happiest day of my life?"

I saw Ruthie now, again looking up at me in the soft moonlight glow. Her eyes held nothing but love. I shook my head violently. "No. I love Ruthie," I said through gritted teeth. "There's only Ruthie for me!"

———

The next several months were mostly a blur. I took an extra class so I could finish my degree by September. I completed my draft obligation, and now Sister Rose wanted me to take that counseling job she was planning. Ruthie and I were also talking more seriously about our relationship. Although neither of us actually mentioned marriage, we both knew that was where we were heading.

It was the middle of April. Spring was slow in coming this year, but I didn't notice. I was so focused on my classes, my plans with Sister Rose, and especially Ruthie, it felt like spring had come already. I was happier than I'd ever been in my whole life.

I was running late for my Wednesday class, but I stopped by the university post office anyway. My advisor was supposed to send me a summer schedule I needed. I opened my mailbox—and then I saw it. A letter with familiar handwriting.

I held my breath as the room spun around and around. The letter shook in my hand. *Don't open it! Throw it away!* But I had to open it— if I could just stop shaking.

Inside the envelope was a note. *"I miss our walks. I miss you. Can you meet me at the Student Union lobby Monday morning at 10 o'clock? Elizabeth."* Just three short sentences. But it was enough to make my heart race and my face flush with all the hunger I was so desperate to forget. "I miss you too, Elizabeth."

It was madness to see her. Not now. Not ever. If I open myself to her again, if I allow my passion for her to come out, like I did so many times, she'll consume me all over again. But I couldn't help myself. I wasn't over her the way I hoped. I closed my eyes. I was back in that borrowed college apartment again. The afternoon light trickled through the darkened blinds. Elizabeth curled up beside me, her bare skin warm against mine.

Then we were in her living room. Her eyes distant now, empty of any feeling for me. My heart was pressed painfully against my chest, just like it was doing now, as if that was all it knew to do. I walked slowly outside and found a bench. It was all I could do to just breathe.

"Ruthie! What about Ruthie?" I said too loud. Someone turned and looked at me.

Ruthie loves me completely. Just tear up the letter!

But I've always loved Elizabeth, and now she wants me!

She doesn't want me. She just misses our walks together—because I'm such a good friend! That's what she called it.

But she misses those walks with ME! That's more than just being friends.

But what about my walks on the farm with Ruthie? What about Christmas night?

"Enough!" I shouted. Several people stopped walking, staring for just a second, then quickly moved past me. The air was quiet now, with just the sound of a bird singing in the tree above me. "It's only a meeting with an old friend. I'll tell her I'm happy now with Ruthie. That'll be it." *But will it? Not with Elizabeth*, a voice whispered again. I kept the letter and I didn't go to class.

That night back at St. Augustine's, I tried to focus on my work, but all I thought about was that letter—and Ruthie.

"Daniel, can you help me with my math homework," Joey called when he saw me staring out the window of the rec room.

"Not now. Can't you get one of the other boys to help you? Maybe Daequan?"

"I already asked him, but he doesn't know how to do it. And teacher said I gotta have it done by tomorrow."

The last thing I felt like doing now was some stupid math problem. "Bring it to me," I muttered.

Tossing all night, I barely got any sleep until near dawn. But then I didn't hear my alarm, and I was late getting to Daequan's school to meet with one of his teachers. "Sorry, Mrs. Benson. My alarm didn't work for some reason."

"No problem, Mr. Robinson. Daequan and I were just talking about how well he's doing in my class. The truth is, he seems to have a real flair for writing. Have you seen his latest story about his mother? It's actually quite good."

"Yes, I did, and I agree. It's a good story." Daequan asked me to read it last night, but I laid it on my dresser and forgot about it.

"That's the reason why I wanted to meet with you." She handed me one of the several newspapers on the corner of her desk. "Although Daequan is only a sophomore, I wanted to let you know he's been nominated to be on the school newspaper staff. It's really quite an honor." Mrs. Benson smiled. She seemed genuinely excited. "I guess there's a lot more to Daequan than anyone realized."

I smiled, remembering my first meeting in this same building with Principal Jackson.

"This is quite an early birthday present for Daequan, don't you think, Mr. Robinson."

"What? Oh, right." Is that this weekend? "We...ah... we've got a little party planned for him at St. Augustine's on Saturday. This news will make it even more special for him."

I scribbled a note to myself as soon as I got back to my car.

That afternoon I met with Sister Rose to talk about the counseling program we were planning. I told her I'd have my degree by the end of summer, but I didn't tell her I hadn't been to any classes all week. *I'll make them up after I meet with Elizabeth on Monday.*

On Saturday Ruthie surprised me by stopping by my cottage to celebrate Daequan's birthday with us. "Don't forget our lunch date Monday." She cooed and squeezed my hand.

Monday? I felt my face suddenly hot. "God, I'm sorry, Ruthie. I have to stay at school for some lab work. Maybe later next week. I promise." I hated lying to Ruthie. She didn't deserve it. But I couldn't stop myself. My head was in the lobby of the student union, waiting to see Elizabeth again. She was already consuming me.

———

My plan was to come late, so she would see I had moved on. I wanted her to know I was happy now without her. But I was there an hour early, pacing the floor, checking my watch, constantly looking toward the door. I couldn't help myself. Finally, at 10:15 I saw her in the parking lot... and she looked even more beautiful than I remembered. My heart raced, my face felt hot and my legs went numb, like they did so many times when I was with her in college. *Dammit! Get control of yourself!* I ran to the men's room and splashed water on my face. I stayed there as long as I could. Maybe she'll think I was late too...like I didn't care.

"Daniel! It's good to see you again," she called out as I walked back to the lobby.

"Elizabeth. I'm glad to see you too, and surprised." My heart pounded hard in my chest. I was sure she could hear it. *Be calm. Just breathe.*

She hugged me easily, the way two good friends would greet each other after a summer vacation. I tried to hug her back, but it felt awkward, and I didn't quite know what to do now. Thankfully, she didn't seem to notice, holding me for a moment longer than just friends normally would. I caught a gentle whiff of that perfume she always wore, and my heart raced again. *Just like I always remembered her!* We parted and stood there, staring at each other. Finally, I blurted out what had been on my mind for nearly a week. "How in the world did you find me?" I tried to sound calm. But that question made me seem anxious now, even hungry for her. *Just breathe. It's only a conversation with an old friend.* "I mean what brought you here to Case Western?"

"I've been taking some classes." She said it so casually.

"But I thought you were teaching elementary school. In Kent."

"I was, for a year. But I realized that wasn't what I wanted to do. So I enrolled here, you know, to see what interested me. And that's when I saw you walking across the campus." A welcoming smile filled her face as she gently touched my arm. "I tried to call out, but I guess you didn't hear me. So I looked you up at the registrar's office and got your post office number."

"But I thought you were living in Kent. Why didn't you just take some classes there?"

"We moved here when Jeffrey started law school, and we liked the area so much we decided to stay when he got a job with a Cleveland law firm."

Jeffrey! Of course, she's married! I cursed myself again for even imagining she had any interest in me. *Not four years ago. Not now. Not ever!* "I don't understand." I wanted to scream the words at her, but I swallowed hard. "Your note...?" I asked instead, as calm as I could pretend to be.

"I've never forgotten all our walks on the golf course and how good you made me feel." Her voice purred the way I remembered it when we were dating. My cheeks flamed. "I've always felt bad for the way I treated you. I really am sorry, Daniel."

My mind raced. I had to control my emotions or I'd say something I'd regret. I just let her talk.

"Don't get me wrong. I love Jeffrey and I'm happy with him. I really am. It's just that he spends so much time at work." She looked down at the floor, then back at me. "What I mean is Jeffrey and I don't talk much, not like you and I did, and I just miss that. God. I know you think I'm a terrible person, but I miss those times we had together." Her face turned red, as tears welled in her eyes. A sob caught in her throat.

I couldn't help myself. I reached over and took her arm, like I did so many times in college. "Let's go for a walk. We can talk."

Elizabeth smiled, wiping her eyes, then took my hand and squeezed it.

CHAPTER 15
A WORLD TURNED BACK TO CINDERS

CLEVELAND, 1973. The room was too dark to see the clock. The only light was the slim line of evening sun that broke through a gap in the curtains of the Starlight Motel. I let my head burrow back into the pillow and closed my eyes again—wait, the Starlight Motel!

O God. What have I done?

The passion we shared all through the day ebbed back in like a slow tide. The smell of her hair as I buried my nose in her dark locks. The feel of her hands wrapped around my shoulders, how her eyes fluttered when I...

God, being with her again was the best feeling—ever. Then why did I feel like shit now? *What time is it?* I ran a hand through my hair, stretched, then grabbed my watch on the table by the bed. *6:30! The boys!* A wave of guilt flooded over me. I opened both eyes wide, and looked all around the room. Even in the dim light, I recognized the cheap curtains, the darkened television on the dresser in front of the bed, the faded wall picture of Lake Erie, and especially the stale smell of cigarettes from a thousand motel guests before us. Another wave of guilt pressed down on me. I had to get up... go back to St. Augustine's...

A sleepy voice moaned next to me. "Mmm?" That beautiful voice... when I turned toward it, there was a rhythm of gentle breathing again. I sighed quietly. I couldn't get up now. I'd wake Elizabeth. But I couldn't go back to sleep either. There was...too much to process. But not now. All I saw was the curve of her mouth, very still now, but for a slight rise and fall with each slow breath. Just hours ago—a lifetime ago—they had been full, insistent lips that welcomed me in every way. Every. Way. I ran my hand along her bare legs, long and slender. How she wrapped them around me... I shook my head quickly, but too late. I was smiling already. *She is perfect.* The air was still and the room quiet, except for the sound of my breathing. Her eyes slowly opened, before she smiled up at me.

"Was I sleeping?" she murmured, drawing me to her.

"Were you?" I teased. Our lips neared and met. We laid there now, holding each other, talking like we did so many times in college, as if the years apart never happened, as if she never got married.

"I've got so much to tell you about all that's happened since I last saw you, and especially my trip to San Francisco." The words came so easily with her now. "You wouldn't believe the two hippies I caught a ride with through Utah."

"Hippies?" She grinned, propping herself up on an elbow. "You're kidding!"

I laughed. "No, I promise!"

I told her about riding in the dope bus, and all the weed, and even the LSD Mellow offered me. "He said it was a religious experience!"

Now it was Elizabeth who laughed.

I told her about Sunshine's astrology, and how she wanted to name their baby *Blue*, because it was her favorite color. "She said it would work for a boy or a girl. Can you believe it?"

A smirk spread over her face. "They sound like characters right out of a Jack Kerouac novel."

"More like Tom Wolfe. Remember that book I read to you that weekend at Shaker Village?"

"You mean the one with the weird title. *Electric* something."

"*Electric Kool-Aid Acid Test.* You thought it had to be fiction. Well, I lived that book on my trip. Believe me, it wasn't fiction!"

"In fact, it was Sunshine and Mellow who told me San Francisco would be the greatest city in the world... but I nearly got killed there."

Her smile disappeared as she fixed her eyes on me. I talked slower now, laying out every detail about San Francisco, from my first day when I got beaten so bad, about panhandling, what happened at that awful church, even about eating out of dumpsters and sleeping on the streets. "It was pretty scary for a while." I shuddered.

She reached over and tenderly stroked my head without saying a word. "That's when I met James and he told me about Elijah's mission. He let me live there and even gave me a job as a janitor." I smiled now thinking of Elijah. "In a street sort of way, he reminded me a lot of Doc Samuels. You remember him from college, don't you?" She nodded, her eyes still fixed on me.

"But James also introduced me to heroin." She caught her breath, the same reaction as Doc. "But not like you're thinking," I quickly added, then inhaled and closed my eyes. "He was just seventeen…" I told her everything about James, why he ran away from home, how boys like him are used on the streets, and how he got hooked on heroin. "He thought he was over it…, but he relapsed a couple times…" I saw Elijah again slump against the door when those two cops told him what happened. "…and that last time killed him." The air went out of me, just like it did every time I remembered James.

Elizabeth pulled me close and held me. "You know his death wasn't your fault."

"I know. That's what everyone tells me. But it still hurts…" My eyes started burning again. This was the first time I mentioned James to anyone since I was in Doc's office. I still felt that same stab in my heart, but it helped talking about him again…especially with Elizabeth.

I sat up in the bed and looked at her, growing more animated. "I forgot to tell you about Bobby. He was this guy I met in Montana. He had been in Vietnam and he was thinking about killing himself, you know, because of all that he'd seen over there. But he changed his mind because of me. At least that's what he told me."

I paused. "What about your brother Richard? Whatever happened to him after he got drafted?"

She smiled again. "That's so sweet of you to remember Richard," she said, leaning in and kissing me. "He went to Germany, just like you promised he would. And he's back home in Kent now, and married. All because of you."

I chuckled at that...me having any influence with the Army! All I remembered was we made love for the first time after that conversation about Richard.

I laid back down on the bed and pulled her close to me again. "I know I talked a lot in college about being a counselor, and I've been sort of offered a counseling job at St. Augustine's as soon as I finish my degree. That's why I feel like I've found my place here, helping kids like Daequan. He's one of the boys in my cottage. Tough background, but he's got the potential to make it." I barely thought of Daequan, or anyone at St. Augustine's since I saw Elizabeth in that parking lot this morning.

Daequan...Francis Cottage...Miriam Cottage...Ruthie! I winced and snapped my eyes shut.

"Daniel?" I felt concern in her voice, something I never heard in college.

Slowly I opened my eyes. "Sorry. It's nothing, really." But it wasn't nothing. Those innocent brown eyes hung in my mind like an apparition. *I love you, Daniel.* I winced again, but forced a smile. "I've been talking too much about me. Your turn now. What have you been doing all this time?"

"My life's not nearly as exciting as yours," she said. "I taught a fourth grade class in Kent for a year, but when Jeffrey was accepted at Case Western, we thought the commute would be too much, so we moved near campus."

Jeffrey. I cringed. *We can never be together, not like I want us to be. But here we are, as if he doesn't exist...as if Ruthie...* I forced both of them out of my mind and focused on Elizabeth.

"I thought about teaching again, but my heart was never in it. That's why I've been taking classes, you know, to find something I really want to do with my life. But then I saw you..." Her lips teased a smile, and she leaned toward me, kissing me gently on my cheek, then on my lips. "...and now I know why I'm here."

My whole body relaxed. I didn't even realize I was so tense. I laid my hand gently on her bare shoulder, moved it slowly across her breast and grinned. "Show me why you're here again. I need a reminder."

She laughed and pulled me on top of her.

———

St. Augustine's was dark when I pulled into the parking lot behind Francis Cottage sometime after midnight. *What am I going to tell the boys? God, what am I going to tell Sister Rose? I'll tell them my class ran too late...that I tried to call, but couldn't find a phone... Maybe they won't even know I was gone...*

I took off my shoes and carefully opened the cottage rear door. The dining room was empty. Several dirty dishes crowded the table, but I didn't see the boys anywhere. *Good. They're all in bed.* I walked down the hall and cracked open Daequan's door. Pale moonlight was coming through the window now and I could see him sitting up in his bed.

"Sorry I was late getting back from my class. Thanks for helping the boys with dinner."

He didn't answer. *Does he know?* I pushed that thought out of my head. "I'll clean the kitchen for breakfast," I said, hoping that would help.

He still didn't answer. I turned away and walked back to my room, flicked on the light...and right there on my dresser, staring at me, was that picture of the whole Drabowski family in front of the Christmas tree. Ruthie had it framed just for me. "So you'll have all of us with you every night," she said. I loved that picture...but now I couldn't look at it. I flipped it over and dropped onto my bed. *What if she knows?* There were those soft brown eyes looking up at me again. *I love you, Daniel,* screamed in my head.

I forgot about the kitchen.

———

Before we parted, Elizabeth had asked to meet me again. "For lunch," but not until Wednesday. "I've got a drama workshop on Tuesday and I can't miss it."

"Me too. I've got my adolescent counseling class. Wednesday then. Lunch." I didn't tell her my class actually met on Wednesday and I'd have to skip it—again. That bothered me, at least until I was with her. Then it didn't matter. Nothing mattered, but Elizabeth. We sat together in a back corner booth in Martini's Authentic Pizza House on campus, talking until four o'clock...just enough time for me to get back to St. Augustine's for dinner with the boys. Then later, after they were in bed, I quietly slipped out the back door and drove to the Starlight Motel. And I did the same thing on Thursday, and Friday. I had to cut both my classes all week. But who cared? Not when I was with Elizabeth. When we were laying together, holding each other, when I saw her smile, heard her laugh, I felt a tingling sensation from the top of my head to the bottom of my feet—like every nerve in my body was on fire! Especially when we talked about something, maybe it was just some line from a book I was reading, and she shared her thoughts about it, I felt she really understood me. And I never felt more alive then. I mean really alive, like everything in my life, everything I had ever done, brought me to this moment—with Elizabeth!

Then why did I feel so bad at the same time? Was it Ruthie? I cared for her. She's a wonderful person. So sweet. I felt like I'm part of her family. And I really liked all of them. But there's something missing...

How can I face her—or her family? Not now. Not after what I've done. But I can't avoid her forever. She's expecting me to be with her on the farm Saturday. Oh God, I've got to tell Ruthie about Elizabeth. I owe her that.

———

I only stayed a couple hours on the farm. I told Ruthie I had a lot of studying to do. But I saw something in her eyes. *Does she know?* For just a minute, I thought about telling her—but I couldn't.

Elizabeth and I met again on Monday, and every day that week. I was careful to be back at the cottage well before dinner. And I never left again until I was sure all the boys were in bed and asleep. I don't know why, but something felt different with them. Did they know..., especially Daequan? There was a look in his eyes... Something I hadn't seen in a long time—like he was seeing right through me. I thought Sister Rose looked at me funny, too. *Does she know I haven't been to class for weeks? Did my professor call her? No, that's crazy. But what if...*

That night, alone in my room, I picked up the picture of me with the Drabowskis, staring at it. Michael sure was excited with that silly toy I got him. I sighed, grabbing the notebook my professor asked me to keep on all the boys.

"Anthony Jackson seems to be adjusting better to his father's death. He still doesn't talk about him much, but when he does, he actually seems engaged in the conversation, like he is not repressing as much as he has in the past."

"Joey Martinelli hasn't cried for his parents in several weeks. He seems to view Daequan Jefferson, who is 15 and the leader in the cottage, as his surrogate father, or at least his big brother."

"Daequan has done surprisingly well in his new school, once he got past the obvious racism he faced initially.

I noticed I hadn't written anything about him being asked to write for the school newspaper. Mrs. Benson told me that three weeks ago, but I forgot. Too busy I guess.

I slammed shut the notebook and tossed it back on my desk.

"Maybe I'll listen to some music." I grabbed a record from the shelf. But it was Beethoven's fifth symphony—one that Ruthie gave me for Christmas.

How'd you know I always wanted this? It must have cost you a fortune. She was so excited about that gift. Now I didn't think I could ever listen to Beethoven again.

———

It was Friday afternoon. I planned to meet with Elizabeth, but she couldn't make it. I was on the playground with the boys, leaning against the swing set and thinking about yesterday with her, when I felt a soft hand on my back. "You okay?" A familiar gentle voice. *What am I going to say to Ruthie now?* I turned around and forced a smile.

"I-I'm fine. Just tired, I guess." Several girls called out. She walked over to them, then quickly came back to me.

"You do look awful tired, Daniel. Is it your classes?" She took my hand and tried to pull me to her for a kiss. Sister Rose told us both to be very careful with our affections in front of the kids, and right now I was glad for it. I leaned in to kiss her forehead, but Ruthie pecked me on the lips anyway, like she did so many times when no one was looking. I smiled, as always, but inside, her kiss hurt more than I imagined it would.

Her smile disappeared. A worried crease formed on her brow, and her lower lip protruded as she gave me that familiar wounded puppy look. "I haven't seen you for a whole week. Is everything okay? I mean with your classes?" But she wasn't really asking about my classes. She never did.

I brushed my hair back from my face. I hadn't slept more than two hours any night this week. Sometimes I dreamed about being on those San Francisco's streets, getting rousted by the cops. Once I even woke up in a cold sweat, convinced those two muggers were coming after me again.

But I couldn't tell her any of that. "Yeah. It's my classes. I've got a paper due this week that's keeping me up at night." That wasn't a lie. I did have a paper due next week, but I missed so many classes I hadn't even started it. I barely thought about it—until now.

"I'm so sorry, Daniel," Ruthie whispered. She put her hand on my forehead, and for a minute her touch made me forget. I closed my eyes, but then all I saw now was Elizabeth, on top of me yesterday, her long dark hair draped over me as we....

I shuddered. *No! Not here!* I opened my eyes and smiled weakly, mouthing an apology.

"Your head feels warm. I'm worried. Do you need to see a doctor? You've got all this pressure with your classes, and now I'm complaining that you're not spending enough time with me. I'm so sorry."

"I-no, no. It's okay. You're fine, Ruthie. It's not you. It's me. I just need to budget my time better. That's all. I slapped my face gently, as if trying to wake up. "I'm the one who's sorry." *You have no idea...*

She pulled me close, holding me tight. "You've got nothing to be sorry for," she whispered. "I'm glad I saw you today anyway. I just wanted to remind you about my mother's birthday tomorrow. You are coming to dinner, right?"

"Um..."

She jabbed me in the chest. "Now listen to me, Daniel Robinson. You. Need. A. Break." She quickly pecked me on the lips. "I'll see you at the farm tomorrow afternoon, Mr. Robinson. That's an order."

I grunted a sound that was somewhere between a sigh and a laugh. "Can't argue with that." She turned to leave with her girls, then stopped and slipped her arms around my neck, like she did so many times on her front porch. "Sister Rose isn't around now," she cooed and pressed her lips against mine. But I didn't feel them, not like I always did. I didn't feel anything...just a sharp pain in my heart.

———

The drive to the farm seemed a hundred miles long. *How will they act? Do they know anything? Maybe I should turn around. Ruthie knows I don't feel well.* But when I stepped out of my car, everyone looked so glad to see me. I guess Ruthie told them I'd been sick. I think the kids really missed me because Janice and Michael kept feeling my forehead. Andy and Paul tried to show me that model car they were building. They said it was a '64 Corvette or something, but I wasn't sure. Joe complained that he had to do all the work in the barn this week without me. That's when Mrs. Drabowski pushed open the screen door, holding a plate piled high with chocolate chip cookies. "The girls made them just for you, Daniel." I wasn't hungry, even for her cookies. But she held them in front of me and waited. "Thank you," I mumbled, and took one.

I missed all of them, more than I thought I would. And what I was doing to Ruthie...to them, it was all I could do to not cry in front of everyone. I picked up Michael and hugged him, then hugged him again.

"So Daniel, Ruth Ann tells me you'll be starting that new counseling program with Sister Rose in the fall," Mrs. Drabowski asked as soon as I sat down at the dinner table.

"What? Sorry...ah...yes..." I forced myself to concentrate. "...in the fall. I just have to finish my classes this summer."

"What sort of counseling will you be doing? Will it be just with the older children, like that one boy Ruth Ann said you've helped so much? What was his name?"

"Ah, uh..." I usually loved it when Mrs. Drabowski asked about my boys. Last month, she even suggested I bring some of them to the farm sometime. I thought it was a great idea...then. But that was the last thing I wanted to think about right now. The kitchen door swung open and Ruthie came in with the cake covered with bright, burning candles.

"Happy birthday, Mama!" everyone shouted, then broke into a song. *Thank God! No more questions.*

I tried my best to join in with the celebration afterward, but it got harder as the afternoon wore on. Especially when the kids said something like, "When you and Ruthie get married..."

Joe didn't help any when he started talking about expanding the farm "when the next generation takes over," then winked at Ruthie and me. She tried to act embarrassed, but squeezed my hand. I was pretty sure she had been talking to him about this long before today. In the end, I couldn't take it anymore, and pulled her aside. "I think I need to head back to St. Augustine's a little early."

"Are you okay?" Her hand covered mine gently. "I can make you some tea if you think that will help. Is there anything I can do?"

I pecked the top of her head. "I think I just need some sleep. I'll be my old self tomorrow." The whole family walked me to the porch with my cookies, now packed in a little box. I promised to be back as soon as I felt better, hugged everyone, then drove away feeling dead inside. Ruthie knew it, because her last look as she closed my car door, wasn't her same warm smile. It was pale and strained.

Somehow, instead of turning toward St. Augustine's, I found my car going toward the Starlight Motel. Again.

"There you are," Elizabeth purred when she opened the door. My heart raced, seeing her standing there, her hair knotted in a bun, and wrapped only in a white towel that hugged her body. "And I thought I was going to have to shower alone."

I couldn't help it. All the stress, the sadness I felt the whole day with Ruthie's family, just streamed out of me in a sigh of relief, and then a smile that quickly turned into a laugh. Here, now, with Elizabeth, I didn't need to pretend. Here I could just be... me! Her gorgeous lips formed an inviting grin. "Finally..." I breathed, and slipped through the door.

———

I pushed back my chair and sighed, looking at the letter from the dean. Passing grades in both classes. Sure, all those classes I missed really hurt me—probably a whole letter grade in both of them, but at least I passed —as long as I turn in my final reports by the end of May. And then just two more summer courses and I'm done. Thank God!

Just then the phone in my room rang. "Francis Cottage. Daniel Robinson speaking."

Fifteen minutes later, I found the boys, all sitting and doing nothing under a tree in the playground. "You guys seen Daequan?" I asked. They watched me without answering. It reminded me of when I first came here. Just guarded, blank stares. Even Joey had that same look now— something I never saw in him before.

"Look guys, I need to talk with Daequan. Where is he? It's important." No one answered still, but Anthony just pointed toward the bench at the back of the parking lot. "Thanks for nothing," I muttered and walked that way.

I found him where the boys said he'd be. "Hey, Daequan. Got a minute?" He didn't answer, or even look up at me. *What's with these guys? Do I have to go through this same routine with every one of them?* I sat down next to him.

"Mr. Jamison said you haven't turned in several assignments. Apparently, they were due weeks ago. And he caught you smoking in the restroom. What's going on?"

"Nothin' you'd care about," he muttered, not even looking at me. He sounded tired, like he hadn't been sleeping much.

"Don't give me that, Daequan. What's going on?" I asked again, but he ignored me and started to walk back toward the cottage.

"Don't walk away from me! Now what's going on?"

He spun around so fast I almost jumped. We were nearly nose to nose. "What's going on with you? I asked for your help with those assignments a month ago. I told you I didn't understand them. But you were never around to help me like you promised!"

I blinked. My mouth opened. But Daequan gave me no time to make up some excuse. "And I'm not the only one who says that. Everyone says it's like you don't even live here anymore."

His chest was heaving. He breathed hard and fast, glaring right at me. He was nearly as tall as me now. I didn't realize how much he had grown this year. He waited...for what? An apology. Okay, he's right. I blew it...but I didn't say anything.

Daequan stormed past me, bumping me—hard. "Thanks for nothing." His voice was dead, numb again. Something I hadn't heard in a long time. I watched him walk slowly back to the cottage. Then the rear door slammed.

———

I set dinner out for the boys that night, same as always. Hamburgers, fries and salad. Their favorite. But Andre and Louis were the only ones to come to the dining room. All they did was grab several plates and take them back to their rooms. Was Daequan behind this? I remembered another meal from a lifetime ago.

"Michael, your turn. What are you thankful for?" Michael Antonelli blushed as everyone waited for him to say something. "Um...I'm thankful for Sister Rose, and for the nuns. And... and for my friends here..."

"God, Mikey, what kind of prayer is that?" Louis teased.

"Let him be," I said. "We're all thankful for the nuns, aren't we boys?" They all nodded, sort of.

"How about you, Andre. What are you thankful for?" Without missing a beat, he nearly shouted, "That I can go fishin' here. I love fishin' 'cause I caught the biggest one."

"No you didn't. Mine was bigger. Maybe the biggest one ever caught here," Daequan chimed in.

"What? That catfish wasn't big enough to make a lousy sandwich? You call that a fish. Mine was way bigger...and you know it!"

"Okay, boys," I finally said, laughing at both of them. "Enough lies about fishing. How about you, Joey. What are you thankful for?"

He didn't say anything for a minute as he looked down at the table, thinking hard. "I'm thankful for Daequan...and for Daniel."

The other boys nodded. I didn't say anything, but turned my head a little, and wiped my eye.

But that was a long time ago. Taking my plate, I walked back to my room and collapsed in my chair. On my bed was the notebook with all the fun stuff I used to plan for them, about their progress, even some of the dumb stuff they did, like Daequan's reaction when he caught his first fish. "I guess I should write a note about him taking up smoking," I muttered.

But then I saw my car keys on the desk. My fingers twitched to grab them, go see Elizabeth again. But I couldn't tonight. She said her drama class was going to a stupid play in Cleveland. Well, at least I've got my lunch date tomorrow with her. I closed my eyes and remembered that last afternoon... at the Starlight Motel. Her hair, dark as night, was draped over me as we made love.

But what have I done to these boys? Everything is a battle now with them... How did it come to this? I tossed the notebook onto my desk and dropped onto my bed. I was the one who changed, not them. I know it.

———

I called Mr. Jamison in the morning, and somehow wrangled an extension on Daequan's assignments. But we talked longer than I planned, and now I was late for my lunch date with Elizabeth. I hurried toward my car when a familiar voice called to me in the parking lot. "Daniel!" Sister Rose and two men stood beside a car parked opposite mine.

"Sister Rose! Hey Jackie. I didn't see you there."

"How's it going, Daniel?" Jackie Enders was the house manager of Benedict Cottage. Although he was younger than me, he had been there longer because he never went to college. From the couple times I talked with him, he seemed like a pretty good guy. He nodded toward the other man. "My brother, Shawn, just dropping by to say hello and meet everyone here at St. Augustine's." I groaned inside. Now I have to get out of all this talk about nothing.

Shawn nodded. He looked maybe ten years older than Jackie, at least from the gray in his hair and beard. "Sister Rose offered to help me find a small apartment here in Cleveland for a bit. I'm thinking about moving to the area. Anyway, it was really nice meeting you, Daniel. And thank you, Sister Rose, for your help."

"Don't mention it, Shawn." Sister Rose gave him a quick smile, but she was watching me carefully. "Ah, Jackie, if you would like to show your brother around St. Augustine's. The other sisters and I will join both of you for lunch shortly."

"Yes, Sister. See you around, Daniel." Jackie locked his car and led Shawn toward Benedict Cottage.

All the while, Sister Rose looked hard at me.

"Is everything okay, Daniel?" she asked.

"Everything's fine, Sister," I glanced down at my watch.

"Your spring classes are completed. And I believe you only have two summer classes remaining until you graduate?"

"That's right, Sister."

"I'm glad to hear that, because you know our counseling program is set to begin in September. Everything depends on you graduating this summer."

I still had those late papers to turn in. I hadn't gotten to them yet, but I figured I could always get another extension. "Anything else, Sister?"

"No. That's all. I was just concerned there might be some problem with your classes. But since there isn't..."

"Okay, then I'll see you when I get back tonight." I reached for my car door.

"Daniel..."

I looked at my watch again.

Sister Rose cupped her hands together and took a small breath, like she sometimes did before saying something important. "There is one thing. You have seemed very distracted lately. I thought it was your classes, but since you say everything is fine with them, forgive me for asking such a personal question..." She paused, glanced at the parking lot for just a second, then looked up at me. "...but is it Ruth Ann?"

I thought her voice faltered. I saw worry in her eyes too. Not like she sometimes worried about funding the counseling program, or even when one of the boys was going through a hard time, like Joey when he first arrived. Her look now was more pained, even personal. The only time I saw that was a lifetime ago when we stood with Daequan outside Principal Jackson's office.

For just a second, I was tempted to tell her she was right, that I didn't know how I felt about Ruthie now, and it's tearing me up inside. I wanted to tell her *everything*, if only for someone to hear what I was going through—someone I trusted. But then I remembered Elizabeth waiting for me in that little deli on campus. "Everything's great, Sister. Trust me."

———

I drove as fast as I could, and might have made it on time, but the only parking spot I found was a dozen blocks away. I was already thirty minutes late when I finally reached the deli, gasping for breath, covered in sweat. I quickly scanned the room. *Thank God, she's not here yet!* I found a quiet booth in the corner, wiped my face with a handful of napkins, all while staring at the door.

Twenty minutes later Elizabeth walked in, carrying a small package from a boutique shop she always talked about down the street. I waved.

"Do you remember that note I sent you in college?" she asked as she sat down.

"What note?" I asked.

"The one I sent you when we were dating? I wrote about all the things I loved about you, especially how good you were to me. Don't you remember that note? It took hours to write it."

"Of course, I remember it, Elizabeth," I gently laid my hand on hers. "It was a beautiful note. What made you think of it now?"

"It was the last part where I said, 'I love most of all how much you love me.' I thought about that just now when I saw you waiting for me. You still do love me, don't you, Daniel?"

For God's sake, Elizabeth, you're a married woman! What does it matter! But that's not what came out of my mouth. "I've always loved you," I said, squeezing her hand. "All I ever wanted was for you to love me back."

I held my breath... *God, why did I say that?* It felt like an eternity, but it was probably just a minute, maybe even a heartbeat, before she took both my hands in hers. "I love you, too, Daniel."

Hearing those words... my heart raced. I've looked in those dark eyes a thousand times, and now they only see me! Gently, our lips met. She pressed her kiss, touching my tongue with hers. *I love you too, Daniel,* was all I heard. Nothing else mattered, not Sister Rose's job, not my boys, not even Ruthie.

Our love making that afternoon was everything I knew it could be. We held each other long afterward, talking, sharing all the things we held back—until now. "Jeffrey isn't what I thought he would be." She buried her head on my chest. "I mean, he's a good person, but...but we never talk. Not like you and I do... and I feel... I feel so alone with him. Does that make any sense?"

"Like living alone together?"

"Exactly. You always know just how I feel, Daniel. Oh God, I've missed these talks with you."

"I felt the same way growing up with my family. I never told you about my old man, but he beat all of us. That's why we all left home... to get away from him." She pulled me close when I told her how much I wanted to be better with my own kids someday. "And my mother left too, but in a different way..." I hesitated, not sure what she would say...if she knew about her. *What if she thinks I'm crazy too?*

But I swallowed hard, then told her about seeing my mother leave in an ambulance so many times. "That's why I said they were dead. I was too ashamed." We both cried as she hugged me tighter. We made love again.

I never mentioned Pastor Duncan.

Instead we talked about her and teaching school. "It wasn't nearly as much fun as I thought it would be," she said. "But I really like my drama class. I might even get involved with a local theater company.

"Mmm..." I traced an idle pattern on her shoulder, "I'm surprised. I mean, I never knew you were interested in that sort of thing."

"I wasn't. Not in college anyway. But when I was in high school, I was in the senior play. *The King and I*... and I really loved it. I wasn't the lead or anything. I only had a small part, but when I was on stage..." Her words drifted off.

"What? Tell me more. I mean there's a whole other side to you I never knew existed."

Her eyes went dreamy. "When I was up there, onstage, I felt...." she hesitated, "...I felt I could live another life, be anybody I wanted to be. Does that make any sense, Daniel? Or am I just being silly, like Jeffrey says?"

I cringed hearing his name again. "Jeffrey doesn't know you like I do, Elizabeth. And when you're in your next play, I'll come see you. Front row. I promise."

She pulled me close, kissing me softly. "You always make me feel so good, Daniel," she whispered.

As the weeks passed, we developed a rhythm to our deceit. I had to be at St. Augustine's in the morning and evenings, and she had to be back after nine when Jeffrey came home—except when he was out of town, which was often. Then we could spend the night together in our motel room. I still went to Ruthie's farm on Saturdays, but it was harder with every visit. My afternoons with Elizabeth were our special times... but that was when my summer classes were held.

Soon I quit even pretending to go to them. I still planned to graduate and be a counselor. I was sure of that, but it would just take longer now. That's all. Elizabeth had to know I dropped out of school, but she didn't ask, and we didn't talk about it. All I wanted to talk about was us. As long as I was with her, as long as she was laying naked in my arms, that was all I cared about. I guess you get used to anything, even lying. After a while, I didn't even notice.

———

But I couldn't live in that motel room forever. Eventually I had to tell Sister Rose my degree would take a little longer than I thought. First, I had to tell Ruthie. The last thing I wanted to do was hurt her, but I had no choice. *It's not like I planned for this to happen. She'll understand.* But I knew she never would—and I hated what I had to do to her.

It kept me awake too many nights, thinking, worrying. I planned to meet with her several times, to tell her, but I couldn't. It was never the right time.

"Don't forget my drama class is taking a trip this week. Will you miss me?" Elizabeth cooed when I held her that night.

"Of course, I'll miss you, but don't worry. I've got something I've got to take care of... at school." *Now I'm going to tell Ruthie... and this time I mean it!*

The next day I waited until I knew her girls were in bed, then knocked on her cottage door. My heart thumped. How many times had I done that? How many times did we sit on that bench, alone in the dark, staring at the night sky? For just a second, I thought about leaving. I gritted my teeth. *I have to do this. I owe it to Ruthie.*

"Daniel?" The door opened just a bit. She stepped out, a smile spreading across her face. "I'm so glad to see you, because I have something for you!" She hurried back inside and came out a minute later with a small box. "Here, my mom and the girls made these for you. Chocolate chip cookies!" I hesitated, then reached for it. But it felt like a knife to my heart.

Ruthie giggled. "So why the surprise visit?" She wrapped her arms around me and tucked her face in my chest. "Oh, Daniel, I haven't seen you in so long," she sighed. "I've missed you so much!" She peered up, angling for a kiss—just like she did so many times... in another life.

Elizabeth's kiss burned through my memory, hot and hungry. Her skin, always warm to the touch, her dark hair fanning over my bare chest when she laid her head on me. I could breathe in her perfume anytime, any day, and feel so suddenly free. There's no one, nothing else, that does that to me. Just Elizabeth.

Clearing my throat, I stepped back from Ruthie. "There's something I have to tell you. It's important... but not here."

Her smile disappeared, and even in the dim light, she turned suddenly pale. "Are you okay?"

My mouth turned dry, my heart throbbing as I took a sharp breath.

"Can we sit over there... where we can be alone?" I pointed toward the bench on the playground, where we often sat together, even in winter, when all we had to keep warm was a blanket and our conversation. I hoped it would be easier talking there. It wasn't.

The words caught. "I...I never told you about the girl I dated in college. Her name was Elizabeth." My head throbbed. Sweat beaded on my forehead. I couldn't breathe. "She came back... and... and I realized I still love her."

The color drained from her face. She tried to say something, but no sound came out. She just sat there staring at me, not moving, not saying anything. Her eyes reddened as tears slowly ran down her cheeks.

"I never planned for this to happen, Ruthie. I never wanted to hurt you..."

She started to shake, just a little at first, then her whole body quaked uncontrollably as she sobbed and sobbed. I looked away, hating myself for what I did to her. *But it's for the best. I had to do it.* We sat there now, saying nothing, and waited. Her eyes begging me to say I love you, not Elizabeth. And I waited for an absolution that would never come.

My mind raced. What would Joe say? I could feel Mrs. Drabowski's hand on my forehead, so worried about me, and those hugs from Janice, Mary, and little Michael. And what about Andy and Paul? They were like brothers to me. *God, they don't deserve this any more than Ruthie does.* I felt sick.

After several agonizing minutes, I stood. "I never meant to hurt you, not like this." I said again. "I'm sorry, Ruthie. I really am." I laid the box on the bench beside her. My legs felt like lead. She looked up at me, still silent, but her eyes pleaded for me to stay. Tears burned my cheeks as I turned away and walked slowly back to my cottage.

"If you need more time..." she cried out, "...I'll wait for you. I love you, Daniel."

I love you, Daniel. Those same words haunted me from my first night with Elizabeth.

Later, back in my room, I tried to sleep, but I couldn't. I got up and sat in my chair in the dark. But all I saw were those wet brown eyes looking up at me.

The sooner I put all this behind me, the better.

I turned on the light and slid an empty cardboard box from my closet. Scanning the room, I looked for everything that reminded me of all of them. There was that book on gardening Joe gave me when I helped him plant those vegetables. And that statue of Mary Mrs. Drabowski gave me when I told her I was having a hard time in one of my classes. "Just pray to the Virgin for help, Daniel. That's all you need do." she said. And that model plane the boys made, and a dozen other little things the kids gave me. All these, and more, I crammed in the box. But two things I saved for last—that Christmas photo of me with the whole Drabowski family, and especially those Beethoven records. I looked all around the room one last time, then folded the lid tight, and pushed it back in the closet. I slumped on my bed just as the morning sun leaked through my window...

Two days later Ruthie quit St. Augustine's. They said she was going to Chicago to help her ailing grandmother, but I knew the truth—and I hated myself all the more for what I did to her... what I did to all of them.

But I had to do it... for her sake. If I said that enough times, I hoped I might believe it.

———

I tried to keep busy with my work, but I was only going through the motions. Finally, one of the nuns came to tell me Sister Rose wanted me in her office. I felt I was sleepwalking all the way there. Everything seemed so gray, so out of focus.

"Daniel, I haven't seen much of you lately. Even when you're here, it seems you really aren't here. I don't know where your head has been, but I know it hasn't been with your boys. Now tell me, what's going on?"

Since leaving Ruthie, I stayed hidden in my room most of the time, without talking much to anyone. I cleared my dry throat. "I guess I've been distracted, with Ruthie."

Sister Rose looked down at her desk for a second. I heard the barest hint of a sigh. "I'm very sorry she left us. She said it was her grandmother, but I think it was something more. But that's none of my business." She straightened. "What is my business is that I've spent months developing this new counseling program, and it all depends on you. You still graduate in August, don't you?" The question hung in the air.

"Like I said, Sister, I've been so distracted with Ruthie." I hated lying to her, but she'd never understand my relationship with Elizabeth.

"Daniel, your personal life is your business, as long as it doesn't affect your work here at St. Augustine's. But based on what I've seen lately, it's clearly been a detriment." An old note of firmness came back into her voice. "Now I need to know the status of your degree."

I could feel the blood rush to my face. "That's the problem, Sister. I... I had some trouble with a couple classes and it looks like it might take a little longer. I'm sorry, but it... ahhh... it couldn't be helped."

Her eyes closed slowly, as if to say 'I knew it.' She never did anything slowly. The rest of the world might call Sister Rose an effective leader, or even a righteous authority. To the other staff, and especially the kids in St. Augustine's, she could be an impenetrable wall. But she let me see past that once, so long ago, talking about her dead husband. I saw it in her eyes then, and I knew I could trust her, like Doc. I saw... hope... when she looked at me then.

Now...those same eyes showed nothing but disappointment... and sadness. "I'm afraid that puts me in a very difficult position. Her voice sounded tired. So very tired. "We have to move on, with or without you." The air drained from my lungs. "I'm sorry, but the board has too much invested in this program to delay it any longer. We'll just have to find someone else."

I grabbed my knee to steady my hand. My first thought was to ask her for more time. *I'll work extra hard next semester to get my degree completed.* But I didn't say anything. *Maybe it's time to move on with my life—with Elizabeth.* Suddenly, miraculously, I could breathe a little easier now. After all, St. Augustine's had too many memories of Ruthie. "Do you want my resignation?" I was surprised how easily the words came out of me.

There was a minute, while she stared at her desk, deep in thought. "It will take some time to find someone suitable for your cottage..." She paused again. "...but you haven't been here with the boys for weeks... at least emotionally. In all honesty, there's not much difference if you stay or leave."

She looked at me, but her eyes seemed far away. "Shawn Enders asked me if I had an opening. I wouldn't really call him the best fit, but he is Jackie's brother, and well... he won't have to pay rent for some apartment in town."

She stood. "Daniel, I will give you a week, or two if you need to prepare your belongings and say your goodbyes. But after that, St. Augustine's will need your room vacant, please. Can you do that?"

So after two years here, it's come to this. I ran my hand over my face. *Well, that's it then. It's best for all of us.*

I nodded. "I'll probably just need a week. And Sister, for what it's worth, I'm sorry."

"So am I, Daniel. So am I."

———

With everything that happened, I needed to talk to Elizabeth. *I should call Doc too...* For a minute, I nearly picked up the phone and dialed him, but I shook my head. Too long of a story. I checked the calendar. Yes! Elizabeth was supposed to be back tomorrow.

The next afternoon, when we were lying together again in our motel room, I told her what happened with Sister Rose. "It's actually a good thing. I made a commitment to stay here two years, and I did. And I learned a lot..."

There are no bad students, just bad teachers. I was back in my room flipping through the boys' files.

Louis Antonelli raised his arms high in the air in the indoor ballfield. He looked so proud of himself.

Anthony Jackson stepped back from the last of my birthday cake. His mouth and hands covered in chocolate. A smile spread across his entire face.

Andre grinned wide as he flipped that fish he caught at the pond.

I shook all of them out of my head, cleared my throat, then looked over at Elizabeth's perfect face next to me.

"Are you okay?" she asked.

"Just thinking about something. That's all."

Her hand traced a circle on my chest. "Think about *this* for a minute," she teased.

I chuckled. "You always make me feel better, don't you? That's why I love you. And that's what I was thinking about... us." My mind was clear now. So clear I saw everything. I jumped out of the bed and paced the room. "Let's get out of here, Elizabeth!" I nearly shouted the words.

She looked confused. "You mean this motel room? Where do you want to go then... for a walk?"

I shook my head as I paced. "No, not this room. This city! I mean I want you to go with me. On a romantic adventure... to San Francisco! You'll love Elijah. He's the Mission director who helped me get over James' death. You remember James, don't you? He was like a kid brother to me."

I couldn't stop talking about our new life together. "Have you ever been to San Francisco? It's the most beautiful city in the world. I could even show you James' *Painted Ladies*. You remember the houses I told you about, the ones he loved so much? Remember how we spread his ashes in the wind so he could live there forever? You'll love San Francisco. I know you will."

I was so excited I couldn't stop talking. The more I talked, the more I paced the room. And the more I paced, the louder and faster I talked. "This is what we've been waiting four years to do together. Remember how you told me you could pretend onstage you're somewhere you've never been? Be anyone, do anything? Well, now you can do it for real! It'll be so much fun—for both of us. How long do you think it'll take you to get ready? I have a week to say goodbye to the boys. I just need them to understand. God, I'm so excited about us. I love you so much, Elizabeth."

I stood there, in the middle of that motel room in nothing but my undershorts, expecting her to be as excited as me about our new life together. This was something we both wanted. At first she looked serious, even worried. Then she smiled.

"You were always so serious in college, Daniel. I'm glad you can joke with me like this. That's why I love our times together. You make me feel so good when I'm with you."

What? I just stared at her. "I'm not kidding. I mean it," I said. "I quit my job and I'm leaving Ohio. I want you to go with me. I love you, and I know you love me."

"I do love you too, but you can't be serious. I can't just leave everything and go with you. I'm married to Jeffrey."

I couldn't believe what I just heard! "Think about what you're saying. You're no more married than I am. Sure, you've got a document that says you are, but you're in my bed. I left Ruthie because I love you. And you can leave Jeffrey because you love me!"

"Oh, Daniel." She looked at me the same way she did on her porch four years ago. "I've got a life here with Jeffrey. I can't give up everything, and just drive across the country to live with a bunch of... of dirty street people! What kind of life is that?"

"What kind of life do you have now with Jeffrey? Are you happy? Be honest, just for once. Are you really happy?"

"I'm happy with you the way it is now. We don't need to change anything. You can get another job. There are plenty of jobs in Cleveland. But I need you to stay here, with me." She started to cry, just a little. This time, I ignored it.

"What you mean is you want to keep your house and your car and your status with Jeffrey, while you have me as your afternoon toy. What am I, some sort of whore? Tell me the truth. Is that all I am to you? Because if it is, then I'm leaving. I swear, I'll leave."

"Daniel, I love you," she sighed, wiping her eyes, "but you're hurting me now with all your threats. Please, just come back to bed with me. I know it's been hard for you at work, and I know your classes have upset you. But don't take it out on me. Let me hold you until you feel better."

I could feel the anger drain from me—leaving only despair. "I can't go on like this," I mumbled, barely able to breathe the words. "It's too degrading." *If you need more time...I'll wait for you. I love you, Daniel. Oh...Ruthie. What have I done?*

Elizabeth seemed deaf to what I was saying. She opened her arms, wet her lips with her tongue, smiled seductively, and waited for me to come to her. But I didn't move. Her smile disappeared. "You're not really serious, are you, Daniel? I mean..."

"I'm dead serious, and I'm not coming back to bed with you, not until you tell me you're going with me. I mean it." I was calm, even cold, as I spoke, and that frightened her. I saw it in her eyes.

"Don't make me choose. I can't. I love you, but I can't leave Jeffrey. I just can't. That would be wrong."

"What we've been doing every afternoon has been wrong. What I did to Ruthie was wrong. I'm asking you to make it right, and come with me. Enough lying from both of us. Let's be honest with each other, just once. I gave up everything and everyone I care about just for you. Now I'm leaving Ohio. I love you and I want you to come with me. That's as honest as I can be. Now you decide." Grabbing my clothes, I first put on my pants, then my shirt, and finally my shoes. I wasn't backing down. Not now. Not ever. No more lies!

"I can't, Daniel. I just can't." She cried harder now.

In that moment, as the full extent of her indifference finally hit me, as if she had punched me right in the gut, I hated her... and loved her still... and I despised me even more. "Then I'm done with you, Elizabeth. I'm done!" I opened the door and walked out, leaving her naked and alone on the bed.

"Daniel, don't leave me. I love you. I need you. Please don't leave me!"

I didn't look at her. If I did, she would pull me back... and I couldn't do that anymore. There was no more life left in me. She took it all.

And I let her.

———

A week, that's all I asked for. But the next two, three days were gone before I knew it. Night or day made no difference. It didn't matter. I just lay on my bed, like a zombie, dead, but not dead, just getting up to put dinner out for the boys. I felt so... so tired, but I couldn't sleep either. Most times I wasn't even hungry. After Ruthie, Sister Rose... and now Elizabeth, I was empty, just a shell. Sister Rose said I needed to tell the boys I was leaving, but I didn't know what to say. It didn't really matter anyway. I left a long time ago. I just didn't realize it until now.

Finally, at dinner time that Friday, I collected the food and stood waiting at the table. I wasn't sure why, especially now. This had been going on for at least three weeks. Two of them would come get the food and take it back to their rooms, so they didn't have to eat with me. It was always two different boys every night, like they planned some sort of schedule. This time Daequan came with Mikey Dugan. They paused a moment when they met my eyes, but then Daequan marched in and took two trays and nodded to Mikey, who picked up two more. Without a word, they started to walk away.

I didn't plan it. I just said it before I could think. "Wait." They stopped, staring at me, without a hint of expression on either of their faces. Just waiting. I blinked, then looked at the ground. *What do I say now?* Daequan surprised me. "Go on," he told Mikey, putting his trays back on the table. "Tell your brother to come get these." Was his voice deeper, rougher? I hardly knew who he was anymore. Mikey nodded, leaving without another look back.

Daequan crossed his arms, staring straight at me. His face showed nothing, except for the bags under his eyes. He wasn't sleeping either. And he looked thinner now, older too.

"You don't look too good." I hadn't planned that, but he looked as bad as I felt.

"Lot you care," he grunted.

"I do, actually. More than I've shown you lately. Want to go outside? I need some air." He studied me, not sure what to do with the sudden personal turn in the conversation. Besides, I knew all the other boys were listening in from every corner in the cottage, and neither of us needed that.

We walked outside, out of sight of the playground, away from St. Augustine's main office building. There was some light from the parking lot, and a bit more from the half moon still hanging low in the sky. He pulled out a cigarette and lit it.

"You know you're not allowed to smoke." I knew it meant nothing when I said it.

"Lot you care." He blew smoke in my direction, daring me to take his cigarette from him. And I could have... but there was no point. It wasn't really the issue. We both knew it.

"When did Mr. Jamison tell you about my smoking? Two... three weeks ago?" He took another drag and held out his hand, dangling the cigarette just a foot from me. "You know, I thought you were going to check my room that night, find my cigarettes. But you didn't even bother to look." He spit the words at me.

He was right. And I felt like shit. Worse than shit, because he was right about everything... more than he even knew. He took another slow, defiant drag on his cigarette. It had been ages since we stood so close together. That's when I noticed it. He's nearly as tall as me, but right now he looked so small, so lost, so alone.

"Nothing to say?"

I opened my mouth.

"It doesn't matter." He shook his head, then looked at the ground. "You know, Joey broke down last week? He said he couldn't take it anymore. He said it was like you were dead and gone... just like his parents. That's when he started having nightmares again...because of you."

I felt like he punched me in my stomach. I wished he did! This felt worse. "You...one of you...should have told me."

"Maybe we tried. Maybe we knocked on your door. Maybe you didn't answer because you weren't there." He spit at the ground, dropping his cigarette in front of him, then pressing hard on it several times. "We didn't need you after that. I got a blanket and a pillow and slept on the floor in his room. I took care of him... without you."

His cool stare hardened now into a glare. All I could do was look at the ground.

"You're leaving, ain't you?"

There was no way around it. He deserved the truth. "Yeh. Next week, Maybe sooner." There. I said it. I thought I'd feel better now, but I didn't. I felt worse...so much worse.

He nodded. I didn't know how to read his face now. Was he angry? Hurt?

"I guess that's good," he said. "Dunno if we can keep going on like this all summer anyway. Michael says he doesn't want to go near your damned ballfield anymore." He spit at the ground again. "He just gets angry when we bring it up."

"What about the others?" I could barely get out the words. I felt exhausted, drained, beaten.

"It don't matter. You wouldn't care anyway," he snorted. "Remember when you asked me to try hard in school? For Andre and Terry and all of them? You said I got what it takes to make a difference with them. Remember that? Huh?"

I didn't know what to say, but I wanted to say something. "Listen Daequan, I... I want to explain. No. Forget that. It doesn't matter now. What I really want to say is I'm sorry."

"Don't." He shook his head without even looking at me. "You're still leaving."

He walked past me now. "We all thought..." His voice cracked. "...I thought you were different," he said as he turned the corner. I heard the cottage door slam shut. I shook.

I couldn't go back to the cottage. Not now. He's probably telling everyone that it's true—that I really was leaving. I couldn't even go back to my room. I just need to walk, to clear my head. God, I would have to walk all the way to San Francisco to do that now.

So that's what I did. I walked. Not to San Francisco, but all around St. Augustine's...all night. But my head didn't clear like I wished it would. And I didn't walk alone. Around me, I saw my family, who knew nothing but pain for generations, and Pastor Duncan, who robbed my soul from me. Walking behind them was Elizabeth, who took my last breath. They were quiet for a time, and I thought they were gone, but they were just waiting for me to invite them back.

This time there were new apparitions with them. Sister Rose turned toward me as she passed by, and I felt the full weight of her disappointment. I heard the anguished cries of the second spirit long before she came into view. *"If you need more time... I'll wait for you."* But there was no more time, and she was gone before I could answer. Behind them all, I saw all my boys... walking behind Daequan. I tried to call out to them—to tell them I was sorry. But they kept walking, without even looking at me.

All my life I blamed the ghosts in my past for the pain I felt. Seeing these new spirits now, I realized, with maddening clarity, that I abandoned and abused the ones who loved me too—just like my tormentors.

I was no different. God, I was even worse. *Everyone I cared for, all of them... they're all gone... because of me.* Just like Billy...like James.

"Oh, God!" I cried out in anguish. "I'm broken from birth, and there's no fixing me." In that moment, I knew what I had to do. It was so simple, I was surprised I hadn't thought of it before. Early the next morning, as soon as I saw Shawn Enders get out of his car behind the cottage, I gathered up all my memories of St. Augustine's—that box with the picture of me with the Drabowski family, those special Beethoven records Ruthie was so excited to give me, and especially my notebook with the stories I wrote about my boys—I packed all of it in my car, then I drove out of the parking lot and south toward Columbus, and then west on Interstate 71 to Cincinnati. From there, it was a long drive south until I came to Wilsonville sometime in the middle of the afternoon. I saw Davis Hall where Doc Samuels had his office, and where I spent so many hours.

I drove past the college, then further south on Rt. 29 to the end of the road, where the Norfolk Southern railroad bridge crossed over the Kentucky River. I parked my car and pulled out the box with everything to remind me of the Drabowski family, and my boys that I hurt so badly. I walked up the embankment onto the tracks, then on to the center of the bridge, where I stopped and stared down at the river two hundred and seventy-five feet below. It was brown and flowing fast. "Good." I held the box with all my memories out over the railing. "There's no fixing what I've done to them," I said, then let it go—down and down—until it exploded in the river, then quickly disappeared in the current.

Now I climbed up onto the railing, lifted first my right leg, then my left leg, up and over, so I now stood out over the river. I took a deep breath and leaned out away from the railing. "There's no fixing me," I said one last time.

CHAPTER 16
LIKE A DEAD MAN WALKING

WILSONVILLE, 1973. "It was the strangest thing, Doc. You know, when I was looking down at the river, I was really going to do it. I was so tired of running all my life with nothing to show for it, but a long list of empty promises and shattered dreams." Doc Samuels was working late at his office when I knocked on his door. I hadn't seen him since I left for Cleveland more than two years ago, and I only wrote or called him a couple times. I was always too busy with my boys or my classes. Now I wished to God I talked to him more. Then maybe... "You know what drove me to that bridge? It wasn't Elizabeth, or even all that crap I lived through growing up in Clairton. It was me."

Doc sat back in his chair, stroking his chin, his eyes fixed, just listening like he did so many times in college. I took several slow, deep breaths, trying to find just the right words. "I know it sounds weird, but I saw all the people at St. Augustine's that I hurt—almost like in a vision... really good people, like Ruthie..." I caught my breath. "...and especially the boys in my cottage who needed me." I looked away for just a second and wiped my eyes. "I hurt all of them... terribly...maybe worse. And now... how can they trust anyone again?" This time I didn't even bother to look away as the tears rolled down my cheeks. I saw all of them walking by me again.

"All my life," my words were barely more than a whisper now, "I raged against my tormentors for what they did to me. But after what I did to Ruthie, to my boys, and even Sister Rose..., God, I can't believe how I treated all of them." My voice broke and the words caught in my throat. "That's when I realized I'm no different...maybe even worse than my tormentors, because I knew what I was doing was wrong... and I did it anyway."

I turned and looked past Doc, seeing all of it, all that I did to those people, as wave after wave of guilt and anguish washed over me again. I wiped my eyes, then looked back at him. "That's why I went to that bridge. I couldn't live with what I'd done."

Doc didn't move, or say anything. He just stared right at me.

"Know what stopped me from doing it? Not what you might think. Nothing noble like thinking about all the good things in my life. God knows there hasn't been much of that. It was a lot simpler. I was standing outside the railing, looking down at the river. And I was ready to let go, really." I leaned back in my chair and closed my eyes. I could see that river now, two-hundred and seventy-five feet below, brown and flowing fast.

"But..." My voice shook. "But...I remembered sitting in this office all those times when I was so desperate... so lost. And I remembered you always had that stupid cup... Yeh, that one." I pointed at a cup on the corner of his desk. "Do you remember what you said when I first asked about it?"

He smiled, and we both mouthed the words. "Life is written in pencil so we can get a lot of second chances."

"I was standing on that bridge, more lost than ever...with more regret and guilt than I could live with..." I shook as a chill ran through me. "...and no hope that it would ever change." I looked up. "Then I remembered that cup... and I thought maybe... just maybe, I can get one more second chance." I straightened and took another breath. "So I stepped back over that railing, walked off the bridge, got in my car and drove here to see you. Sounds crazy, huh, Doc?"

Doc didn't say anything. It could have been just a second. But it seemed like forever. "Not crazy at all, Daniel," he said, reaching over and squeezing my hand. "I think it's the sanest thing I've heard in a long time. And for what it's worth, I'm very glad to see you. More than you'll ever know." He squeezed my hand again, a smile spreading across his face.

"I know that. I really do. That's why I'm here." I fell back in my chair again, too drained to speak, and breathed in the healing I felt so many times in this room. We sat there, without saying a word now, both of us so glad to be together again.

"So what are your plans?" Doc finally broke the silence. It was an obvious question, but one I hadn't thought about.

"I think the first thing I have to do is write Sister Rose and apologize. I feel really bad for the way I let her down. And I think I should write to the boys, especially Daequan. He had a really rough start, you know, trusting people. But I thought he was going to make it..." I saw him standing in front of me again. *"You're leaving, ain't you? We all thought...I thought you were different."* I saw him walk away. I heard the cottage door slam shut. "But I don't know what I can say to any of them."

I took another breath. "And I should write Ruthie too. I saw her shaking. I felt again the desperation in her voice. *"If you need more time...I'll wait for you. I love you, Daniel."* Now she was gone.

"But I don't know what I can say to her either. Not now." I looked at Doc, waiting.

He gently stroked his chin, as if trying to absorb everything I had told him. "You might want to wait on that letter to Ruthie," he finally said. "She might not hear you. Not yet anyway. Maybe someday."

I nodded. It was all I could manage.

"You know what really eats at me?" I asked slowly, as the guilt washed over me again. "How many times did I rant, right here in this office, about what Elizabeth did to me. But I did the same thing to Ruthie. That's why I feel so bad. And there's nothing I can do to make it right, is there?"

"Probably not. But time can heal a lot of wounds, as you know firsthand."

"I believe that, Doc, I really do. But I have one question. Something I've thought a lot about since I left that bridge... and maybe even since I met Elizabeth. You know, Peterson always said we were never really a couple—at least not in her mind. He used to drive me nuts when he said that. But now... after all this, maybe I knew all along he was right. I guess what I'm asking, what I can't stop thinking about... Why did I go back to her again and again, knowing the whole time she would never love me?"

Doc sat very still, brow furrowed. The silence between us now was deafening. A minute passed, then two, maybe more. I shifted in my chair, waiting for him to say something, anything, but still he was silent.

Finally, he cocked his head just a little. "Let me ask you a question."

I raised an eyebrow.

"You said you knew the whole time she never loved you. How did you know that? Or a better question is do you even know what love is?"

"I think Augie loved his wife Marie," I said. "You remember him, don't you? The guy who joined the Peace Corp to honor his dead wife."

Doc slowly shook his head. "Think about what you just said. I asked if you knew what love is, and all you can think of is a stranger you once met who spoke well of his dead wife. Does that tell you something?"

He was beginning to irritate me with his questions, but I let it go. "He sold his farm and travelled all the way to Uruguay—because of her. That's love, isn't it?"

"That's not what I'm asking...and you know it. Have you actually seen how people in love treat each other?"

I heard my mother screaming at the old man as she smashed that lamp on his head. Rage contorted his face as he slapped her hard—once, twice, three times.

I shuddered at the memory. "What about you. I've been to your house. I see how you and your wife treat each other. That's love. Right?"

He shook his head again. "You've seen how two people act when they have company. For all you know, we could be fighting all the time when no one's around."

I couldn't even imagine... "You're not...are you?"

He smiled. "No, Daniel. For the record, my wife and I aren't fighting every night, and yes, we do love each other. But my point is you haven't actually seen how we treat each other when we're alone. And that brings me back to my original question. Do you know what love is?"

I just stared at the floor.

Doc pulled his chair next to me, and put his hand on my shoulder, like he did so many times. "I know you as well as anyone knows you. Right?"

I nodded, still looking down at the floor. "I think it's fair to say that you've wanted the one thing you could never have—someone to love you. Fair statement?"

I nodded again.

"Then Elizabeth came along, and we've never talked about this, but she was your first, and my guess, your only sexual encounter."

My face suddenly burned. How could he know that? But how could he *not* know that? I nodded.

"To you, that was love. But really, it was just two lonely, desperate people groping for one another in the dark."

"Jeffrey isn't what I thought he would be...we never talk." Elizabeth said in my memory. *"I feel so alone with him."*

"Like living alone together," I mumbled.

"Exactly. And lonely, desperate people, stumbling in the dark, hurt each other... like Elizabeth hurt you, and like you hurt Ruthie... and your boys at St. Augustine's."

I squeezed my eyes shut, dropping my head onto my chest as guilt pulsed over me again. Fresh tears welled up. Suddenly, I felt so very tired, so old. I didn't know how long I sat there, motionless. When I finally looked up, Doc was holding a pencil in front of me. I rubbed the tears from my eyes.

"Life is written in pencil so we can get a lot of second chances, Daniel. His voice was barely a whisper, but it thundered in my head.

"But..." He pulled it back. "...if we don't look hard at ourselves, if we don't take responsibility for our mistakes..." He let those words hang in the air. "...we're condemned to repeat them over and over—and that only leads to that bridge on the Kentucky River."

"What are you saying?"

"What I'm saying is you hurt a lot of people. You can't erase the damage you've done... but you can rebuild."

I turned and sighed, looking out the window at all the students walking by. "I thought I was doing that... with Ruthie. Now I don't know if I'll find someone like her again." That was the closest I came to describing how I felt on that bridge, the guilt and remorse, all morphed into an abyss of hopelessness.

"I don't know, Doc." I shook at the memory of that river calling me. "You know what scares me even more?" I looked up at him. "Even if I did meet someone...someone really special... how do I know..." I bit my lip, struggling. "...how do I know I won't do the same thing again? I mean, can I ever trust myself? Truth is, Doc. I don't think I ever want to feel anything again. It's too dangerous."

"I understand, Daniel. I really do. All I can say is there are a lot of erasers in life, and I do believe you'll find the woman you're looking for." He laid his hand on my shoulder again, looking me in the eyes. "And when you do, I know it will be different. I know *you* will be different. I mean that. I really do."

"That's my only hope, Doc...." Saying that word—hope, for just an instant I felt I might somehow climb out of this chasm I had built of old and new sorrows. Maybe I will find a place to call home, and maybe I will find someone who will love and heal me, and maybe I won't ever be normal, but maybe I'll find happiness.

Maybe was just another word for hope.

"So let me ask you one more time," Doc said now. "What are your plans? I mean after you write Sister Rose."

"I really don't know. I'll probably go back on the road and see where it takes me. I've never had a home anyway..." Ruthie's farm flashed through my mind. "I always thought the next place would be better. I guess you could say the road's my home."

"Why don't you stay here? You could work at the school, at least for a while. Or even in Lexington."

"I'd love to, but I think I'm still too raw inside. Too many memories here. Except for you, I've had nothing but pain in this place. I think it's best that I start over again. I do that pretty well, you know. Start over. That's the only hope I have." I grabbed a pencil out of his cup. "Lots of second chances."

"I understand. I really do. But maybe I can help with a direction."

He opened the desk drawer and pulled out his address book. "I've got a friend in Detroit. A pastor, but I think you'll like him. He's really unorthodox, at least by Methodist standards." He quickly thumbed through the book. "Here it is. Nick Blanton."

I shook my head. "Thanks, but I don't see myself working in a church."

"I don't expect you would. Besides, it's a small church, and they can barely pay his salary. But he might know of a job in Detroit. He's made a lot of contacts there."

"I don't know, Doc. I was thinking about going back to San Francisco. Elijah said I could have my old job back anytime."

"I don't blame you. I just thought you remind me a lot of him. And maybe this could be a way to put your second chance thinking into practice. What better place for that than Detroit? Why don't you stay at my house for a couple days and just think about it?"

———

I noticed a change in the weather when I drove through Toledo on Interstate 75 and entered Michigan. It was colder than Ohio, almost immediately. It was just September, but I felt fall in the air. It wasn't so much the cold that bothered me. I just spent three winters in Cleveland. But Michigan seemed different—darker, especially when I got closer to Detroit. I passed through a dozen small towns, like Rockwood, Woodhaven, Southgate, Lincoln Park, but they all seemed part of the same dark industrial monolith. In every direction, all I saw were factories—hundreds of them, each one belching so much smoke and dirt and filth into the air that I couldn't tell where the blackened dome of sky ended and the soot covered ground began. As far as I could see, it was all one huge panorama of dirt! *God, this place reminds me too much of Clairton.* I shivered.

I drove on through downtown Detroit and headed north into the surrounding neighborhoods, but they looked to be a wasteland of abandoned and burned out buildings. For just a minute I thought about turning around and heading west to San Francisco. But I kept driving north for several miles where it seemed more habitable, yet only barely. I drove to the northern edge of Detroit at Eight Mile Road. Doc said this was like some sort of dividing line with the whites living in the north suburbs and the blacks in the city on the south. The church was somewhere in between. I drove slowly west. Not sure. Where was I going? Why was I here?

Finally, I saw a sign. 'Reconciliation Methodist Church.' It looked like it once had been a beautiful building, but those days were long gone, like most of the buildings I saw coming through the city. The front door was locked, so I walked around to the back where there was another door with a sign. 'Church Office.'

There are so many of you people asking for help. If you don't go away, I'll call the police. I shivered again, but pushed a buzzer on the wall anyway.

"Come on in," the box said. I almost jumped.

"I'm Daniel Robinson." I answered cautiously, surprised anyone answered. "Doc Samuels sent me."

"Been expecting you. Like I said, come on in."

A scraggly looking man, not much older than me, opened the door. He was wearing jeans and a flannel shirt, his hair hung well below his collar, and he looked like he hadn't shaved in days.

"I'm looking for the pastor," I said.

"That's me." He grabbed my hand and shook it. "Nick Blanton."

I tried to hide my surprise, but he noticed and laughed. "You think I look more like the janitor, don't you? I hear that a lot. Even my bishop tells me that sometimes. But in this neighborhood, it helps if you don't look too much like a cop."

Is this guy serious?

He ignored my reaction. "But that's a discussion for another day," he said, motioning for me to come in. "You must be exhausted. You can stay with my wife and me 'till you get settled. We've got a little house nearby. It's not much, but it's close to the church and pretty safe because the neighbors watch out for me."

God, what have I got myself into? "That's good, I guess," was all I said.

———

The next morning I was ready to tell him I wasn't going to stay. But I kept thinking about all those burned, abandoned buildings I'd seen, and what Doc said about second chances here. And there was something about this Blanton guy—something I couldn't quite figure out yet. *Maybe I could stay a couple days. Just to learn more about what he's doing.* "So what brought you here, Nick?" I asked over breakfast.

"I grew up in Detroit," he said, pouring milk on his cereal. "Well, actually just north of here, a place called Southfield. I lived in the city when I was going to Wayne State and one thing led to another and I got married and ended up in seminary in Kentucky. That's when I met Doc Samuels. He was teaching a seminar in Lexington on making a difference in our community, something he called 'street faith.' He made me rethink everything I believed."

I smiled. "He has a habit of doing that."

"You got that right. Anyway, after I graduated, I planned to come back to Southfield. I was even assigned to a nice church there."

"What happened?"

"The riots."

"I don't understand."

Nick's face suddenly grew dark. He seemed to be looking past me now, like he was seeing something else. "There was a section of Detroit called Virginia Park. Maybe 60,00 people lived there, mostly black. But the Detroit Police Department was all white then and they treated that neighborhood like Vietnam. The car plants were laying off a lot of people, so there was tension in the entire city. It was July 23, 1967. Nobody here can forget the date. The cops raided a blind pig on Clairmount Avenue..."

I gave him a confused look. "Blind pig?"

"Sorry. It's an illegal bar, pretty common in the city, but the cops raided it in front of maybe two-hundred people on the street. That got the crowd pretty worked up, you know, screaming about police abuse and racism and stuff like that. One thing led to another and pretty soon a thousand people surrounded the cops and all hell broke loose."

I saw that Kent State crowd screaming at the soldiers again. Shots rang through the air. A kid lay on the ground with his blood and brains all over my shirt. I shivered. "How bad was it?"

"Before it ended forty-three people were killed and hundreds wounded, and more than a thousand buildings were burned. It changed everything for Detroit...and me."

"I don't understand. Were you involved?" I asked.

Nick laughed. "I get that look a lot when I tell this story. The answer is no...if that makes you feel any better, but let's go for a drive. It'll make a lot more sense if you can see what I'm talking about."

I still wasn't sure what to make of this guy, but I got in his car and we drove west on Eight Mile Road, then south on Woodward Avenue. After a couple miles he turned west again on some other street. By now I was totally lost. Finally, he stopped the car in the middle of an empty intersection, where a bent sign said Linwood Street.

"Over there. That vacant building. See it?" He pointed toward any one of a dozen burned out and boarded up shells.

"Which one? They all look vacant?"

"The three-story gothic revival with the gargoyles on the fascia."

I gave him a blank stare.

"The stone building with all the garbage and tires stacked in the front yard," he answered, obviously disappointed I didn't understand even the basics of Victorian architecture. I smiled thinking of James again. "That's where I lived when I was going to school. I loved that building. Every room was filled with ornate Victorian woodwork. You just don't see that sort of craftsmanship anymore. A great neighborhood too—or at least it was."

James would like Nick. But I was glad he wasn't here. I couldn't handle the two of them blathering on about gables and cornices and dentil moulding like he did every time we were anywhere near his beloved *Painted Ladies. God, I still miss him.*

Nick pulled the car to the side of the street, but he could have parked anywhere. There were few cars, and even fewer people in sight. Just blocks and blocks of empty burned out buildings in every direction. He didn't say anything for several minutes while he scanned the block. "Over there. On the corner. That was our first apartment when Pam and I got married," he said, then turned silent again, staring at what was left of his old neighborhood. "After we moved, and then the riots happened, I kind of forgot about this place. That is, until I met Doc Samuels and everything changed."

Suddenly, he put the car in gear and turned onto Clairmount Avenue. "Now I'll show you why I didn't take that church in South-field." We drove east again to Woodward Avenue, then north. "Do you see it?" Nick asked.

"See what? All I see are the same abandoned buildings everywhere. I don't understand."

"That's my point, Daniel. This is Highland Park. We're miles from the riot. But it all looks the same. Do you know why? Because all the white people here got scared and moved out, to places like Southfield." His voice got louder. "Sorry. I don't mean to get on my soapbox, but whenever I come back here, I remember what this city used to look like..." He took a deep breath. "I turned down a fancy church in the suburbs and came here to all this shit that our city became, because I wanted to make a difference. I wanted to know if my faith was real."

"Well, is it?" I didn't mean to ask that. I hardly knew this guy. But there was something different about him—something I liked, and I wanted to know more about him.

"In ways I never thought possible," he answered without hesitating. "This may sound strange, but faith comes easier for me here." He caught himself again. "Sorry to be rambling on, but does that answer your question?"

I didn't understand all he was talking about, but I was pretty sure I knew why Doc wanted me to come here. "I think so."

"Good," Nick said as we headed back to his house. "Now let me ask you a question. Why are you here?"

I had thought about that all morning driving through the city with him. Now Daequan was back in my head. *We all thought...I thought you were different.*

I shivered hearing his voice again. I couldn't undo what I did to him and Joey and all the other boys, but maybe I could do something here. Call it penance.

"I could tell you I just need a job. And that's true. But after talking with you, I think I'd like to help here, you know, make a difference. I've got two years experience working with city kids in an orphanage. And I'm just a couple classes short of my Master's degree in counseling."

At one time I thought I could make a difference with them, but...

Nick shook his head. "We really don't need a counselor. Not yet anyway." Then his face brightened, like he just thought of something. "But I could sure use some help remodeling the church basement."

"You mean did I get a broom with my degree?"

He tilted his head, his brow scrunching.

"Sorry. Just something a guy asked me once, you know, in a job interview. It was kind of a joke between us after that."

"Okay." Nick's face brightened again. "We desperately need to get our homeless shelter up and running before winter hits. It can get pretty cold on the streets for a lot of people in this neighborhood."

"I'll be glad to help, but I do need to look for a paying job right away. Any ideas?"

"Actually I do have an idea. I've got a friend who owns a fuel depot. He can't keep drivers on his city route, so I know he's got an opening. You interested?"

———

"You ever drive a fuel truck before?" Bruno Pagglioli barked. "You're not a drunk, are you? My last driver got drunk and hit two parked cars. Don't need another drunk working for me."

Bruno was short, fat, balding, smoked a rancid cigar and somehow managed to yell orders to three different people at once in both English and Italian. And from what I could tell in the few minutes I'd known him, he wasn't an easy boss. Once I convinced him I wasn't a drunk, he gave me a short driving course around the depot in a Kenworth diesel fuel oil truck and told me to come back at five the next morning. "Congratulations, kid. You're a teamster now." Bruno tossed me a set of keys and a map of the city, then stomped back to his office, all while yelling instructions to another driver on the lot.

"Not much on training, is he?" I grumbled to Nick as we walked back to his car.

He laughed. "Look on the bright side. At least you won't see Bruno all day when you're on the road."

———

I made it through my first week as a teamster, and soon after that, with my first paycheck in hand, I moved into my own apartment. An older couple in Nick's church had what they generously called a 'finished' basement. There was a bedroom, a tiny living area with a kitchen, and a dimly lit bathroom with an old metal shower. Granted, the ceiling was nothing more than exposed joists, ducts and wiring, the floor was bare concrete, and there were no windows, so it was always dark as a cave, but it did have a separate entrance, making it private. And it only cost $100 a month. There was even a library two blocks down the street where I could read all the books on the list Doc gave me. I planned to help Nick with his shelter too. I wasn't wasting my second chance. Not this time.

———

Even though every muscle in my body ached by Friday, I liked working with Nick on Saturdays because it got my mind off my job, at least for a couple hours. And it also gave me a chance to talk more like we did that first day.

"How's your job going?" he asked when I walked into the church basement.

It's like working in a sewer all day long with all the smoke and dirt that I have to breathe in every day, And everyone drives like they're crazy in this lousy place. I get the finger a dozen times a day. And my customers aren't any better. All they do is complain. They make Bruno look like a saint!

I shrugged. "It's a job." I paused, just for a second. "But..."

"But what?" We were waiting for the electrician to arrive, so we had some time to talk. I hesitated again. "It's like there are two different cities, even two different worlds. There's the white world north of Eight Mile, then there's the black world in Detroit. It's like two warring countries separated by this single road. Like a Berlin wall!"

God, I shouldn't have said that. I don't even know this guy. How's he going to react?

But he didn't seem upset at all...or even surprised, like this was something he heard every day. "Good way to put it. I never thought of it quite like that, but I guess you're right."

I relaxed a bit, enough to tell him what I *really* thought about Detroit. "Aside from some of the boys in my cottage at St. Augustine's in Cleveland, I've been pretty oblivious to this whole racial thing. But here..."

"Race is everything. Right?"

"Exactly! But it's not just that. It's the hatred I feel on both sides. It's not like I get shot at, or anything like that. But the way black people stare at me. I can see the hate in their eyes. And all I ever hear from my white customers is 'nigger' this and 'nigger' that. God, I feel exhausted —and I've only been here a couple weeks. But you've been living and working right in the middle of this racial shit, for what, five years now? Doesn't that get to you?"

"It does. Sometimes I feel like I've been beaten up and left bleeding in the middle of Eight Mile Road."

"I know what that feels like."

"Let me ask you a question, Daniel. Don't you think this is exactly where I should be if I want to make a difference? In the middle of everything?"

I had to think about that for a minute. "Couldn't you preach the same message from a safer part of town?" I asked.

"Believe me, I've thought about that, but..."

The basement door opened and the electricians walked in. "Looks like we'll have to finish this discussion some other time."

———

I helped Nick the next Saturday, and the Saturday after that, like I said I would. I even started attending his church. There weren't many people there, maybe a hundred on a good Sunday, but usually about half that. Most of the members were black, like I expected. But I was surprised to see as many white people as I did, especially with what I was hearing from all the whites on my route. *Maybe Nick's on to something.* I still had a lot of questions for him, so I hung around the church one Sunday morning after everyone else left, I found him locking the door.

"Let me ask you something. When we first met, you said you gave up that church in Southfield and came here because you wanted to know if your faith was real. Remember that?"

Nick grabbed a chair and pointed toward another one nearby. "Sounds like this is going to be a sit down conversation."

"Maybe."

"So ask. Pam's at her mother's for the afternoon and I've got nowhere to go for a while."

I sat down next to him. "When you drove me into Detroit, you showed me the Clairmount Avenue area where you used to live. Remember that conversation?"

He nodded.

"I think all your ideas of living out your faith in real ways are good, and from what I can see with these people here, it may be the only way to bring this city back together, but...."

"But what?"

"I mean, they can barely pay your salary and you've got a wife and a baby coming soon. I guess what I'm asking is do you ever regret not taking that big church in Southfield?"

Nick leaned back in his chair. "To be honest, Pam and I have had this discussion...a lot."

"And?"

"And we both agree we're happy here because what we do is making a difference. Isn't that all that matters?"

I didn't answer. I wasn't sure what to think.

"Let me put it this way," Nick said, now leaning forward in his chair, his eyes fixed on me. "Faith, at least for Pam and me, comes down to simply trying to help the people who cross our path. And this 'Berlin wall,' as you call it, is the people who crossed our path. It's where we're most needed. Besides, we've never been much interested in getting rich anyway. We've got a roof over our heads here, and we like what we're doing. Does that answer your question?"

"Maybe, for now anyway."

———

I planned to spend more time helping Nick with his remodeling project like I promised. But November weather seemed to drain what little energy I had. It bothered me when I missed my first Saturday, but I couldn't help it. Bruno had me working extra hours all week, and I was too tired to leave my bed until noon. I didn't make it to church the next morning either. I told myself I'd make it up next week. But the weather didn't improve any, and neither did my disposition. I spent both days reading. Nick called me Sunday afternoon to see if I was all right. "I'll be there next Saturday. And church too. I promise." But I overslept again.

One week led to another, and by December, Nick stopped calling. Just as well because I wanted to spend more time reading anyway. But I lost my library card and never got around to replacing it. Instead, I just watched television alone in my basement apartment. I didn't really mind that... until Christmas when all I thought about was Ruthie's house.

Daniel's here, Ruth Ann!

What do you have for me?

Is that big present mine?

I warned you, Daniel, they're a handful on Christmas.

"Ruthie," I called out into the dark. It was part prayer, part regret, part good-bye. *If I had only...* I wiped my eyes and pushed that memory out of my head.

———

February passed. Then March. Bruno told me my job was seasonal, but I was still surprised when he let me go in early April. *Maybe this is a good thing. Now I can go to San Francisco, like I always planned!* But when I checked my bank account, I only had a couple dollars. I remembered seeing a sign about some uniform company needing a route driver. So I took the job, but just until September. *Then I'm going back to San Francisco!* In June I remembered the birthday party Ruthie and the boys gave me at St. Augustine's, and I thought about having a little party for myself, but I didn't bother. *Too many bad memories.* I don't remember much about the summer. I drove my truck all day and watched television alone all night until I fell asleep in my chair thinking...

Anthony's mouth and hands were covered in chocolate from my birthday cake. He looked like the happiest kid in the world!

Andre was so proud of that fish he caught at the pond. Sunlight flashed off its scales.

But then...I heard Daequan's voice. "You're leaving, ain't you? We all thought...I thought you were different."

I rarely called Nick.

Finally, September came and went, and I still didn't have enough money saved for my trip. Maybe by spring, I promised myself. But when Christmas rolled around, I remembered Ruthie again. This time I spent most of my savings on a new color television.

It was some evening in the spring, or it could have been summer. It didn't matter. All I knew was every day had no beginning and no end, just one long blur of grey nothingness. I drove my route alone all day, then sat alone in my chair all night, too weary in body and soul to do anything but watch my television screen flickering until I fell in and out of sleep. Then I got up in the morning and did the same thing again another day... and another day... and another day. I didn't know when it was, and maybe it was a dream, or a nightmare. I couldn't tell. All I knew I was back on that bridge in Kentucky, leaning out over the rail, looking down at the river again. But this time I couldn't step back. There was no one to help me. No one cared if I jumped.

"God! I'm so alone!" I cried out in the dark of my basement room. I sat there, seeing nothing, feeling nothing.

———

I was driving my same route on Woodward Avenue on the north side of the city. On Mondays I always got a hamburger for lunch at Dewey's Grill. But it was a cold, grey October day and Dewey was always a grump anyway. That same bridge nightmare woke me again last night, and I didn't have the energy to listen to his complaints. I parked my van in the alley behind the Uptown Diner instead.

"What are you doing here today?" Kate smiled. She was my regular waitress for the past year I'd been eating lunch there, but we never talked much. She was always too busy for any conversations anyway. Fine with me because I enjoyed the quiet.

"Just had a taste for corned beef. Got any ready?" I didn't smile back at her. Sometimes even a smile felt like a lie.

"Of course. Usual place?"

"Yep. In the corner. I'm peopled out and it's only Monday." I said dully, slumped into the booth and flipped open a book I brought. But after ten minutes and no lunch yet, I dropped my book on the table, checked my watch and looked toward the kitchen. "She knows I've got a schedule to keep," I mumbled. But still no Kate and no lunch. "Where is she?" I checked my watch again. *Damn! Now I'll have to take it to go.* "I should've gone to Dewey's," I grumbled, walking toward the kitchen.

"I wish he'd notice me."

That sounds like Kate. I leaned on the counter next to the kitchen door to hear what she was saying.

"Then ask him out. This is 1975. Women can do that now, you know. We've been liberated."

Is that Maggie?

"Not me. I couldn't do that. I haven't been on a date since high school. And I know he'd never go out with me because I'm divorced."

"Maybe I would, Kate." I said half out loud, surprised I even thought that. Sure, she's pretty enough, but I was too numb to notice or care—until now. My face flushed.

"That's no big deal anymore. Hell, I've been divorced three times and I never have any trouble getting a date? Just offer him something he wants."

"That's disgusting, Maggie!"

"I meant dinner. Offer him one of your special Irish dinners, whatever you people eat. Obviously he likes it. All he orders is corned beef, for crying out loud."

"I don't know what to say."

"Then I'll do it for you," Maggie said, as if that settled it. I turned around too quick, tripped on the stool next to me, caught myself, and hurried back to my booth.

"Daniel, right?" Maggie barked, when she reached my booth. If there ever was someone who embodied Detroit, or at least the white Appalachian migrant Detroit that lived north of Eight Mile Road, it was Maggie. She was certainly pretty once, but time and too many troubles —in her case three ex-husbands—now gave her a weatherworn appearance. She was maybe forty-hard-years old, give or take a few miles either way. She was about five-foot seven and lean, something she advertised with her too-tight jeans that left no doubt exactly how lean she was. That is, except for her ample breasts, more than evident through the stretched buttons of her blouse. Her skin was dark from too many days laying in the sun when she was young, and now seemed more leather than tan. But it clearly accented her long, bottle-blond hair that was pulled back in a ponytail so severe that it tugged at the sides of her eyes. I had the impression she got her training at some interstate truck stop where she developed the ability to scare the living bejesus out of any customer who dared complain about any deficiency in her service, real or imagined.

"Kate wants to know if you'll have dinner with her sometime. She'll cook it. She's very good. You'd be an idiot to pass it up. You game?"

My face was on fire. Maybe it was the afternoon sun, now shining in the window for the first time in weeks, or maybe I only wanted a free meal, or maybe it was the way Kate seemed so shy, so vulnerable, looking at me from the kitchen door...and waiting. I glanced at Maggie, then over at Kate and smiled, just a little. This was the first time I'd done that in a long time.

"Okay."

CHAPTER 17
HOPE CRUSHED TO EARTH WILL RISE AGAIN

DETROIT, 1975. "Hope I'm not late," I said when she opened the door. It was all I could think to say. I was so nervous I arrived an hour early and parked around the corner, trying to get up the nerve to knock on her door. It was a cute house, small, but well-maintained, not like most of the other houses in this Royal Oak neighborhood that needed more care than their owners seemed willing, or able, to provide. It was obvious she spent a lot of time maintaining it. There were even yellow mums blooming in the front yard. I was impressed—and nervous. I tried to sound relaxed, but I wasn't doing a good job and she had to know it.

"No. You're right on time."

For a second I remembered another first date a lifetime ago. The smell of fresh hay mixed with cow manure seared my senses. *Daddy! Let him at least say hello to mother before you drag him off to the barn!*

I quickly shook that memory away. All week I thought about our date tonight, but now that I was actually here at her door, I had no idea what to say. I just stood there, frozen. *What am I doing here?*

She looked at me, then at the flowers in my hand, then back at me.

"Oh, sorry." I held them out to her. "I brought these, ...ah...for the dinner table."

She smiled, brushing her hand against mine as she took the flowers. "They're lovely. How did you know red roses are my favorite?"

"I heard you talking to Maggie about it once." I shrugged and rubbed the back of my neck. "Guess I just remembered."

She looked quickly down at the roses, her face glowing as she smiled again. I never noticed that smile before, at least beyond the cursory nod she gave everyone at the diner. It was shy, yet radiant now, with her full cheeks flush against her fair skin. Just then the evening sun broke from behind a passing cloud, and her red hair glistened with hues of gold. Maybe because the diner was always dark, and I was usually worn out by lunch, so I never paid much attention, but now she seemed transformed into a totally new person. For the first time in so long, my heart pattered.

Don't stare at her! But I couldn't help myself.

Just then she glanced up from the flowers and saw me looking at her. My cheeks burned.

"Do you want to come in and sit down?" she asked, holding the door open wider. Her green eyes had turned lush and emerald in the evening sun glowing across her hair. *Simply... gorgeous.*

"Oh, sorry. I mean, yes." I followed her into the house. *Not a good start!*

"Why don't you take a seat here in the living room while I put your flowers in water." She walked on into the kitchen, leaving me to decide where I should sit. I stood there, staring awkwardly around the room. It was as simple as the outside, but clean too. The rug in the center was faded, like it had come from some old house, but it added warmth, especially with the oak floor. The ebbing sunlight flowed through the window, over two stuffed chairs facing a coffee table and modest green couch with soft red pillows on the opposite wall. *If I sit in one of these chairs, she'll think I don't want to be close to her. But if I sit on the couch, she'll think I'm expecting something.*

I hovered, unsure what to do, then stepped toward the couch, where I spotted several photos of a little girl above it on the wall. She looked to be two or three years old, and judging by her red hair, she had to be Kate's daughter.

But I still didn't know what to do, so I moved back to the middle of the room and just waited. Kate finally came back, sat on the couch and patted the cushion for me to sit beside her.

Thank God!

But our conversation still wasn't much better. We stared awkwardly at one another. My mouth was dry as sweat beaded on my brow. *Say something! Talk about the weather, her work, anything, but don't just sit there!* But I still couldn't think of anything, and so all I did was look down at the floor, then around the room. Finally, I blurted out. "Your daughter?"

"I'm sorry?" She looked like she had no idea what I was talking about.

My face flushed again. "I meant the pictures on the wall. Is that your daughter?"

"Yes. That's Susan. She's three years old this month." I thought she would be glad to talk about her daughter, but she just looked down at the floor quietly.

God, did I do something wrong? "Cute kid," I somehow managed. "She has your hair, too. Is she here?"

"She's with the sitter." Kate seemed to relax, just a little. But that was about it, and the maddening silence crept on for another minute. Maybe more. Finally, I just blurted out the first thing that came into my head.

"Fitzgerald. Is that Irish?" I asked. *Why did I say something stupid like that?*

Apparently it wasn't as stupid as I thought because she laughed. "To the core. Just ask the nuns."

Now I didn't know what to think about her. "Why? Were you going to be a nun?" It seemed like an obvious question.

"God, no!" She laughed again, but this time anger filled her eyes briefly.

"Tell me more... please!"

"Let's just say after twelve years at St. Benedict's School, the nuns were glad I graduated."

"Why's that?" I was beginning to think there was a whole other side to this shy, sensitive waitress and single mother than I realized.

"Well, for starters, in the second grade I refused to pray the *Hail Mary* with my class."

"Is that bad?"

"Bad? Sister Angelina Marie called my parents to the school and told them I'd be an atheist before I turned eighteen."

I felt my eyes grow wider. "What happened then?"

"She made me stay after school 'to save my soul,' as she called it." Her face tightened. "You must pray ten Hail Mary's for your defiance," she said in this weird voice, then slapped her knuckles. Whack! Whack! whack! "Are you ready to pray like a good Catholic girl now, Mary Kathleen Fitzgerald?" Whack! Whack! whack! She slapped them again, this time even harder.

I didn't know what to say...or even think. *Is this some Catholic joke?* But she wasn't laughing. "So what did you do?" I asked.

"I was just a skinny little seven-year-old girl who didn't want to spend eternity in purgatory," she said, looking surprised I even asked. "What could I do? I prayed the damned Hail Mary's—all ten of them in one breath!"

And she rattled everyone off right there—in one breath!

I just sat there, my mouth dropped wide open, staring at this shy, gentle, sweet woman—who apparently wasn't any of those things! "What did that nun do?" I finally got out.

"She threw up her hands and walked out of the room," she said, sticking out her chin, the way I imagined her doing to that nun!

"God, I had no idea nuns were like that...and I had no idea you were like that either!" I said, still staring at her, not quite sure if I was fascinated or frightened by her story. I had a hundred questions now, but all I could think to say was, "Why do I get the feeling there's more to this story than just your second grade?"

Without missing a beat, she said, "Do you mean my junior year in general when they moved my homeroom desk into the office? Or specifically that time when Sister Mary David made me wear scotch tape on my ears all day because I complained I didn't hear her when she told us to turn in our math assignment. Or we could talk about that incident in my senior year with Sister Monica Ann?" She practically hissed that name.

For the past year, this petite, gentle, shy waitress had been quietly serving me lunch, for maybe fifty times, and now I'm sitting here with someone I didn't even recognize! "Tell me about Sister Monica Ann," I mumbled, almost in a daze.

She hesitated, then smiled again, like Frankie Denardo when he did something so outlandish, so unspeakably stupid, but he couldn't stop himself from bragging about it.

"I always hated my red hair. The kids all teased me about it. So just before graduation I dyed it strawberry blonde. I thought it would make me more popular."

"And...?"

"Sister Monica Ann saw me when I walked into school." Her eyes tightened and her jaw clenched at that name. "She was the school principal for as long as anyone remembered, and everyone was scared to death of her, even the other nuns!"

"Why?" I edged forward in my seat.

"We all called her 'the ghost' because her face was this sickly white color, like Lenten candlewax, and her black veil made her skin even more creepy. Then every time she prayed, her face got all pinched, like it really hurt to talk to God. But it was her voice...." She stopped for a second, like she was hearing that nun again. "...it was a cold, fingernails-on-chalkboard-make-your-skin-crawl whine that never changed, whether she was talking about the glories of heaven or the sinful nature of patent leather shoes, there was always that same sanctimonious disapproval, like everyone except the Blessed Virgin..." She quickly crossed herself. "...was destined for hell."

"Ah...um...so w-what did she do...whack you on the knuckles, too?"

"I wish! She nearly had a heart attack! She grabbed me by my hair and marched me right into her office...and the whole time whining at me in that awful voice—but now ten times louder. I don't know what hurt more—my hair or my ears!"

"What did she say?" I couldn't believe what she was telling me now.

"What has it been, five years? But I can still remember her exact words, like yesterday." Her face contorted, 'Good Catholic girls don't dye the hair God gave them! Do you understand me, Mary Kathleen Fitzgerald? You will remove that sinful color immediately!' "

"And...?"

Her body stiffened. "I dyed it platinum blonde instead, of course!"

I shook my head. "You've got to be kidding! I'm afraid to ask what happened next."

"She called my parents to the school and threatened I wouldn't graduate if I didn't get rid of my so-called harlot-colored hair."

"And of course, you did. Right?"

She stuck out her jaw again. "Of course. I dyed it jet black!"

I tried to act surprised—and I was, but all I could do was laugh. She laughed too, but defiantly, like she was standing in front of Sister Monica Ann again and daring her to stop her now. The entire year I ate at the diner, I thought of Kate as this shy, sweet, gentle person. Maybe that's why I always sat at her table. But what I saw now was...a force of nature, a girl who actually *liked* to break the rules! "I'm afraid to ask," I said, still staring at this person I never knew existed until this very moment, "but how did that nun react?"

Her shoulders slumped. The color drained from her face. "I graduated, but she said I couldn't 'defile' the ceremony. Those were her exact words! Can you believe it?" Her defiant tone was gone. "She mailed my diploma to me two weeks later...in a plain brown envelope, like she didn't want anyone to know I'd gone there for twelve years—like I didn't even exist to God!"

I remembered how small Sister Rose made Principal Jackson feel —and he deserved it. But not Kate. Sitting here with me, her green eyes now wet and red as she forced back her tears. She looked so hurt, so vulnerable, as if holding that envelope all over again. I wanted to put my arm around her, tell her that nun was wrong. "It must feel weird to see those nuns at church on Sunday," was all I could think to say.

She stiffened. "I'm not Catholic anymore," her tone hardened again. "After my divorce..." She caught herself and looked away. "It's a long story and I'd rather not talk about it. Okay?"

"Is it something I said? I didn't mean to hurt you. Believe me."

"No, it's not you...not at all. It's just that I was always taught good girls don't get divorced... it proved those nuns were right...about me, I mean."

I felt a knot in my stomach. "Do you miss him?" Maybe she only asked me to dinner to get over him.

"Not a chance. I'm glad to be rid of him." She started to reach for my hand, but paused. "And I-I've looked forward to this evening with you. It's just that...twelve years of Catholic teaching is hard to forget."

Whew, so I'm not just a rebound date! "That's good, that you...ah, ahem, that you're glad he's gone." I thought about taking her hand, but hesitated. *It's just ...just dinner. No promises I can't keep. Just a simple date.* Then a faint whiff of something cooking tickled my nose and my stomach growled. "Uh...I was kind of looking forward to dinner."

"Me too, Daniel." She smiled at me. "For a long time."

"And for what it's worth, I'm glad you're not a blonde anymore. I think your red hair is really beautiful. I mean it."

She smiled again as a timer sounded in the kitchen.

"I know Maggie said you wanted corned beef, but you have that all the time at the diner, and I wanted this dinner to be special." She led me to the kitchen and pulled a pan from the oven. A rich, savory smell quickly filled the room and I began salivating. "It's called chicken lichter, and it's the specialty at Machus Red Fox in Bloomfield Hills. I've only eaten there a couple times, but it's my favorite restaurant, and I've always wanted to make it myself. I hope you like it." I could tell she was nervous—at least until I finished my second helping!

After dinner, I didn't feel nearly as awkward now, and I think Kate must feel the same, because our conversation flowed so easily, like two friends relaxing together at the end of a hard day. I told her about going across the country, about Bobby, and Mellow and Sunshine, and especially James. She talked about growing up with nine brothers and sisters. "You know, a good Catholic family that filled the entire pew every Sunday!" I was surprised when she said it was actually lonely growing up in her house. Her father was always working and her mother was always having babies.

"Like living alone together, huh?"

"Exactly." She pointed at me and nodded. "I determined I'd be different when I got married...." She turned her face away. "...but that didn't go like I planned, did it?"

I tried to change the subject. "You said you're not Catholic anymore. Do you still go to church?"

She looked back up with a quick breath. "I do. You might know the place. It's Nick Blanton's church on Eight Mile Road."

"You're kidding! He's the reason I'm in Detroit? He even helped me get a job here. Good guy. I've been going there, well sort of, since I got to Detroit a couple years ago."

"I know," she said. "I saw you at church once."

"You did? When? I mean, why didn't you say something to me?"

"I tried, but you left before I could say anything. I was sort of hoping I'd see you the next Sunday, but you never came back."

"I was going through a hard time then... for the past ten years actually, but I wish I'd known that was your church. I would have come more often."

She smiled, averting my gaze, as if surprised by the intensity. I blinked. It had been so long since I talked with a girl like this.

I saw Ruthie on the bench behind St. Augustine's... waiting, crying. I saw the Kentucky River below, flowing brown and fast... A sudden chill rushed through me.

Kate looked at me. I thought she wanted to say something. But I forced a quick smile. "So now I'm really curious," I said. "How in the world did you ever get connected with Nick Blanton?"

"That's another long story."

"I've got nothing but time."

Kate took a deep breath "I was really struggling. You know, with my divorce." She cleared her throat. "Not because I wanted him back. Believe me, after I caught him with his third girlfriend, I was more than happy to get rid of him. That's why I changed my name back to Fitzgerald. I didn't want anything to remind me of that asshole."

"But...?"

"But I just had Susan. And I knew we couldn't live on what little child support he was supposed to pay me. So I had to get a job, but I couldn't afford a babysitter."

"I don't understand. How did Nick Blanton's church...?"

"They didn't. Not at first. It was Pastor Nick's wife, Pam, who got me going there. I met her when I started working at the diner. She used to eat there a lot. Anyway, we were talking and I mentioned how hard it was to find a sitter for Susan. Next thing I know, she showed up with Pastor Nick and said they'd do it for free." Her eyes were suddenly wet. She reached for a tissue and wiped a tear from her cheek. "I'm sorry. But I do this every time I think about what they did for me."

"I understand. I really do, Kate. Nick calls it 'street faith.' You know, living your faith by helping people."

"I can't imagine any of the nuns offering to help me with anything! It only seemed right that I attend his church after that. I've been going there ever since."

"I'm really glad they helped you like that. I haven't had a lot of good experiences in church myself."

"I know how you feel." Kate clenched her jaw again. "After what I went through with the nuns, I was skeptical too. But I never would've made it without Pastor Nick and Pam. I mean it. They saved my life."

"I had a friend in college, a teacher. He did that for me too. His name was Doc Samuels. He's the one who sent me here to connect with Ni—."

The clock chimed twice. Darn! "I had no idea it was this late."

We stood. "I feel like we just started talking."

She smiled. "Me, too.".

Kate walked me to the door. As I turned to face her, she swallowed, clearing her throat. "Well, ah, thanks for coming, Daniel—"

I hadn't planned to say it, but the words just came out. "Are you free next Saturday?

She offered a shy smile. "What did you have in mind?"

Now I didn't know what to say. This was supposed to be just one dinner. But now...? My cheeks felt warm. "I just...I mean, I really liked talking with you. And...ah...maybe we can go somewhere." My mouth was suddenly dry. "If that's what you want...."

Her green eyes glistened. "I'd love to do something with you... next Saturday, Daniel."

An idea quickly formed in my head. "But let's make it in the afternoon." I spotted the pictures on the wall behind her. "And bring Susan. I'd love to meet her."

She looked so...radiant now, standing in front of me. "We both would love that...whatever you have in mind."

We stood there a long minute, our eyes locked on one another. She started to lean forward, closer. *Wait, no—*

"Well, good. I'll be back next Saturday afternoon," was all I managed to say. She looked disappointed, and I really did want to kiss her, but...

She managed a quick smile. "We'll be waiting for you."

I smiled back. "And dress casual," I said, walking out the door.

––––––

Both girls were sitting on the porch when I arrived early Saturday afternoon. "You must be Susan. How are you?" I held out my hand to her, and she shook it carefully. Kate must have practiced that with her.

"I'm glad to meet you, Daniel," she said. Her voice waivered, and she blinked several times, but managed to keep looking at me. Then she turned toward her mother, as if asking if she did alright. Kate gave her a broad smile, then turned to me, with a sheepish look.

"I hope you don't mind, but before we go, I need to water my flowers. I forgot to do it yesterday and they're starting to wilt." She reached for the hose, turning on the faucet. "I'm sure Susan can entertain you for a couple minutes. That is, if you don't mind?"

"No problem at all." I sat down on the step so I was at eye level with Susan. "I'd love to talk with her." She looked at her mother again, then at me.

"Did anyone ever tell you how much you look like your mother?"

"Sometimes." She lowered her head, shuffling her feet. "But I don't like my hair."

"I don't understand. I think your hair is really pretty. Why don't you like it?"

"Because my friend Jenny, she lives next door and we play together all the time. She said red hair is ugly." Then she fell silent, staring at her shoes.

"I'm sorry she said that to you, Susan, because my brother Robert told me my hair was ugly too, so I know how you feel."

253

She looked up at me again. "Is it okay if I ask you a question?"

She nodded. "Did you know that your mother is the only person I know with red hair? And I know lots of people. Everyone else has boring brown hair, including me. Does Jenny have brown hair?"

She nodded again.

"Did you also know your mother has strands of gold in her hair? That's true. Look at her now. See how the sun makes the gold sparkle."

Susan turned around and looked toward her mother watering the last two flowers where the sun was now shining right on her. "I think I can see it," she said.

"That means your mother is very special. Of all the people in the world, only a couple of them are lucky enough to have red hair, and only the prettiest ones, like your mother, have those special gold strands. Do you think your mother is pretty, Susan?"

She nodded again.

"In fact, with the sun shining on you now, I think I can see some gold in your hair, too."

She reached for her ponytail and held it up in the sunlight.

"Now if your mother is special and pretty, and you look just like her, doesn't that make you special and pretty too?"

She didn't say anything, but I could tell she was thinking about it. "Maybe," she finally answered.

"Then maybe Jenny is just jealous because you're so special and pretty. Just something to think about, Susan."

She smiled, just as Kate turned off the faucet and walked back toward us. "Now what have you two been talking about? You both looked so serious."

I stood and dusted off my pants. "Nothing much. Just talking about how pretty the sun makes everything."

Kate cocked her head. "Okay, I guess." She started to ask something, but changed her mind and smiled at me. "So where are you taking us today?"

———

As the three of us drove twenty miles north to a remote part of Oakland County, I thought about where we were heading. When I first arrived in Michigan two years ago, I used to go to this place a lot because Nick said it was where he went to get away from 'all the craziness in the city.' That's what he called it. It wasn't really a park. More of a nature preserve—virgin woods that hadn't been over-developed when Detroit was awash in automobile money. Now the money was gone, and Nick said some Ford executive donated the land as a tax write-off. It was just woods for miles, sycamores, maples, hemlocks and even an occasional birch. But it was the pines I liked most, because it was the only place in the entire city where winter was actually pretty. The trails were laid out so you could walk all day and never meet anyone else. And aside from the wind, the only sound I ever heard here were my footsteps. A perfect place, well... until I lost interest in it—and in everything for a while. I shuddered thinking about those days again. Ruthie and all the boys flashed through my mind for a second.

"Why the somber look on a beautiful day like this?" A teasing voice interrupted my thoughts.

I glanced to the side to see Kate grinning at me. "You look like you've been driving on Woodward Avenue in Friday traffic. Am I that hard to be with today?" She scrunched her lip and pretended to be hurt. I couldn't help but smile.

"Sorry. This was my first trip back here in more than a year, and I'm really glad to have you and Susan with me."

"Well, maybe you should tell that to your face....," She offered that same teasing smile again. "...because you don't look like you're having much fun."

"Just thinking. That's all."

"Well, a penny for your thoughts." She reached into her purse and held out a handful of coins to me. "There. That should get me about thirty minutes of non-stop conversation from you, Daniel Robinson."

I couldn't help but smile. Where did this girl come from? "Agreed." I reached for her coins. "Do you want to know what I was thinking? I was thinking I don't even recognize you. I mean, you were always so serious at the diner. But now, you're... you're..."

"I'm what?" She stuck out her lip again, pretending to be hurt.

This time I laughed. "That's what I'm talking about. When I get you away from the diner, and away from talking about those nuns, you're a funny person."

"So now you think I'm funny? You really know how to compliment a girl."

"That's exactly what I mean, Kate. I've never had this much fun just talking with a girl." I dropped the coins back in her hand. "But if you'd rather I shut up and didn't say anything..."

She looked at me for a second, then down at the coins now in her hand, and smiled. "I'll take the conversation with you."

We soon turned off the highway onto the dirt road into the park. "I used to come here sometimes, just to walk and think." I pulled into the empty parking lot at the end of the road. "All the noise and traffic in the city really gets to me. But when I'm here I can recharge my batteries."

"It's beautiful, Daniel, and so quiet. I never knew this place was even here. Is this where you bring all your girlfriends?"

I shook my head and smiled. "This place is too special. I haven't shared it with anyone... until now." She took my arm as we walked down the trail, and I almost flinched. As much as I wanted that... I wasn't sure. Not yet. It's just been so long since I was with someone... like this. I closed my eyes for just a second and breathed in the crisp fall air. The touch of her arm on mine felt so... warm, so calming, so right. I opened my eyes and smiled at her.

Suddenly the sun came from behind a cloud and the entire forest exploded in a sea of fall colors. Kate drew in a sharp gasp. Susan stopped in her tracks in front of us. The oak leaves blazed in brilliant red, the maples an intense yellow, and the pines the deepest green I had ever seen. They all burst into a magnificent bloom as golden light spread over them. In that moment, here now with Kate and Susan beside me, Michigan never looked more beautiful. We all stood there, in silence, just breathing in this sanctuary.

Finally, I nodded toward the trail and we started walking again.

"So how do you do it?" I asked as we rounded a bend in the trail. "I mean work full time and care for Susan too? That's got to be hard."

"Pastor Nick has been a godsend for me."

"You mean the babysitting?"

"That's part of it, but not what I really mean. All through school the nuns said I was going to hell because I wasn't a good Catholic. When I got divorced, I thought my life was over. Pastor Nick showed me that faith isn't a bunch of rules, and that God can forgive anything, even divorce." Her eyes glazed over, and we fell silent for a moment. *Looks like Kate has her ghosts too. We thought you were different... If you need more time... I'll wait for you.*

Finally, I cleared my throat. "I like to think life is written in pencil," I said slowly. "We get lots of second chances." I meant it for her, but I needed to hear it too.

"That's what I'm learning, Daniel," she said, wiping her eyes, then she took my arm again and squeezed it. A hundred thoughts raced through my head. *I've known her for a year, sort of. But after just two dates, she's not like anyone I've ever met. She's really different... and I'm different with her. Maybe both of us can get a second chance. Maybe.* Her hand slid down my arm and touched my hand as her fingers gently intertwined with mine. I let out a silent breath, letting my heart slow as we walked on down the trail in silence, watching Susan run ahead of us, poking bushes with a stick.

"You know, Daniel," Kate said after a while. "Other than the fact you drive a truck for a living, and your trip to San Francisco, I really don't know much about you. I'd like to know a little more about the person I'm spending all Saturday afternoon with." She turned to me and grinned impishly. "Unless you're some sort of spy. You don't secretly work for the government, do you?"

I smiled. "No, I'm not a spy."

"Good," she feigned a relieved sigh. "For a minute I was worried."

I couldn't help but laugh with her now. "Fair enough. What would you like to know about me?" I finally asked.

"Well, for starters, tell me about your family. We've talked for hours on both of our dates, but you haven't said a word about them."

Oh. Them. The brilliant fall colors all around us seemed suddenly dim. I stared at the ground.

"Why do I get the feeling you don't want to talk about your family?"

"I left home at sixteen. I think that says it all." All those awful memories of Clairton rushed over me again. I saw the old man drunk, my mother crying in her bedroom, the ambulance taking her to Woodville, that night when Robert nearly killed the old man.

"Daniel? Are you okay?"

I blinked. "Sorry? I was just remembering..."

"About your family?"

The sun slid behind a cloud, and now all those brilliant colors that had looked so alive, were darker, cold grey. "It's a long story... and it's getting late." She gave me a smile, but it seemed worried and small, almost like she did in the diner when she asked me out. We didn't talk much on the drive back to her house.

That evening, after Susan had gone to bed, Kate brought two bottles of beer from the kitchen and sat beside me on the couch. But all I saw was my old man sitting across the room in his chair, eyes bloodshot from drinking all night at the bar, cigarette dangling from his lips, fumbling with his lighter. I heard him yelling at Mum again. *Goddamn it, get me some fuckin' matches!* I clenched my hand around the bottle. My throat felt tight.

"You're blockin' the fuckin' television!" I shook, like I had to duck my head again.

Kate noticed and turned toward me. "Are you okay, Daniel?"

"I'm not feeling too good." I stood. "Maybe something I ate coming back from the park." My hand was trembling as I set the bottle down beside the couch. "I've got to go. I'm sorry, I really am." Then I hurried out the door without even saying goodbye.

I should have been used to my ghosts coming at me like this, but I laid awake all night, staring at that frightened look on Kate's face when I left her house. *Why did I do that? What's wrong with me?* It was sometime near dawn, when Doc's words floated back in from a lifetime ago. *Whatever happened to you, whatever has been choking you all these years, It wasn't your fault.* His words swam around and around in my head. *It wasn't your fault.* I knew what I had to do.

"Kate. It's me, Daniel. I'm sorry to call you so early in the morning, but I couldn't sleep at all last night. I just want to say I'm sorry for leaving you like that. I wasn't really sick. I was just upset about something. No, not you. Something in my past that I need to tell you. Can I see you tonight... please?"

Kate looked so scared when she met me at the door, and that made me feel even worse. We sat on the couch as I took a deep breath and just blurted it all out—all the pain I called my home growing up. I told her how my old man was always drunk, how Robert nearly killed him over that stupid car, and how he broke Billy's arm and then beat up my mother and we had to call the cops on him. "That all came back to me last night when you brought out that beer. It was like I was living it all over again. I guess that's why I don't drink. Too many bad memories. Sounds crazy, huh?"

"Not crazy at all." She took my arm. Her green eyes were soft, not even a hint of criticism in them. "I had no idea the beer bothered you so much. But I understand. I really do... and I won't have it here again."

"No, Kate. You don't have to do that. They're my ghosts and I have to deal with them."

She kissed my cheek gently. "But you don't have to deal with them alone now."

"But there's more," I said. "My mother was... sick... but in a different way." I told her about all her trips to Woodville, and the whole time I talked, she never let go of my hand.

For the first time in a long while, there were no ghosts that night when I was alone in my room.

———

The next Saturday I planned a surprise dinner at that Bloomfield Hills restaurant she mentioned on our first date. The only fancy restaurant I ever went to was the Shaker Village Inn with Elizabeth, and it was nothing like this place. I found out I actually had to wear a coat and tie to get in! So I had to spent all afternoon looking for a decent sport coat and matching tie at Hudson's. And I had to iron my new shirt when I took it out of the package because it was all wrinkled. Then it took me another hour to get that damned cowlick of mine to lay down. But all that trouble was worth it when she met me at her door, wearing a soft green dress that hung delicately on her shoulders, revealing just enough, but not too much. Her matching heels added perfectly to her five-foot six-inch frame so she fit easily beside me. A modest pearl necklace accented her red hair that rested gently on her shoulders.

"You look...absolutely stunning!" I stuttered as I helped her slip into her coat. She smiled and took my arm as we walked to the car.

"Oh Daniel, I can't believe we're actually going to Machus Red Fox!" she squealed when we pulled into the parking lot. "I haven't been here in years because it's so expensive. I mean, how did you ever get reservations?"

I shut off the engine, pulled the key out of the ignition and turned toward her. "Kate, you said it was your favorite restaurant. That's all that matters."

She leaned over and kissed me on the cheek. "And being here with you makes it even more special."

I didn't tell her I'd been thinking about coming to this place all last summer. Apparently, some big shot union guy named Jimmy Hoffa was last seen eating here just before he disappeared. I saw FBI people in the parking lot for months when I drove by on my route, and I thought it would be kind of cool to look inside the place, maybe even run into some gangster types who might be hanging out. But now, actually walking into Machus Red Fox with this gorgeous woman on my arm, seeing a gangster at the table next to me was the last thing on my mind.

"A quiet table in the corner," I told the maître d. Until this week I never even heard of that word. I practiced saying it all week!

"You know I was afraid to go on that first date with you," Kate said after our waiter had gone back to the kitchen. He offered wine, but Kate declined. I tried to tell her it was okay, but she insisted.

"I kind of got that impression. But just so you know, I was nervous too. I hadn't been on a date in a long time."

"That's what I wanted to ask," she said. "We've talked a lot about my divorce, but you haven't said anything about... about your old girl-friends. I guess what I'm asking is have you ever been married? It's okay, I mean, but I kind of sensed there'd been someone in your life."

Even sitting here across from Kate in the fanciest restaurant I'd ever been in, Ruthie was still nearby, crying alone on that bench, her eyes begging me to stay. *I never meant to hurt you, not like this. I'm sorry. I really am.* I looked down at my glass of water and didn't answer. Forks clinked on the plates around us. Someone behind laughed. Finally, Kate whispered, "It's okay. You don't have to tell me." She took my hand and squeezed it, then looked up at me, her green eyes glowing in the soft light of the restaurant. "All that matters is you're here now... with me."

We talked instead about Susan and how well she was doing in daycare. We talked about Kate's church and how much she was learning about her faith from Pastor Nick. The waiter came back with the special for the night. I had no idea what it was. I just know we both said it was the best *something* we ever had. We talked a lot about Doc. And my job. But we never talked about Ruthie—and especially Elizabeth. That conversation would have to wait for another day.

CHAPTER 18
TENDER MERCIES

DETROIT, 1975. Thanksgiving was nothing special growing up in my house. The old man would watch television and get drunk, and the rest of us would stay out of his way. And after the way I left the boys and Ruthie...I didn't want to even think about Thanksgiving for a long time. So when Kate asked if I had any plans for the holiday, I gave her a shrug. "Read a book I guess...unless you've got something in mind?"

"Of course." She smiled. "Holidays are always special in my house."

Kate wasn't kidding. I got there a little late because of some construction on Woodward Avenue blocking a couple streets near her neighborhood. But when I pulled in front of her house, it was already decorated and waiting for me. There were several pumpkins on the porch, while a huge wreath of leaves, pine cones and miniature pumpkins, hung from the door, capped with a large orange bow.

"There you are. I was starting to worry!" Kate gave me a tight hug in the living room. Susan stood next to her, smiling as excitedly as her mother. There were more decorations inside the house. A large picture of a pilgrim family with a huge turkey hung in the window. Taped along the wall leading to the dining room were several more pilgrim pictures that Susan must have drawn. A huge multi-colored Thanksgiving cloth covered the table, topped with a wreath that was bigger and brighter than the one outside. In the center stood a tall, spice-scented orange candle—all lit and waiting for me. But I was surprised to see five chairs and place settings at the table.

"I see you've brought some dinner guests I haven't met yet, Susan," I said, sitting down beside her. "Can you introduce them to me?"

"This is Nancy, Daniel. I just got her this week." Susan snuggled Nancy against her chest, and handed me another doll. "And this is her sister, Julie. But she's real shy."

"Well, I'll keep her right next to me, how about that?" I said. Susan giggled, and Kate smiled at me. "I'm glad to meet both your friends, Susan, and I hope they're as happy as I am to be here today." Now it was me who smiled at Kate.

"I'm glad you're here, too, Daniel," Susan said. "And so are Nancy and Julie." She pointed toward their stitched-on smiles. "See!"

"Turkey's ready!" Kate chirped, pulling a gorgeous roasted bird out of the oven. Susan clapped and my stomach growled in approval as all those Thanksgiving smells tickled my nose.

It was... hands down, my best Thanksgiving dinner—ever!

Afterwards, when the last piece of pumpkin pie, topped with vanilla ice cream, was shared with Nancy and Julie, I took Kate's hand. "I've got a little Thanksgiving surprise of my own." Both girls looked up at me, eyes wide.

"What is it, Daniel?"

"You brought Nancy and Julie to meet me today, and I'd like to have both of you meet a friend of mine. Someone very special."

Susan looked all around the room, and Kate just looked confused. I laughed and reached for the phone. "I'd like to call a special friend. He was my teacher in college, and he saved my life, like Pastor Nick saved yours. I've already told him about you and Susan, but I'd like to finally introduce the three of you...if that's okay, I mean?"

Kate smiled and nodded.

"I know you'll love him," I said, dialing through all the numbers. "It's ringing. Hey, Doc. It's me. Happy Thanksgiving! Yea, I'm with them now. Can you talk? Great. I'll hand the phone to Kate now."

"Hello...?"

I pulled my chair next to her, then squeezed her other hand. She seemed to relax, a little anyway.

"Yes, it's Kate, but it's actually Mary Kathleen Fitzgerald."

She laughed. "Yes, it is Irish...to the core, as Daniel says." She laughed even harder now. "Yes, I think Daniel is really special, too." She squeezed my hand and smiled at me.

"Of course, I'll take good care of him for you. I promise."

"A visit?" She raised her eyebrows at me. I nodded.

"Tell him maybe in the spring," I whispered.

"My daughter? Of course, we'll bring her. And thank you for asking."

Her eyes were wet now. I squeezed her hand again.

"And I'm glad to meet you too, Dr. Samuels. Okay, Doc. As long as you call me Kate. And happy Thanksgiving to you, too." She set the phone down on the cradle, reached for a napkin and wiped her eyes.

After that call, I cleared the table while Kate put Susan and her dolls to bed for a nap. When she came back into the kitchen, she took my hand and said, "Let that stuff go for now. I've been looking forward to talking with you all week. Let's sit on the couch and just relax, at least 'till she wakes up."

She raised my hand to her lips and kissed it.

Our eyes met for a heartbeat, and my pulse jumped. "I'd like nothing better." I wanted to pull her close, to kiss her full on the mouth...but I didn't want to hurt her too. I couldn't do that again. I just couldn't. But Kate didn't seem to notice and was already sitting down, and patting the couch beside her. She squeezed my hand.

"I can't believe how much Susan has grown this year." Kate said as we both put our feet up on the coffee table and stretched our legs. But I had to loosen my belt a notch after that meal before I could feel comfortable. "I haven't eaten like that since... ever!" I patted my stomach. She smiled and leaned into me, resting her head on my shoulder. "I'm glad you liked it. And I'm glad you called your friend today. I think I like him."

I wrapped my arm around her and gently stroked her hair. We sat there now for several minutes, just listening to each other breathe.

"Susan's going to be taller than me someday," she finally said. "And smarter, too. Not like me." Her voice trailed off.

"What do you mean?" I asked.

"Nothing. I just never did well in school. That's all." She stiffened a little, like she always seemed to do whenever she mentioned school.

"From what you told me, those nuns didn't exactly bring out the best in you. Or were you just pulling my leg with all those stories? I mean, about whacking your knuckles and everything?"

"Oh, they're all very true. Trust me." she covered her hands quickly, and her eyes dropped to her lap, as if she was thinking about those nuns again. Strange that just a simple word like school could quickly change a very enjoyable afternoon. But I remembered all the ghosts that interrupted my conversations so many times.

"You know, Kate, I actually did better in college than I ever did in high school. Ever think about going to college?" I thought that would make her feel better.

"Me?" She shook her head. "I'm not college material. I'm just a waitress, and that's okay, really. But not college. That's for people like you."

People like me? "Something to think about," I said. "...but someday if you ever want to take a class, I'll help you with it." She didn't say anything, so I changed the subject. "How do you like your job at the diner?"

"I like seeing you there." She smiled up at me.

"I hope so. I eat there almost every day now." I patted my stomach again. "But what I mean is that something you want to do forever?"

"God, I hope not."

"I don't plan to drive a laundry truck the rest of my life either."

"What then?" she asked. "I mean what sort of job do you want to do?"

"I used to think I wanted to be a counselor, but not anymore."

"What changed your mind?"

I remembered St. Augustine's and how I let everyone down. Sister Rose, Daequan and the boys... Ruthie. "It's complicated..."

Both of us stared awkwardly at each other. "Maybe we can watch a football game or something. After all, it is Thanksgiving," I got up and turned on the television. It looked like the Lions were getting trounced by the Rams, but I didn't care.

"Good idea," was all she said as I sat back down beside her, but it was obvious—to both of us, there were too many uninvited ghosts in the room today.

———

I hated December in Detroit. The sky was always dark, and the temperature hovered at 35 degrees—just cold enough to be miserable, but not cold enough to snow and cover all the dirt in the city.

The days I wasn't with Kate, when I spent my time alone in my basement apartment were the hardest. I tried watching television, or reading a book. But too many times I just remembered...

"We'll just have to find someone else."

"You're leavin', ain't you?"

Some nights I could actually see Daequan walking away from me. That cottage door slamming...again and again.

But other nights...I saw Ruthie sitting on the bench, crying out to me. *"If you need more time...I'll wait for you. I love you, Daniel."* Sometimes, when I woke up soaked in sweat, it was Kate sitting there. *"I love you, Daniel,"* she called out to me.

"Oh, God!" I cried out. The first time that happened. My chest ached so bad I thought it was a heart attack. The second time, and then the third time, I just laid there, staring into the dark void of my room.

No matter which ghost walked by me, they all said the same thing. *"I thought you were different. We all thought you were different..."*

Kate was the best thing that ever happened to me. But if I hurt her... like I did all the others... But what could I do? If this went any further... she needed to know all of it...

The next day I met her in the diner at lunch. "Can you arrange for a sitter for Susan on Saturday? I'd like to take you to Oakland Wilderness again, but alone?"

She looked confused. I never asked that before. And I never liked going there in December.

"It's okay, Kate. I just need some time with you. Something I've been thinking about. That's all."

"Okay." but the look in her eyes said volumes.

———

We drove the twenty miles in silence. Both of us tried a couple times to say something, but it didn't help. We mostly just stared at the road in front of us.

When we finally got to the park, we walked the trails like we always did, as if this was just another normal date. There was a fresh dusting of snow, absorbing the sound of our footsteps. All we heard was the sound of our breathing against the rustle of the pine branches above us. Even on a grey December day, the park was beautiful still.

"What are you looking at?" she finally asked when she caught me staring at her. There was that same hint of worry in her voice.

"I was just thinking how beautiful you are...and that I'm the luckiest guy in the world to be here with you."

She almost smiled, but stopped herself. "You said you wanted to talk with me...alone. Daniel, is it something I've done? You're scaring me." She held her breath, eyes wet.

The words caught in my throat, and I reached for both her hands like I did so many times. "When we were first dating, you asked me if I had ever been married. I wanted to tell you about someone...but I couldn't." I hesitated, struggling for the right words. "But you need to know the truth."

She stiffened, and even in the dim light of the grey forest, her green eyes flashed angry. "You're *still* married, aren't you, you sonofabitch!"

I jumped back, covered my head instinctively and laughed. "It's okay. Really. I've never been married. I swear to God!" She relaxed and her whole body leaned into me again.

"Then what is it, Daniel. What couldn't you tell me?"

I took her hand, squeezing it, but I wasn't laughing now. "Her name was Elizabeth. We met in college. I guess you could say I loved her too much."

I bared all the hurt that was Elizabeth. I told her how much I wanted to date her, and how she toyed with me, how we finally started dating, and that we even talked about getting married. "Or at least I talked about it. She married someone else... someone with better job prospects—whatever that means." I looked away and shut my eyes as she pulled me close. She felt so warm against me as we held each other in the cold winter air.

"I thought I was over her. I really did." It was barely more than a whisper, but my words seemed to echo through the whole forest.

"I was dating someone. Her name was Ruthie, and she was a really good person. She said she loved me and I was happy with her. But when Elizabeth showed up again..." I sighed as that memory rushed over me. "I lost Ruthie, lost my job, abandoned the boys I was supposed to protect, and nearly lost my mind over her." My wet cheek stung against the cold air. I didn't know if she could see it, and I didn't care.

"You don't... still love her... do you?" she asked. Her lip trembled, and the fear in her voice was palpable.

I shook my head. "I'm through with her. Both of them. I'm sure of it, but..." She caught her breath as tears rolled down my cheeks. "...but I hurt a lot of people..." I saw all of them again, all those good people who cared for me, who needed me, they all walked by me one more time, and on down that trail into the darkness of the forest.

There I said it. Now you know who I really am. Blame me... Hate me... Leave me... "All I know is I'm so sorry for what I did..." I sobbed uncontrollably in that vast ocean of silence in the forest. I never felt colder, more lost, more alone.

Finally, she took my face in her hands. They were so... so warm. "Listen to me, Daniel." She pulled in closer. "Someone once told me that life is written in pencil. He said we get lots of second chances. Do you believe him? I do."

I just breathed—slow, deliberate breaths of guilt and pain and remorse, and all the while she held my tear stained face in her hands. "Some people..." I finally said. "...they confess their sins..." Every ragged word tore at my throat now and cut at my heart. "...and they're forgiven. But not me. I've had to live with all the people I've hurt. Every. Single. Day. B-because...some things can never be made right."

My shoulders slumped. "I guess what I'm saying..." I sighed, "...all

I've ever known is hurt…and-and hurting others, and now that I'm with you… I keep thinking I might h-hurt you, or Susan…" Tears filled my eyes and ran down my cheeks again. "Oh, Kate, I don't want to hurt you or Susan. God, that would kill me if I did. I mean it." I reached up and took both her hands in mine. "So if you want to… l-leave me… I understand… because you don't deserve to be hurt."

Kate reached up and lightly wiped my cheeks with her hand, and kissed me, softly, tenderly, then took my face in her hands again and looked right at me. "I want you to know something, Daniel Robinson. Don't you worry about me or Susan. I think I know you better than you know yourself. And our commitment is written in ink. And you can't erase ink. But…" She pressed her finger against my lips. "…we can't do any of this without you. Do you understand what I'm saying, Daniel Robinson? Do you?"

How many nights did I lay awake, wanting to love her, but so afraid I would hurt her? But maybe… if we can lean on each other…together we can be strong. Maybe I can be forgiven, and maybe even be normal. I am finally safe…with her.

I wrapped my arms around her and kissed her lips. Not with the desperation and hunger that left me so empty with Elizabeth, and not with the comfortable acceptance I had with Ruthie, but with total, final forgiveness. "You're what I've been looking for all my life, Kate," I said, kissing her again, fully.

———

With Christmas coming, I wanted to give Kate something special, to let her know how I felt. But what? She didn't seem interested in jewelry. Clothing was boring. *How can I tell her that everything I've done, every place I've been, has led me to her?*

"I know what I'll get!" I banged open the closet door in my basement apartment. "It's in here somewhere," I muttered, digging through several old boxes on the floor. Finally, at the bottom of the last box was a large envelope filled with all the photos I took since I left college. "Thank you, Augie," I said, spreading them out on my bed. "And thank God those two guys didn't steal the film canisters in my jacket."

Seeing him in his old John Deere hat made me smile. All my same feelings about Bobby Saunders came back with that picture of him waving goodbye on that Montana trail. I laughed at Mellow and Sunshine's clothes. And the dope bus! It's a miracle it lasted as long as it did. It was hard seeing that picture of James, but he looked so happy standing in front of those houses he loved so much. I wondered if I'd ever see Elijah again. Sister Rose looked a lot like the nuns Kate described, but she sure didn't act like them. I stared at the picture I took of Daequan and the boys for several minutes. The old ache was still there, but draining away bit by bit. I closed my eyes, imagining them on the playground, laughing. *I hope you boys can forgive me someday.* A tear dropped on their photo, but I was at peace.

All of Ruthie's pictures were at the bottom of the Kentucky River. I sighed. *Maybe she's found someone else like I have. Maybe she's happy now too.* Doc's picture was bigger than all the others. I couldn't wait for him to actually meet Kate in person. I knew he'd like her.

I wrote a little verse with each photo, but the last one was my favorite. During one of our trips to Oakland Wilderness, I asked some hiker we met to take a picture of me with Kate and Susan. I thought we looked like a real family, all of us standing together, holding hands and smiling, like we fit perfect. And that's what I wrote. *My long journey and all these people led me to you because we were meant to be together.*

She cried when I gave it to her and we spent the rest of that night sitting on the couch, holding each other and staring at the Christmas tree. When she first asked me to help her decorate it, I didn't know what to say. Growing up we only had one a couple times, and it was always some aluminum thing the old man picked up at K Mart if he wasn't too drunk, or if he even remembered it was Christmas. "A real Christmas tree, of course!" Kate said when I asked about it, "Is there any other kind?" It was tall, nearly touching the ceiling, and covered with row after row of alternating red, white, blue, green and yellow lights, topped by an angel with a glowing white halo. The colored glass balls and icicles that covered the tree made all those lights glisten even more. Kate gave Susan the job of putting Baby Jesus' crib and all the Wise Men under the tree.

Late that night, long after Susan was in bed, we dimmed all the lights in the room and just held each other, staring at the tree and breathing in the pine smell of the room. Who knew how long we stayed there, listening to each other's heartbeats? It was perfect. I hadn't felt this happy...in forever.

"Merry Christmas, Kate."

"Merry Christmas, Daniel."

———

I wanted to stay in that moment forever, but in January Kate came to me crying. "I was told I have to work the dinner shift at the diner, but I can't ask Pam to watch Susan every night. I'll just have to find another job...somewhere."

"Maybe not," I said. "What if I watch Susan until you get home? Then you won't have to worry about bothering Pam, or paying someone else. Besides, Susan and I get along great. Right?"

"I don't know, Daniel. I'll have to work late most nights, maybe even 'till midnight. And you have to get up so early in the morning for your job. I couldn't ask you to do that."

I pulled her into my arms. "You're not asking. I'm offering. Besides, I can catch some sleep on the couch after Susan goes to bed. Trust me. I'll be fine. Besides, it'll give me some special time with her."

"Are you sure? I mean, about being here so late?"

"Trust me. We'll both be fine."

The next night, I set up a card table in the kitchen and covered it with a white tablecloth I found in the closet. In the center, I put a large candle set into a wooden holder, along with four cups and saucers from the cupboard that sort of matched. There was no tea pot, at least not a fancy one, so I washed out a glass pitcher I found in the refrigerator and filled it with tea.

I never had a sister, so who knew what went on at one of these things, but after a few days I started to think I could serve a pretty good tea party for Susan and her dolls—even if she did have to correct me more than once when I got their names wrong.

"No, Daniel. Her name is Nancy and the other doll is her sister Julie. She's the shy one. Remember?"

"Sorry, Susan. I guess I'm not too good with girl's names."

"That's okay. I'll teach you."

"Thank you. I need a good teacher sometimes. But I do have one question. I see you've got a new doll, and she has red hair. What's her name?"

"She's Mary, because that's my Mommy's real name. And you know what, Daniel? When I play with Mary, and the sun is shining through the window, I can see the gold in her hair. That's why she's my favorite."

"She's my favorite, too. And I won't forget her name."

As much as I enjoyed my tea party time with Susan, getting only four hours sleep every night was exhausting—and Kate noticed. "Daniel, I'm home," she whispered in my ear when she found me asleep on the couch sometime after midnight.

"Daniel," she said again, shaking my shoulders.

"Huh? Oh, sorry. I didn't hear you come in." I wiped my eyes and tried to shake the sleep out of my head.

Kate sat next to me on the couch and gently stroked my hair. "I'm worried about you. I really love what you're doing with Susan, but I don't know how long you can go without sleep, especially driving your truck all day in the city." Her eyes softened. She caught her next words, then finally said slowly, still struggling as she spoke. "Maybe you should...you know, stay here tonight...or every night...so you can get enough sleep."

I sat up and took her hand in mine. "Don't think that hasn't crossed my mind, Kate. I'd love to be here with you at night...and every night. I really would. And maybe if I met you before... before Elizabeth or even Ruthie, I might say yes. But you're too important to me. Don't ask me to explain it. God knows I don't have any good memories about marriage, but there's a part of me, especially since I've been with you these past four months..." I took both her hands now in mine. "Call me old-fashioned, but I still believe marriage is special...and I don't want to cheapen it by just moving in with you and pretending we're married. I can't do that to you... and Susan."

Kate just looked at me for several long minutes. Finally, she smiled and kissed me. "Thank you, Daniel."

Over the next six months, the three of us made more trips to the

Oakland Wilderness. Every Saturday, even when snow still covered the ground, it was our hideaway from all the noise of the city. Sometimes we walked and talked about nothing. It didn't matter. We were together. But our favorite times were those rare Michigan days when the winter sky was crystal clear and so cold we could see our breath freeze right in front of us and then float up into the trees. "If you look close," I whispered to Kate, "all those crystals are shaped like a thousand little hearts —just for us." She squeezed my hand.

When spring finally arrived, we often sat on a blanket on the ground for lunch and stared up at the trees above us, just breathing in the smell of the pine needles. There was a pond about a hundred feet from the spot where we were sitting and I happened to notice a pair of swans gracefully moving through the water together. "I've always admired them," I said to no one in particular.

"What?" Kate asked.

"Oh, sorry. I was just thinking out loud how much I admire those swans. I heard they mate for life. I always thought they were smarter than most people."

Kate only smiled.

Two weeks later we finally made our special trip to Kentucky to see Doc Samuels. I was nervous the whole drive. *Will Kate like Doc? Will he like her? Sure, they talked on the phone a couple times, and they both sounded fine. But what if...*

None of that mattered at all. As soon as they met, they were talking like old friends. Even Susan got into the conversation when he asked about her new doll. "His name is Daniel," she said, "because all my girls needed a brother." I never saw Doc look as happy as he did then.

It was sometime near the end of July. We were sitting on the swing on her back porch, enjoying the evening breeze and staring at the night sky. For most of the day it had been the color of wet gray aluminum as a summer drizzle slowly made its way through the city. But now the sky was clear and a half moon was just rising into view, a thick, white sliver that seemed carved into the dark horizon. Above it there were thousands, maybe even millions of stars now shining down on us. I thought we could almost reach out and touch them all. We were talking, like we always did, about anything and everything, mostly about us.

"I know you said you came to Detroit because of Pastor Nick. But do you remember when I asked why you weren't going to his church... at least until we started dating." She squeezed my hand. "Remember what you said? That you were going through a hard time for the past ten years? What did you mean by that?"

I really wasn't ready for that question. "Let's just say there was someone in the church when I was a kid...someone I trusted, like your nuns...and he did some things in the name of God..."

You go ahead and tell this little story you just made up, Daniel. No one's going to believe you anyway.

"...things I've spent a lifetime trying to forgive. So let's just say I believe God isn't offended by our doubts. But he is deeply offended by all the abuse that's done in his name. Does that make any sense?"

"Sort of," was all she said.

"So let me ask you a question, Kate, since you brought up the subject. I know we talked about those nuns, and I know Nick and Pam have been good for you, but we've never actually talked about what you believe. I mean, how do you get what those nuns did out of your head?" I think that question was meant more for me and my ghosts than hers.

Her face hardened and her eyes tightened, like they always did when I mentioned the nuns. "I felt I was never good enough for them... or even for God." She said slowly, measuring every word. "I mean, the nuns *were* God, at least in St. Benedict's School. Then when I got divorced, I thought they must be right, because now they had proof that I was going to hell. I felt... abandoned by God." She pulled a tissue from her pocket and slowly wiped the tears from her cheek. "I hate it when I cry like this... but I can't help it sometimes."

"But you don't believe that now, do you?"

She smiled, dabbing her eyes once more. "Pastor Nick said something when I first met him. He said if we were perfect, then God's light would bounce off us. That it's our scars that catch his light...like my divorce. He said I shouldn't pray to be perfect, but just pray to be forgiven, because that's one prayer God always answers."

Her eyes filled again. "So to answer your question, I guess you could say I believe in forgiveness."

"You mean second chances?" I asked.

"Yes, and maybe third and fourth chances, too."

Kate took my arm and slid close to me, resting her head gently on my shoulder. "But what about you, Daniel," she said softly, even carefully. "You believe in God, don't you?"

I hesitated for several long seconds, not sure how to answer. "It's complicated," was all I managed to say.

She sat up, looking right at me. "No, it's not. You believe in God or you don't. It's that simple."

I fell back into the couch, staring up at the ceiling, as thoughts of Pastor Duncan and Doc Samuels rushed over me. "Maybe it's simple for you, but God has been a mixed message for me."

She reached for my arm again, her eyes searching mine for an explanation.

"I think what I'm trying to say is I want to believe, and at times I really do believe in God... especially since I met you, but...

"But what, Daniel?"

I sighed slowly. "I think life is like running a marathon. Some people are lucky enough to start at the front of the crowd where running's easy for them. But some of us were born with a club foot and every step we take is a struggle. It seems no matter how hard we try, we can't catch up. The best we can do is limp behind everyone else. Well, that's how I think of God. Sometimes believing is a real struggle... but now you're here and all I know for sure is you're the best reason I ever had to believe in God. Does that make any sense, Kate?"

She pulled me close again and whispered, "I love you, Daniel."

I knew she wanted me to say that to her, too, but the words caught in my throat.

"I'm sorry, Daniel. I shouldn't...." She started to cry again.

I lifted her chin so I could look into her red eyes. "No, it's me who's sorry, Kate. You didn't say anything wrong. God knows I've wanted to say that to you a hundred times. But there's something I haven't told you..." My throat tightened again. "Something bad."

She caught her breath, then whispered, "Whatever it is, you know it's written in pencil." She gently kissed me, then pulled me so close I could feel her heart beating against my chest. I had to tell her...everything. But how?

"Some things...they never go away." My mouth was suddenly dry. "My family was a mess." I struggled with every word. "But what I didn't tell you was I moved in with my pastor when it got really bad at our house. He was like the father I never had, and I was glad to be with him. But one day..."

Her green eyes were fixed on me.

"I was just seventeen... just a kid... and... one day he started touching me..." My voice quivered. I felt her heart pounding.

"I keep thinking it was my fault...like there's something in me... like I don't deserve to be loved." My whole body convulsed as I wept in her arms. She knew my secret now... that awful part of me I hid from every-one. And now she would say I was... too dirty.

But she didn't. "It's our scars that catch God's light, Daniel," she whispered, gently pulling me to her. "Let me love away ALL your pain." Her lips pressed to mine tenderly. We both held each other silently as our two broken hearts bonded together into one. There, in that moment, I found the missing part of me. I touched my lips against her ear and whispered, "I love you too, Kate."

———

The bright September sun streamed through the stained glass windows and filled the entire church with a rainbow of magnificent colors—all of them coming to rest right on us. It made the gold in her hair even more dazzling. Nick Blanton walked to the front of the altar, smiled broadly toward me and Kate and Susan standing in front of him, spread his arms to the congregation, "We are gathered together today in the sight of God, and in the presence of friends and loved ones, to unite Daniel Robinson and Mary Kathleen Fitzgerald in holy matrimony."

I didn't hear much of what he said after that, but I heard every word of his prayer. It had more meaning than anyone there could ever under-stand. "Lord, don't hold back your tender mercies from these two people. Troubles may have surrounded them in the past, sometimes too many to count. And sometimes they couldn't see their way out. But you brought them through it all to be here today, together." Nick looked directly at me, then at Kate, and said, "As God has given his tender mercies to both of you, so now you are to give them to one another."

We kissed each other so long Nick finally asked if he could finish the ceremony. We both laughed and turned to the congregation, our eyes wet, as he said what we both waited all our lives to hear. "I would like to introduce to you Mr. and Mrs. Daniel Robinson!"

The audience applauded, but one tall man in the back stood and clapped the loudest. It was good to see Doc Samuels again.

CHAPTER 19
I'M RUNNING AS FAST AS I CAN

DETROIT, 1977. Married life was much more complicated than I ever imagined. On the one hand, there are the obvious pleasures of physical intimacy. But it was far more than that for me. Lying next to Kate through the night, holding her, feeling the warmth of her body next to mine, the smell of her hair, even the sound of her breathing, all were constant reminders that I was no longer alone. Many times, long after she had gone to sleep, I would stare at her in the window's dim light, memorizing everything about her, imprinting her onto my mind and soul. Gradually, in our shared love, I began to emerge from my cocoon of loneliness, and now with Kate beside me, I was becoming someone new, someone I always wanted to be...someone normal.

On the other hand, there were the not-so-obvious everyday issues that can distract and derail even the best marriages. I knew it wasn't going to be a good day when Kate woke me at six a.m. Driving my route through Detroit traffic all week was always exhausting, and I wanted to catch up on some sleep before church.

"There's no hot water, Daniel!"

I rolled over, too tired to open my eyes.

"Daniel!"

I cracked open one eye, then the other. "Huh? What?" I mumbled, looking up at Kate standing over me wrapped in a towel. She didn't look happy.

"I said we don't have any hot water!"

I rubbed my eyes for several minutes, stretched my arms and yawned, all while she glared at me, tapping her foot. "I'm awake," was all I managed to say, dragged myself slowly out of bed and stumbled down the basement steps in my underwear. Ten minutes later I met her in the bathroom with the bad news. "Looks like the water heater's broken. We'll have to replace it."

"Can we afford that?" Her face softened now. "I mean, we just paid for new tires on my car last month."

"No choice, unless you don't mind more cold showers."

Money was an ongoing issue since we got married, and now it seemed we owed just about everyone. Both the electric and the heat bills were a month late, and the car insurance company sent a threatening letter about terminating our policy. Kate's Pinto was five years old and constantly breaking down, but at least it was paid for. The Cutlass I bought while working at St. Augustine's was in better shape, but I was still making payments, and now I was behind and the bank was sending me notices. We did okay for the first six months, but when she got pregnant, the doctor said standing on her feet and carrying those heavy trays all day was too hard for her. She had to quit her job. But that nearly halved our income and I had to take any extra shifts I could get at work just to make ends meet. That would have helped...if everything in the house wasn't falling apart. Now I had all these doctor bills to worry about.

———

I was hunched over the checkbook and a pile of unpaid bills spread over the kitchen table when Susan called me from the living room. "Are you coming to our tea party like you promised?"

"Maybe later," I mumbled.

"All the girls are waiting... and you promised." I didn't answer.

Five minutes later Kate walked into the kitchen. "You promised Susan all week..." I tried not to look at her. I saw that expression too many times lately. Not angry, not even hurt, but disappointed. I didn't need this discussion again. Not now.

"I'm too busy, Kate," I snapped without looking up from the checkbook, then caught myself. "I'm sorry. You're right. I did promise I'd play with her," I sighed, "but I was just trying to figure how to pay all these damn bills. Half of them are already late..."

Kate came up behind me and rubbed my shoulders. "Have you thought any more about that position they offered you at work?" She asked that a lot, and every time I told her no. Since I started driving my route for Detroit Industrial Uniforms three years ago, I'd been offered the route supervisor's job several times. I was the only driver with a college degree.

I laid my pencil down and reached for her hand. "We've talked about this a dozen times, Kate. Sure, it's a promotion, but it'll mean sixty hours a week, and I'd feel like I was single again—and so would you. That's why I turned it down."

"I understand." She looked at the bills scattered over the table, then at me. "But what are we going to do, about the bills, I mean?"

That was a question I couldn't answer. "We'll just have to be more careful. That's all." But it never was.

———

"Susan starts kindergarten next week and she needs new clothes," Kate announced when she found me at the same kitchen chair a week later, hunched over the same checkbook and another pile of unpaid bills marked 'Past Due!' in red. "And I forgot to tell you the doctor wants to see me tomorrow. Just another routine exam, you know, because the baby's due in November."

"And just another damn bill." I regretted saying that immediately, but it was too late. She walked out without another word. "Sorry," I called to her. "I didn't mean that," then turned my attention back to the bills. When I finally came to bed two hours later, I found her crying. "What's wrong?" She'd been crying a lot since she got pregnant.

She looked up at me, with wet, swollen eyes. "I just know you're going to leave me," she blurted out, then buried her face in her hands and sobbed.

I wasn't ready for this discussion. Not tonight. "What in the world are you talking about?"

She caught her breath. "With all our money worries, and now with a new baby due, it's only going to get worse. You never say anything, but I know it worries you too."

I sat down on the bed. "Sure, I'm worried about the bills, Kate. But what makes you think I'll leave you?" I tried to sound calm, but mostly I was just tired. It was another exhausting day for me, and I didn't need this conversation.

"Because you say all the time you hate your job. And you hate living in Detroit. You've been all over the country. I just know some day you're going to say you can't take the pressure anymore and just leave me."

I pulled her to me. "Lots of people hate their jobs, and everyone hates living in Detroit."

Her eyes wide now, she hesitated, like the words caught in her throat. "All men leave," she sniffled, then buried her head on my chest. She felt so small, so fragile—and so frightened now.

I gently stroked her hair, like I did so many times when we talked in bed. "I'm not like most men. You know what kind of family I came from. You and Susan—and our baby now, you're the only real family I've ever known."

"That's why I'm so scared, Daniel. You never had a family, so why should you stay with us now?" she wept even harder as she sunk deeper into my arms. Her heart pounded against my chest.

"That's exactly why I will stay, Kate," I said and held her tighter, hoping that would somehow calm her. "You're what I've been looking for all my life. I'm not going to leave you now just because I'm worried about money. I love you too much. Do you believe me?"

"I want to..." Her voice quivered, "...but I'm so scared."

I didn't know what else to say. In my family words were used like weapons to chip away the wall we all built around us. Words were meant to hurt, not heal. What could I say? I held her close in my arms and whispered what she needed to hear. "All I know, Kate, is my heart would break into a million pieces without you." She didn't say anything, but she didn't let go of me all night.

We didn't talk about my job, or the bills, or anything else that upset her after that. Instead we drove to Oakland Wilderness after church on Sunday. That was our sanctuary, the one place we all felt free to be a family again. "Are you sure you're okay here by yourself," I asked Kate when we parked the car.

"My ankles are too swollen to walk," she said. "I'll just sit here with the windows open and breathe in all the fresh air. I'll be fine, but you and Susan go on and enjoy yourselves." It was September and the first hint of fall was in the air. I always loved September, even more than spring. To me September was never the end of something, but a new beginning. September was when I started college and when I met Doc Samuels my sophomore year. September was when I got a second chance on that bridge. I married Kate in September. And now this was September again, our first anniversary together. "Breathe it all in," I called back as Susan and I walked down the trail.

"I hope Mommy is having a girl. Then I can play with her like I do my dolls," she said when we stopped to look at a solitary bent tree at the top of a barren rock mound in the distance. It had grown at an angle from the persistent winds that blew from the west and across that hill-top, and now its long branches waved awkwardly, a deformed but defiant gesture of survival. I always liked that tree from the first time I saw it, as if I could understand how it felt growing there against impossible odds.

"I think that's a great idea, Susan, but won't that leave me outnumbered in the house?"

"What do you mean, Daniel? I mean, Dad." She had been calling me that a lot since I started the adoption process last month. Susan probably felt we were a real family now, too.

"There are already two girls in the house. If your mommy has another girl, that will make three of you and only one of me. That doesn't sound very fair, does it?"

"I guess not... but I still want a sister."

"Okay, Susan. We'll both pray for a sister for you."

On Thanksgiving Day Kate gave birth to a beautiful seven-pound, six-ounce healthy boy. I was there when the nurse first handed him to her. She wrapped her arms around him and buried her nose against his face, her eyes closed as she breathed in his scent. "I want to name him Jonathan," she whispered, holding him up to me for the first time. "It means 'God's gift,' because he's our reminder that we've been given a new life together."

I never thought much about a name for our baby. All I wanted to do was hold him close to me, kiss his perfect skin, and breathe in his fragrance. "I can feel his heartbeat, Kate!" I said as I held him against my chest. "He feels so... so helpless." I kissed his right cheek, his left, then his forehead again and again. "I'll always be here for you, Jonathan. I promise," I whispered in his ear.

Kate watched me, tears running down her cheeks. "I know you'll never leave me now, Daniel." She held out her arms to both of us. "I can see it in your eyes when you look at our new son."

I kissed her, then Jonathan again. "We're a family, Kate. We're going to be okay now."

On Monday morning, I accepted that office job.

———

It took me nearly two years to finally get caught up on all our bills, and we even had a little money in the savings account now. Best of all, right after Jonathan's second birthday, Kate announced she was pregnant again!

"Oh Mommy, I know it's going to be a girl this time. I just know it!" Susan squealed. I didn't care. All I knew I was going to be a father again!

I was so happy, for a few minutes at least, because I almost forgot about the Cossack. That's what I called Ivan Volkov, my short, stocky boss at the office. He came from somewhere in Russia thirty years ago and acted like he was still running a Siberian gulag. He had a wide, pale face, red nose and bleary, dull eyes that I had seen too many times in Clairton. His hair was gray-speckled and cut short in no apparent style. He often came to work unshaven, a foul-smelling cigarette dangling from his mouth, and wearing a wrinkled suit that looked slept in. I thought it ironic Detroit's largest uniform company was owned by someone who looked like the men in Elijah's mission.

But now that I was a route supervisor and working alongside him every day, especially when he was drinking, all I heard was my old man, but with a Russian accent. "Where fookin' report I ned?" It didn't matter he forgot to tell me about it until that morning. The first time it happened, I didn't know what to say, so I apologized. But he only pounded my desk and screamed, "Don't abologize, goddammit. Just ghet dun." I tried to complain—once, but he just waived his hand in the air and said, "Yuh khan kwit!" But I couldn't quit—not with a family to support now.

Slowly, one day, one week, one month after another, Ivan's rants weighed down on me more until I felt I couldn't breathe. Being home at night with Kate and the kids was the only thing that made my job tolerable.

"It's nearly midnight, Daniel. I didn't hear you come in?" Kate said when she found me watching the kids sleep from their bedroom door. "Are you okay?"

"Just thinking," I said, still staring at them. The only thing I ever wanted my entire life was a family. And now I had that, but I never saw them anymore. Instead I felt adrift in an ocean of abuse that washed over me every single day at work.

"Oh!" she cooed as she wrapped her arms around me. "I just felt the baby move."

"That's all that matters, Kate," I said, but I wanted to say so much more to her. I just couldn't. Not now.

I wrapped an arm around her. "Just thinking we need to look for a bigger house."

"Oh, Daniel, I'd love that, but can we afford to move?"

I patted her belly. "We really don't have a choice, do we?"

A month later Kate and I found a perfect three-bedroom house in the same neighborhood for just $100 more a month, and it even had a fireplace! "I know this is going to be our best year ever," she said when we signed the new lease.

"I hope so, Kate." But hope could be a delicate thing, and easily damaged if handled too much.

I never paid much attention to politics, not since Kent State. So when Kate mentioned something about protesters taking over our embassy in Iran, I didn't think much about it. That was six-thousand miles away and didn't affect me. When President Carter declared an embargo on all the oil from Iran two months later, I ignored it. But when gas lines formed all over Detroit and Ivan screamed that my drivers weren't making their deliveries on time... "Where the hell is Iran?" I yelled at my secretary. Now this dot on the map, in the middle of nowhere, that I never heard of before, was the only thing I worried about all day, every day, while I frantically tried to keep my trucks on the road.

When summer finally arrived in early June, I hardly noticed. It was just another exhausting week for me stuck inside my windowless office listening to the Cossack scream at everyone. There were plenty of days when I missed the peace and solitude of my route truck. There were no rantings from Ivan, no calls from angry customers, no mindless chatter from the dozen people sharing my office, no perchloroethylene from the plant constantly choking my lungs.

When I got home one Saturday near midnight, Kate found me again standing in the darkened hall by the kids' new bedrooms. "Are you okay?" she asked.

"I was just thinking how much they've grown this year. Susan will be going into the third grade this fall... and God, Jonathan is nearly three now. They're both growing so fast...and I haven't been here for them..." I wanted to say I couldn't tell where my work ended and I began anymore. It all blurred together, and everything seemed so gray, undefined, and terrifying, because this wasn't how I wanted to spend my life. But I had no choice. I had a family who depended on me, who needed me to go to work every day, no matter how hard it was. This was my life now. I didn't say anything.

When our new baby was finally born in August, I barely made it to the hospital in time. There was no gas anywhere in the city and our customers were all screaming for their uniforms to be delivered yesterday or they would tear up our contract. Ivan was drinking more than ever, threatening to fire everyone of us if we didn't "get fookin' johb dohn." That was his answer for everything. When Kate called and

285

said Pam was taking her to the hospital now, I had to sneak out the back door of the plant so he wouldn't see me leaving. I didn't need another fight with him, not now. Not ever.

"A girl!" Kate gently kissed our new baby on the forehead, then handed her to me. "She has your blue eyes, Daniel. And she looks so happy, doesn't she?"

For the past two years I felt like a man who had been half-asleep, moving in blurred motion, unmoored from those who anchored my life and gave it meaning. And now holding my new baby girl in my arms, I felt all those long-buried emotions well up in my throat. "I want to name her Emma," I said and kissed her gently on the forehead.

"Why Emma?" Kate asked, genuinely surprised. This was not something we had discussed. We hadn't discussed anything lately.

"That was my grandmother's name." I wiped my eyes.

"You never mentioned your grandmother before, Daniel."

"There's not much in Clairton I like to talk about. But I do remember... I don't know how old I was, maybe five or six... my mother sometimes took us to my grandmother's house to get away from the old man. She had blue eyes, just like me and Mum. And she always made us this special cake with wild raspberries that grew behind her house. It only happened a couple times because she died when I was pretty young, but that raspberry cake at my grandmother's house is probably my only good memory growing up. And when I saw our baby's blue eyes, I just thought of my grandmother... and Mum." *What would she think about naming her Emma? Where is she now? Is she...better?* I shook my head and handed the baby back to her. "But it's not really that important. Whatever you want to name her is okay with me."

She pulled me close and kissed me gently. "I think Emma is a beautiful name for our baby."

———

I promised I would take time off from work when they both came home from the hospital, but there was another crisis at the plant. One of my drivers quit unexpectedly and I had to run his route all day, then do all my office work until midnight. I complained repeatedly to Ivan, and he promised to hire a new driver, but one week led to another, then another, and by the end of the month, I was putting in eighteen hours every day.

"I can't take it anymore, Kate." I collapsed on the bed beside her sometime after midnight, too exhausted to even undress. She had been in bed for hours, but never slept when I wasn't home. She turned on the lamp, then laid her arm across my chest.

"What's wrong, Daniel?"

How could I tell her the best part of my life was slipping past me... and I was losing the ones I care about most? "I took this office job when Jonathan was born. I knew it would mean a lot of hours, but we needed the money. He's nearly three now, and the only time I see him is at night when he's sleeping. Susan is growing so fast I hardly recognize her. And now with Emma..." I took a slow breath and pulled her to me. "I think what I'm saying, Kate, is I feel like I'm losing you and the kids, not because of anything bad I've done, but the good thing I'm doing all wrong. Does that make any sense?"

"I don't understand," she exhaled the words. Worry and fear mixed in her eyes.

I took another breath. "I can't really explain what I'm feeling, but I just know my old man was never there when I was a kid." I stared up at the ceiling as she took my hand and squeezed it. "I swore I'd be different. But our kids are growing up without me—just like my old man... and it's killing me, Kate. Something's gotta change. That's all I know."

"What are you trying to say?"

"I'm not sure."

Neither of us said anything for several minutes. "If you quit your job...," exhaling every word, as if they were too much for her to say out loud. "...what will you do?" She held her breath now and just looked at me... waiting.

I wasn't sure how to say it, so I just blurted it out. "I've always wanted to be a counselor, I lost track of that dream for a long time, but I think I still might like to do that?"

We both laid there holding each other, just staring at the ceiling in silence. "Why don't you call your friend Doc Samuels?" she finally said. "Maybe he can help you."

"That's a good idea, Kate," I finally said, then reached over and turned off the light. We held each other until we fell asleep.

———

To my surprise, Doc said he expected this call someday. "I never saw you as a truck driver." Just hearing his voice again gave me hope. For the first time in nearly three years, I could breathe.

"The good news is you've got most of your grad work done already. Where was it, Case Western? But you really need a PhD to get a counseling job that can support a family. But that could take four years or more, and full time. It's a pretty rigorous program."

I felt my excitement evaporate.

"But there is another option," he said.

I held my breath.

"A growing field actually. Pastoral counseling."

Silence for a long minute.

"I know what you're thinking, Daniel. Too many ghosts in the church," Doc finally said. "But think of it this way. What I'm doing is pastoral counseling. Do you think you could do what I'm doing?"

"You mean like a college counselor?"

"Maybe, but not necessarily. Remember I started out as a missionary in India. I've never talked much about it, but I had my share of ghosts in the church too, and not just that boarding school I told you about. But eventually all that led me here. Pastoral counseling for you might be in some college, or it might be in some ghetto church like Nick. As long as you feel you're helping people, that's all that matters, isn't it?"

I remembered all those afternoons in his office. All those times he helped me when I was so alone and so desperate. He was the reason I walked away from that bridge. He saved my life again and again. *Could I help somebody like Doc helped me?*

Something's gotta change. That's what I told Kate. For our family... for her and the kids... and for me too...

Over the next several months I called him nearly every day with a growing list of questions.

What school do you suggest? How will I pay for it? How long will it take to get my degree? What sort of classes will I need?

And the most important question, *How will I support my family while I'm in school?*

He suggested United Seminary in Dayton, Ohio, because it had a program that would accept my classes from Case Western. "All you'll need are some specialty courses and you can probably get your degree in a year or so. And they might even allow you to pastor a small church while you're in school," he said. "It won't pay much, but often you're provided free housing, so you won't starve until you get your degree."

———

In early December, I drove to Dayton to meet Marvin Nicholson and ask him about a student assignment. He was the superintendent for the Western Ohio District of the United Methodist Church. When I entered his office, he just motioned toward a chair in front of his desk. He looked to be in his early fifties. His graying hair was cut short, but still parted carefully on the left side in a military style. His dark suit was pressed perfectly, not one wrinkle. But it was his eyes I noticed most. He never looked directly at me, even when he shook my hand feebly. I got the impression he wasn't comfortable with people.

Everything in his office seemed to be placed carefully in order. The wall behind his desk was decorated sparsely, with only a single formal photo of him with another clergy that might be the bishop. Shelves covered the walls on both sides of the room. They were filled with perfectly lined books. His oak desk was polished and bare, except for a photo of several unsmiling children I assumed were his grandkids.

He pulled out several manila folders from a file cabinet and placed them on his desk. "I'm afraid there aren't a lot of churches available, not until the summer at least." He thumbed through the folders without looking up at me. "If you could wait for a year, I'm sure I could find a suitable church for you, especially when you have your degree finished."

"I'm afraid not, sir. I've got a wife and three kids, so I need to work. David Samuels—he's my mentor from college. He said there might be a small church I could pastor while I'm in school."

"Normally we'd have something. There are a lot of small congregations in the area that can only afford a student pastor. But like I said, if you could wait, at least until June..."

June? What now?

He shuffled through the folders a second time, rubbing his chin in thought. "The Salem Hill Church is open again," he said, pulling out a thick, worn folder from the back of the cabinet drawer. "That's in Shawnee County, about halfway between here and Cincinnati. It's a small congregation, but there are about 15,000 people in the town. I'm sure you could grow the church with a little extra effort."

"Why do I have the feeling there's more to this story?"

"May I be candid, Daniel? It's not an easy church. It has a history of conflict. To be honest, nobody wants it. But it's all I have available. Are you interested?"

I didn't hesitate. "Yes, sir, I am."

"Good. I'll start the paperwork in the morning."

I stood up and was about to leave when Superintendent Nicholson said something, almost as an afterthought. "It means peace."

"What does, sir?"

"Salem Hill. It means peace in Hebrew. I think it'll be a good town for you."

"So do I, sir."

CHAPTER 20
LET THE WIND OF CHANGE CARRY US

SALEM HILL, OHIO, 1981. We drove into Salem Hill at the beginning of January. Several inches of fresh clean snow layered the ground, but the sun was shining and everything glistened. It looked just like the new beginning we hoped it would be.

"It's absolutely beautiful, Daniel. I love it here," Kate said looking all around as we drove.

On the edge of town we passed a large factory. 'Crown Glass Company' was emblazoned in large letters on the gate. Cars filled the whole parking lot.

"Even the factories are clean here," I said.

We were driving past what must be the city park when Kate pointed toward a hill in the distance. "Look, Daniel. See all those kids sledding!"

"Can we go there, Mommy? Please?" Susan and Jonathan both chimed in at once.

"Maybe tomorrow," she said. "After we get the truck unloaded."

I couldn't help smiling as I watched Kate talk with the kids like this. *I only wish I had that with my mother. If only...* I shook that thought out of my head. Our new adventure excited me as much as the kids, and the last thing I needed now was dwelling on the past. "Let's drive through downtown and see what it looks like too, Kate. What do you say?"

We drove west past the park on Main Street. The trees gave way to large homes on both sides of the street. "They remind me of the houses I told you about in San Francisco. You know, the ones James loved so much."

"They are beautiful, Daniel," she said staring out the window.

We turned onto Broadway into the downtown business district. "I know where the kids will want to go," I said pointing at Jenkins Ice Cream Shoppe. "Look. At the end of the block. There's a movie theater, too."

For just a second, I thought again of my mother, what she would think of Salem Hill... what she would think of my family.

"What's that huge stone building in the center of town, Daniel? The one with the bell tower on top."

I pushed that thought quickly out of my head. "Looks like city hall. Impressive, isn't it?"

"What did you say Superintendent Nicholson called this town?" she asked.

"The city of peace."

Kate turned toward me, her rust colored hair glinting in the sunlight. "I think we're going to do just fine here," she said, smiling. She never looked more beautiful to me.

———

"You must be Daniel Robinson. I'm Roberta Stewart and I'm on the church board." She met me in front of the parsonage right after we arrived. "I wanted to be the first to meet our new pastor." She appeared to be in her late forties, though it was hard to tell with the winter hat she wore pulled down on her forehead, and especially the makeup that seemed too heavy. Her coat looked expensive, but barely warm enough to fend off the cold wind. I got the impression she wore it today for my benefit, rather than comfort.

"Glad to be here, Mrs. Stewart."

"It's just Roberta. We're like family here in Salem Hill," she replied, eyeing our furniture as it was carried into the house by some of the men from the church.

For some reason I thought she had been sent here to inspect the new pastor. She probably would be calling everyone with her report as soon as she got home. "Then I'm just Daniel. And this is my wife Kate. That's Susan, our oldest on the porch. She's eight. Jonathan is the one in the red hat. He's three. And that is our baby, Emma." I pointed toward the blanketed bundle in Kate's arms. She's just six months old."

She glanced in Kate's direction, but didn't even look at the kids. "Superintendent Nicholson tells me you're from Michigan. What part?" she asked instead.

"Detroit. I was in business there."

"What brought you to Ohio?"

"It's a long story." I didn't think she'd be interested in hearing about James or Daequan, and especially Mellow and Sunshine!

"I'd love to hear your story," she answered, but I had the feeling she was hoping to flush out any hidden secrets. I chose my words carefully. "I always wanted to be a counselor. So when pastoral counseling was suggested, I ended up at United Seminary."

"Well, Pastor, we're all really glad to have you here." She seemed disappointed there wasn't any salacious gossip to pass through the church. "I just don't know how much counseling you'll be able to do. People in our church all seem pretty normal to me."

I thought she was kidding, but she didn't smile. "After living in Detroit, it'll be nice to be with normal people again," was all I could think to say.

———

Roberta Stewart was right. The only counseling call I got was from a mother in the congregation asking if I could help her son with his application to Ohio State University. So my time was spent visiting with my church members and talking about the weather, something everyone complained about in Ohio, just like they did in Michigan. We sometimes talked about the high school football team. "Next year we'll have a winning season," they all said. But I never much cared for football, so I just nodded and tried to look interested. Mostly what we talked about, especially with the older members, was their ailments.

"Just a lot of talk about nothing," I complained to Kate. "It seems like a waste of time."

"Be patient," was all she said.

"What do you mean by that?"

"I mean you're expecting people to tell you their personal thoughts and feelings, but they don't even know you."

I was hoping for a little support, not criticism.

"Let me put it this way," Kate said, ignoring my irritated look. "When you first met Doc Samuels, what did you talk about?"

"My classes. But what's your point?" The conversation was really beginning to upset me now.

"My point is you didn't talk about anything personal with Doc until you developed a relationship with him. And that took a lot of conversations about your classes—about nothing according to your definition."

I remembered all those times in Doc's office.

"How long was it before you felt safe enough to talk about your family, or Elizabeth? And especially that awful pastor of yours?"

She was right. "Okay. You win." I mumbled.

She smiled.

———

I didn't tell Kate there was something else about the church that bothered me even more. From my first conversation with Doc Samuels, my intent was to focus on counseling. Yet even with a student church like this one, the people still expected I would offer them the assurance of unquestioned belief in God—like I had growing up in the Clairton Baptist Church. But where was God when the old man broke Billy's arm? Hiding in the bedroom with Mum? Where was God when Pastor Duncan 'prayed' all over me? And what about all those times I begged God for some sign I wasn't alone? I got nothing but silence. What can I say on Sunday mornings about a God like this? How do I tell them I had more questions about what I believed than answers? And that made my role as a leader in the Salem Hill United Methodist Church... uncomfortable at best.

It was early March when I stopped at the Shawnee County library for a book, and I noticed a woman playing in the corner with her son.

Their clothes were dirty, and not nearly warm enough for the freezing temperatures. The boy looked to be the same age as Susan. There were also several bags on the floor behind them. The woman, probably his mother, opened one of the bags and removed first a notebook, then a pencil, and finally something to eat, giving each one to the boy. When he was done with each item, he would give it back to her, and she carefully returned it to the bag, pulling the cinch tight. The affectionate look she gave him as he drew in his notebook... I felt a sudden pull in my chest. Did Mum ever look at me like that?

I blinked—and I was back in the library. Were they homeless? They didn't seem like the people I saw in Elijah's Mission. I got the impression being on the street was new to them, and they were trying desperately to maintain some degree of normal living.

"Do you know anything about that woman? The one with the boy?" I asked the librarian.

"I think they're homeless," she whispered, as if embarrassed to even say the word. She motioned for me to come into her office. "I've seen them here a lot since the cold weather hit last week," she said in a hushed tone. "Some of our patrons have complained because we're getting so many of those people here now."

I thought of Sister Rose, and I wanted to ask if she meant those *homeless* people or those *black* people, but I let it go. For now.

"I feel bad for the boy," she said, as if that somehow made her comment okay, "but I don't know what I can do to help."

"Maybe I have an idea." I walked over to them.

"I don't mean to intrude, but my wife and I were supposed to meet a couple friends at Bob Evans for dinner." The woman stiffened as she looked up at me. Neither she nor her son said anything. "We had gift certificates given to us, but they can't make it, and they expire today. I hate to see them go to waste, and we don't want to eat alone. So I was wondering if you and... is this your boy?"

The woman nodded, but still didn't say anything.

"I was wondering if you and your son would like to keep us company for dinner. Our treat."

The woman stared hard at me, as if considering her words, until the boy pulled on her sleeve and nodded several times. "The boy might like dinner," she finally said. "I appreciate the offer."

"Great. Just wait here and I'll go get my wife. She's expecting me. Then all of us can drive to dinner together. It looks like it might rain soon."

She glanced out the window. "Okay."

Neither of them said much at Bob Evans, not until they had devoured fried chicken, potatoes, green beans, two baskets of rolls and several pieces of pumpkin pie. Then the conversation flowed. She said her name was Lettie Davis. "And this is my boy, Damien. He'll be nine next week."

"Glad to meet you, Damien." I shook his hand, but he barely looked up at me. "I've got a daughter about your age, in the third grade. What grade are you in?"

"Fourth." He looked at his mother, who nodded. "I like school a lot, but I'm not going right now 'cause we got kicked out of our house..." Lettie cleared her throat and the boy hushed.

"Damien does real good in school, but sometimes he talks too much," she said. For a moment, neither of them said anything.

Better change the subject. "Based on your accent, my guess is you and Damien aren't from around here."

"No sir, at least not originally. We came from a little town in Alabama called Marion about two years ago. There wasn't much work in all of Perry County, least not for black folks, so Antoine, that's my husband, he brought us north so he could find a job." She handed the last roll to Damien. "And he got a factory job right away. Good job, too, making parts for cars. But it didn't pay much, not at first. That's when I got a job as a waitress, you know, to help with bills. And we thought we was going to be okay... then Antoine got the cancer..." The words seemed to catch in her throat. "He died right after Christmas."

There was nothing I could say, so I just nodded. Rain started falling.

"Me and Damien were just getting over his death when I got fired at the restaurant. They said I missed too much work. But I couldn't help it." Her face was solemn, yet filled with sorrow and anger. "Antoine was so sick and he needed me with him. I told my boss that, but he fired me anyway. I been looking for work since then, but I ain't had no luck. Then we got kicked out of my apartment..."

"Where are you living?" Kate asked. That rain wasn't going to let up anytime soon.

"Here and there. Wherever we can find a place."

I remembered walking those streets in San Francisco, digging through garbage cans for food, sleeping in the park. Those were lost, alone days... But Elijah offered me a safe place to stay. "What are you going to do?"

"Don't know. I can survive, but I'm worried for my boy." There was fear in the set of her jaw, but beneath it, a determination... a protectiveness, almost. There was nothing she wouldn't do for her boy. I could see it.

"Damn you, William!" Mum smashed a lamp on the old man's head.

I blinked again. *Not now. Focus on her!* I looked out the window, then toward Kate. The rain had now turned to snow. She nodded.

"Listen Lettie," she said, "we might have something temporary for you."

That night Lettie and her son moved into the basement of our house. The next morning Damien enrolled in the Salem Hill Elementary School, and by evening Roberta Stewart was on the phone asking if it was true that I had a *colored* family living in the parsonage. "I know adjusting to life in a small town like ours can be difficult, Pastor, but I do need to remind you this is not Michigan. We're good Christian people here who like things to change slowly, if you know what I mean."

"I know exactly what you mean." I felt my face heat. "But actually, it wasn't a family. Just a woman and her son... and it was snowing when I saw them in the library..."

There was a heavy silence for a minute, but it seemed like forever. "My God... Do you mean you brought a colored woman into our house..." It wasn't really a question at all. She nearly shouted the words over the line.

"What do you suggest I should have done? Let them freeze to death on the streets?"

"Of course not, Pastor. But bringing them here to Salem Hill, *in the church's house*... People will talk..." She nearly hissed.

"But they were homeless," I protested. "Kate and I *both* felt it was the right thing to do." I felt my face grow even hotter. "It's only until she gets a job."

"I just think they would be more comfortable with their own kind. That's all." All I heard was Principal Jackson.

I wanted to tell her who we invited into our house was my business. I wanted to tell her she was a bigoted hypocrite. But I just hung up the phone.

The church board called an emergency meeting the next evening and Superintendent Nicholson was asked to attend. Although he applauded what he called my "Christian charity," he suggested I should have considered other housing options "better suited for a single woman in Dayton." His implication was clear—and the board agreed. A vote was called and a resolution approved unanimously. Use of all church property, including the parsonage, would first have to be approved by the board. "To maintain the integrity of the neighborhood," declared Jane Thornhill, the board chairman. Her husband was Dennis Thornhill, the manager of the Crown Glass Company, and the largest employer in town. They were generally thought to be the biggest donors in the church.

I walked out of that meeting feeling like I was in an alien country where they were speaking a different language. All I felt was alone—and angry. "Dammit, Kate!" I shouted and slammed my notebook on the kitchen table when I got home. "I know what it's like to be homeless. I know what it's like to be hungry. If Elijah hadn't helped me, I might not be alive today. But Reverend Nicholson and the board said Lettie and Damien can't stay here. They said they have to leave!"

I felt terrible when those two men beat on me in that alley. But this felt far worse, like they beat on my soul. That same fear and rage welled up in my throat as I looked at Kate. "I tried to do the right thing. I tried to do what so many people did for me. But where was God tonight? Tell me that, Kate."

Her face hardened as her cup shook in her hand. "Damn those people!" she said through clenched teeth. "That could have been me and

Susan sitting in the corner of some library in Detroit... The only difference is she's black... and I met Pastor Nick..."

We both stood there, too angry to say anything. Finally, she pulled me close and wrapped her arms around me. "Believe me," she whispered. "God had nothing to do with that meeting."

We just held each other in silence.

"What are you going to do?" she finally asked.

I knew what I wanted to do. "I'd love to quit... but I can't. At least not yet. We've got three kids to think about... and I still need to finish my degree. Maybe then, when we're more stable, I can transfer to another church where I don't have to put up with this bullshit."

"But what about Lettie and Damien? How are you going to tell them?"

I thought a lot about that since the meeting ended, and I had an idea. "The board didn't actually say they had to move out *right now*. Maybe if Lettie can get a job, maybe at some restaurant in town. I thought I saw a couple places that were hiring."

"That might work," Kate said. "Then we can help them get their own apartment." For the first time since I got that call from Roberta Stewart, I felt hopeful... but I didn't say anything to Lettie. Not yet.

Danny's Family Restaurant on Broadway and the Dew Drop Inn both had 'Help Wanted' signs in their windows. But once they saw Lettie, both managers said the positions were filled. We even tried to apply at Crown Glass, but the guard said they weren't hiring anybody either. By the time we picked up Damien at school, Lettie had applied at a dozen places, but couldn't find a job anywhere in Salem Hill. A week later I bought them both a bus ticket back to Marion, Alabama. Lettie's face had been blank as she thanked me, her voice hollow, but all I saw was my mother when she got into that ambulance back to Woodville. Now here were two more people I had failed.

"I just wish I could have done more," was all I could say that night. The silence that followed pressed down on both of us. For the first time in a long while, Daequan was back in my dreams.

———

After that I tried not to think about Lettie and just focus on my classes, avoid any more conflict and bide my time until I finished my degree. But it wasn't easy. I kept seeing them again in my mind, so alone except for each other. Over and over, Lettie's sad face climbing up those steps into that bus...

Mum, where are you? Are you okay?

Meanwhile, attendance increased a little each week. By the end of my first six months, we averaged ninety people every Sunday. "A twenty percent increase!" Jane Thornhill announced to the congregation.

That night when I climbed into bed, Kate asked what I thought about Mrs. Thornhill's announcement.

I didn't answer. She slid next to me and pulled me close. "That was good news about the attendance, wasn't it?"

"The attendance? Yeah, that's good, I guess."

"What's wrong, Daniel? You act like you're not even listening."

"Sorry, Kate. I've just had something on my mind lately. That's all."

"You're not second guessing what you did for Lettie again, are you?"

I sighed. "I don't think I'll ever be able to let that go, completely. But besides that... Lettie and Damien have been reminding me of something... someone."

She reached over and turned on the lamp. I looked toward her and took her hand.

"Ever since I saw them, I've been thinking more and more about my mother. Lettie's story about her husband... the way she looked at her son... It all reminded me time is short. And my mother—well, I remember her face when Robert left her... and especially when they took Billy away. You know, maybe if I had stayed with her, maybe she might not have gone back to Woodville."

"Daniel, you were just sixteen. There was nothing you could have done."

"I know you're right, but I still wish I did more."

"Do you know where your mother is...or if she's even alive?"

"No. But I was thinking of calling my Aunt Mary. You know, she's the woman who took in Billy. Maybe she might know something about my mother. What do you think?"

She sat up in the bed and looked at me with a hundred questions in her eyes now. We sat there quietly for a while. "How many years has it been since you saw her?" she finally asked. "Do you even know where she lives now, or even how to contact her?"

I slid out a note pad from the nightstand drawer. "I called information a couple days ago. You know, just to see if she still lived at the same address in Pittsburgh." I opened the note pad. "She's still there. And here's her number." I looked at Kate and waited, anxious for her to say something, anything, now.

"I think you should call her," she said, as if that settled it.

"What should I say? I mean, it's been seventeen years." I put my arm around Kate and pulled her to me. "What I really mean is I'd like to have you with me... if I call her. I don't know if I'm strong enough to bring back all those memories...at least not without you."

She squeezed my hand. "When can we call her?"

———

The call started off awkward, and my first impulse was to hang up, but I met Kate's eyes and took a deep breath. "I'm married now...with three kids," I said.

"That's good." Aunt Mary sounded just as uncomfortable as me.

"I guess why I called..." I spoke slowly now, trying to gather my strength. "I...ah... wanted to find out about Mum."

She didn't say anything, and my words echoed in the silence. I held my breath.

"Your mother is still alive, Daniel," she finally said, and I heaved a relieved sigh. Kate nodded, reading my look. "But she's not well."

"You mean..." Aunt Mary must have known what I was thinking.

"No, not that. She hasn't been back to Woodville for years. I mean her health isn't good."

"Aunt Mary?"

"Cancer."

I felt the blood drain from my face. Kate pulled her chair next to me. "What is it?" she whispered.

"Cancer," I mumbled.

"But I think she'd love to see you," Aunt Mary quickly added, as if trying to somehow soften her news. It didn't. "She's in a nursing home in Pittsburgh."

My mind reeled. I felt elated and devastated at the same time. Without even thinking, I heard myself ask, "What about Robert? Where is he?"

She didn't answer.

"Is he okay?"

My question drifted in the air.

"Aunt Mary?"

"I'm sorry, Daniel," she finally said. "He was killed in Vietnam..." I slumped back in my chair. I didn't know what to think or feel. I hadn't thought much about Robert all these years, but hearing now that he was dead... the air still drained from me. "...I wanted to tell you when it happened, but I didn't know where you were."

"What is it?" Kate mouthed. I shook my head toward her. "Killed in Vietnam," I whispered.

She shook her head, squeezing my hand. The solidness of her touch calmed me.

"What about Billy?" I asked. "Is he still living with you?"

The silence that followed pressed hard on my chest. I didn't know if I could handle any more bad news. "Aunt Mary?"

Her voice was barely audible now. "He hasn't lived with me for eight years."

"Do you know where he is?" I asked. "I'd like to see him too, you know, when I come to Pittsburgh."

I could hear her breathing. "I'm not sure how to say this, but Billy was in and out of jail a lot. But a year ago, after he got out the last time, he left for Florida. He always said he wanted to live by the ocean. And I got a letter from him once, but I don't know if he still lives there. I'm sorry, Daniel."

We were never close growing up. I mean, we were all just trying to survive. But they were the only brothers I had. "If you ever do hear from him, tell him to call me... please. Tell him I'd really like to talk to him." It was all I could think to say.

I hung up the phone and reached out for Kate. For half my life, I felt like I lost my family. Then for a couple minutes I thought I found them, and maybe we could somehow be together again—but I was wrong.

———

The lobby reeked of urine and disinfectant. I looked around the room for a nurse, an orderly, anyone who could tell me where my mother was. On the left side seemed to be a waiting room, illuminated with what looked to be a dozen obscenely bright fluorescent bulbs that surely were intended to make it feel warm, but only looked harsh. There were several chairs and a few tables, with an old RCA television in the corner. A couple people were staring at it, but they didn't seem to be watching, or even caring what was on the screen. We walked down the hall to the right and found several people sitting in wheelchairs. I started to ask them if they knew where my mother's room was, but they only stared up at us with blank, unseeing eyes. *Does my mother look like this now? What will I say to her?* With every step my mind raced with more questions.

"Aunt Mary said her room is B31. Do you have any idea where that is, Kate? God, does anyone work here?"

Finally, I gave up trying to find someone to help us and walked down a hall, hoping it was the right one. As we passed several open doors, I noticed the bare rooms had two beds, where small, frail people lay sleeping, or just staring at the ceiling. I wasn't sure I could go through with it now. Kate noticed and took my arm as we walked. That helped—a little.

"There's B corridor, Daniel." She pointed to the hallway on the right. "I think room 31 is at the other end."

I took several deep breaths as we walked, but it didn't help. My heart pounded harder with each step.

"Do you want me to go in with you?" Kate asked when we reached her room. I just grabbed her hand for support. Then with another deep breath, I opened the door slowly.

A woman sat by the window, staring out at the parking lot.

Her hair was gray, but Mum's was turning gray when I last saw her. Living with the old man can do that. But this lady was thin, too thin.

She looked frail, a lot older than Mum's fifty-nine years. *Will she even recognize me?*

"Mum?" My voice shook.

Slowly, she turned. Her blue eyes were the same as I always remembered. "Daniel!" she said and held up her arms.

I quickly walked across the room and wrapped my arms around her. We both cried as she patted my back, then stroked my hair. She weighed half what I did, but I felt so small in her arms. The only words that could describe what I felt now were grief and guilt and regret, all mixed together into a weight that squeezed the air out of me. I should have done something, anything, to help her... but I didn't.

"I'm sorry, Mum," I choked out.

She didn't say anything, but just held me like I always wanted her to do when I was growing up.

"I'm so sorry." I said again.

She took both my hands in hers. Her face had aged so much over the years. "Now why are you saying that, Daniel?"

"I'm sorry I wasn't stronger for you..."

"Daniel." Her hand traced gentle strokes on my cheek. "I'm the one who's sorry. I should have been stronger. I should have been there for you."

I wrapped my arms around her frail body and whispered, "I guess we both can start over now, can't we, Mum?"

"I hope so, Daniel." was all she said, but to me, it was volumes.

Kate stood by the door the whole time, watching us with a quiet smile.

"And who is that beautiful girl with you, Daniel?"

"That's Kate, Mum. We've been married for nearly four years."

Kate came across the room and hugged my mother.

"Thank you for loving my son." Mum said.

"Thank you for giving him to me."

I was so excited now, for a minute I even forgot about the cancer. "And we have three kids!" I said. "Susan, Jonathan and Emma. We named her after grandma."

"Emma? Oh, Daniel..." Her eyes filled as a tear ran down her cheek.

"I can't wait for you to meet all of them." I squeezed both her hands in mine.

"I can't wait to meet them, too. Now you both sit here and tell me all about them."

All we talked about our whole drive back to Salem Hill that night was my mother. "I feel like I've been given a second chance with her. Like we can be a normal family. At least until...." The words caught in my throat. "Now that I've found her, I don't think I can handle losing her again."

It was dark in the car, but I knew Kate saw the tears in my eyes...and I didn't even try to hide them. She squeezed my hand. "You won't be alone this time."

Dear Billy,

I'll bet you're surprised to hear from me. Aunt Mary told me you were living in Florida, but she wasn't sure you were still at this address. She also told me about Robert.

I guess that's the reason I'm writing you, because I want to... you know, start over. That's why I went to visit Mum with my family. Surprise! I'm married—and I have three kids now. I'd love for you to meet them if you're ever in Ohio. So if you get this letter, write me back. I'd love to talk with you again. We can... well, maybe our family can have a second chance.

I tore up the letter and started over again—for the tenth time. I didn't know what to say. I didn't know what I could say. Dear God, please give us a second chance.

Church attendance dropped that summer. The new families who came when I first arrived all moved on to bigger churches with more to offer. At the next board meeting, Jane Thornhill suggested I join both the local Rotary and the Kiwanis to get more people to come here. I did, but I felt I didn't fit in, no matter how hard I tried. I got the impression there was a long list of pastors before me who were told to fish for new members there. After the third meeting I found myself sitting alone.

I tried to forget about Jane Thornhill and the church by taking another trip to see my mother. This time we took the kids with us. All they talked about was meeting her, and the closer we got to Pittsburgh, the more questions they had.

"What does Grandma look like?"

"Will she know who I am?"

"Why haven't we met her before?"

"How long 'til we get there?"

By the time we reached the nursing home, I was exhausted—but excited. Mum was waiting for us when we walked in her room. She looked like she just had her hair done, and she appeared much younger this time. She seemed to come alive with the kids.

"I'm very glad to meet you, Grandma," Susan said, hugging her. "And I made this for you." She handed her a large crayon drawing of all six of us holding hands together. Mum cried.

"And this is Jonathan. He'll be four this November." Susan pointed toward her brother.

"Nice to meet you, Grandma," he said, holding out his hand to her, just like Kate taught him to do all week.

"My, aren't you the most handsome boy I ever saw. You look just like your daddy when he was your age."

"Would you like to hold Emma, Grandma?" Kate asked. "But she's getting pretty big now, so if you want me to hold her for you, that's okay."

"I've waited too long to hold a baby again, dear. Hand her to me."

The time passed too soon, and all of us hated for our visit to end, especially me. "Something I want to ask before we go, Mum," I said, hugging her one last time. "I know raising three boys was never easy. So how does it feel to have three girls in the family now?"

"It feels wonderful, Daniel. Just wonderful."

The kids slept most of the trip home while all I thought about was Mum... until I reached Salem Hill and found a half dozen complaints from Jane Thornhill on my answering machine. I ignored all of them, wrapping myself with the warm memory of our time with Mum.

———

It was sometime in early October. I was sitting at the kitchen table reading the newspaper, when Kate handed me a letter, postmarked Florida. My hand shook as I opened it.

Daniel,

Thank you for your letter...

It was hard to pick out the scratchy words. But I knew it was Billy.

...I'm glad you're married and have kids. I'm not married, but I got a girlfriend here, and a job in construction.

Thanks for asking me to meet with you, but I don't think I'll ever be in Ohio.

So good luck. And no need to write me again. What's done is done. I'm okay.

Billy

There wasn't a day these past sixteen years when I didn't wish I could somehow undo what happened to Billy. Now it was too late. Some things could never be made right. I hoped they could, but hope is such a fragile thing.

I gave the letter to Kate without a word. She read through it quickly, then slid a chair next to me and took my arm.

"I'm so sorry, Daniel. I know how much you wanted to see your brother again. But you did write him. You did try to make it right. Sometimes that's all you can do."

"Maybe... but now I wish I never wrote to him. I mean, not hearing from him... I think that would have been easier. But knowing he doesn't want to see me..." I slumped back in my chair and dropped my head onto my chest.

Kate pulled me close and kissed me softly on the cheek. "But you changed where you came from. What happened to you and Billy won't ever happen to your kids. Sometimes that's the best we can do."

I sighed. "That's the only hope I have, Kate... But I can't do it without you." We held each other for a long, long time.

———

When it was reported at the December board meeting that attendance was still declining, Mrs. Thornhill suggested I visit all the homes in the neighborhood. "You know, invite them to church on Sunday." she said.

"You mean go door to door, like a salesman?" I didn't even try to hide my frustration.

"Not at all," she said slowly, her words oozing with condescension. "Just be a good neighbor and tell them how friendly everyone is in our church."

"Doesn't that seem a little... pushy? The only people who do that are the Jehovah Witnesses and the Mormons. I'm not really comfortable doing that."

"Let me be frank, Pastor," Mrs. Thornhill said, her voice now taking on a decidedly sharper tone. "Attendance, and offerings I might add, have been declining. We all feel it's your job to fill the pews. That is, if you want us to keep paying your salary."

I bit down hard on my lip.

The next morning Kate found me sitting alone in my church office, staring out the window.

"What's wrong, Daniel? Is it your mother?"

I motioned for her to sit in the chair next to me. "Not Mum. Visiting her has been the only thing I look forward to. It's the church. For the past year I've tried my best to fit in. You know that."

She nodded.

"But that issue with Lettie, and now what the board is telling me to do. Kate, my heart's just not in this anymore."

"But you just completed all your classes at the seminary. Are you thinking about asking for a transfer to another church?"

"I'm not sure another church would be any different."

"Then what are you thinking?" she asked, her eyes focused right on me. She held her breath.

"I don't know. That's why I wanted to talk with you."

She took my hands, like she did so many times. "What's your passion, Daniel?"

"What do you mean?"

"I mean what brought you here?"

"I thought it was counseling, but all my time is spent fighting with the board... and who have I really helped since I got here?"

"What about Lettie and her son?"

I saw them both again, boarding that Greyhound bus in Dayton, turning toward me at the last minute and waving goodbye. And going back to what? An even more hopeless future in Alabama. "Lot of good I did them."

"You got them off the street in the middle of winter, didn't you?"

I sat back and rubbed my chin like I saw Doc do so many times.

"You thought you wanted to be a counselor. It didn't work out exactly like you planned. But you got Lettie through a crisis. Isn't that what a counselor does?"

"Maybe..." I answered slowly, still thinking about what she said. "... but I should have done more." I sat there for several minutes, not saying anything. "Maybe I'm just in the wrong place," I said slowly now.

"Do you mean another church, a bigger one, near a college campus?" Kate asked.

"I don't know. There's a part of me that thinks the problem is just this church. But there's another part that says it's more than that. Like I told Doc when he first brought up this sort of counseling, I just don't know if I fit in a church. Too many ghosts." I turned and looked out the window at the dark clouds that were again forming in the sky. "But where would I go? And what would I do?"

"Have you thought about calling Doc Samuels?" Kate asked. "He might be able to help you answer that."

I remembered all those hours I spent in his office, all those times he helped me through one crisis after another. "Yeah, I can call Doc," I said, smiling slightly for the first time since meeting with the board.

I pulled her close. "You always seem to say exactly what I need to hear."

CHAPTER 21
DISCERE DE VIA NEGATIVE

SALEM HILL, 1982. "Kate is right. Counseling does come in many different forms." I was glad to hear Doc's voice again. "I guess what I'm asking, is what do you want to do, Daniel?"

"I think something like Elijah does in San Francisco," I said. "You know, what we did with Lettie."

"Street faith."

"Exactly."

"That can open up a lot of options. But I'd suggest you talk with Francis Webber at Xavier University near you in Cincinnati. He's got a program I think you might like. It's called Social Justice and Theology."

"I'll call him today. And thanks again, Doc. I mean it."

———

I stood in front of Dr. Webber's office for several minutes. The door was open, but he wasn't there. From the middle of the room, a single green lamp cast its glow from a large desk. Alongside it several books lay open next to a legal pad that he was apparently writing in. The floor was bare, and the only other furniture was a wooden chair directly in front of the desk. It didn't look comfortable, only functional.

Book-filled shelves covered one side of the room. Along the other wall was a kneeler, like the ones in St. Augustine's chapel, with a picture of St. Francis above it.

"You must be Daniel Robinson." someone behind me said. Startled, I turned around and saw a man wearing a simple black suit and clerical collar. I knew Xavier was a Catholic school, but for some reason I never expected Dr. Webber to be a priest. Thoughts of Father Ken's boring sermons flashed through my mind. "Please, have a seat," he said, pointing toward the chair.

With his gray, thinning hair, I guessed him to be fifty or so, but it was hard to tell because his thick, heavy framed glasses filled his face and made his eyes seem larger, more intense. Yet there was a relaxed, even welcome air about him.

"I was reviewing your application for my program, and I have a couple questions," he said when we both were seated. My chair was as uncomfortable as it looked, and it didn't help me relax. He must have noticed because he quickly added. "There's no problem. It's just that most of my students come from within the traditional confines of our faith. But your resume is much more, how should I say this, eclectic. To be candid, it's not every day that I get someone applying for a doctorate in theology who lists 'homeless shelter janitor,' 'orphanage house manager' and 'truck driver' on his resume."

He smiled, and I breathed for the first time since getting his note three days ago asking me to come to his office. "That's why I wanted to meet with you before our first class. I'd like to know more of what brought you here, if I may."

I paused, not sure what he wanted to hear. "Let's say that my journey has taken a lot of twists and turns." It wasn't much of an answer, but it was all I could think of.

"How so?" he asked.

"I mean I've made a lot of mistakes..." I paused again, then quickly added, "...but I think I'm heading in the right direction now."

"Discere de via negativa."

"I'm sorry?"

"It's Latin. It means 'learning from the way of the negative.' "

"Well, you might say I've had a lot of negative in my life... but I think it made me a better person. At least that's what David Samuels always told me."

"I agree with him. Some would even say that's how Augustine became a saint. His journey of faith took a lot of twists and turns, as you call it, and apparently he did alright, don't you think?"

I couldn't help but smile at that comparison. "I don't see me becoming a saint," I said shaking my head just a little. "Truth is, I've got a lot more questions than I have answers right now. All I want to know is how to make what I do believe real in the street where it's most needed."

I immediately regretted my words. *He's a priest. How could he understand my doubts? Will he change his mind about accepting me in his program?*

But instead, he nodded. "This program is a good place to start your journey."

I breathed a sigh of relief.

"Besides," he said now, offering me a slight smile, "I can't do much about the saint part anyway. I'm still working on that in my own life." He rose, and our conversation drew to an end. "But I do think we can help you with the application of your faith."

I stood. "I'm really glad to be here, more than I can tell you, Dr. Webber. I mean it."

"I'll see you in class after lunch then... and it was good talking with you, Daniel," he said, shaking my hand as I turned to leave.

———

"I think I'm going to like my professor," I called out to Kate when I walked in the door. "He's a priest. But not like the ones I met at St. Augustine's. I mean this guy's really interesting. I think I could actually become Catholic if everyone was like him."

"Not if it includes me," she called back from the kitchen.

I laughed, thinking about all her stories about those nuns. "Not literally, Kate," I said. "I just mean Dr. Webber said what we did with Lettie and Damien is what the church is supposed to be doing. I know it's only my first day, but I think I'm going to like this program."

"I'm glad you like school so much." She walked into the room and gave me a kiss. "When you talk like this, I know why our kids are so smart."

"How's that?" I asked, not sure what she meant. Her smile faded and she looked down.

"I guess I was worried they might be, you know, like me."

Now I was more confused. "What do you mean?"

"I just mean college is not for people like me. That's all." She turned and walked quickly back into the kitchen, cutting the conversation.

I followed after her. "Why can't you go to college, Kate?"

"Dammit, Daniel," her voice suddenly echoed loud in the room, "I'm just too old to sit in a classroom with a bunch of teenagers." She glared, as if daring me to say anything more. "Just let it go...please," she finally said, her tone softening now. It was more of a plea than a demand. With wet eyes, she turned and left me alone in the room.

God, what did I say?

That night when we were both in bed, talking about the kids like we always did, she seemed like her old self. Now, it might be a good time...

"About college..."

"I told you I'm too old for that nonsense, Daniel. Now don't bring it up again." She rolled over and turned off the light.

I didn't mention it again for several days, but it still bothered me. On Friday night, after the kids were in bed, we were watching television in the living room. "Did you know there's a community college nearby. Shawnee College. Most of the students there are second career." I tried to sound casual.

"What?" She looked over at me.

"You said you were too old to go back to school. But I checked and a lot of students there are your age. Even older. They told me they actually focus on people like you."

Her face flushed. "What do you mean 'people like you'?" she snapped. "Are you saying there's something wrong with me? Because I don't deserve that. Not from you!"

"All I meant was people with kids. People who have been out of school for a couple years... like you. That's all. I got up, but she reached for my hand.

"I'm sorry," she said, much softer now. "I didn't mean it. I'm just not college material. That's all."

"Why not, Kate?" I sat back on the couch with her. She didn't say anything, but just stared at the floor.

"Do you really want to know why, Daniel?" she finally said. The words seemed to catch in her throat.

I nodded.

"Every time you bring up this idea of me going to college, I feel like I'm twelve again and sitting in Sister Monica Ann's classroom." Her voice cracked and she shook as she spoke. "I can still see her pointing that damned ruler at me whenever I got a wrong answer. She'd slap my knuckles and say, 'Mary Kathleen Fitzgerald! We're wasting a good Catholic education on someone...'" Her eyes filled with tears. "'...someone who's obviously retarded.' Do you know what it feels like to be called retarded for twelve years by your teachers?" A tear ran down her cheek. "So no more talk about college, please. For my sake." She looked so hurt, so angry, and so fragile, all at the same time. Everything in me wanted to hold her, but she stood, and walked quickly into the bedroom. The door clicked shut.

I sat on the couch for several hours, staring out the window and thinking about what she said, about being so hurt by someone you trusted, someone who was supposed to protect you. Those nuns were no different than Pastor Duncan...

You go ahead and tell this little story you just made up. No one's going to believe you anyway. I'm your pastor—your priest—your nun... Suddenly I felt sick.

When I came into the bedroom near midnight, the light was off.

"Kate, are you awake?"

"Yes," she mumbled.

I sat on the bed beside her and took her hand. "I've been thinking about what you said... about feeling like you're retarded."

She didn't say anything, but I thought she had been crying.

"The way I see it, you can let what that nun said eat at you forever, or you can come with me Monday to Shawnee College. At least look at what they have to offer. That's all I'm asking."

Before she could answer, I gently touched my finger to her lips. "Just think about it," I said. "Please."

She nodded, just a little, but enough to let me know she would be okay now. I pulled her close and held her until she fell asleep in my arms.

———

"Mrs. Robinson, I can't say for certain until I get your high school transcript, but from what you've told me, your grades were not particularly good."

Kate tapped her foot for the next thirty minutes as the Shawnee College counselor talked. It was obvious, at least to me, she wanted to leave his office as soon as we walked in.

"He said I need remedial courses," she grumbled when we got in the car. "That's so humiliating. I can't do that." She sounded angry again. But there was a quiver in her voice this time. She looked so hurt... so scared.

I didn't say anything. Instead, I drove on past our house and turned into Shawnee Park. "Let's go for a walk," I said, turning off the engine. The air was damp from a morning rain, and the leaves hung low overhead, giving us a cool retreat from the summer heat. The only noise we heard was a pair of birds calling to one another, and the gentle sound of our footsteps.

"Remember all our walks at the Oakland Wilderness when we were dating?" I took her hand. She smiled just as a beam of sunlight broke through the trees and picked out the golden hue in her red hair. She never looked more beautiful. We walked on until we came to the creek that meandered through the park. Here we found a large rock by the water's edge and sat down. "Did you know I had to take some prep courses in college? Doc Samuels helped me get through them." I wrapped my arm around her shoulder and pulled her close. "I'll help you, too. Just like Doc helped me. I know we can do it—together."

"I'll think about it," was all she said.

———

I was surprised when Walter Manchester walked into my office one Monday morning. He was a member of my church, but I had only talked with him a couple times in the eighteen months I had been there. I heard his wife died several years ago, and I thought he had been a school teacher, or something like that, but I wasn't sure. Someone told me he had family, but he never talked about them, at least not to me. Mostly all he did was shake my hand and leave after church, like most of the members.

"I just wanted to say I appreciate what you said yesterday... in your sermon."

"Thanks, Walter. I'm glad to hear that." I motioned for him to sit, but he shook his head. It was obvious he was uncomfortable talking with me, but I had a feeling there was something more he wanted to say. "I really need a cup of coffee this morning. The kids kept me up all night and I need something to help me wake up. I could use the company. My treat."

He nodded.

Neither of us said much as we walked the three blocks to the Java Shoppe on Broadway. The coffee wasn't great, but it did have a couple booths that were private enough for someone to talk, yet public enough so they could leave if the talk got uncomfortable. I called it my outside office.

We both sat there for several minutes, sipping our coffee and talking about the football game Friday. *A lot of talk about nothing.* But I remembered what Kate said about Doc talking about nothing with me until I felt I could trust him.

"You were a teacher, weren't you?" I asked. He nodded. "I taught history for thirty years until I retired in 1972." He seemed to relax now.

"Do you miss it? I mean, the interaction with the students?"

"Not really. Teaching changed a lot in the sixties. There wasn't the respect in the classroom, not like there used to be." He signaled for the waitress to refill his cup. "I was ready to retire anyway. Mary and I were planning to spend a lot of time at our cottage in Vermillion, on Lake Erie. But she got sick and..."

Is this what he really wants to talk about? "You mentioned the sermon yesterday..."

He took another sip of his coffee. "I appreciate what you said about your mother, about meeting with her again after all those years."

I thought about telling that story a couple times since my first visit with my mother, maybe in a sermon about the prodigal son, but from the son's perspective. Kate thought it was a great idea, and I wrote out some notes. But every time I put them back in my desk. "Too personal," I told her.

"Thanks, Walter. But to be honest, it wasn't easy for me... you know, to talk about it. I thought the people might see me as..."

"Human?"

I laughed.

"You know, I've been going to this church nearly seventy years, but that was the first time I ever heard a pastor who actually understood what I'm feeling."

He took another sip from his cup, paused, fidgeted with his napkin, then looked up at me. "About your mother... I mean, can you really forgive her for... for not being there for you, like you said?"

I saw something in his face—like this wasn't really a question about my mother. "I get the impression, and forgive me if I'm wrong, but are you asking me if I really meant what I said about my mother and me starting over? About getting another chance to be a real family?"

His hand shook as he looked away and quickly wiped his eye. He took a deliberate breath, as if trying to regain control of himself, then turned back toward me. "I said some things to my son a long time ago... things I really didn't mean. But we were both angry over something... I don't even remember now what it was." He took another breath. "Mary always told me I needed to talk with him, you know, to make it right. But I couldn't... Then Mary died."

I never took my eyes off Walter.

He leaned in, his eyes fixed on me. "What I'm asking...what I need to know.... Do you think he'll forgive me?"

I remembered hugging my mother at our first meeting. I remembered how safe I finally felt in her arms, even after all those years. "I know he will, Walter." I laid my hand on his arm. "All you need do is ask him."

Both of us sat there for several minutes in silence. Finally, he stood and took my hand. "Thanks, Pastor." was all he said, then walked quickly out the door.

I didn't see Walter for several weeks after that. Then on Labor Day weekend he was back in church, but this time he wasn't alone. Sitting beside him was a young man and woman with two little boys. All of them were smiling.

––––––

In September Kate started her first class at Shawnee Community College, but it wasn't easy. Every night I found her sitting at the kitchen table reading assignments two and three times, checking and re-checking, even triple checking her answers. Sometimes I helped, but what I did most was encourage her, like Doc did for me.

"Here," she said four weeks later when she walked into the house. Her hand shook as she gave me an envelope. "My first test. I can't open it. I know I failed." I thought she had been crying all the way home from school, because her face was flushed and her eyes were red. She stared at me now, not moving, not even breathing... just waiting.

Please God, a passing grade. I held my breath as I tore open the envelope. I looked at it... breathed again, smiled, and handed it back.

Her hand shook even harder as she reached for it. She stared at the large red letter at the top of her paper. "I got an A!" she whispered, barely able to breathe now. Her eyes filled with tears as she hugged the test, then hugged me. "I'm not retarded, Daniel. I know I can do it now!" She buried her face in my shoulder and cried while I wiped a tear from my own cheek.

That night I drove to K Mart and bought a frame to hang her first test on the wall above her desk in the bedroom. I added a note beside it. "Life is written in pencil. We get a lot of second chances!"

––––––

"Are you ready for Halloween?" Kate called out when I walked in the house. Growing up we never made much fuss about holidays, because we never knew if the old man would be on a bender. We set our expectations low so we were never disappointed. But not Kate! Christmas presents were planned, bought, wrapped and hidden from the kids six months ahead. Easter was a forty-day celebration of festive self-denial ending in an ever-expanding egg hunt throughout the house and yard, and sometimes half of the yards on the block. The Fourth of July was an all-day fireworks display, and even Memorial and Labor days were noted for her picnic feasts in the park. When I dared complain—only once I might add—about all the fuss on every imaginable holiday, all she said was "I'm Irish," as if that settled it.

So I wasn't really surprised when I found her with the kids all dressed in matching costumes on Halloween—Kate as the proud lioness with her three cubs in tow. But what I definitely was not prepared for was the massive lion's head and costume she held out to me.

"You're not expecting me to actually wear this...in public, are you?"

"Please, please, please, Daddy," all three kids begged while Kate egged them on.

That night, long after they were finally in bed and asleep, we were sitting together on the porch swing in the dark, staring at the harvest moon and enjoying the quiet of the crisp night air. "You know, I never thought I could do it," I said.

"Do what, wear that costume?" she asked. "It looked great on you, and the kids loved it."

"That too." I smiled when I remembered the look on Walter Manchester's face when we knocked on his door tonight. "But I was thinking more about this whole church thing."

"I don't understand."

"Do you remember when Doc Samuels first mentioned pastoral counseling? Remember how nervous I was about it? Too many ghosts."

She nodded.

"That's only part of it. The real reason is that I wasn't sure I believed enough."

"What do you mean, Daniel? Are you saying you don't believe in God?"

"Not really. I think what I'm saying is that I wasn't sure I believed in the church...or at least my place in the church. But seeing Walter tonight with his grandkids, I guess I realized that maybe Reverend Nicholson is right. Maybe Salem Hill is the city of peace for us after all."

She took my hand and squeezed it. "I know it is, Daniel."

CHAPTER 22
THE CRUCIBLE

SALEM HILL, 1982. Thanksgiving was almost here—the end of what looked to be our best year together. Then why did the hairs on the back of my neck stand up when Reverend Nicholson called? He just said he wanted to meet with me. That was something he tried to do every quarter. "I'll come by your office, before the holiday weekend," he said.

On Monday, when the district superintendent walked into my office, I knew something was wrong. I could read it on his face after he closed my door. "I have some unsettling news," he said as soon as he sat down.

I had no idea what it could be. Other than Jane Thornhill, there had been no complaints in the church. "It's personal," he said, looking even more serious now.

I didn't know what to think.

"It's about your church... I've had a call..." He looked down at the floor, clasped his hands together and rubbed them nervously. The man was clearly uncomfortable with the conversation. "I'll just get right to the point," he finally said, looking up. "Someone in your church, a woman, has said you made inappropriate comments to her. You may even have touched, or kissed her. That was not made clear to me. But the caller was quite adamant there was sexual harassment on your part."

He looked at me now, satisfied he had done his job as district super-intendent, and he waited for me to say something—a confession, an apology, anything to justify his obvious struggle to deliver this difficult, but necessary message.

I didn't know what to say. I wasn't even sure I heard him right. "I'm sorry. I don't understand," was all I managed to mutter.

Sighing, Reverend Nicholson rubbed his hands together, then slowly repeated, "a woman in your church was quite adamant there was sexual harassment by you." His temples throbbed and his jaw clenched as he again waited for me to offer some mea culpa. But I had none to give.

"Whatever you heard, it's not true. I guarantee it!" I said instead, thinking that would settle the matter.

"I believe you, Daniel, but there's so much misconduct being reported in the media lately, even by clergy. So for the good of your church, and all the churches in the district for that matter, we have to take every allegation very seriously."

"I agree, and I am taking what you say seriously. Believe me. So who said this? Because I have absolutely no idea what they're talking about?" I wracked my brain to think who could say something like this. *Was it Sally Lincoln? She always complained to me about her husband. Or maybe Carolyn Nixon? She told me she might get a divorce... and I did offer to talk with her if she needed help. Did she think I was coming on to her? Did anyone think I had a sexual motive when we brought Lettie into our house? Or was it...*

"It was an anonymous call," Reverend Nicholson said. "In fact, it wasn't even the victim who called, but somebody else. She said she wanted to protect her friend. That makes it more difficult for us to deal with this situation. But it's still important that we respond immediately."

"What do you mean?" Now I was more confused—and frustrated—than ever.

"I want to help you deal with this properly, for your sake, and for the sake of your church."

"I still don't understand. What do you mean, 'help me deal with this properly'?"

"Well, counseling of course. The district has ample resources available for you. I'm sure we can arrange something, perhaps even as early as next week. With good progress at each session, I don't see any need to involve anyone else in this. It shouldn't impact your role here as pastor. That is, as long as there is some sort of monitoring in place to limit your unsupervised contact with women in your church. Just standard procedure, you understand."

No. I don't understand at all! I wanted to scream out at him.

"If you'd like, I could arrange for your first session with a counselor."

I felt like I was in Pastor Duncan's office again. I saw him praying, felt him rubbing all over me, and I couldn't make him stop.

"I'll make that call today if you'd like." Reverend Nicholson's voice seemed to come from a distance. "It's best we handle this right away. For the good of your ministry. Don't you agree?"

I shook my head, trying to force Pastor Duncan from my mind. The hairs on my arms prickled. "Not today," I said.

"I understand, Daniel. I'll call you later in the week, say Wednesday... once you've looked at your schedule."

"No. Not Wednesday." My face was suddenly hot.

"We really shouldn't delay this. It's important we address this issue immediately. For the sake of your church. Friday then? But we really shouldn't delay getting this process started beyond then... for your sake."

Pastor Duncan flashed through my mind again. His Old Spice burned my nose. *God, make him stop!*

"Not Friday either. Or next week or even next month for that matter." I nearly shouted the words at him. "I can't do it."

"Please don't make this more difficult than it already is." His face was red now, his temples throbbing. "Denial only makes it much harder for us to resolve this." Reverend Nicholson never liked confrontation. He fidgeted with his pen as he spoke, clicking it open, closed, then open again. "I know it's difficult to face these issues, especially for ministers," he said, not even looking at me. "But you'll just have to trust me on this."

Click... click...

"Let me see if I understand you," I said, trying hard to remain calm. "You claim someone in my church, but you don't know who, said I harassed someone else in the church. But you don't know who that is either. And you're not really sure what I'm actually accused of doing. Does that sound about right?"

He didn't answer, but just clicked that damn pen again. Click, click...

"Then how do you know it's true?" My voice grew louder with each word I spoke. Reverend Nicholson looked at me, his face now bright red as the veins on his neck bulged. "Daniel, much of this information is confidential... to protect the victim. We can never be absolutely certain of truth in these situations."

Click, click...

"Yes, sir. I understand that, but it sounds like you believe it's true. That's what really upsets me. You came here with your mind made up." I nearly spit the words at him.

"The fact you're upset shows me counseling would help you." Reverend Nicholson seemed genuinely offended I didn't agree with him. "I see this as a learning experience. It's something that can help you become a better minister."

Click, click... click, click...

I stood up and pushed my chair against the wall with a thud. My body tense. My head ached. "What about the truth?" I didn't even try to hide my anger now.

"Truth is such an elusive thing, especially in these matters." He sounded so condescending, like I was some kid in the principal's office who wasn't smart enough to realize he was trying to help me. "Quite frankly, perception is really all that matters. If someone perceives they've been harassed, that's all that concerns us." He stood and moved toward the door like he wanted me to just agree with him, so he could leave and end an obviously uncomfortable conversation.

But I couldn't. It simply wasn't true! I felt caught in a drain that sucked me down and down and I couldn't make it stop. My mind reeled. I was going to explode! *Just breathe*, I repeated over and over in my head. "But you don't even know who said this," was all I managed to say. "Doesn't that bother you, even a little?"

He sighed. "Of course, that bothers me." He shook his head slightly. "Being a minister sometimes means trusting those over you, even when you don't understand where they're leading."

"But what about the truth?" I asked. "How will you ever know the truth if you don't investigate this?"

He sighed again. "Even Jesus asked, 'What. Is. Truth?' " He pronounced each word carefully, as if trying hard to finally help me understand what was clearly obvious to him. "My role as the spiritual leader of the district is to do what's good for the whole United Methodist Church, not just one minister."

In that instant, I realized what I always sensed. For him, faith was a set of laws, not a spiritual experience. He didn't speak from any personal conviction. His trust was in the rules of the church, that they would speak for him. Any real feelings of compassion for others... if that was even part of his vocabulary... simply was not part of his faith. I wanted to scream now, but I just shook my head in disbelief.

"Think of this as a growth experience. I know this is quite a shock. It's not easy to look at ourselves like this. But from time to time we have to do that as ministers. So just think on it for the next few days. Talk to your wife. I'll call you next week, say Monday afternoon. Now I think we should pray together about this, don't you?"

"Our good and forgiving God, we ask..." he began, but all I heard was Pastor Duncan. *No one's going to believe you anyway...someone whose mother is at Woodville? They'll think you're crazy too.* I desperately wanted to cover my ears and block out both of them.

———

I couldn't relax while I waited for Kate to come home from her afternoon class. Every word of our conversation with Reverend Nicholson replayed in my head, over and over until I wanted to scream.

A woman in your church...

What do you mean help me deal with it...?

It's important we address this issue with counseling...

What about the truth...?

Think of this like a growth experience...

Our good and forgiving God...

"What's the absolute last thing you'd ever expect to hear about me?" I asked as soon as she walked in the kitchen door.

"What are you talking about?"

"Reverend Nicholson came to my office today."

She frowned, tightening her lips. "That creep makes my skin crawl." That was her favorite name for him. *Creep*. Now I understood what she meant.

"You're not going to believe it, but he said some woman in our church accused me of sexual harassment."

She dropped her books on the table with a loud THUD! "You've got to be kidding. That's the most ridiculous thing I've ever heard."

"That's what I told him."

"Who is it? I mean, who said that about you?"

"He doesn't know. It was an anonymous call. He's not even sure what she says I've done! It's all innuendo and third-hand hearsay."

"And he believed it?" Her face turned deep red. "That's absolute crap!"

"That's what I told him. But it gets worse. He wants me to see a counselor."

Her body stiffened and she grabbed the chair so hard her knuckles turned white. I never saw her this angry before. "So what did you tell him?"

"I said I wouldn't do it. That would be admitting to a lie. I can't—I won't do it!"

"Good," she said, as if that settled the matter.

"It's not good actually. He insisted I get counseling. He said it would be a 'growth experience.'"

"He really is a creep. You know that? He reminds me of Sister Monica Ann." Shaking her head, she dropped into the chair, then looked up at me. "This makes me sick to my stomach."

"Me too, Kate. I feel like I'm in a bad dream and can't wake up. The whole time he was talking to me, all I heard was Pastor Duncan again. God, it was awful. What is it, seventeen years later and I still felt that pervert rubbing all over me when I was with Nicholson."

Just saying Pastor Duncan's name out loud made my blood run

cold. Suddenly weak, I fell into the chair beside her. My eyes closed and I dropped my head onto my chest, exhausted. I was drowning. "God, make it stop," I sighed as I heard the scrape of wood over the floor, and then Kate's arms wrapped around me. We held each other for a long time, just us in a middle of this maddening sea of lies.

"What are you going to do now?" she finally asked.

I guess I'll call Bishop Payne. I don't know what else to do."

"What if the bishop agrees with Reverend Nicholson? What will you do then?"

"I guess I'll start over somewhere else. All I know is I can't do what he's asking. I couldn't live with myself if I did."

"And I won't let you," she squeezed both my hands. "But I want you to know one thing...and I mean it!" She looked directly at me, eyes flashing wide with anger. "If you ever think about taking another church, for any reason, you can do it without me. I thought the nuns were cruel. But what these people have put you through—especially that creep Nicholson, it's just evil, and I'm done with it. I mean it, Daniel."

"So am I, Kate. But we just need to get through this. Then we'll see what happens after that."

Bishop Payne was my first call the next morning.

"We have ample rules in place to address these situations," he assured me. "You can trust me to get to the bottom of this."

I hung up the phone, relieved that my nightmare would soon end.

We tried to focus on Thanksgiving dinner. We still wore our usual Pilgrim hats, and Kate still hung a few decorations, but it wasn't much of a celebration. No matter how hard we tried, neither of us could get Reverend Nicholson's allegation out of our minds.

"It will soon be over," I promised her.

But the first week of December, then the second, passed with no word from Bishop Payne. I couldn't stop thinking about that allegation. When I was in church on Sundays, I scanned the congregation constantly, even in the middle of my sermon, trying to think who accused me. *Alice Miller hasn't spoken to me for several weeks. Was it her? The Sheltons haven't been in church lately. Maybe she... Should I shake hands with any of the women after church? When am I going to hear from Bishop Payne?* To keep my sanity, I focused on Christmas with my mother.

———

"You're right, Mr. Robinson. Your mother does seem to be doing much better than we expected at this stage in her cancer," said Dr. Berkowitz, the nursing home's primary doctor. He had been treating her since she arrived. "To be honest, she's doing far better than we ever expected."

I noticed a change in my mother with every visit I made to Pittsburgh these past eighteen months, especially when Kate and the kids came with me. She was gaining weight, the color seemed to be coming back to her face, and she looked so happy. I started actually thinking she might get better. That was why I had to talk to Dr. Berkowitz. I had to know for sure.

"Is her cancer in remission? I'm hesitant to be that optimistic," he said. I got the impression he was asked that question too many times, giving everyone the same answer. "My best advice is to spend as much time with her now as possible."

———

"I thought you would like this. I made it myself," Mum said when she handed Susan her present.

"Oh, Grandma, it's beautiful!" Susan held up the knitted hat. "How did you know green is my favorite color?"

"I just thought green would complement your beautiful hair. I'm so glad you like it."

"I love it, Grandma. Do you have a mirror so I can see how it looks on me?"

Kate pointed toward the bathroom, smiling. She seemed as excited by the present as Susan.

Emma struggled to get the ribbon off her present. Kate got up to help, but Mum stopped her. "Let me do it. I've waited a long time for this Christmas, and I want to enjoy every minute of it."

"Thank you, Gamma," Emma said as she held up her own knitted hat. "I made that for you too, honey. I hope you like it."

"I love it, Gamma."

Jonathan watched his sisters open their presents, his brow furrowing. Mum noticed and smiled toward him. "Now don't you worry, Jonathan. I raised three boys and I know you don't want a knitted hat, too. Why don't you look in my closet? I think there's something special for you in there."

Jonathan ran to the closet, opened the door and stared at the genuine Wyatt Earp pearl handled cap gun and holster set—and it even had a Marshall's badge with it. He didn't move at first, not sure if he could believe his eyes. "How did you know that was what I wanted most for Christmas, Grandma? And it even has four rolls of caps too!"

Mum winked. "Let's just say I had a little help from Santa Claus."

Kate and I sat on the couch and watched the Christmas celebration I always wanted—and for a little while we forgot cancer and Jane Thornhill and Reverend Nicholson and Bishop Payne, and for one beautiful afternoon we were happy.

I thought about my mother the whole way back to Salem Hill. "I just wish there was more we could do," I told Kate.

———

It was early January when the bishop finally called. He asked me to meet with him and Reverend Nicholson at his office in Cincinnati the next morning. *Thank God this nonsense is finally over,* was my only thought driving there.

"Daniel, Superintendent Nicholson and I were just talking about your involvement in several service clubs in Salem Hill," the bishop said, shaking my hand and smiling as I walked into his office. Bishop Payne was considered 'a rising star' in the church. Possessing Hollywood looks and a politician's sense of opportunity, he arrived in Ohio ten years ago with a degree from Harvard Divinity School, a rarity for most Methodist pastors in this region, and an eye that looked well beyond the mundane confines of parish ministry. After only a few years as senior pastor at the largest Columbus church, he was soon appointed superintendent in that district. Even though he was much younger than Rev. Nicholson, he quickly passed over him when the bishop's position opened in Cincinnati last year. This was the first time we had met.

"We certainly encourage our pastors to be involved in the community," he said as he motioned for me to have a seat in front of his desk. Reverend Nicholson was seated beside him.

Those same hairs on the back of my neck tingled again.

"Now about that nasty business we discussed in November. I promised you we'd look into it, and we did. Superintendent Nicholson and I spent a great deal of time talking to many people in Salem Hill. All of them speak highly of your sermons. Perhaps a bit too long, but we all hear that, don't we?" He chuckled.

I heard Roberta Stewart saying, *People in this church all seem pretty normal to me.*

"I wanted to meet with you today so I could tell you myself that we could find no hard evidence of misconduct."

I smiled slightly, and let myself breathe in relief. Thank God my nightmare was finally over. Reverend Nicholson glared at me.

"However..."

My stomach came up into my throat. *Oh God...*

"...we do have some concerns with your response to this situation. As you know, being a minister is not an easy calling. There are times when we have to look beyond our own interests and needs, times when we have to put the interests of the church first."

I heard the board voting against what I did for Lettie.

"Superintendent Nicholson and I both feel it would be in your best interests to address some of your anger and uncooperativeness issues. We have ample resources available for you."

My head throbbed. A sharp pain radiated from behind my eyes to the base of my neck. His words sounded so distant now. "You mean counseling?" I muttered, not sure if I heard him right.

"I like to think of it as a support program, Daniel," the bishop said, still smiling genially. "I can assure you it's very beneficial. And we have an opening next week. What does your schedule look like?"

My whole body felt on fire. I couldn't answer. *How would Doc handle this?* A sudden calm moved over me. It was all so clear now, as I met his gaze head on, then chose my words deliberately. "Let me see if I understand you, Bishop Payne." I paused, letting them hang onto my words. "Two months ago, Reverend Nicholson came to me with an unsubstantiated, anonymous allegation, and insisted I have counseling to deal with what he called 'my problem.' I appealed to you, and you found there was nothing to this allegation." I paused again.

Both men looked right at me. Rev. Nicholson started to say something, then caught himself.

"But now you're telling me I need counseling because I refused to admit to something you now know I didn't do. Is that about the gist of it?"

The bishop's smile froze. His eyes turned icy. "That is such an unfair analysis of the situation, Daniel." He spoke slowly now, his words controlled, but with that same condescending tone as Reverend Nicholson had used. "You're a very gifted man, and you have a bright future in the United Methodist Church..." His politician's smile crept back on his face. "...especially with your doctoral studies. We could certainly use more ministers with your passion."

Reverend Nicholson glared at the bishop.

"But we have to think in terms of the whole church, not just one pastor. What I'm saying is if you were more cooperative with your leadership, if you were more of a team player, I'm sure you could easily pastor some of our biggest churches in Ohio."

I heard Jane Thornhill saying, *It's your job to fill the pews if you want us to keep paying your salary.*

"I am trying to think of the good of the church, sir," I said. "But if I were to accept this lie, as you both suggest, then what would I have to offer any church I would pastor? Isn't truth the foundation of our faith? So how can I accept a lie, just so I can get a bigger church?"

Bishop Payne folded his arms. "Truth can be so elusive." He lifted his eyebrow. "Even Jesus asked, 'What is truth?'"

My mind raced. I wanted to tell them I was learning to listen to the members of my church like Walter. I wanted to tell them how much I tried to help all the broken people I met. I wanted to tell them I felt safer taking homeless people like Lettie and Damien into my house than I ever did with either of them. But I didn't bother. It was so clear to me now. Pastor Duncan, Kate's nuns, Jane Thornhill, Reverend Nicholson, Bishop Payne, all of them who try to kill compassion in the name of virtue, they simply wouldn't care. So I just said, "It was Pilate."

"What?" Bishop Payne asked.

"It was Pilate who asked, 'What is truth?' Not Jesus. So before you embarrass yourself with your limited understanding of the Bible you claim to believe, I suggest you read it again." I walked out of his office, took a deep cleansing breath when I reached the parking lot, then got in my car and drove home to Kate. I felt freer than I had in a long time.

CHAPTER 23
IN THE MARGINS OF UNCERTAINTY

SALEM HILL, 1983. Driving back home all I could think about was what just happened in Bishop Payne's office. I should have been livid with their manipulation and deceit, but to my surprise, all I felt was relief. They forced me to quit something I was never comfortable doing. Too many ghosts in the church. But I really did try to fit in for two years. Especially when I saw Walter sitting in church with his family, I actually thought I could make it work. But I was wrong, and now I was glad to move on.

But what am I going to tell Kate? She was so excited with her classes this term... I don't want to ruin that for her. But I've lost my job—and our house... My confidence faded with each passing mile. *Did I do the right thing? I've got a wife and three kids to support. And there's Mum in that nursing home. If we have to move away to find another job, then I might not see her again...*

My mind raced with questions. For the first time the full impact of my decision hit me. *God, what am I going to do now?* Driving mindlessly through Cincinnati, I found myself in front of Xavier University. *There's Hinkle Hall. Maybe I can talk with Dr. Webber before I go home.*

He was out, but his secretary said I could see him if I came back in an hour. Even with the January weather, I thought I'd wait out front by the statue of Francis Xavier. I always enjoyed sitting there alone between classes, just to think. But today that statue only reminded me of St. Augustine's... how I let down Sister Rose... abandoned Daequan... what I did to Ruthie. And now I'd failed my family too!

"Please God," I whispered. "I really screwed up my life again... and I need some direction." It wasn't much of a prayer, but it was all I could manage. I never felt so alone.

When I came back, I found Dr. Webber in his office. I told him about the accusation, and what Bishop Payne wanted me to do. He leaned back in his chair. "I'd like to tell you that sort of thing doesn't happen in the Catholic Church, but I'd be lying." He crossed his arms, shaking his head slightly. "Sometimes I think we're our own worst enemies in the church. And it doesn't matter if it's Protestant or Catholic."

I was glad I came to see him. He often reminded me of Doc Samuels, especially now.

"What are you going to do? Pastor another church?" he asked.

"I doubt it. Even if I wanted to, my wife said she's had it with the politics in the church."

"I feel the same way most days. Although I have more independence here at the university, I'm not sure I could do it if I were a parish priest again."

I felt better hearing that, but it made what I had to tell him even harder. "I really want to finish your program..." I had to force my words out. "...but I can't."

"I don't understand." Dr. Webber didn't normally show a lot of emotion, but he looked genuinely surprised. "I'm sure we can work out something to fit any change you may have in your schedule now."

There was so much I wanted to say, but I wasn't sure he would understand. Still, I just said it. "We've never talked about it before..." The words came slowly. "...but there have been other people in the church... who have hurt me... I think what I'm trying to say is faith hasn't come easy for me. But now, after what just happened, I don't know what I believe anymore." I lowered my eyes, swallowed, then looked up at him again. "I think what I'm trying to say is I have more questions now than I have answers... and this is a Catholic school.

Anyway, I've got to find another job now, and I can't stay in your program. I just wanted to thank you for all I've learned so far, and especially for listening to me today. I really needed that."

I got up to leave, but he stood, reaching for my arm. "Would it surprise you that I have days when I'm not sure if I believe anymore?"

I wasn't sure I heard him right. I just stared at him, like I did Doc Samuels when he told me about that boarding school he went to.

"Do you know what I've learned in my thirty years as a priest, Daniel?"

I didn't answer. I just stood there.

"I've learned that God isn't offended by my doubts. Unlike many in the church, God isn't even offended by unbelief. Do you know why? Because honest questioning will only lead to God. To be perfectly candid, there are too many priests who have never questioned their faith, and as far as I'm concerned, they're worthless as priests!" His voice was suddenly much louder. I never saw him react like that before.

He put his hand on my shoulder. "The same thing applies to my program here at Xavier." His voice gentled. "Daniel, the Department of Correction has been putting a lot of pressure on me to finish my rehabilitation proposal. You've seen the numbers. More than half the people coming out of prison get re-arrested within three years. I could really use someone with faith like yours to help me full time with my research. Maybe you could even teach a few classes here. That would free up a lot of my time. Are you interested?"

———

Kate had only one question. "Does this mean we have to move to Cincinnati?" But I knew what she was really asking. Will she have to quit school?

"We'll find something here in Salem Hill." I reached across the table and squeezed her hand. "At least until you graduate I can drive to Xavier every day. It's only about an hour away. Besides, I'm already driving there twice a week for my classes. What's a couple more days?"

She leaned in and hugged me gratefully.

I planned to rent a house, but everything we looked at was either too expensive or too small for the five of us. One week passed, then two, and still we found nothing. Finally, after a month of searching, I happened to drive by an old house across town on Phoenix Street—and that's when I got my idea.

"Remember those houses I told you about in San Francisco?" I asked Kate the next afternoon when she got home from her class. "You know, the ones that James loved so much, and where we spread his ashes after he died? You're not going to believe it, but I found one here in Salem Hill. And it's for sale!"

She walked past me into the kitchen. "We can't afford something fancy like that," she answered, not even looking at me. Clearly, she didn't think I was serious.

I followed her. "This house is different. It's in foreclosure, so the bank really wants to sell it. I think they'll come down a lot on the price. Besides, there's an apartment on the back. If we rent it to someone, that should pay most of our mortgage. So it'll almost be like getting a free house."

"A free house?" She dropped her books on the counter and looked up at me. "You're not making any sense."

I grabbed a cup from the cabinet, poured coffee into it, then held it out for her. "Of course, it's not as fancy as the ones in San Francisco. But with a little remodeling, I'm sure it can be a great place for us."

She shook her head as she sat down at the kitchen table, then took a sip from her cup, making it clear she thought the discussion was ended.

But it wasn't over. Not for me anyway.

I grabbed a chair and sat next to her, reaching for her hand. "Just look at it. That's all I ask."

She started to say something, but took another sip instead, all while tapping her foot like she always did when she was upset.

"It can't hurt to just look at the house. What do you say?"

Finally, she nodded, but with little enthusiasm.

I tried to prepare her as we drove across town. "The neighborhood's sort of in transition.

And the house isn't much to look at either, but it has potential." I tried to sound as positive as the realtor who showed it to me yesterday, but I wasn't very convincing. Kate just looked at all the decaying houses on both sides of the street and shook her head.

I stopped in front of a two-story unpainted frame house with the 'For Sale' sign in the front yard. The afternoon sun had melted most of the snow, exposing parts of the house I hadn't seen before. It looked even worse than I remembered. The front porch sagged badly. Several windows on the second floor had broken glass, and from the ground, the sashes looked like they needed to be replaced. And the roof didn't look nearly as good as the realtor said it was.

If James were here, how would he describe this house to Kate? "Look at all the intricate details on the porch columns, the ornate corbels and gable decorations on the eves, and especially that stained glass window on the front door, they're all irreplaceable art." I tried to sound as positive as I could pretend to be. "I can't even imagine all the work that went into building this place."

She just stood on the sidewalk, staring blankly at the house.

"Let me show you what the inside looks like. It's even better," I said, undeterred by her lack of appreciation for what James would call 'a masterpiece of Victorian architecture at its finest.' "It still has all the original woodwork."

Nobody was living there, so the realtor gave me a key when I told her I wanted Kate to see it. "The electricity's turned off, but I think there's enough light coming in the windows to get a pretty good view of the downstairs at least," I said as I unlocked the door and motioned for her to follow me. A choking, rotting odor rushed over us as soon as we stepped inside. Kate stopped abruptly and covered her nose.

"What's that awful smell?" she asked through gritted teeth. "It's like something died in here."

I noticed that yesterday with the realtor, but ignored it, and I wasn't about to tell her that now. "The house has been closed up all winter. That's probably what you smell. Once the windows are opened in spring, it'll be fine."

That didn't satisfy her at all.

"Look at the hardwood here in the foyer!" I said, propping the door open to flood the house with fresh air. "I'll bet there's not another floor in town with this parquet pattern. But just watch your step. A couple boards might be loose." She glared at me, still holding her nose while grumbling something I couldn't quite hear.

"There are four bedrooms upstairs." I took her arm and led her toward the staircase. "But be careful with that railing. It's a little loose... but I can easily fix it."

"I've seen enough!" She turned and started to walk back toward the door, but I quickly grabbed her arm.

"Let me show you the living room instead...please. I think you'll love the ten-foot ceiling and all the great woodwork."

I pulled down several large cobwebs in the doorway and led her into a large room in the front of the house. The sun was at a perfect angle and every corner of the room was basked in light that cascaded through three tall bay windows. "What do you think? Of the woodwork." I pointed toward the ceiling. "I haven't seen crown moulding like that since San Francisco. And look at the paneling with those corbels above the fireplace. Can you see us sitting in front of a romantic fire every night?" Just then, wood creaked somewhere.

"What was that?" Kate squeezed my arm, her eyes wide, as she frantically looked all around the room. "Did you hear that? I think it came from the dining room, or maybe the hall."

I took her arm. "Probably just the house settling... I mean, because the heat's been turned off all winter. Nothing to worry about. I'll get the furnace turned on long before we move in."

"What do you mean 'before we move in'? Not with me!" She spun around and hurried out of the room.

"It's really not as bad as it looks," I called, running after her. "It just needs some cleaning, and I can save a lot of money doing the repairs myself. I figure it'll only take me a couple months to get it looking great again."

She stopped at the door, started to say something, but turned again to leave. I reached for her arm to stop her. "I'll be honest with you, Kate," I said. "We've got to move soon and we're out of options. This is the only house we can afford."

She shook her head. "We need to rent a house somewhere. Anything is better than this place." She stomped out the door, making it clear she was done with the tour. I ran after her again, reaching for her arm, but she pulled away.

"Kate. Please. I need to tell you the real reason I think we should buy this house. It's not the woodwork, or even the price. It's something more personal."

She faced me, her foot tapping again.

"It's my mother."

"I don't understand."

"She's the reason I think we should buy this house."

"What are you talking about, Daniel?" Her foot tapped even harder now.

I took her hands in mine. "When I found my mother, I felt like I was given a second chance with her. But she's dying. Every time I leave her, I think it might be the last time I'll see her. Dr. Berkowitz made that clear at Christmas."

"What are you saying?" The tapping slowed and her face softened a little.

"I'm saying I want my mother to come here, to live with us, in the apartment on the back of the house. At least for the little time she's got left, she can be part of our family. I want to do that for her... and for me."

I waited, my chest heaving slightly.

She relaxed, then pulled me close. "Then I think we should buy it," she said and gently kissed my cheek. "And one more thing. If your mother is going to live with us, then she needs to have one of the bedrooms in the house, not that apartment on the back. She's family, Daniel, not a renter."

I wrapped my arms around her. "I love you, Kate." I wanted to say so much more, but I just held her close. That said everything I felt right now.

———

We moved into our new home in March. I had a list of repairs I wanted to do before Mum arrived, but it kept growing almost daily. I expected we'd have to do a lot of cleaning, and painting. Replacing the kitchen cabinets was too expensive, so I repainted them instead. Not what I wanted, but all I could afford. But then the kitchen and bathroom both had plumbing leaks, and all the bedroom lights flickered. "Needs a new circuit breaker box," the electrician said. I was hoping we could heat the house with the fireplace, but when I started my first fire, the living room filled with smoke. "Looks like you need to rebuild those chimneys. There's a lot of flue damage, so I wouldn't use it till it's fixed," the contractor warned. Fortunately, Walter Manchester stayed in contact with me after we left the church, and he knew someone who gave us a deal on a new furnace.

"I wanted to have everything done when Mum gets here." I dropped onto the bed, exhausted, after another long weekend working on the house. "But it's taking a lot longer than I thought... and I don't know how much time, you know..." I couldn't say it.

Kate squeezed my hand without saying anything. Finally, she pulled me close. "I don't think your mother cares about living in a perfect house, Daniel. She just wants to be with her family."

I slept better than I had in ages. In the morning, I called Dr. Berkowitz.

Mum seemed so happy to be with us, and for a while I thought Dr. Berkowitz was wrong, and that she really was going to get better now. She was as excited as me the day I stripped old wallpaper off Susan's bedroom wall and found a note scribbled on the plaster. *Installed by Benjamin Noble, 1884.*

"That was the year my mother was born," she said, smiling. "In a way, this house reminds me of her. When I was growing up, our house wasn't as fancy as this one, but it was big, and it had wallpaper, just like this room."

"I don't remember much about Grandma because she died when I was little. I just remember going to her house for that raspberry cake she always made. Remember how Robert and I used to pick the berries in the woods behind her house?" My mouth was suddenly wet. "I can still taste them."

She smiled again. "I remember that, too. And I'm glad you named Emma after her." She walked to the window, standing there for several minutes, not saying a word, just staring into the distance.

"Do you miss her?"

"Everyday..." She wiped her eyes. "...but I'll see her soon," she said, dropping down into the chair by the window. I watched her for a minute, then picked up my scraper and started stripping another piece of wallpaper. Mum just watched me in silence for the rest of the afternoon. It was a good day for both of us.

What I liked most were our dinner times together, especially when she entertained the kids with her stories about growing up in Coal Valley without a car, or even indoor plumbing.

"You mean your bathroom was in the backyard, Grandma?" Susan asked. "Where did you take a shower?"

"We didn't." They just gaped at her. Mum laughed, then quickly added. "But I did take a bath every Saturday night."

"But where, I mean how... you know, if you didn't have water in the house?" It was obvious Susan couldn't imagine anyone, especially her own grandmother, living without a bathroom.

"It wasn't so bad, dear. We carried the water in from the well in buckets and heated it on the wood stove. Then we all took a bath in the tub in the kitchen."

"In the kitchen!" Susan's fork fell to the floor. Jonathan's mouth dropped open.

"And all of us used the same water too," Mum said, almost as an afterthought, like this was a perfectly normal thing to do in a family.

"Gross!"

"No way, Grandma!"

"Ewww."

Kate and I laughed about her story for days after that. And the best part was the kids never again complained about the construction mess we lived with.

———

I didn't think much about it the first time Mum missed dinner. She said she didn't sleep well and just needed a nap. The second day I was a little worried, but when I brought dinner to her, she seemed fine, especially when the girls walked behind me. "Hi Grandma," they both called out, running to hug her in her bed. For a couple days she seemed to be her old self again.

"You know, Kate, when I was growing up, I only remember seeing my mother smile once. But you'd never know that now, would you? She seems so happy when she's with the kids—and so do they."

"I'm glad she's here with us, too, for their sake. They'll need these memories of her when..."

"When what, Kate?"

"When she's gone."

I suppose I always knew this day would come, but she was doing so well! *This is just a temporary setback. She's going to beat the cancer. She's not going to die!* But no matter how many times I screamed that in my head, I knew Kate was right. It didn't make it any easier.

It was a month later when Emma said something really strange. I was sitting in the stuffed chair in my bedroom, where I studied in private, away from all the noise in the house—but close enough to Mum's room, so I could keep a close watch on her now. Emma saw me and climbed up on my lap, nuzzling under my arm, like she always did when she wanted to be close to me.

"Someone was in Grandma's room talking to her this morning," she said, like it was something normal. But no one from Hospice was scheduled to come today. Not sure what she meant, I laid the book down.

"Who was with grandma, baby?"

"I don't know who she was, Daddy, but she was old like Grandma... and she had pretty blue eyes too."

Oh, just one of her pretend games, okay. I played along. "What else did you see?"

"She called her Mama, and she seemed real happy to see her."

What? Mama? "So... what did Grandma and her Mama talk about?"

"Raspberries, Daddy. They talked about picking raspberries again real soon."

A chill ran through me as I caught my breath. I just pulled her close and wiped a tear from my cheek.

Two days later Mum passed away peacefully in her bed. She wasn't in much pain, not with the medication Hospice provided. And I was glad she was still herself until the end. The kids all spent time with her, especially Emma. Even though she was not quite three years old, and had no real understanding of death, somehow she sensed her grand-mother was very sick.

"Did you notice how Emma stayed with Mum right to the end?" I asked Kate that night after the funeral. We were watching the last soft rays of the evening sun fade in the living room, trying to adjust to the empty feeling in the house now. "It was like she knew."

We were quiet for several minutes. Finally, I told her what Emma had said.

"She saw Mum talking to someone..."

"I don't understand. No one's been here to see her."

I reached for her hand. "She said Mum was talking to her mother, my Grandma Emma."

"That just sounds like one of her pretend games."

"That's what I thought, too. But..."

"But what?"

I hesitated. "She said.... they talked about...picking raspberries. How did Emma know about that? I mean, I never told anyone but you about doing that at Grandma's house when I was a kid."

Neither of us said anything now. "You don't think....?" I finally asked.

"I don't know what to think, Daniel, but I'm not really surprised." She took my hands in both of hers and held them tight. "Emma's my sensitive one. Sometimes I think she's got a second heart for hurting people..." She pulled me close. "...just like you, Daniel."

I wrapped my arm around her shoulder. "When I first talked about bringing my mother to live with us, I never thought it would erase all those lost years, but I think it helped. Having her here with us these past couple months...," I wiped my eyes. "...sometimes I actually felt like all that shit I grew up with never happened. Does that make any sense?"

"A whole lot of sense, Daniel. It means you've changed where you came from."

I pulled Kate even closer to me. "All I know is when I met you, I found what I was looking for all my life."

"Me too, Daniel." She nuzzled against my chest.

———

After Mum passed, I mostly focused on my new job with Dr. Webber. I spent hours in the library poring through stacks of books, reading dozens of articles, compiling pages of notes. Even teaching two under-grad classes wasn't nearly as hard as I thought it would be. "Just like preaching a homily," Dr. Webber said. Then he added with a grin, "but you give a test at the end of the term."

But it was my prison visits that first year that turned my life upside down. Part of my job was to interview wardens, corrections officers, case workers, chaplains, and especially inmates. Dr. Webber said I needed to understand how being in prison really felt from multiple perspectives.

I didn't know what to expect on my first prison visit. I thought London Correctional would be a dark stone dungeon, like in the movies. But it looked more like my college dormitory—at least until I got inside. Here I found one locked gate after another, all under the intense scrutiny of dozens of guards who constantly checked and rechecked me, and an untold number of cameras that recorded every movement I made.

It didn't smell like my dorm either. The hot, stagnant air mixed with sweat and foul cigarettes from a thousand men in the summer made me want to retch, though after a dozen trips, I barely noticed. I was surprised how much light there was in prison, too much, in fact. Every hall and room, glared with artificial light. I was sure there was some security reason for it, but all I thought of was Charly's experiment box in my college psych class. But what I never got used to, what kept me awake at night, was the sound of metal doors slamming shut behind me. I felt trapped, like I was locked up too, forgotten, never to go home again—like these expressionless men, reduced to just the numbers on their shirts. That's why I always opened all the windows when I drove home, even in winter. I needed to feel the wind on my face. I needed to feel free again.

———

"Daniel, I'd like you to go to Mansfield Reformatory this week," Dr. Webber said when I walked into his office. "The chaplain wants to talk about one of his men there."

I'd been there a couple times the past year, but I never got used to it. Of all thirty-five prisons in the state, I dreaded going to this one. I read somewhere that it was built a century ago as a 'model for humane rehabilitation'—that was the actual phrase they used when it was opened! But today it was only known for rats, inedible food, disease, and especially violence. From my first visit, I heard stories of inmates being beaten senseless, sliced with shanks, or even thrown from six-story walkways, all over petty grievances. Critics repeatedly called for the prison to be closed because of what they called 'brutalizing and inhumane conditions,' but nothing ever changed. I think the chaplain described it best. "Not fit conditions for an animal." Dr. Webber wanted to change that, and that was why I was going back to Mansfield again.

"Glad you could come here on such short notice, Mr. Robinson." Chaplain Stanton shook my hand in the main lobby. "I've got a guy I'd like you to meet. He's been in the East cell block for most of the past twenty years, but he's up for parole again."

I shuddered. I'd only been in that cell block once, but I still had nightmares about it. Two men caged in a six-by-ten metal box barely big enough for one person, with only a steel bunk bolted to the wall, a toilet, sink and a single light.

Most men adjusted to almost anything in prison. The rancid food, the constant threats...they even learned to ignore the cockroaches and rats that crawl over them at night. But what no one ever got used to, what drove too many crazy, was the sheer size of East block. Six hundred vermin infested cells stacked row after row, six stories high. "The tallest cell block in the world," the warden said, like it was a good thing he could cram twelve hundred men in one cavernous cement block room, hovering over ninety-five degrees in summer, and near freezing in winter. The noise, the never-ending screams, was maddening—and those who hung themselves with a bedsheet, or cut their wrists with a metal shard and bled to death, proved it.

"His name is Charles Vickers." Chaplain Stanton handed me a thick file. "He's been denied parole twice and if he doesn't find a place to go soon, they'll deny him again."

I tried to focus on what he was saying, but all I heard was 'twenty years in East block.' I shuddered. "Where's he from?" I finally asked.

"Cleveland. But he's got no one there, or at least no one willing to help him."

Of all the chaplains I worked with, I identified with Warren Stanton the most. An Episcopal priest for fifteen years, he burned out on church politics and took the chaplain's position at Mansfield. "It might sound crazy," he once told me. "but I feel safer here in this hell hole than I ever did with my church board."

"Doesn't sound that crazy to me," was all I said, but since then, I didn't mind going to Mansfield nearly as much.

"So how can I help, Chaplain?"

"I was hoping you might know a place he could live in your part of the state."

"I'm sure we can help him find an apartment somewhere in Cincinnati or Dayton." I said.

"There's actually more to his story."

"There always is." I settled as best I could in the vinyl chair in his cramped cinder block office.

"It's his crime. He was convicted of raping a girl. It was in all the papers when it happened. Although it was twenty years ago, I'm pretty sure he won't be welcome anywhere in the state."

"Is he dangerous, Chaplain?"

"I'm not even certain he's guilty."

I leaned forward in my chair, not sure if I heard him right. "I don't understand. You said he's been in prison for twenty years. If he's innocent, how was he ever convicted?"

"My opinion? Politics. The girl was sixteen and Vickers was eighteen then, and they were sort of dating."

"Doesn't sound like rape to me. I mean, she was at the legal age for consent. And it was consensual, right? Wouldn't the Romeo and Juliet exemption apply? I don't see how they could even call that sexual battery—and definitely not rape."

"The girl was slow, and the DA said that met the legal requirements for rape. The problem was Vickers' IQ wasn't much higher. Apparently they were in the same special class. Her parents didn't like their relationship, so they pulled her out of the school. But they still saw each other secretly."

"I don't understand. Vicker's IQ should have been used in his defense. Even then, I would think the most he could get for rape was maybe ten years, not a life sentence." I was still trying to make sense of what he was telling me.

"Let me put it this way. It was 1963. Cleveland was changing. You know, with lots of blacks moving in from the South. The girl was white and he's black. White people were scared to death of that sort of thing."

Principal Jackson's words filled the room. *We can't allow our children to be put at risk from these people.*

"When her parents accused him of rape, it played right into everyone's worst fears. It didn't help that the DA was up for reelection. He was under a lot of pressure to send a message, and that's exactly what he did—a twenty-year message."

"If we don't help, what will happen to him?"

"The parole board will deny him again and again until he dies in here," the chaplain said. "Which might not be too long."

"Is he sick?"

"I wish he was. Then they'd move him to the infirmary where he'd be safe."

"I don't understand."

"Ever hear of the Aryan Brotherhood?"

"Sort of. White power stuff. Like the Klan." I heard Roberta Stewart again. *Is it true you have a colored family living in the parsonage?*

"The Klan burns a cross in a black man's yard." Chaplain Stanton's eyes narrowed. "Aryans here aren't nearly that subtle, especially with sex offenders like Charles. They send a message in the shower room, if you know what I mean."

Pastor Duncan's office flashed through my mind. I shuddered.

"The threats got so bad for Charles, the warden finally moved him to solitary where he'd be safe. But he's no better off there. Do you know anything about that place?"

"Just that it's called 'the hole'...and I'm guessing for good reason."

"You got that right." He shook his head. "Even the most hardened men here dread that place." He paused, then spit out the words, "It's a dark, dank, solitary confinement cell, with nothing but a toilet and a bunk, and where prisoners sometimes have to sleep on the bare concrete floor."

He paused again. "Charles is locked down twenty-three hours a day, alone in a bare metal room with the only light coming from the slot in the door. Most guys go crazy after a week, but he's been in there almost a month." He stared at me now, letting his words hang in the air. "But he can't go back to the cell block because the Aryans will kill him. That's why I'm so desperate to find him a place before his parole board hearing next month."

Both of us sat there, not saying anything, as Daequan's final words screamed at me. *You're leavin', ain't you? I thought you were different!* A cold chill ran through me. That's when I got my idea. "I might know a place," I said and leaned back in my chair. "But first I need to meet him. Then I have to talk to a couple people. I'll call you later this week."

Charles was much smaller than I imagined, maybe just five-foot, six inches, and slight, not more than one-hundred and thirty pounds. *No wonder the Aryans targeted him.* What I noticed most was the way he greeted me. He looked me right in the eyes, and shook my hand with confidence. I didn't get that often in prison.

"Glad to meet you, sir," he said.

"And I'm glad to meet you, too. Chaplain Stanton speaks very highly of you, Charles."

"He's a good man, sir. I learned a lot from him. You know, about my faith."

Talk like that was common with inmates. "Everybody loves Jesus in jail," Dr. Webber told us in class. He said too often faith can be just another con in prison, and that we have to take a lot of the religious language we hear with a grain of salt. "But..." he quickly added, "...don't become so jaded you miss genuine faith when you see it. Sometimes God can be most present in prison."

How can I know if he's not conning the chaplain—and me? For some reason I remembered my first conversation with Walter Manchester. "Chaplain Stanton said your mother was quite a special person. Can you tell me about her?"

He looked up at the ceiling, as if trying to picture her in his mind, then looked toward me. "At home it was just me and Mama. I didn't have any brothers or sisters, and I never knew my daddy. Mama said he died when I was little."

"Were you close?"

"Real close. She had a beauty shop in our house and I helped her a lot with it."

"I understand she used to visit you every Saturday. It must have been hard when she died. When was it, five years ago?"

"Yes, sir. It was real hard for me. But that's when Chaplain Stanton came here, and he helped me get through it without doing something... you know, stupid."

"You mean hurt yourself? I hear that happens a lot in here."

He nodded. "I don't think I could have made it without Chaplain Stanton."

"I'm glad to hear that, I mean that he helped you. I just lost my mother last year, and I don't think I could have made it without my wife's help."

He tilted his head, just a little, as if surprised by this sudden personal turn in the conversation.

"Do you know what's been the hardest thing for me to deal with? Regret." He just stared at me. "My father was pretty abusive and I left home when I was still in high school. I don't regret leaving, but I do regret leaving my mother behind... with him." All those same emotions rushed over me again. I turned away, for just a minute. "But we got together again last year," I finally said. "She lived with me for several months until she died. It wasn't much time... but it helped us both. A lot."

He still didn't say anything, his eyes wide, listening to every word.

"How about you, Charles," I asked now. "Do you have any regrets?"

He looked up at the ceiling, as if trying to think of what to say. "My mama told me I had no business dating a white girl. She said nothing but trouble would come of it. I wish I listened to her, then maybe..."

"Maybe what, Charles?"

"If you're asking did I rape her like they said I did, no, sir, I didn't. Sure, we kissed, and she told the police that, but they didn't believe her...or me."

Was he telling the truth? I had no idea. But that really didn't matter. A life sentence, even for rape, was a gross violation of the moral basis of the law. And from what I could tell, it had everything to do with race.

"Well, I'm not an attorney, so I'm really not qualified to discuss legal issues with you," I said. "But the reason I'm here is to ask how you're doing, I mean, in the isolation cell. That's got to be hard." I thought he would go off on the Aryans or the guards, especially if he was innocent like he claimed. But he didn't.

"I'm okay. It's quiet there, and I get to read my Bible more," was all he said.

Has he somehow made peace with his situation? I wasn't convinced. "I understand you're going to see the parole board again. Any idea where you plan to go if you get released?"

"No, sir. Not yet. I got no family in Cleveland anymore. Chaplain Stanton said he's trying to help me, but he's not sure what he can do."

"What if your request is denied? What are you going to do then?"

"I've been denied a lot of times, and they might deny me again."

"But I hear the Aryan Brothers have made some threats. I guess what I'm asking is you've been locked up half your life for something you say you didn't do. Doesn't that bother you?" *Someone in your church, a woman, has said you touched, or even kissed her.* I only lost a job because of that lie, but it still made me seethe every time I thought of Reverend Nicholson. Charles lost twenty years of his life for something he said he didn't do. That had to be eating him up inside.

He just looked down at the floor, then back at me.

"Yes, sir, it does... or it did for a long time. But Chaplain Stanton told me something when I first met him. I still remember his exact words. He said, 'hate can't drive out hate. Only love can do that.'"

"What do you think he meant, Charles?" I needed to know—for me, too.

"I think he meant someday I'm going to get out of here. But if I don't let go of my hate, I'll never be free, no matter where I am. And that's what I did for the past five years—let go of my hate."

Driving back to Salem Hill, all I thought about was our conversation. I had degrees in both psychology and theology, but this guy who could barely read, and who's been in prison all his life, knew more about forgiveness than me. I didn't know what to think of Charles Vickers, but one thing was sure. I needed to know everything about him.

The next morning I asked Dr. Webber to make several calls to Columbus and have his records faxed to me. Two days later, surrounded by dozens of files and hundreds of pages about his entire life, I was convinced that Chaplain Stanton was right. That night I shared my thoughts with Kate.

"You don't actually think he's innocent, do you?" she asked. "I mean, twenty years for something he didn't do? How can that happen?"

"Innocent people can be accused of anything." The thought of Reverend Nicholson heated my face.

"But I thought you said he signed a confession?"

"He did, but he couldn't read. Not then anyway. When he got to prison some volunteer took pity on him and taught him to read at maybe a fourth grade level. I'm not surprised he signed a confession because he probably thought it was a letter to his mother, or whatever those cops told him."

Kate tapped her foot hard against the table. "Even if he couldn't read, if he's innocent like you say, how could he go to prison for something he didn't do? He had an attorney, didn't he?"

"Sort of. He had a public defender with too many cases and no time to read his file. He told him he'd spend forty years in prison if he didn't confess. Believe me, I've seen that too many times in my research this past year. You remember how much pressure the bishop put on me to go along with him if I wanted a bigger church. Is that any different?"

"But you didn't do it, Daniel."

"But most people would, and that's my point."

"I still can't imagine..."

I took her hand and squeezed it. "The apartment on the back of our house is separate from the kids, and it's empty. I think he deserves another chance," I said. "God knows, he's earned it. But this has to be our decision, not just mine." I leaned back in my chair—and waited while she thought about it.

Her foot stopped tapping, but she didn't say anything for a minute... two minutes. She just stared at the floor, thinking. Finally, she looked up at me. "I have just one question. Would he be a threat to our kids?"

I leaned in and took both her hands again. "Believe me, I've asked myself that question a hundred times. All I can say is I've read his file and I've talked with him for several hours. The chaplain has known him for years."

"I don't know, Daniel. What if... just what if...?"

"You remember our first date?"

She blinked. "What?"

I looked down at our hands and smiled. "When we started talking at the table...I had this feeling... I just felt so... so safe being with you... like I could be myself."

She smiled a little too, her warm green eyes welcoming me. "If I remember, we talked until two in the morning. I guess we both felt the same way." She squeezed my hand.

I cleared my throat. "What I'm trying to say, Kate, is even with all the baggage we both brought to that table, we both knew *inside*...." I laid my hand on my heart. "...we knew we were right together. And now with Charles, everything inside me feels right... that he's not dangerous, and bringing him here is the right thing to do... for all of us."

I paused, then took a deep breath. I wasn't sure she would understand what I wanted to say. I wasn't sure I even understood it myself. "I went to Mansfield to help Charles." I chose my words carefully. "But when I was with him in that hell hole he called home for the past twenty years, I felt like he was the one helping me. I know that doesn't make any sense, but what I'm saying, Kate, is I think—no, I know—Charles is the real thing, and we're the only hope he's got."

She was quiet again for several minutes, sitting there thinking. Finally, she squeezed my hand. "Do you think Charles will like living in Salem Hill?"

Four weeks later I met him at the Mansfield gate. He seemed so small in his prison issue suit. It was much too big, and he looked so lost standing there, clutching a small plastic bag that held everything he owned. He looked frightened too—like a boy waiting for the bus on his first day of school. I saw Daequan again, walking away from me, so hurt and angry. He would almost be a man now. Maybe I couldn't change what happened then, but I *would* do the right thing now with Charles!

"Feel strange to be on the outside?" I asked as we walked to the car.

He looked slowly all around at the open fields that surrounded the prison, his eyes wide, his mouth a little open. "Like nothing I ever felt." His words were deliberate, even stunned, as if desperately trying to understand what just happened. He reminded me of Emma when she saw her first snowfall. "I keep waiting for someone to take me back inside," he muttered, more to himself than me.

What could I tell him? He'd been locked up for twenty years—more than half his life. Prison was the only world he really knew. I couldn't even begin to understand what Charles felt right now. I remembered when I rode that bus out of Pittsburgh a lifetime ago. It was June and the fields that surrounded the prison were green. I opened the windows and the car filled with the smell of new life. "Breathe it all in, Charles."

CHAPTER 24
THE VALLEY OF THE SHADOW OF DEATH

SALEM HILL, 1984. "Daniel, you're not going to believe what happened in class today," Kate called out as she walked in the door from school. "You know that guy I told you about? The one who's always interrupting the teacher?"

"I think so. What was his name? Anthony something? Why?"

"Anthony Turner. They escorted him off campus!"

"You're kidding? What happened?" I grabbed a kitchen chair and waved her over. "I didn't think he was that disruptive. What did he do?"

"Neither did I, but like I said, he was always interrupting the teacher." She started talking faster. "When he did it the first day of class, Dr. Bennett tried to answer his questions. Even when he did it again, none of us said anything. I guess we thought he'd settle down, or drop out. But he kept coming to class and arguing with everyone. He made all of us nervous." She had to stop and catch her breath. "But today he got really upset, yelling something about God's vengeance on all sinners! It was scary." She shook her head, as if struggling to make sense of it. "All of us thought he was going to hurt someone."

I stared at her, my eyes as wide as hers. "Were the police involved?" I finally asked.

"No. Just campus security" She slowed her breathing. "He left with them, but he was yelling at Dr. Bennett the whole time. More crazy stuff."

"Unbelievable. What class was that, Kate?"

"Crisis intervention!" She offered a slight smile. "Ironic, isn't it? Dr. Bennett called it field experience, like it was something that happens all the time."

"Look on the bright side," I smiled back at her. "You won't have to worry about him anymore... at least until he gets out of prison someday and asks us for help." It was a joke, but she didn't laugh.

———

All the changes in our lives this year had exhausted both of us. I was still feeling my mother's death, especially when I looked into her bedroom, that Emma has now claimed as her own. But with all my work for Dr. Webber, helping Kate with her classes, and the ever-growing house project list, I was too busy to dwell on it, especially now that Charles was with us. Even if he was living in the apartment on the back of our house, I wasn't sure how the kids would adjust. As I expected, Jonathan was slow to accept him. "He's shy with most new people," I said. "Give him time."

Charles raised his eyebrows. "It's okay. Not like Emma, huh? She makes friends with everyone she meets."

"You got that right. Sometimes I wonder if they're even related." We both chuckled.

A couple days later, I found Charles and Jonathan bent over a jigsaw puzzle I had promised a week ago that I'd do with him, but never had the time. Both of them were so focused, I just gave Charles a thumbs up and mouthed, "Good job." when he looked up. He nodded, then plucked for a puzzle piece off the table. "Here it is!" He held it up as they high-fived each other. I don't know who was more excited—Charles or Jonathan.

It was Susan who seemed most comfortable with Charles, especially after he helped her with some of her chores. She was nearly twelve now, and one of her jobs was to rake the yard after I mowed it. Not a big project, but still a lot of work, especially this year with the June temperatures nearly 90 degrees every day. One afternoon he came out of his apartment, grabbed another rake and started working next to her. *Well, how about that?* I watched them from the kitchen window, sipping my coffee. An hour later when I looked out the window again, they were both covered in sweat, dumping the last pile of clippings in the garbage can. Charles held up his palm for her, and she gave him a solid high-five, just like Jonathan did. I walked back into my office smiling.

But Charles made it clear he wanted a job more than anything else. That was something he dreamed about every day in prison—to have a normal life again. Every inmate I talked with had the same dream. They all said that was the only thing that made prison bearable—dreams. "But they have no idea how hard actually getting a job can be." Dr. Webber always cautioned us in class. And Charles was no different. He never had a real job before, and finding one in Salem Hill, especially when Crown Glass announced they were shutting down at the end of the month—sending fifteen hundred unemployed workers into the market... well, I wasn't optimistic. "Whatever it takes, he's got to get a job," I told Kate. "I'm not buying him a bus ticket back to Cleveland, or Alabama, or anywhere else, not like I did Lettie and Damien."

A week later Charles announced he got hired at Miller Brothers Egg Farm. "He should be okay now," I told Kate at breakfast the next morning. "Maybe we can take him out to dinner tonight? You know, to celebrate his new job." It had been so long since we did anything fun, and we both needed the break.

"That's a good idea." She smiled, taking my hand. "But let's go someplace special, like that Italian restaurant in Dayton, near the river."

"La Focaccia? Great idea." I squeezed her hand. "But let's take the kids and make it a family celebration."

Before she could answer, the phone rang. It was Sally Murphy, a reporter with the Salem Hill newspaper. I had no idea why she would be calling, especially at this time of the morning. "I want to ask you about Charles Vickers, the convicted rapist who's living in your house."

The conversation quickly went downhill from there. I tried to say he wasn't a danger to the community, that he benefitted from a lot of programming in prison. I even tried to say he might be innocent, but all she wanted to know was why we brought him to Salem Hill.

That afternoon all the details of Charles' crime was the lead story—especially that he was now living with us. There was even a picture of our house! "This is going to get ugly," I grumbled at Kate, throwing the paper in the garbage. *Should I tell Charles about this. No. It'll only upset him. We'll just ignore it.* But two hours later there was another call we couldn't ignore. "The city council is gonna run that nigger rapist out of town. Maybe you, too." Then the line went dead.

Kate didn't say anything, but I saw something in her eyes. It was more than worry...but not quite fear. A foreboding, maybe. We cancelled our dinner plans and spent the night at home, sitting wordlessly in the dark long after the kids had gone to bed... just thinking about what might happen now.

———

I had never been to a city council meeting before, or even inside city hall for that matter. The council chamber was on the second floor, at the far end of the hall. It was a room intended for maybe seventy-five people, but the dark paneling made it seem smaller. There was a long table at the front of the room for the council members, mayor, city attorney and clerk. Above them was a large plaque with the city motto—'Salem Hill: the city of peace.' All the council members kept looking at the people forcing their way into the room. It was obvious they weren't prepared for the angry crowd now filling every chair, and many of them held a copy of the newspaper. I found the last two vacant seats in the rear by the door.

"My name is Larry Miller and I live at 703 Phoenix Street." a man standing at the podium up in front told the council when the meeting started. It was hard to understand his words from where we sat. Apparently, I wasn't the only one.

"You need to speak up, Larry, so everyone can hear you," Chairman Donald McKenzie said.

"Sorry, Don. I never done this before." He looked down at something he was holding, then back to the council members.

"It's okay, Larry. Take your time."

He took a deep breath and reintroduced himself, gripping the podium hard as he spoke. "...and I read that article in the Salem Hill News last week about what this Robinson guy is doing at his house."

He held up the paper and pointed toward the headline. "It says he's got that rapist Charles Vickers living there. He called it his moral responsibility to give him a second chance. Salem Hill has got a lot of kids." His voice grew louder. "What about his moral responsibility to them?"

"Damn right, Larry," someone shouted.

"We'll have no outbursts here," Chairman McKenzie warned the crowd. "Everyone will get a chance to speak, but only from the podium."

Several people stood and pushed through the crowd, lining up behind him.

"I'm not done with what I got to say, Don," Larry Miller's voice was louder now, more confident.

"You tell 'em, Larry," a woman yelled.

He quickly scanned the audience behind him and nodded toward her. It was obvious, at least to me, he was enjoying this moment. "Those of us here ain't the only ones upset with what Robinson is doing." He looked back toward the council members. "I got a bunch of petitions I passed around my neighborhood... and I got 450 signatures on them in just four days!" Someone nearby handed him a stack of papers. He slowly walked the five feet to the clerk's desk, holding them high in the air above him, then dropped them on the table with dramatic flair in front of her. "EVERYONE wants the city to stop Robinson and get Vickers out of our town. If anyone's got a moral responsibility, it's YOU council members."

"I bet he practiced that move all day," I whispered to Kate.

Apparently, it worked. Several people clapped as he walked back to his seat, nodding toward the crowd with each step.

"Thank you, Mr. Miller." Chairman McKenzie looked at the people still coming into the room, and those filling both side aisles, then at the clock on the back wall, and finally back toward Mayor Wayne. "Is there anyone else who has something to say to the council before we move onto our regular agenda?" It was obvious he was irritated his meeting was getting out of control before it even began.

"I got something to say," a woman standing behind Larry Miller called out, moving toward the podium.

"State your name please." Chairman McKenzie said.

"You know who I am, Uncle Don."

"Course, I do, Becky, but you gotta say your name for the record. It's the rules."

"Sorry, Uncle Don. I mean Chairman McKenzie. My name is Becky Wallace and I live across the street from Robinson. We bought our house two years ago. We planned on living there all our lives. This year we had our first baby." She was young, maybe twenty-five or so, a little heavy. She seemed familiar, and I vaguely remembered seeing a pregnant neighbor a couple times, but we never talked, other than just a nod hello. She looked angry now. "Because of what Robinson done, my husband and me are afraid to have any more kids, at least not in that neighborhood. We got our house up for sale now. The realtor said it'll be hard to sell with Vickers living next door. It ain't fair he can come into our town and ruin our lives. It just ain't fair. Thank you."

The chairman's face was suddenly crimson. "Mr. Livingston, I want you to look into this," he barked at the city attorney. "See if there's some legal issue that needs to be addressed. Then get back with the council at our next meeting."

"I can certainly do that, Mr. Chairman."

"Alright then, if there's no more comments from the audience, I'd like to move on with our agenda."

We slipped out the back of the room and hurried home. Neither of us slept much that night.

———

The next morning I was running late for a meeting with Dr. Webber when someone knocked on my door. It was a woman I thought I recognized, and there was a man with her carrying a large camera pointed toward me.

"Mr. Robinson. I'm Cheryl Atkins, with Channel 7 News in Dayton. I want to ask you about Charles Vickers. Do you have a minute?" I only met her once at some media event Dr. Webber held, but

I never actually spoke with her, not like this. She was taller than I remembered, and her television makeup seemed out-of-place in person, especially here in Salem Hill. I definitely didn't want to talk with her now.

"I really don't have any time. I'm late for a meeting. But maybe later." I started to close the door.

"Did you know there was a petition brought to the Salem Hill city council meeting last night with 450 signatures? A lot of people are upset about Charles Vickers living in your house. Do you have any comment, Mr. Robinson?" She shoved a microphone in front of me.

Be calm. Don't react. "Yes, it's true Mr. Vickers is living in an apartment behind our house," I answered carefully, still trying to gather my thoughts. "But I want to make it clear he's legally free to live anywhere in the state. The prison chaplain asked us to give him a place to stay until he can get back on his feet. He's convinced—and I agree with him—that he's actually innocent. I'm sorry some people in Salem Hill are upset, but I can assure you, Mr. Vickers is not a threat. In fact, he's got a job now, so he's actually contributing to the community."

The camera man moved closer with every pause I took, adjusting his lens.

"The council asked the city attorney to see if there were any legal options for the neighbors. Do you have any comments about that, Mr. Robinson?"

The lens closed in with a low whir. My mind raced. I wanted to push that damned camera out of my face—and both of them off my porch. What would Dr. Webber do now? *Just relax and speak slowly.* "I feel confident we have not broken any laws or city ordinances by offering Mr. Vickers a place to live," I said now as calmly as I could. "But the council is certainly welcome to look into the issue."

All the details of Charles' crime, and my answers to her questions, nearly verbatim, were the lead story on the six o'clock news.

I clicked off the television, shaking my head. "I can't believe people are making such a big deal about Charles living with us. I don't get it."

Kate looked toward me. "I thought the chaplain warned you this could happen when he was released."

"Sure, in Cleveland—maybe. But not Salem Hill. That's why I agreed to bring him here. I guess we were wrong."

She was quiet for a minute. "Have you told Charles yet, about that meeting last night...and now this?" nodding toward the television, and looking as worried as me.

"Not yet. I mean, how do I say, 'Welcome to Salem Hill, and by the way, everyone wants you to leave?' That's not a conversation I'm looking forward to."

The next day, waiting for Charles to come home from work, I thought a lot about what Daequan had to face. His only crime was being black in a white school. But Charles spent twenty years in prison for something he didn't do... The judge pounded his gavel. *Guilty as charged!* That metal cell door slammed shut! I shuddered. Daequan... Charles... Salem Hill... I bit my lip. *I won't let him down. Not this time...whatever it takes!*

Although Charles had a kitchen in his apartment, it only seemed natural for him to have dinner with us and talk. How are you settling in Salem Hill? How do you like your job? The kids wanted to know if he liked pizza. What kind? What was his favorite television show? The usual questions. Afterward, when Kate and the kids were gone upstairs, he stood to leave too, but I asked him to stay with me. "You know, so we can talk without the kids." He sat back down, his eyes searching my face.

"You want a Coke?" I asked.

He nodded, and I grabbed two cans from the refrigerator.

"Amazing, ain't it?" He snapped the tab open, then took a long drink.

"What?"

"That you don't need a bottle opener for Coke now. It's little things like that I'm still getting used to."

"I never thought about it, but I guess you're right."

There was a long silence, both of us just sipping our Cokes. His eyes met mine. "Are you okay?" he asked.

"Not really." My hand shook, just a little, as I set my can down on the table. I hated what I had to tell him. "There's something you should know. I-I'm sorry I didn't tell you sooner."

He looked quietly at me, waiting.

Everything came out then. Each detail of the meeting, the newspaper, the anonymous call, the television interview. I felt sick telling him this, like I had let him down, but...I had to tell him. I owed him that.

Charles didn't move, or even blink. Finally, when I said it all, he took another drink from his can and set it back down, nodding.

How can he act like nothing happened? He doesn't even look surprised! "Are you...ah...I mean, did you know about...?"

He lifted his can one more time and emptied it, then gently set it on the table. "I heard some talk at work. Oh, and there was that newspaper in the garbage can a couple days ago."

"So-so you knew about this? The whole time?"

Charles shrugged. "I didn't know some stuff. Like the phone call. The television interview. I know you gave me a TV for my room, but I never watch it much. I prefer books. Learned that in prison." He looked me right in the eyes. "For what it's worth, I appreciate what you said, I mean, about me deserving another chance... and especially that you know I'm innocent. That means a lot...more than I can say. I mean, you left me with your kids while you both were at that meeting. I—"

He clasped his hands. "Besides Chaplain Stanton, I never had no white man believe in me like you."

My mouth dropped open. Everyone in this damned town was so afraid of this guy, yet he's the gentlest, most forgiving person I ever met.

"I've got to know, Charles. For my sake. Will you be okay? Please, tell me the truth."

He nodded. "I'm okay. I really am." His voice was calm, his face relaxed. Not even a hint of worry or anger. "Like I told you in Chaplain Stanton's office. I had to let go of my hate if I ever wanted to really be free, no matter where I am. That's what got me through prison, and that's what I'll do now. I know God will take care of me here too."

I nodded. But I envied Charles. His faith seemed to come so easy for him.

———

Two weeks later the city council chamber was again packed with people, but this time reporters from the Dayton newspaper and several television stations were there. For just a minute, I was standing in the parking lot at Kent State again, looking at the angry mob in front of me, drawn in by the intense emotions, but frightened by it at the same time. Chairman McKenzie stared toward Kate and me in the front row. We never actually met, but he seemed to know who I was. The air in the room was already stifling. Sweat beaded on my forehead in minutes. Several people fanned themselves.

"Before we begin our regular agenda, is there anyone who would like to address the council," he asked, but he already knew the answer. A dozen people were lined up behind the podium, and all of them looked angry.

"My name is Linda Zimmerman and I live on Second Street, right behind Robinson's house. I'm a teacher at the elementary school, and I came here because I love the children in our town. I respect that he wants to help people, but he's putting our children in danger with that rapist living there. If you ask me, they should have executed him twenty years ago." Mrs. Zimmerman shook, crying softly. "I'm sorry for being so upset," she said, wiping her eyes. "I told my husband Tom I didn't want my emotions to get the best of me tonight. But I'm just so scared what might happen if that predator ever gets his hands on one of our children."

She took several breaths to calm herself. The man standing with her whispered something. She shook her head, then looked back toward the council table. "I'm a Christian and I believe in helping people, but not that pervert. Not in a neighborhood with innocent children."

The room erupted with applause. This time the chairman allowed it to continue.

For God's sake, woman, he's been with my own kids for a month! How dangerous can he be?" I wanted to scream at her, but she wouldn't hear me. None of them would.

"Thank you, Mrs. Zimmerman," the chairman finally said. "All of us on the council share your concerns for our children. And I want to say how much we all appreciate your many years of service at the elementary school."

"Thank you." She wiped her eyes again, but this time carefully in front of the cameras, then sat down.

"Mr. Brothers, I believe you're next," the chairman said.

"My name is Robert Brothers and I have a real estate office in that neighborhood. My dad started our business thirty years ago and I still run it. I live right down the street from Robinson's place where that predator is living now." He turned and glared at me. "So I'm really worried about what he's doing to our town, and how it's affecting our property values."

"Damn right, Bob!" someone shouted.

"Maybe if he saw all the work we've done to fix our house, he wouldn't worry so much about property values," I whispered to Kate. She nodded.

"Folks, you can't be talking out of order," the chairman said with little enthusiasm. I got the impression he agreed with them. "All of you will get a chance to speak about what Mr. Robinson is trying to do here in Salem Hill. Okay, go ahead, Bob."

"Thanks, Don. When I first heard a minister bought the old Allen house and was fixing it up, I thought that's a good thing. Be good for the neighborhood. Boy, was I wrong. I've got a ten-year-old son, and he plays in the neighborhood all the time, like I used to do when I was his age. Now I'm afraid to let him even go outside. Robinson says he wants to give people a second chance. What about our kids? They deserve a chance too!"

"You tell em, Bob!" someone shouted behind us. Kate shook, then quickly grabbed my hand. I squeezed it, my eyes still focused on Chairman McKenzie, who forced back a smile.

This time he banged his gavel, but with little enthusiasm. "I won't tolerate these outbursts," he said looking toward the camera.

I jumped to my feet. "Mr. Chairman! I want to address this issue!"

"Alright, Mr. Robinson. The council will hear from you now. But you gotta come to the podium." He didn't look happy, but I didn't care.

"First of all, I object to the term 'predator' that both people have used. It's inflammatory, and only creates unnecessary fear and anger in the community. Second, when Mr. Vickers was released, he was legally free to live anywhere in Ohio, but he had nowhere to go. We agreed to let him stay with us until he got a job and a place of his own."

"He can live in hell!" Robert Brothers called out from his seat. The woman next to him nodded and yelled something I couldn't hear.

"I won't have any more outbursts like that." the chairman barked, banging his gavel harder. He couldn't afford to have his meeting get out of control in front of the television cameras—not in an election year.

I turned and quickly looked around the room. *There's my mailman sitting by the window. And the woman behind him is the clerk at Kroger's who always talks about her kids to Kate. Isn't that Susan's teacher in the back of the room? These are my neighbors. People I see on the street every day. We say hello to each other.* But all I saw now was Kent State. The tension in the room was suffocating. *Don't react. Just present the facts.* I turned back toward the chairman. My legs were shaking. I took a deep breath and gripped the podium.

"What I'm saying is that our house actually makes the neighborhood safer." I tried speaking slowly now, just like Dr. Webber taught me to do in front of the cameras. "The data is very clear that housing is the key to reducing recidivism. All we're trying to do..."

"If the city don't get rid of Vickers, we'll do it ourselves!" a woman yelled. I quickly glanced at the exit, then turned toward Kate and mouthed, "Are you okay?" She nodded, but her eyes nervously scanned the room.

Chairman McKenzie banged his gavel several times, then growled, "Thank you, Mr. Robinson," all while looking toward the city attorney. My turn was done. I dropped back into my seat and took Kate's hand again. "We were planning to hear from Mr. Livingston later in the meeting," the chairman said. "But I think it's best if he gives his legal opinion on this issue at this time. Mr. Livingston."

"Chairman McKenzie. Council members. I've researched this situation extensively the past two weeks and I believe there are two pertinent factors." He shuffled through several papers on the table. "First, Mr. Vickers is on parole. That means, by definition, his rights are limited by law. Second, technically he is a Cuyahoga County resident. That means he should be under their jurisdiction, not ours. If the council should pass an emergency ordinance prohibiting felons from other counties from moving here, I feel it would stand up to legal scrutiny."

Chairman McKenzie tried to look serious for the cameras, but he seemed relieved, even elated. Everyone knew he planned to run for mayor in the next election. I suspected he hoped to use Charles Vickers —and me—as his ticket into office.

"Then I move that Mr. Livingston draft an emergency ordinance to be voted on at our next council meeting on September 4," McKenzie said. "All those in favor, signify with an *aye.*"

It was unanimous.

———

Kate and I both tried to put the council meeting out of our minds for the next two weeks.

After my conversation with him, and especially with all the tension in Salem Hill, he had dinner with us every day. And now, it was a good time to see how he was handling it. That's when he told me what happened at the farm. "They said they didn't need me anymore."

Kate and I looked at one another. We both knew Ed Phillips, the farm manager. I thought he was a pretty good guy, and nothing like those rednecks screaming for blood at the council meeting. "What happened? I mean, did they tell you why they let you go?" Work was slow in Salem Hill since Crown Glass closed, but the last time I drove by Miller's, I saw they were adding another chicken barn.

"They just said they didn't need me anymore."

"Are you okay? Anything I can do to help you find another job?"

"No sir... I mean Daniel."

I never felt comfortable with Charles calling me 'sir,' especially since he was living with us now. But after twenty years in a white man's prison, old habits were hard to break. "I've already been to the job center and found a couple places that might be hiring. But thanks for offering."

"Maybe it's only a temporary thing, Charles. Maybe when that new chicken barn is completed, maybe they'll call you back then."

"You're probably right." There was little enthusiasm in his voice. It was obvious he didn't believe it—and neither did I.

I didn't know what else to say to him. I remembered Lettie... the defeat in her eyes as she climbed the steps of that bus back to Alabama. *No! Not this time!*

I called Ed first thing in the morning to see what he could do.

"We just had to make some cutbacks," he said. "Charles was our last hire, so I had to let him go. That's all." He sounded nervous. I got the clear impression he really didn't want to talk with me.

"Do you remember when we first met at Rotary? What was it, three years ago?" I asked. "I was new in town and I felt really awkward being there. But you sat with me when you saw me alone in the corner. I always appreciated that. That's why I was glad Charles was working for you. So tell me what's really going on, Ed."

There was some shuffling on his end, growing fainter. Then his office door shut. "I don't like it anymore than you do," he said when he picked up the phone again. "But I didn't have a choice. It was old man Miller. He said having Charles here was bad for business. He said he got a lot of calls from people in town, and I think city hall too, but he wouldn't say who."

"Ed, for what it's worth, I'm convinced Charles never did it. I've studied all his court records, and it's obvious it was nothing but race. For God's sake, Ed, you're from Cleveland. You know how political that city can be for a black man. I got a glimpse of that here at the city council meeting last week. Is there anything you can do for him?"

"You're probably right. Truth is, I liked the guy. But this is Salem Hill..." His voice barely a whisper now. "...people here are scared of Charles... and they want him gone." His breathing was heavier now. "I don't agree with it, but there's nothing I can do. I'm sorry. I really am."

There was nothing I could say. "For what it's worth, thanks for trying," was all I could manage. I started to hang up the phone when he said something faint, hesitant. "Just be careful, Daniel." Then the line went dead. Was that fear in his voice?

———

It was two days later when I stopped in McDonalds for a hamburger. The lobby was crowded, and the line was longer than usual. I was waiting for my turn to order, still not sure what I wanted to eat. For some reason, the line seemed unbearably slow. That's when I noticed an older woman staring at me. After several uncomfortable minutes, she stepped right in front of me.

"Are you that Robinson guy I read about in the paper?" she hissed.

Who is this woman? I looked straight ahead at the menu board without answering, but she moved closer, just inches from my face. A smell of cigarettes hung from her breath.

"You're the one who brought that rapist to town. If you lived in my neighborhood, I wouldn't put up with your shit."

I tried again to ignore her, hoping she'd go away, but that only made her madder. "I've got seven grandkids..." Her voice was louder now. People turned and stared at us. Several moved back. They looked as nervous as me. "...if that animal you got living in your house ever comes near any of them..." she snarled, "...I'll kill him myself, and I'll kill you too."

My heart pounded in my chest like a jackhammer. All I could think to do was raise my hands in front of me. "Lady, I just want a hamburger." It was more of a plea than a protest. But that only made her madder. Her face contorted with rage, getting so red I thought it would explode. "I'm not that hungry after all," I muttered, turning away, and walking out the door. My hand shook as I fumbled for the key. Voices bombarded me as I drove out of the parking lot.

We're the only hope he's got.

I got a petition I passed around my neighborhood.

People are scared of Charles and they want him gone.

I'll kill him myself, and I'll kill you too.

I was still shaking so much I drove two miles across town before I realized I was going the wrong direction. I pulled into the empty Crown Glass parking lot, slammed on the brakes, and pounded on the steering wheel. "What the hell have I gotten us into!" I didn't know how long I sat there, unmoving, not even thinking. Just staring at that woman in front of me again. I turned the car around and drove back home. I needed to hold my kids again. I needed to hold Kate.

That night, long after dinner, I was sitting alone in the living room, trying to make sense of all that happened, when a loud knock on the door shattered the silence. I sat straight up in my chair. *Is it that crazy woman from McDonalds? Did she follow me home?* I pulled back the window curtain, just a little. "Thank God! It's only Jim." I breathed a sigh of relief and unlocked the door. Jim Richards was the pastor of the Salem Hill Presbyterian Church downtown. He never seemed to like confrontation. Maybe that was why his congregation had been growing. He made everyone feel good. I always envied that. But there was also something... unsettling about him. That's probably why I hadn't talked to him since I quit my job at the Methodist Church. But I was really glad to see him now.

"I heard what happened to you," he said when I opened the door. "Are you okay?"

"Little shook up, I guess. It's not every day someone threatens to kill me in McDonald's. But I'm fine." I led him to the living room and waved toward a chair.

"The reason I'm here, Daniel," he said, before he even sat down, "is that all of us in the ministerial association are very worried for you, and for our community, especially after that incident today at McDonalds."

"I could sure use your help, Jim. You know, with Charles' situation. He's not dangerous like some people make him out to be. Truth is, I'm convinced he's innocent. But that's another story."

"Like I said, Daniel, that's why I wanted to see you... you know, before this situation gets out of hand. All the ministers in town have given this whole thing you're doing a lot of prayer and...." He looked down at the floor, took a breath, then looked up at me. "...we all agree what you're trying to do for Mr. Vickers is a good thing, but... but we're not sure it's best that you do it here. Maybe if you helped him get a place in Dayton, you know with...."

For just a second, Principal Jackson flashed through my mind. "With who, Jim? *His own kind?*"

His face flushed. "I didn't mean... for it to... to sound like that," he stammered. We're just worried what all this is doing to our community. All of us, I mean, all the ministers, we all thought he'd be better off in a city like Dayton, not a little town like Salem Hill. That's all."

"That's okay, Jim. I know what you meant. And I'm glad you stopped by." I stood and walked him toward the door.

He turned and shook my hand feebly. "We'll be praying for you... and Charles too."

"Thanks." was all I said, then shut the door.

"Who was that?" Kate asked when she walked into the room.

"Just someone who came by to remind me why I'm not a pastor anymore. That's all."

"I don't understand."

"It doesn't matter, Kate. It's been a long day. Let's go to bed. I need to feel safe with you for a little while."

———

Charles didn't have any luck finding another job, but he didn't seem discouraged by it. "It's still better than being at Mansfield," was all he said. We offered to take him with us to the Shawnee Park, but after someone yelled something about a 'nigger rapist,' I bought us a family pass to Kings Island Amusement Park. "At least no one knows us in Cincinnati," I told Kate as we climbed in the car.

"Can I ride The Beast this year, Dad? Please?" Susan begged all the way there. That was all she talked about since we saw the park advertised on television six months ago. Now that we were actually going there, she wouldn't take no for an answer. "It's the biggest and fastest roller coaster in the world! All my friends at school have already been on it."

Kate would never go near that thing, and I wasn't too excited about woofing my cookies all over the park either. "Ask Charles if he'll ride with you," I finally said when we drove into the park. He looked at me in the rearview mirror, his face contorted in exaggerated pain. But he shot Susan a broad smile, then looked helplessly back at me again. "You owe me, Daniel." he mouthed.

"Better than Mansfield," I called out as both of them walked toward the entrance line. That was the first of their four trips on The Beast—and all both of them talked about the rest of the day.

"I was never so scared and so happy at the same time!" he said over and over in the car on the drive home.

"You sure didn't look happy," Susan snorted. "I never heard anyone scream that loud before."

"I wasn't screaming! I was laughing!"

"Then I never heard anyone laugh like that either."

Now it was all of us who laughed, but Charles laughed loudest. Even in the dim light in the car, I could see him smiling the whole ride home. When we finally reached Salem Hill, it was dark. All three kids had been asleep for the past thirty miles. Even Kate had her eyes closed.

"You know what I felt on that ride?" I heard Charles' soft voice from the back seat. "It was like I was flying through the air... completely free, without anyone holding me down."

I didn't answer. I wasn't even sure he was talking to me. All I knew was that was the best day of the summer for everyone—especially Charles.

———

September 4 finally arrived and the council chamber was again packed. This time more reporters and cameras lined up around the back of the room, jostling for the best position. The air conditioner was running, but it wasn't doing any good. It was obvious the system was intended for only the handful of people who normally attended these meetings. Someone tried to open the windows, but they wouldn't budge. The meeting hadn't even begun, but the air was already stifling. Several people were fanning themselves, and my shirt stuck to me. Chairman McKenzie whispered something to Mayor Wayne, who nodded, and both men removed their coats and loosened their ties.

The chairman wiped his brow, turning toward the audience. "Before we begin our regular agenda, is there anyone who would like to address the council."

Shawnee County Commissioner John Brookfield stood and walked quickly to the front of the room. "My name is John Brookfield." He gripped the podium tight as he spoke. "As you all know, I'm a county commissioner. But I'm here tonight as a resident of the neighborhood where that predator Vickers is living. I'm here to say that we don't need his kind in our community."

"No, sir, we don't!" a woman yelled out.

"Amen!" someone called out from the other side of the room. The chairman banged his gavel for quiet, but that only seemed to make Brookfield angrier.

"I grew up in this neighborhood. Now I have three kids of my own and I want them to grow up here too. But I have proof Vickers was stalking my daughter." His voice was louder now and his eyes bulged. Sweat ran down his face. "I saw him myself, standing in the alley, staring at my backyard, at my little girl!" He nearly screamed the words.

"I woulda shot that son-of-a-bitch!" shouted a man from the back of the room. The cameras swiveled in that direction as the reporters furiously scribbled in their note pads.

Brookfield paused, turning toward the audience. "I yelled at him, and he ran down the alley. God only knows what he was thinking." He looked around the room, then directly at the cameras, as if pleading for help. "Now I can't let my kids even go out in our own backyard."

The audience erupted, almost with one voice. "Get that nigger rapist out of town!" that same man in the back of the room called out. "Robinson too!" someone behind me yelled. Several cops standing in the hall moved into the room, eyeing the crowd nervously. One of them said something into his radio.

I jumped to my feet. "Mr. Chairman, I object to Mr. Brookfield's accusation," I yelled over the noise. "When did this incident happen? Did you call the police?"

"I d-don't have to answer those questions!" Brookfield stammered, clearly caught off guard. McKenzie again banged his gavel several times, but I ignored him.

"You have to answer my questions, Mr. Brookfield, if you're serious about keeping the community safe! If someone was stalking your daughter, especially if you believe it was Mr. Vickers, did you call the police? Because I'm sure Mr. Livingston can verify that. But we both know you didn't, don't we?" Because it never happened!"

I let that statement hang in the air. Brookfield glared at me. But I wasn't done with him. "I'm extremely offended a county commissioner would intentionally feed the community fears with such an inflammatory allegation such as this, without even an attempt to prove it. It's irresponsible, even contemptible."

"Mr. Robinson, you're out of order," the chairman slammed his gavel hard on the table. "You need to direct your comments to the council, not Mr. Brookfield!"

"No sir!" I shot back. "It's Mr. Brookfield who's out of order. His comments are so outlandish, I must address them for the safety of the community."

"Mr. Chairman! Mr. Chairman!" Brookfield shrieked like a cornered animal, furious that I had challenged him so publicly, and in an election year. "I demand the council vote immediately to get that bastard Vickers out of town!" With each word, he thrust his finger into the air furiously, as though Charles was in the room. "I demand, we ALL demand you vote now!"

The room erupted. Several people stood, shaking their fists in the air. I looked quickly all around. Two more cops moved in from the hall. One of them said something into his radio, then signaled to his partner.

"Don, you've got to take a vote on this before these people go crazy," Mayor Wayne yelled to the chairman over the uproar.

McKenzie quickly banged his gavel repeatedly until the audience finally stopped yelling. "The council is prepared to vote on the emergency ordinance to amend the zoning laws of Salem Hill. The clerk will now read the ordinance. Mrs. Johnson."

"*Emergency Ordinance 84-21053 to restrict the residency of felons under supervision with state or county legal authorities, and whose residency is from outside Shawnee County. Said felons are hereby prohibited from establishing residency in Shawnee County until they are released from supervision.*"

"Please vote aye or nay regarding this ordinance when your name is called."

My head was going to explode! I wanted to scream at all of them, *Charles is a human being, not some monster!* Kate gripped my hand hard. I held my breath, but I already knew what they were going to do. I always knew.

Unanimous vote—again.

Cheers erupted through the audience, followed by more threats toward Charles and me. "Run 'em both outta town!" they began chanting.

I frantically searched the room. "Where are those cops?" I called to

Kate over the screams. She didn't answer, but I saw fear in her eyes. "We gotta get out of the room before the crowd comes after us!" I grabbed her arm and moved quickly toward the door.

"I'm not surprised by the vote," I yelled to her as I shoved our way through the crowd, "but I'm really worried about these people. I haven't seen anything like this since Kent State. Stay close and keep your head down."

Once we were out of the room, I pushed past several more shouting people in the hall, and moved as fast as we could toward the stairs, but the crowd blocked my way. Brookfield yelled something behind me. Some guy tried to push us back, but I grabbed Kate's arm even tighter and elbowed him. Hard. We ran past him, down the steps and out the building.

Thank God, we made it out of there in one piece! I frantically looked all around. "Where did we park the car, Kate? Wait—the back side of the lot!" I grabbed her arm again. "Hurry! Before one of Brookfield's goons comes after us!"

We ran a dozen feet across the lot, when suddenly several camera lights flashed on, nearly blinding me. "Mr. Robinson! Mr. Robinson!" two reporters called out, before a woman shoved a microphone in my face.

"Cheryl Atkins. Channel 7 News. Could I ask you a question? What do you think of the decision by the city council tonight?"

I stopped, looking back at the city building. No one had followed us. I took a quick breath to calm my nerves and faced the camera. *How would Dr. Webber answer this?* I took another deep breath. "Obviously, I'm disappointed, but I'm not really surprised," I said slowly, trying my best to sound calm. "Even though Mr. Vickers has been freed by the Department of Correction, and can legally live anywhere in Ohio, too often fear and bigotry, and especially politics, make it difficult for men like him to get a second chance, as was evident with this vote."

The noise from inside the building got louder...louder, until the front door banged open. "Daniel!" Kate tugged on my arm and pointed at several people on the steps. I glanced over, then back at the reporter. "Unfortunately, we really have no choice now, but file a lawsuit to overturn this ordinance. I hate to do that, but the city has left us..."

"There he is!" someone shouted. Footsteps thundered toward us—then a loud THUMP! A brick bounced off the pavement right next to me. Several more rocks landed nearby, and the reporter and I both jumped back, ducking our heads. I grabbed Kate's arm, as I frantically eyed the crowd. "Get behind me. Quick!" My heart raced. My whole body shivered from sheer adrenaline. But there was nowhere to go. Suddenly blue uniforms and silver badges cut in front of us! "Thank God you're here!" I called out to the two cops.

"Follow me, sir!" one of them grabbed my arm and his partner took Kate's. The officers led us quickly to the far side of the lot where our car was parked.

I tried several times to check the mirror as we drove out into the street, but my hand shook too much. "Daniel. You're bleeding!" Kate cried out as we passed under a street light. "There's blood on your forehead. Are you okay?" She reached over and dabbed my face with a napkin from the glove box.

My head throbbed. I felt sick. "It's nothing. Probably a scratch or something." I tried to sound calm, but I wasn't very convincing. Neither of us said anything as we drove the eight blocks back to our house. When I pulled into our driveway, I shut off the engine, then sat there for several minutes, in silence. "You know what really bothers me?" I finally said, staring out the front window. "How could I be so naïve—or maybe stupid—that I didn't think this could happen. After what the church did to Lettie and Damien, why am I surprised? Maybe if I did something different. Maybe if we moved away from here when we had the chance. Maybe..."

I turned to her. "I'm sorry I ever got you into this mess, Kate. I really am."

She took my hand and pulled me to her. "Remember what Nick said at our wedding? 'Troubles may surround us, sometimes too many to count. Sometimes we can't see our way out. But God will bring us through it all together.' Together, Daniel," she whispered in my ear. "I'll always be right by your side, no matter what happens." I held her hand tight, both of us now staring out the window in the dark silence.

CHAPTER 25
ISLAND OF RELIEF IN A SEA OF DESPAIR

SALEM HILL, 1984. The light was still on in Charles' apartment, but I didn't want to talk with him. Not yet anyway. We walked up the stairs, then stood in front of each of the kids' rooms, watching them sleep in the soft light of their night lamps. They looked so... peaceful, without a care. There was nothing under this roof like the madness we just went through. All that fear about Charles... and the safest place in town is right here with him watching over my three beautiful babies. I couldn't help smiling at the irony, but it still left a bitter taste in my mouth.

We laid in bed, listening to the clock in the stairway sound off every hour—one o'clock—two o'clock—three—four—five. All I could think about all night long, was what to tell Charles. When the clock finally rang six times, I dragged myself to the living room. "Maybe Channel 7 will have some news about last night." I switched on the television.

"As you can see, the situation here is quite tense," Cheryl Atkins said into the camera, pushing back some hair from her face. "Threats against Daniel Robinson and convicted rapist Charles Vickers have now turned violent. It's clear this story is not over yet." The sound of yelling and chanting in the background almost washed out her voice. She glanced quickly behind her, then spoke louder now into the camera. "The next battle will likely be fought in the courts. This is Cheryl Atkins, reporting to you live from Salem Hill, the city of peace—or at least it used to be."

"Oh God, what have I gotten us into?" I clicked off the television. "How do I tell Charles about all this?"

I found him raking the yard just after breakfast. "I'm glad you didn't go to that meeting last night." Yesterday, I thought about asking him to come with us, maybe even speak to the council, so they could see he wasn't the monster people feared him to be. Bad idea, Kate said. Now I was glad I listened to her. Brookfield and his mob would have killed him if they had the chance.

Charles stopped raking and tilted his head toward me. "Why? What happened," he asked.

His eyes went up to my forehead, where the cut was still swollen and tender.

"They passed a new law that could affect you."

He laid the rake against the house. "What does that mean?"

"Maybe we should sit down." I nodded toward the bench under the tree. All the anger I felt in that meeting rushed over me again. The shouts, McKenzie banging that gavel, Brookfield's damned lies about Charles, that crowd charging at us. *Damn, my head is still killing me. I should have taken a couple Tylenols.*

"They said nobody on parole from another county can live here. It's bullshit and they know it! And it really pisses me off they would even try something so blatantly illegal... but they did." I hesitated telling him the rest. How could I say I brought him to live in a place that was more dangerous than prison?

He deserves the truth from me. I took a slow breath.

"I never told you about a woman... It was a couple weeks ago, in McDonald's. Just a normal fifty or sixty-year-old lady, but she was so angry..." I shook, seeing those eyes wild with rage in front of me again. "She threatened to kill me...and you."

Charles eyes grew wide.

"I figured she was just some crazy old lady, and that was the end of it..." I swallowed. "...but at the city council meeting last night... the room was filled with a hundred people just like her... maybe worse. I mean, some of their threats were... Let me just say two cops had to escort me and Kate to our car."

Charles was silent for a minute. Finally, he folded his arms. "I was wondering about that cut on your head."

I nodded. "Remember how they moved you out of East block because of the Aryans? Well, I just think it might be better for you to stay around the house for now. And I'm going to call your parole officer... you know, to see what he thinks we should do."

A heavy silence settled around us. The only sound was the rustling of leaves in the maple tree behind us. Charles just stared at the ground. His eyes kept moving, as if trying to understand it all. Then he stood and grabbed his rake again.

"Are you okay?" I asked.

"Yep." His back was to me. "I'm sorry to hear all that, but I'm fine 'cause I know God will take care of me." He started raking the leaves again, making a large pile in front of us.

But I wasn't fine. All I felt was the crushing weight of rage, guilt and sadness pushing down on me. My head throbbed with pain. Where was God last night? I wanted to scream at him. But I didn't. I just sat there on that bench, listening to the sound of the rake grabbing more leaves with each stroke. "How... how do you do it?" I finally asked, my voice raspy.

He turned and looked at me, leaning on his rake.

"How do you get up every day for the past twenty years in prison, and now here in Salem Hill where you were promised a second chance, and everywhere you turn you get the same shit, just because you're a black man living in a white man's world?" I shook my head, looking across the yard. "How do you still believe God will take care of you?"

The wind picked up for just a second and scattered some of the leaves he had just raked.

"It's like raking these leaves." He quickly pulled a small pile back toward him. "The wind stops for a little time. You go inside, thinking it's done. Then the wind kicks up and you gotta rake them all over again." He made several more swipes with his rake. "You learn to take whatever comes at you. You *learn* to be okay." Saying that, he pressed hard on the rake, like he had to remind himself of it.

He stopped raking again, his eyes still and calm. "This is no different than what happened growing up in Cleveland. Any time my Mama and me went shopping downtown, I could always feel the white people watching us. Mama warned me to keep my head down and don't look them in the eyes."

I shuddered. The way I felt in that council room, all those people glaring at me... He must have felt that a hundred—a thousand—times over.

"I didn't know what she meant, but this one time... I was only ten years old. We were in Woolworth's, and there was this girl in front of us. She looked to be my age, and she had pretty blond hair... I'd never seen anyone with blond hair before. Not this close anyway." His gaze was miles and miles away now, all the way back to Cleveland.

"I don't know why, but I just touched her hair... She screamed loud, like I did something really bad. The managers came running and grabbed me and Mama. Then the police came."

He fell silent for a moment, staring down the alley. "Mama always told me never trust white people. I guess she was right, 'cause dating Mary... that was her name, Mary Chesnicki. She was in school with me, and she treated me like I was... normal. But when her parents said I did those terrible things... all them white people believed it."

The wind kicked up again and tossed more leaves around our legs. Charles gave me a slow, tired smile. "Do you see now? There's always gonna be wind sooner or later. Wind...white folks... they're always there."

He shrugged and started raking. "You learn to be okay," he said again. "That's what I mean when I say God will take care of me."

I sat there wordless for a long time as he raked more leaves into his pile. My head filled with his story, and the memories of last night, and the throbbing of the cut on my forehead, and too little sleep, and—

I just needed to think, for a long, long time. But right now...

I looked up at the sky. A row of dark clouds was blowing in from the west. It started to rain. "Maybe we can finish the raking later... after this storm blows over..."

———

"Have you told Charles what happened yet?" Kate asked when she finally came downstairs. She slept late and this was the first chance we had to talk since we both fell into bed last night, exhausted. Now she had a hundred questions for me. "What did you tell him? About the threats, I mean. Is he okay? What are we going to do now? We can't just let them get away with this, can we?" She sounded calm, too calm. I knew she was as angry as me.

"I told Charles I was going to talk with his parole officer. I'm hoping he might have some advice for us. But I think we'll have to call an attorney, too. We've got to overturn that damned ordinance."

"Good!" she said, as if that settled it.

But it was far from settled. When Kate came home from school that night, she found me sitting in the kitchen with the lights off.

"No one will take the case." I turned on the light. "At least no one here in Salem Hill. The attorneys who would even talk with me called it a 'career killer.'" What little energy I had left drained from me as I spoke, the words falling frayed from my lips.

"So what!" Her statement was innocent enough, but it hit me sideways. I shook my head. "You really don't understand politics, do you?"

"I saw enough last night to know I don't want anything to do with it," she said, pouring a cup of coffee.

"Neither do I, but I'm afraid we have no choice. I brought Charles here and I'm not going to let a room full of ignorant bigots intimidate me—not this time."

"We..."

"What?"

"*We* brought Charles here," she corrected. "It was my decision too."

There were times when I realized how very glad I was to have her with me. I reached up and touched her bare arm tenderly. "I know I couldn't do this without you," I said, then braced myself and pulled another chair for her. "I'm afraid there's more bad news, and I think you need to sit down."

She looked at me, confused at first, then worried. I took her hand. "I got a call this afternoon from Mr. Livingston. You know, the city attorney. He said because of the new ordinance, Charles can't stay at our house any longer because it's inside the city limits. He said he has to move out as soon as it takes effect."

"I don't understand. He has nowhere else to go. We're the only place he's got in the whole state. What are they going to do, put him back in prison?"

"Almost." I hesitated. It felt like there was a tumor inside my chest, pushing on my lungs, robbing me of air. I had to fight just to breathe. "Craig Bowers, you remember him, don't you? He's Charles' parole officer. He called me right after Livingston..." I felt what little strength I had left drain from me. "...he said they're going to put him in jail for now."

Her eyes narrowed. "Can they do that? I mean, is it even legal?"

I shook my head. "As long as he's on parole, they can do anything they want with him. Craig is as mad as we are, but there's nothing he can do."

She slammed down her cup, spilling coffee all over the table. "Twenty years in prison for something he didn't do—and now this! Dammit, Daniel, when will this shit end for Charles?"

"It gets worse." I struggled even saying the words. "Craig asked *me* to tell him, you know, so he can prepare." I looked up at her. "But that would be like betraying a friend, and I don't know if I can do it." I slumped back in my chair. "But I don't have a choice, do I?"

Her eyes narrowed again as she pursed her lips. "I wish we never moved here, Daniel. I really do."

"Me too, Kate. God, I feel sick about all this," I muttered as a wave of exhaustion spread over me. I felt suddenly old now, full of pain and very tired.

She dropped into the chair next to me and grabbed my hand. "So what are you going to do? I mean, about those creeps on the city council?" It was more of a demand than a question.

I heard her, but barely, as though I was on a raft, surrounded by miles of ocean, as wave after wave washed over me. *Was this how it felt to be seasick?* "I've been trying to answer that question all afternoon, you know, since I talked with Craig." I looked up at her, hoping for some word, some sign of encouragement. "All I can think to do is try to get a Dayton attorney—someone who's not in bed with everyone in Salem

Hill." I breathed through my nose several times. It didn't help much. "You learn to be okay," I muttered, then yanked open the cabinet drawer and grabbed the phone book I kept there.

———

The jail entry room was empty, no chairs, or even pictures on the faded gray walls. Not even any signs. There was only the dark, impenetrable, glass partition on the far wall. My feet felt too heavy to move as I stepped toward the intercom in front of me and pressed the button. "I'm Daniel Robinson... and... I-I'm here with Charles Vickers."

"A deputy will be right out. Just wait there," a metallic voice replied from some invisible place behind the glass. I turned away. Guards, locked metal doors, lifeless voices... How did Charles bear it for twenty years? How will he handle it now?

I looked toward him, his face placid, eyes fixed on something beyond this room. He breathed softly. I noticed he already had his hands behind his back. Waiting.

"You make it look so easy," I said. "Faith, I mean."

He gave me a sad smile. "Even Jesus struggled to keep his faith when the soldiers came to arrest him. No, Daniel, faith never comes easy." He suddenly looked so tired, like he had aged a lifetime in these few minutes. I hardly recognized him.

"Charles, I..." The words caught in my throat.

"You don't have to say anything, Daniel," his words sounded no more than a whisper. Then he looked back toward that glass wall. "Remember, you learn to be okay, even in here."

I opened my arms to hug him, but the steel door on the side wall suddenly clanked open and two deputies marched toward us, their foot-steps growing louder with every step. "Turn around," one of them commanded. Charles complied. The other deputy brusquely patted him down, then slapped handcuffs on his wrists, and spun him around. Without looking back, both of them hustled him out, and the door slammed shut. A cold chill ran through me.

I forced myself out, my feet so heavy I struggled to move them one labored step, then another. Somehow, I managed the fifty steps to my car, dropped into the seat, then pounded the steering wheel again and again, as hard as I could until I fell back exhausted. I wept.

———

Apparently Douglas Baintree had no connections with Salem Hill politics, so I was surprised he actually knew James Livingston. "We went to law school together and I thought he was a prick then," he said. "And from what you're telling me, he hasn't changed much. Hell yes, I'll take your case."

"I guess I should ask what you think this will cost." Our bills were all paid, for now anyway, but money had been a worry since we moved to Ohio, especially with all the remodeling costs I never expected.

"My fee is $200 an hour. If we settle out of court, it'll probably cost you $5,000 before we're done. But if it goes to court, it could be $10,000 or more. You never can predict how long these cases will last."

Probably as long as my money lasts. But I pushed that out of my head. "Okay," was all I said. I had no choice.

That afternoon I met with Dr. Webber to talk about Charles' situation. I told him Douglas Baintree had agreed to take the case.

"I'm surprised."

"Why? Do you know him?"

"Not personally. But I've heard of him."

"And..."

"It's just hearsay, you understand." He leaned forward in his chair. "But I've heard he makes his living defending drug dealers and petty criminals he knows are guilty. Again, it's only a rumor, but he's well known to close down most of the bars in Dayton on any given night."

"That may explain it," I said.

"Explain what?"

"I thought he took my case just to stick it to Livingston, but maybe he's got a guilty conscience he's trying to satisfy."

Dr. Webber leaned back, grinning. "He's an attorney. That's a given. Trust me. My confessional is filled with attorneys every Christmas and Easter."

"So you're telling me the only hope for an innocent man like

Charles, is for a sinner like Baintree to kick the ass of an even bigger sinner like Livingston in court? Who says God doesn't have a sense of humor?" It felt good to laugh again.

———

When Baintree filed our lawsuit against the city in October, I thought it would be settled by November, or maybe December at the latest. But there was one delay after another, and that only gave Brookfield and his people an excuse to fill the newspaper with more of their fearmongering.

"Did you ever hear of a group called 'Citizens for Safety?'" I called out to Kate, and slammed the paper on the kitchen counter. "You need to read this article. I'll bet Brookfield is behind it."

She turned off the stove, grabbed the paper and quickly scanned the article. "'...common interest in seeing our town as a clean and safe place to live... Doesn't sound like anything to me."

"Read the rest of it." I pointed to the next paragraph.

She shrugged and picked up the paper again. "'As lifelong citizens of Salem Hill, we intend to educate the community of any issues that are a threat to safety, develop an action plan to address that threat, then form a group of committed citizens willing to make the necessary changes to restore peace and safety in our neighborhoods...' I still don't understand what you mean."

"Read between the lines, Kate." I took the paper from her. "'As lifelong *WHITE* citizens of Salem Hill ...educate the community of any issues that are a threat to safety from *BLACK MEN LIKE CHARLES VICKERS*, develop an action plan to address *BLACK MEN LIKE CHARLES VICKERS*, then form a group of committed citizens willing to make the necessary changes to remove *BLACK MEN LIKE CHARLES VICKERS* from our neighborhoods...' That's what they're really saying!"

"Oh, God, Daniel. You don't really think they're making a threat?"

"That's exactly what I think, and that's why I'm calling Baintree. Before this escalates."

———

To keep our sanity, I tried to act like a normal family, especially when Christmas arrived.

"Are you sure we can do this, Daniel? Are the kids allowed to come with us?"

Kate had never been inside a jail before—and her face showed it when the steel door slammed behind us. She pulled the kids close and scanned the long corridor. "Follow me," the guard barked, and Kate made an instinctive glance in my direction, her eyes asking if it was safe. I heard that sound a hundred times since I started working with Dr. Webber, but it still bothered me too. I took her hand as the kids looked cautiously at both of us.

"It's okay," I said trying to sound as calm as I could. "Craig Bowers called me yesterday and said it was approved by the sheriff himself. We're going to meet with Charles in the attorney's room. It's separate from the regular visiting area, and a lot more private."

The guard opened a door at the end of the hall, where there stood a metal table dividing a small, gray cinder block room. There were two stools on our side of the table, along with several folding chairs that had been brought in for the kids. There was a single stool on the other side for Charles. Behind it was a metal door that probably led into the cell area. A single, harsh fluorescent light on the ceiling illuminated the room, washing out everything and hurting my eyes. There were also several cameras pointed at us.

"Can we get the table ready, Dad?" Susan asked, crouched beside a box on the floor. Ever since I told the kids we were going to celebrate Christmas in jail with Charles, she was more excited than I was. Almost everyday I heard, "Can we have a Christmas tree? Can we give Charles a present? Can we have dinner with him? What should I wear?" and a hundred more questions.

She looked different today with that black eye of hers, but she wore it like a badge of honor. Kate and I should talk about that later, but for now, part of me couldn't help but feel proud.

"Sure, Susan. You can decorate the table while we wait."

She quickly pulled out a green holiday cloth and spread it over the cold metal table. Then, one by one, she pulled out several paper plates, plastic utensils, and a bag of Christmas-colored cookies all three kids baked by themselves just this morning. Finally, while all of us watched, she set up the most important decoration of all—a 12-inch tall, battery-powered, Christmas tree with lights! Susan then nodded toward Jonathan and he flipped a small switch on the base. Like magic...the room was awash in Christmas colors!

Five minutes later the rear steel door swung open and Charles walked in. At first the kids didn't recognize him in his black and white striped uniform. He had lost weight since my last visit. "Merry Christmas!" the kids all screamed when they realized it actually was Charles. From the look on his face, it was obvious no one told him Kate and the kids would be here today—and especially that it would be a Christmas party!

"This is the best Christmas present I ever got." He stepped toward them, but flinched, stopped and looked at the guard. When he nodded, Charles quickly leaned over the table and folded all three kids in his arms.

There were the usual questions from them. What's your room like? Who else is here with you? What do you do all day? And Charles had questions for the kids too. But he also noticed Susan's blackeye.

"What happened to you?"

"Nothing," she grunted, but he raised an eyebrow.

"Come on now...what happened?"

"Just some boy in my class said something I didn't like."

"Oh no. I'm sorry to hear that. What was it?"

Susan glanced at me. "It's okay. You can tell him," I said. "I think he already knows anyway."

She looked back toward Charles. "Joey Brookfield said everyone hated you and you should go back to Cleveland with all the other niggers," she mumbled.

"And what did you do?"

"I popped him right in the nose," she said without any hesitation. "And I would've won too, but his friend Danny Evans grabbed me from behind, and then Joey slugged me in the eye."

"That does look like quite a shiner," Charles said, looking intently at her face. "Did you tell your teacher they provoked it?"

She looked away.

"Susan?"

She shifted in her seat, then looked toward the floor.

"I get it. So what happened?"

"I got detention," she mumbled, then added, "but I don't care!" She looked up at him, her chin stuck out.

Charles seemed to think for a bit. Finally, all he said was, "I met a lot of bullies in prison too, Susan. And I got into a lot of fights, at first anyway."

His calm brown eyes met her wide green ones.

"But God told me those bullies were more scared than I was, and I needed to ignore them."

Susan didn't say anything, but I know she heard him. *You learn to take whatever comes at you. You learn to be okay.*

Now it was my turn. I tapped on the metal door twice. A deputy strode in carrying an angel food cake with a large green candle, burning bright. "Merry Christmas, Charles," I said.

Everyone clapped and clapped, including Charles. He was smiling from ear to ear!

That night after the kids were in bed, Kate and I were sitting in the living room, staring at the Christmas tree, and talking about our visit that day. "Ironic, isn't it?"

"What is?" she asked.

"That I was supposed to be the one to help Charles, because I've got all the degrees. But I think he's the one helping me."

"I don't understand."

"Think about it, Kate. He spent twenty years in prison for something he didn't do. Now he's locked up in jail again because of those bigots on the city council. Yet he's been a model prisoner, and the deputies know it. Why do you think the sheriff allowed us to have that party with him today? He's done more to change attitudes in Salem Hill than I ever could with all my talk about reducing recidivism, or even with our lawsuit. I used to think he was naïve with all his talk about God taking care of him, but I'm not so sure now."

"You're not thinking of dropping the lawsuit, are you?"

"Absolutely not. The only way God can take care of us now is in court. I just don't know when we'll ever get there."

———

January led to February, and now it was March, and we still had no court date in sight. "How long do you think it will take?" Kate asked when she found me opening another letter from Baintree. She constantly worried how we were going to pay his bill, especially when it only grew larger with every delay. I had asked myself the same question too many times.

"He said this happens a lot." I knew my answer wouldn't satisfy her, but it was all I could think to say.

It didn't. "How long, Daniel? I need to know," she asked, her brow furrowed, and her eyes now filled with worry.

"He said the city's just trying to pressure us to quit. He thinks we can win this, but he doesn't know how long it'll take."

"But he must have some idea...," she persisted.

"He says it could take all year if they keep delaying our court date," I finally admitted.

She didn't say anything for a minute, then asked the question that kept me laying awake every night. "How long can we afford to keep fighting this?"

"As long as it takes, Kate! We made a commitment to Charles, and we can't go back on that. We can't."

"Then I'm going to get a job," she announced, as if this was something she had been thinking about for a long time. "Maybe as a waitress at Flannery's, just 'till this case is over."

"You mean quit school? That's not even something I want to discuss. You're too close to graduating, and if you quit now, just so we can pay Baintree, you'll never know those nuns were wrong. No, Kate, that's not something I want to consider, even if it means I have to repay him $100 a month for the rest of my life."

She looked at me without saying anything, her eyes wet now, then pulled me close, wrapping her arms around me. "I love you, Daniel Robinson," was all she said.

Baintree called two months later. "Looks like we're actually going to court Friday."

"That's what you said the last time, and every time before that, too."

We'd been disappointed by too many delays. Why should it be any different now?

"Anything's possible," he said. "But every time the city asks for a delay, it just makes our case stronger. And I'll argue that. But what I need to know... are you ready to testify?"

For nearly all of the past year the Salem Hill News was filled with too many inaccurate articles, biased editorials, and what seemed like hundreds of hateful letters to the editor. I wanted to rebut all of them, but Baintree always told me to say nothing. "Wait for your day in court," he said every time I complained.

Now that day was finally here.

"More than ready. Believe me."

Four days later Kate and I stood in the marbled hallway near the courtroom waiting nervously for Baintree to arrive. Benches on both sides were filled with attorneys poring over papers, making last minute notes, while talking with their clients waiting to go into one of the courtrooms. I recognized a couple of them from my trips to the jail. They must have recognized me too, because they nodded, like they knew why I was there. I remembered what Jim Richards said to me. *All the ministers in town have given this whole thing you're doing a lot of prayer and we're not sure it's best that you do it here. Maybe if you helped him get a place in Dayton.* Ironic. The only support I got in Salem Hill wasn't from the ministers, but from these felons.

Several armed deputies also stood nearby talking, their boredom broken only when a particularly attractive young clerk made the occasional walk to the prosecutor's office at the end of the hall.

It was probably just ten or fifteen minutes, but it seemed like hours before Baintree finally arrived. I expected he would give me some last minute instructions, but he barely stopped to talk. "I have to meet with Mr. Livingston in the judge's chambers first. It shouldn't take long. Just wait here for me," was all he said.

After all these months, all those sleepless nights, we were finally here now... just waiting. Fifteen minutes went by, then thirty minutes, and still no one came out of the judge's chambers. One by one, the hall emptied. Even the deputies disappeared into the clerk's office, and still we waited. "What do you think is happening, Kate? Should it take this long? What if there's another delay?" The more I waited, the more I paced the hallway, with only the sound of my nervous steps echoing around us. Finally, Baintree appeared, followed by Livingston, who immediately walked away from us, out of the building. I didn't know what to make of it.

"It's over," Baintree said smiling broadly. "Technically we didn't win. The city agreed to rescind the ordinance. So there's no longer any need for our lawsuit."

This was all I hoped and prayed about for nearly a year. Now it was finally over, but I didn't know what to say. I just stood in the hallway, too numb to speak, or even think. I could barely breathe.

"Why'd they do it?" Kate finally asked. "It's like they just quit at the last minute."

"Mr. Livingston told the judge there was a 'procedural error,'" Baintree said.

"What's that mean?" I was still struggling to understand what just happened.

"Officially it means Mr. Livingston determined there was a technical problem with the ordinance. That's what will go in the record. But unofficially, he knew it was a lousy law from the beginning. He was betting you'd back down if he delayed long enough. Happens all the time. But you didn't, so here we are now. Congratulations."

After all the legal wrangling, dozens of malicious articles and threatening letters in the newspaper, a violent attack by an angry mob, death threats from strangers, my kids abused and even assaulted at school—and especially what happened to Charles—it was finally over. I fell back onto the bench behind me. I didn't know what to say. I didn't know what to feel. I didn't know what to do. All I could do was breathe in and out.

"Charles! We've got to tell Charles!" I jumped to my feet, hugged Kate, then hugged Baintree, who stiffened awkwardly. "Can we get him?" I asked. "I mean, will they release him now with this court ruling?"

Obviously, no one ever hugged him like that. He only muttered something about taking a few hours to process, then took a quick step back to regain his composure. "My bill," he mumbled, handing me an envelope. I opened it slowly. There was no way I could afford it.

No balance due. "I don't understand." I stammered.

Baintree offered an embarrassed smile, looking away like he was suddenly uncomfortable with the attention, then sputtered something about spending twenty years defending guilty people. "Call it penance," was all I caught.

"But your bill must have been $10,000 or more."

"Don't worry about it," he coughed, grabbing his briefcase from the bench next to me. He began walking away. "My three ex-wives would say I owe a hellava lot more penance than that. Let's just call it a down payment."

That's when the idea came to me. "I have something that might satisfy even your ex-wives." I smiled broadly as I put my arm on his shoulder. "I've got a friend who spent twenty years in prison for something he didn't do. He needs a good attorney to clear his name. Mind if I walk you to your car while we talk?"

———

"How do you like Italian food, Charles?"

"I newer had anyfwing like this befwore," he managed with a stuffed mouth. "Whaw's it cawled again?"

"Ask Kate. She's the food expert."

"Veal parmesan, the best in the city. We've been planning to bring you to La Foccacia for a long time. Too long." She winked at me.

"And wait till you taste the Tiramisu." I closed my eyes and wet my lips. "Mmmm... Don't ask me what's in it. But trust me, your taste buds will fall in love with it." All three kids squealed. They had acquired my sweet tooth all too well.

———

Summer settled in Ohio early in June and the temperature was well into the nineties every day. When the kids, Charles, and I finally found our seats in the Shawnee College auditorium, the air was already stifling. If the air conditioning was even working, it wasn't doing much good. Even though all the doors were propped open, everyone was sweating profusely. Several people even tried fanning themselves with their programs. It didn't help, but no one seemed to care. From what I heard about the school, most of the students were the first in their families to go to college, just like Kate. The room was packed with a thousand sweaty, but excited relatives, all focused on the stage, waiting anxiously for the ceremony to begin. But something in that room made me nervous. Even though our legal battle was over, there were still angry letters in the newspaper. I scanned the room. *Is that woman at the end of our row staring at Charles? Didn't I see that guy in front of me at one of those council meetings?*

"Where's Mom?" Susan yelled over the noise in the room.

I forced my focus back to the stage—and Kate. "I don't see her yet," I yelled back. "Maybe we can see better from those seats over there." I pointed toward the open door on the side of the auditorium. I didn't say anything, but I thought it was also a safer place... if anyone in that crowd came at us.

Finally, the ceremony began. One by one, the graduates walked across the stage. "Mary Anderson." "James Forsythe." "Alice Johnson." With each name called, there was a frenzy of applause and cheering from all over the auditorium. "Donald King." "Sandra Owens."

"I can't see Mom. Do you see her?" Jonathan asked.

"There she is, coming up the steps now!" Charles shouted toward us. Even from this distance, I could see she was crying.

"Mary Kathleen Robinson. Honors degree," the president announced. Kate was shaking so much, I didn't think she'd make it across the stage.

We jumped to our feet and cheered louder than anyone else in the entire auditorium. "Honors degree, Dad! Why didn't you tell me?" Susan shouted.

"I didn't know, and it looks like your mother didn't know either!"

When she finally made it to the back of the hall, she was still crying. She hugged all of us again and again.

"Thank you," she whispered in my ear.

"For what? You did all the work."

"For never letting me quit. Now I've got proof I'm not retarded."

I pulled her to me. "I never even came close to getting an honors degree," I said, kissing her gently. "All I know is the smartest thing I ever did was marry you."

She buried her head on my chest, hugging me fiercely.

———

We had so much to celebrate now. Our lawsuit was over, Charles was back with us, and best of all, Kate was now a college graduate. "Maybe we can go to Kings Island again, or even take everyone to Hocking Hills for a long weekend camping," I announced over dinner that night. "We haven't been hiking in a long time. It'll feel good to be a normal family again. I know this is going to be our best summer ever."

Then Lynn Mitchell disappeared.

CHAPTER 26
HEART OF DARKNESS

SALEM HILL, 1985. It was June 25, my thirty-seventh birthday. We had just gotten home from a long day at Indian Lake with the kids. I turned on the television, dropped exhausted into my chair, and propped up my feet. But suddenly *Breaking News Alert* flashed across the screen. Cheryl Atkins from Channel 7 was standing in front of the entrance to Shawnee Creek Park.

"Kate! You better come in here to see this!"

"Salem Hill police and Shawnee County deputies have been searching all day for a missing college girl named Lynn Mitchell," she said into the camera. "She was last seen jogging here in Shawnee Creek Park more than thirty-six hours ago. She's not been seen since, and authorities are conducting an extensive search of the area."

"This isn't good, Daniel," was all Kate said. I didn't answer.

The next morning the Dayton newspaper headlined the story along with her picture. 'Salem Hill girl missing!' She graduated from Salem Hill High School a year ago and was now attending Shawnee Community College. The article said she was planning to be a nurse. "She really liked helping people, even volunteered at the hospital when she was still in high school," her mother told the reporter tearfully.

Apparently she left her house on Monday morning to go jogging in the park before school, her usual routine. "Six hours later when she still hadn't come home, we were frantic and called the police," Mrs. Mitchell said.

"When she still wasn't home by Tuesday morning..." Mr. Mitchell added, "...we knew it was bad. And so did the police." There was a picture of them holding each other. Mrs. Mitchell was sobbing.

The newspaper reported that patrols had been stepped up all over town and around the county. A search dog was brought in to look for her scent along the trail by Shawnee Creek. At one place, police thought the dog found something, but it lost the scent near the parking lot.

Television crews soon descended on the town, interviewing everyone and gearing up for the lead story on the evening news. The whole town was upset. Nothing like this ever happened in Salem Hill.

I tried to focus on my classes at Xavier, but Lynn Mitchell wouldn't stop floating around the back of my mind. Just as I walked into my office on Thursday morning, Dr. Webber called to me from the hall. "Have you read this article in the Salem Hill newspaper?"

"No. Why?"

"One of my students just showed it to me. I think you need to read it." He bit his lip as I took it.

The headline was impossible to miss. "Vickers suspect in girl's disappearance!" I cancelled my class and drove back to Salem Hill.

"Have you seen today's paper?" I called out to Charles when I found him mowing the rear yard. Since he had come home from jail, he had been looking for another job, but so far he hadn't found one.

"No. Why?" he asked, wiping the sweat from his face.

"Then we need to talk..." I looked up and down the alley. "...but inside your apartment."

I handed him the newspaper. He stared at it for several minutes, then dropped into his chair, without saying a word. I saw worry in his eyes. "Are you okay?" I asked, but he only stared blankly at the newspaper. I wanted to say something, anything, to help my friend. But what?

"I'll be in the house... if you need me." I laid my hand gently on his shoulder, and walked slowly out the door.

Friday came with another story. "Police close to an arrest" was headlined right over a picture of Charles. There was even a copy of his confession from twenty years ago. Nothing was mentioned about the fact he couldn't read then, and had no idea what he signed.

"Is it true?" Kate asked. "You don't think...?"

"I know what you're thinking. And no. I already called Craig Bowers. He said if the cops had the slightest suspicion he was involved, they would've locked him up already."

"Then why would they print something like that? I mean, if they know it's not true?"

"I don't know, and that's what worries me."

After making several calls, I learned the editor was a guy named Jacob Donaldson. He tried several times to get elected to any open office, but he never even got his name on the ballot. I had a feeling he saw Lynn Mitchell—and Charles—as his next campaign.

Donaldson held a public meeting in Shawnee Creek Park on July 4, near the spot where Lynn Mitchell was last seen. More than a hundred people, including John Brookfield and his mob, showed up waving both American and Confederate flags and shouting angry threats for the benefit of the reporters, who seemed to outnumber the protesters. That evening Cheryl Atkins had the lead story on the six o'clock news.

"Salem Hill, the city of peace, is again in turmoil. It has been nine days since Lynn Mitchell disappeared while jogging in this park. Yet the police are no closer to solving this mystery. Many residents have vowed to take matters into their own hands."

"I'm so scared with that rapist out of jail," one woman said as she wiped her eyes carefully for the camera. "I blame the city for not stopping Vickers when they had the chance."

John Brookfield made that same unfounded allegation that Charles stalked his daughter. "If I hadn't run him off, there's no telling what might've happened to my little girl too."

Every day after that, Donaldson's paper printed dozens of letters to the editor, all demanding something be done immediately to make the town safe again.

"Predators shouldn't be allowed in Salem Hill!"

"How long before someone else disappears like Lynn Mitchell?"

"If the city won't protect us from that predator, then we have to protect ourselves."

The Dayton and Cincinnati papers both called me. With each new article, the tension escalated in town, and in our home. "Why do you even bother reading that damned newspaper?" Kate snapped. She had been asking that a lot lately.

"Because I need to know what Brookfield and his goons are planning."

"For what purpose? It only upsets you."

"So I'm not blind-sided again with another petition or letter from the city attorney." I snapped, then caught myself. "Sorry. I didn't mean to bark at you. I just..."

"I know that, Daniel." She laid her hand on mine. "But every time you read the newspaper or watch the news on television, all it does is make you angry, and then you're impossible to live with the rest of the night. And I'm not the only one who sees it."

"What do you mean?" I stiffened.

"The kids have all come to me, even Emma, asking what's wrong with Daddy?"

I threw the newspaper in the garbage and walked out to the porch. She was right, but I couldn't stop thinking about it.

It was a Friday night, near the end of July, sometime after eleven. I was half asleep. Suddenly, there was a loud noise... shattering glass downstairs... then squealing tires in the street. I sat straight up, wide awake now. "Did you hear that?" I shook Kate awake. "I think some-one's breaking into the house!"

I jumped out of bed and pulled on my pants. "I'm going downstairs. You call the cops!" Grabbing a baseball bat from the closet, I moved slowly barefoot down the stairs in the dark, grip-ping the bat at the ready. My heart beat faster with each cautious step until I reached the foyer. Holding my breath, I quickly scanned the room as best I could in the dark. "The cops are on their way!" I shouted, but the only sound I heard was a curtain flapping loudly somewhere. I took two steps into the living room, but felt a sharp pain underfoot. I slapped at the wall switch! The couch and most of the floor sparkled with hundreds of glass shards as light flooded the room. A large brick lay by the now shattered glass coffee table.

"The police are coming, Daniel. Are you okay?" Kate called from the top of the stairs.

"I'm okay, but don't come down here barefoot. Someone threw a brick through our window. There's glass everywhere."

When two officers arrived ten minutes later, I showed them the brick and all the broken glass. They both quickly eye-balled the room.

"Did you see who did this, sir?" the younger one asked. He was slight, and much shorter than me. Honestly, he looked more like a boy in a man's uniform. But he seemed to wear it well, like this was what he always wanted to do. Somehow, there was something familiar about him.

"We were in bed when I heard the glass break," I said.

He looked to his much older partner, who probably was his boss, judging by his sergeant's stripes. The sergeant nodded, scribbling something in his notebook.

"Has anything like this happened before, sir?" the young one asked, and I remembered now where I saw him. He was the cop who got Kate and me out of the parking lot when that mob attacked us. He seemed much taller then.

"You mean other than someone trying to kill me at that council meeting last year?"

For a second there was something in his eyes. I thought he recognized me, too. He seemed about to say something, but didn't. Instead, he looked to his partner again, as if waiting for orders. But the sergeant only shrugged, slapped his notebook shut against his huge belly, and pointed toward his watch. "That's all we can do now, Mr. Robinson," he wheezed, heading toward the door. "Call us if anything else happens."

But the young one hesitated. "I'll ask some of the other officers if they saw anyone suspicious tonight, sir," he said, closing his notebook.

"Thanks. And for what you did that night in the council parking lot too."

"Just doing my job, sir," he grunted as he left. I got the impression he wanted to do more now, but couldn't.

"Is it me, Kate," I said, locking the front door, "or did you notice that fat cop didn't seem too concerned?"

"I caught that," she said.

"But the young one..." I turned toward her. "...he was different. He's one of the cops who got us out of the parking lot that night Brookfield's mob attacked us. I think he's as worried about what happened as we are."

Two hours later, after nailing a plywood sheet I found in the garage securely over the window, I finally climbed into bed. But Kate was still awake, just staring at the ceiling in the dark. Neither of us slept much that night.

————

Most of August passed slowly with still no news about Lynn Mitchell. But there were no more incidents either. The tension in town seemed to calm, just a little—until Donaldson interviewed Lynn Mitchell's parents. He had a picture of both of them crying. "Why can't the police make Vickers tell us where our daughter is, so at least we can bury her," they pleaded. The police chief said his detectives were working hard to solve the case. Mayor Wayne promised he would do everything he could to help the Mitchells. Even John Brookfield was quoted. "I've been demanding all summer that the council rezone the whole city to keep predators from ever coming here." Shortly after that article appeared, Chairman McKenzie announced they were finally prepared to act. "A public hearing will be scheduled at our September meeting and we're going to present a new ordinance that will protect all the children in Salem Hill. We're not going to let something like this ever happen again."

————

It was near dawn when I heard loud pounding on our door. "Who in the world is that?" I mumbled, struggling to find my pants and a shirt in the dark. I didn't want to wake Kate. The pounding continued as I stumbled to the front door. It was Charles.

"You got to look at the back of your house!" He was shaking.

We walked quickly to the rear yard where he pointed to his door.

Nigger! Where's Lynn Mitchell? was spray painted in large red letters. There was a crude cross smoldering in the yard. I kicked it over as hard as I could.

"Damn Brookfield!" I turned around to ask Charles if he was okay, but he was gone. I found him sitting at his apartment table. He was shaking more now. Even in the dim light, I could see him breathing hard.

"You okay, Charles?"

He just stared at the floor, shivering, as I put my hand on his shoulder. He still didn't respond, but he did seem to breathe slower now. "All this reminds me of what happened when I first went to prison," he finally said. His gaze stayed frozen.

"I can't go back there again," he mumbled, more to himself than me. Trembling harder now, he looked up, but I had the feeling he was barely seeing me. "They did stuff to me... bad stuff... cause of what they said I did." He caught his breath, then muttered. "...but I feel like I'm already back there." He slumped into his chair, arms dangling at his side. All his strength seemed drained from him. For a minute, he was still, completely still. Then he started to cry, softly at first, then much harder. I saw Bobby Saunders again, caught in a past he could never escape, and desperate to find a way out. I pulled a chair next to him and put my arm on his shoulder, holding him, just like I did Bobby. "I won't let that happen, Charles. I promise."

The same two cops arrived a couple minutes after I called for help.

"Probably the same guy who threw the rock through my window." I told Good Cop. That's what Kate and I called him now. We called his partner Lazy Cop, and like that last time he was at our house, he didn't ask any questions, only scribbled a couple notes in his book and kept checking his watch, like he had to be someplace else.

"Did you or Mr. Vickers see anyone, sir?" Good Cop asked.

We both shook our heads. "But this is different. It's more personal... and it's going to escalate if you don't stop him," I said, not even trying to hide my concern.

He looked at Lazy Cop, who nodded toward their car in the alley. It was obvious he thought I was all worked up over a stupid prank by a couple kids with too much time on their hands. Lazy Cop took the same report, offered the same half-hearted we'll-patrol-the-area-more-often platitudes, and motioned for his partner to get going, this time emphatically.

"They said you've got nothing to worry about," I told Charles, but we both knew it was a lie.

"That's what the guards told me when I got to prison," he said numbly, then walked into his bedroom and closed the door. A stiff breeze suddenly blew by as the hairs on my neck stood.

Wind... white folks... they're always there.

———

I was late getting home from Cincinnati. Dr. Webber's research was scheduled for review, and he had me putting in extra hours every day. "The city council is going to talk about that new ordinance tonight. I need to be there," I called when I walked in the door. "No time for dinner."

Kate didn't answer. She walked up the stairs and shut the bedroom door. I wanted to ask her if something was wrong, but I was already late for the meeting, so I let it go. *I'll talk to her when I get home.*

It was sometime after eleven when I finally came to bed. The room was dark. "They're going to try and push through that same ordinance again." I kicked off my shoes. "Livingston thinks he can take care of that 'procedural error' this time. Can you believe it?"

She didn't answer. "You awake?"

Still no answer. "Kate, you awake?"

"I can't take any more of this!" she finally said.

Turning on the lamp by the bed, I found her sitting up, holding her legs tight against her chest. Even in the dim light, I could see her eyes were red and swollen. I sat on the bed and reached for her, but she brushed my hand away. "You just don't get it, do you?"

"What? What did I do?"

She turned toward me. Her eyes narrowed. "I'll tell you what you did, Daniel Robinson, if you really want to know." Her lips tightened and her teeth clenched. "First, it was all those ugly people on the church board. And those horrid allegations from that creep Nicholson. Then that petition from the neighbors, and all the awful things they said about you. And let's not even mention your lawsuit that was all you thought about for a year. Now it's another fight with the city, and another lawsuit that will consume you again."

I had no idea where all this was coming from. "I'm sorry, Kate," was all I could think to say. "How can I help?" I reached for her, but she pushed me away.

"How can you help?" She managed to sound calm, but there was a cracking in her voice that grew more intense with every word. "Can you stop people from pointing at me and whispering whenever I go to the grocery store? Can you stop the horrid things they say in front of our kids when we're at the park? Can you stop those awful children in Susan's class from telling her we're responsible for Lynn Mitchell's death? This was her first day of eighth grade. It should have been a special day for her. But she's been crying ever since she got home. Can you stop any of that, Daniel?"

I remembered promising Susan I'd take her for ice cream after school today. It was supposed to be our special time. I felt my face grow hot. "I had no idea... I mean about all that... and I know Susan started school today, but I just forgot... you know, with all that's been happening."

"That's my point. There's always something happening that's more important than us and I can't take it anymore." She looked away, wiping her eyes. A small, strangled, desperate sound came from deep in her throat. "I just can't!"

A wave of regret and guilt washed over me. "I never wanted any of this either, Kate. And the absolute last thing I ever want to do was hurt you and the kids. Believe me." I reached for her hand, but she didn't respond. "But when..." I breathed in. "...when I think of what happened to Lettie, and especially Charles now, I can't just let it go. Does that make any sense?"

The quiet between us now seemed enormous, endless. Finally, slowly, she looked back at me, then wiped her swollen eyes again. "I've always admired your passion to help people, but I don't know how much of this I can take." It was more of a plea than an ultimatum.

I reached for her hand. "I really am sorry, Kate." She seemed to soften, just a little.

"I know you're sorry, but it just feels like... like you don't love us anymore." She started to cry again.

I pulled her close. This time she didn't resist, but I didn't know what to say now. She had always been so strong, no matter what happened to us. Now she seemed so unsure about us. "What are you saying?"

"I'm saying I just want our family to be normal. Is that asking too much?"

Normal was all I ever wanted, too, but in my world that was something that rarely—if ever happened. "No, Kate, not much at all," I whispered. Charles' story about him and his Mama in downtown Cleveland came floating back. *The wind stops for a little time. You go inside, thinking it's done. Then the wind kicks up, and you gotta rake them all over again.*

For several long minutes, we stayed just like that, holding onto each other, worn and quiet. Only the sound of our breathing filled the air. Finally, I cleared my throat. "Normal is... being able to leave all this behind. If you want me to sell this damned house and move somewhere else, if that's what you really want, we'll do it, Kate. I mean it. God knows I'd love to have a normal life too."

She buried her head in my chest. "You'd do that for us, Daniel?"

"Absolutely. If that's what it will take for us to be normal, I'd do it in a heartbeat. But..." I breathed in. "...we have to remember, one of our family would never get to be normal just by moving to another town."

Her eyes went up to my face, but she sat completely still, listening. "All his life," I went on. "Charles has lived every day as an outsider, hated by everyone just for the color of his skin. The closest we ever came to that was...well..." I sighed. "...all of this. Being pointed at, or whispers in the checkout line in Kroger's. The mean things they say to our kids. That crazy woman in McDonald's, and even Brookfield's screaming mob."

All those times we talked together, shared our thoughts, feelings, hurts and dreams. Now looking into her eyes, I thought she really heard my heart, and I loved her all the more.

"You and me and the kids... we're white, like all the other people in Salem Hill. We can always leave, move to another white town and disappear. But Charles... he could never disappear in a white man's world." I leaned my forehead against hers lightly.

"When all this is over, Kate, we'll look at moving away. Some place where we can start over and put all this shit behind us. I promise. Just help me get through this, for Charles' sake. That's all I'm asking."

"For Charles' sake," she said, her voice cracking. "I..." She looked down at her arms, at mine, so pale under the lamplight. "I never thought about it like that before."

"I kissed her forehead. "Really puts things in perspective, doesn't it?"

"You have to keep fighting this, Daniel, okay?" She pulled her head back, and there was my strong, determined Kate again. I saw it in her eyes. "He's our family too. Thank you for reminding me." She kissed me on the cheek, then quickly added, "But you need to talk with Susan. Maybe at breakfast, before she goes to school."

"Believe me, Kate, that's at the top of my list."

The next morning I was up early, sitting at the table, with breakfast waiting for Susan. At first, she didn't know what to say, but just stood there, staring at the table, then at me, then at the table again. "Think of this like our little ceremony to start your special year," I said, lighting the single candle in the cinnamon roll by her plate. "I know eighth grade is really important, so I wanted to have this time together... just you and me. Like we did with our tea parties!" She stood there, not moving, her eyes wide as her mouth dropped open. "And that's not all," I said. "I know you've been asking about going to Indian Lake again. Well, I thought we could go this weekend, maybe rent a boat or something. You know, to celebrate your new school year. After all, eighth grade only happens once in your life."

She hugged me. "Oh, Dad. I'd love that!" Then she stepped back. Her hair glistened gold in the morning sun coming through the kitchen window, just like it did that day I first saw her on Kate's porch step. My beautiful little girl... now almost a grown woman. "I-it's been hard not seeing you lately," her eyes were wet as she looked up at me. "Thank you so much for doing this for me. I've missed you so much. I love you, Dad." She wrapped her arms around me and squeezed, then harder.

I hugged her back. "I missed you, too, baby. So..." My voice cracked. "...so much." We stayed like that. I didn't want this moment together to end... ever.

Livingston's new ordinance wasn't scheduled for a hearing until the middle of September and all of us needed to get out of Salem Hill, so we could act like a normal family, at least for a couple days. The kids—especially Susan—loved our weekend together, and Kate looked happier than I'd seen her in months.

———

"I've got a lot of research data I want to present to the council tonight," I said, walking into the city building. "You know, be the voice of reason. That's what Dr. Webber said I should do." Kate started to say something, caught herself, then just took my arm instead.

The room was packed, and the reporters and television cameras were again positioned along the rear wall. But I thought it was surprisingly quiet this time, and so did the reporters. They looked all around the room, with their notepads in hand, anxious for something to happen. Chairman McKenzie asked for comments when the meeting opened, but no one stepped to the podium, not even John Brookfield. He sat quietly in the front row, without even looking at anyone. *Hmm, strange.* I waited, but still no one came forward. I grabbed all my papers and stepped to the microphone.

"Like everyone here, I am deeply concerned for the safety of our community. That's exactly why Xavier University, and the entire Department of Correction, is so committed to helping men and women coming back from prison get a new start." I tried to remain confident, speaking as calmly as I could pretend to be, but it was hard. The tension in the room felt like a weight pressing down on me from all sides. *Just breathe normal. Be the voice of reason.* "The vast majority of people in prison are coming back home. About ninety-five percent of them actually." My heart thudded like a drum, and for a second, my voice nearly squeaked.

I forced myself to speak each word slowly. "In Ohio there are more than 15,000 people getting out of prison every year. All of them simply want to restart their broken lives. Shawnee County is no different. On average we have about fifty men and women come back from prison every year. All I'm doing is offering one of them a second chance."

"Vickers ain't from here!" someone shouted from the back of the room. McKenzie banged his gavel for order. A half dozen reporters scribbled in their pads as cameras clicked wildly.

"I'll address that," I said, glad my voice was even now. Those times I practiced this with Dr. Webber paid off. "He's right. Charles Vickers is not from Shawnee County. He was originally from Cleveland, and normally we would not have accepted him. But he served his time and literally had nowhere to go. The Department of Correction asked if we would take him in. We felt it was the humanitarian thing to do."

"Tell that to Lynn Mitchell's family!" someone else shouted. This time McKenzie didn't bang his gavel. I wasn't surprised. All the council members were thinking the same thing. I could see it in their eyes. But somehow, I can't explain it, I felt this undeniable calm come over me, like I was doing the right thing. It was as if I could see everything so clear now. I looked right at Mr. McKenzie with all this new confidence—even power. "In spite of the outrageous things that have been written by some in the community, Charles Vickers has never been a police suspect in the disappearance of Lynn Mitchell."

No one responded this time. I paused to let that statement sink in, then made one final attempt to appeal to what Dr. Webber called 'their better angels.' "I believe we're all better than the worst thing we've ever done. We all deserve a second chance... even Charles Vickers."

Chairman McKenzie's face flushed. Eyes wide and shoulders tensed. I thought he might explode, but caught himself. "Is there anyone else who would like to speak?" His voice was a low, controlled growl.

Mr. Livingston leaned over to him and whispered something.

The chairman repeated it, but louder. "Is there anyone else who would like to speak?" No one did.

"Something's wrong," I whispered to Kate when I sat down. She nodded.

"Then we'll move on to our regular agenda," McKenzie said,

banging his gavel. I grabbed Kate's arm and we hurried out of the room. I had to clear my head.

"I can't sleep," I said, throwing off the blanket. I had been staring at the clock on the dresser for two hours, but all I could think about was that council meeting.

"Are you okay?" Kate mumbled, barely awake.

"I'm fine. I just need to clear my head. Think I'll go for a walk or something."

"Okay," she hummed and rolled over, already back to sleep.

It rained an hour ago, and the air still hung heavy and wet as I walked slowly down the alley behind our house. I breathed it in to fill my lungs, like I did on that bus going to Kentucky a lifetime ago.

I made a B in Abnormal Psych, Doc! Congratulations, I knew you could do it, I heard him tell me.

I came to Glacier to kill myself, Bobby said again. *But after talking with you, I'm heading back home. I owe you my life. I mean it.*

I'm going to get my counseling degree. I owe it to James... I'll miss you more than you know, Elijah.

Lettie and Damien waved goodbye as they climbed up on that bus. *I just wish I could have done more.*

His name is Charles Vickers... he can't go back to the cell block because the Aryans will kill him.

I took a deep breath, just like I did when Charles first walked out of that prison. "Breathe it all in, Charles," I said out loud, but this time I meant it for me. I looked up and spread my arms wide, as if trying to take in the entire night sky. "Thank you, God," I said. "I know why I'm here."

I turned around and started walking back home. It was still dark, but I could see everything so clear now. I couldn't wait to tell Kate all about it.

Suddenly headlights flashed directly in front of me. They had to be just six feet away. Then, without warning, they swerved right at me. I tripped over a garbage can, falling hard behind a pole. At the last second the car jerked away, but smashed into the garbage can, crushing it against the pole right in front of me. "God...!" the driver screamed—I couldn't make out the words. Then he revved his engine hard and sped off, squealing tires all the way down the alley. I laid there for several minutes, too afraid to move, shaking too much to even stand. *Maybe he's coming back for me!* I leaned on what was left of that garbage can and forced myself up off the ground. "Nothing broken," I said, feeling all over my body, then hobbled as fast as I could down the alley.

"Did you report it to the police," Kate asked when I shook her awake and told her what happened.

"Not yet. I wanted to tell you first."

"You've got to call right away so they can find him."

"Okay, but I can't even say what type of car it was. I think it was white, but the alley was dark, and it happened so fast."

I was hoping Good Cop would come, but this time Lazy Cop was alone. Even in the dim light of my front porch, his eyes were plainly bloodshot, and the few questions he did ask sounded a little slurred. I wanted to think he was just tired, but I saw that look too many times in Clairton. He took the report, but it had nothing in it. "An unknown type of car, possibly white, driven by an unknown suspect, possibly a white male, may have driven too fast down an alley and nearly hit someone walking in the dark. There may be some damage to the front bumper."

Another sleepless night.

———

We didn't say much at breakfast. I was glad the kids weren't up yet. I didn't want them to know anything about last night.

"I've got a bad feeling about all this," Kate finally said, breaking the silence. "It's one thing to smash a window, or paint vile words on our house. But someone tried to kill you! These people are really sick—and dangerous!"

I said nothing, but I was thinking the same thing.

"I know we talked about helping Charles, but you could get killed. I never agreed to that, Daniel. I'm scared."

From the kitchen window, I noticed a dark row of clouds on the horizon. For some reason, they reminded me of the mill smoke in Clairton. I shivered just thinking about that place again. Bile rose up bitter in my throat.

"You know... it's been twenty years."

"What did you say?" she asked.

"I said it's been twenty years, but I can still remember it like it was yesterday." I kept staring out the window.

"I don't understand."

"Twenty years since I was in Pastor Duncan's office. But I can still see every detail of that room. I can even smell the aftershave he wore. Old Spice. God, I hate that smell. I'm thirty-seven years old, but even now, every time I close my eyes, I still feel like a seventeen-year-old kid getting raped by the one man I trusted."

I turned and looked at her. "You know, Kate..." I breathed a long sigh. "...you never really get over something like that. They say you do... but you don't. A wounded body can heal, but a broken soul stays broke, and I've spent my entire life trying to undo the damage he did to me." I sighed again. "Some things... we just carry them forever."

She didn't move. Her eyes fixed on mine.

"You know, it's not really about sex. Rape, I mean. It's about power. People with power are always raping those of us who have none. The city council is just the latest in a long line of powerful people trying to rape little people like me, or Lettie, or Charles."

I was back in Clairton again, hiding in the corner of my bedroom, alone and so afraid. I dropped in the chair next to her, reaching for her hand.

"I know I haven't been here for you and the kids lately. I know living with me hasn't been easy most of the time. But one thing I'm sure of. You're the best thing that ever happened to me. Without you... none of this makes any sense."

Tears filled my eyes as I fought for the right words. "The other night, I didn't tell you the real reason I've been so obsessed with this fight with the city." I forced myself to breathe. "It's not just about giving Charles a safe place to live. It's more personal than that."

She took my hand in both of hers and squeezed. Her skin felt so soft, so warm, so safe. I took another slow breath. "It's about saying no to Pastor Duncan, and Elizabeth, Rev. Nicholson, and three generations of neglect and abuse I call my family. It's about everyone who tried to crush my soul."

I could feel my heart pound hard against my chest. She squeezed my hands tighter.

"That guy who tried to run me down last night was no different. If I quit now because I'm afraid, then what will be left of me?" I leaned back in the chair and closed my eyes. Tears ran down my cheek. "But I can't do this alone, Kate." I breathed out the words. "I'm not strong enough without you."

She pulled me close, then gently kissed both of my cheeks. "I'm so sorry, Daniel. I didn't know. We'll fight this together. I'll never leave your side. Never." she whispered softly in my ear, then kissed my cheek again and again, mixing my tears with her own.

———

There were no more incidents after that. I focused on my response to what I knew would be the final council vote. Baintree had already drafted our next lawsuit. "Tortious interference," he called it. "The city is intentionally writing a law that is targeted toward you. I know we'll win in court. But this time we're going for damages. My fees, your lost income, pain and suffering, the whole bit. At least a million dollars."

"Is that really necessary?" I asked. "It's not about money. Not for me, anyway. I just want men like Charles to get a second chance. That's all I care about."

"Money is what matters to those pricks. Sometimes you have to hit them in the nuts with a two-by-four if you want to get their attention. And a million dollar lawsuit will definitely get their attention."

I still wasn't convinced. "Won't that make it look like they're right— like I'm only doing this for the money? What if we sued for a dollar, to make a point?"

"Listen, Daniel, you can make all the points you want in one of your classrooms. But when it comes to these assholes, who think they can write any law they want, with no regard to the Constitution, then you have to speak the language they understand. Trust me. A million dollar judgement is the universal language."

———

When Kate and I arrived at the council meeting for the final vote on October 2. I noticed that ordinance had an emergency clause attached so it could go into effect immediately if approved. *Those pricks!* I had no idea that was planned, and I doubt Baintree did either. The room was again crammed with that same angry mob, talking loud, looking anxiously at the council members now filing in through the back door. They all wanted just one thing—a vote that will finally make Salem Hill the city of peace again. There were several television crews and a dozen more reporters stuffed along the back wall, already scribbling notes, and ready to record what all of them knew would be the lead story on tonight's eleven o'clock news. The room fell silent to Chairman McKenzie's gavel, but tension and heat still fumed the air.

"Is there anyone present who would like to speak to council before we begin our meeting?" No one came forward, just like the last meeting. I was the only one to stand. But this time I didn't plan to reason with them.

"Baintree's right," I whispered to Kate as I got up and walked toward the podium. A dozen people standing in the aisle glared, but stepped back to let me pass.

"As you all know, I'm opposed to this proposed legislation," I said calmly, looking directly at Chairman McKenzie. "Not only will it put the community at more risk, but I'm convinced it's an unjust and immoral law intended to deny what God, and the state of Ohio, has deemed the inalienable right of every person to a second chance in life." I paused to let my words settle, then looked directly at Mr. Livingston. "That said, my attorney has asked me to warn you this proposed zoning law will never survive a legal challenge. He said I'm to make it very clear if you should pass it, as you intend to do tonight, we will immediately file a one-million dollar lawsuit. He guarantees me that six months, a year, or even ten years from now, when we finally do enter a courtroom, simply calling your decision here tonight a 'procedural error' will not make your financial responsibility go away this time."

Livingston's face flushed crimson with anger. He clenched his fist so tight, he broke the pencil in his hand. He didn't say anything, but it was clear to everyone in the room my comments were directed right at him.

Ten minutes later the council voted what they thought of my threat. The ordinance passed five to zero without any comments. But the audience wasn't silent. They all erupted into cheers, nearly with one voice. Chairman McKenzie wasn't in any hurry to bang his gavel for quiet this time. He seemed to be enjoying the moment. "Forget about staying for the rest of the meeting," I said to Kate, but my words were smothered in all the yelling from the crowd. I motioned toward the door and grabbed her arm, as we both made our way out of the room.

Cheryl Atkins met us in the hall. "Mr. Robinson, do you have any comment about the vote tonight?" She shoved a microphone in my face. The room suddenly flooded with blinding light, surprising me for just a second. But I expected this vote, and I was ready to speak to the reporters. I took a small breath to calm my nerves, and looked right into the camera.

"Obviously, I'm disappointed, but I'm not surprised. Too often with emotional issues such as this, a bad law can result, as was the case tonight. So we have no choice, but take the city to court again. This time we'll be seeking a million dollar judgement. We're very confident we'll prevail—again." I hadn't planned to add that last comment, but I was so tired of the arrogance of the council, and especially Livingston, I said it without even thinking.

"Do you have any comment on the news about Lynn Mitchell?"

"What news?" My face grew hot hearing that poor girl's name again. I had no idea what she was talking about.

"We have a report that deputies found her body today in a barn owned by a local man named Harold Davenport. He's been arrested and charged with her murder. Do you have any comment on this?"

My mind reeled, while I tried to grasp her words. The camera lights glared right at me, while she pushed her microphone again into my face. I didn't know what to say. Since that girl disappeared, I'd been accused, harassed and threatened, even nearly killed. All because everyone was convinced a black ex-convict from Cleveland was obviously guilty—and it was my fault because I brought him here. No local person, no one born and raised in Shawnee County, no one without a criminal record, would ever do something this terrible. Apparently, they were wrong. It was too much to take in. I wrestled with her new information, trying desperately to think and talk at the same time. "I-I'm very sorry to hear they found her body," was all I managed to say. "We were all hoping—"

"God's vengeance!" I glanced back toward the door just as a man barreled from the room, shouting. In a few seconds, he was standing in front of me, his face knotted with fury.

In a blink, he pulled a pistol from inside his coat, pointing it right at me.

All at once, the hall filled with a dozen or more screams and running footsteps. One man standing next to me... He tripped on the camera wires, then fell back into the attacker.

The room exploded! Smoke seared my eyes, singed my nose. For just a second, there was an awful silence. Just a deafening ringing in my ears.

How did I end up on the ground? I could barely see people, but they were screaming now, running, pushing...all around me.

Several cops rushed out into the hall. One of them knocked the gun from his hand. Another one wrestled him to the ground. "God's vengeance!" he screamed again and again.

I laid there, dazed, scared. The gun powder smoke still burned my nose. My ears rang. I couldn't hear, couldn't see. I felt caught in a silent world of my own, while people ran all around, knocking me left and right. I just stared at everything, but not seeing anyone, not feeling anything. *Was I dead?* Slowly, I lifted first my right hand, then my left. *Alright, they're fine.* I reached slowly for my legs. *I could still feel them. I'm okay. I'm okay.* I tried to get up, but I was too weak, too confused. *Where's Kate?*

"Kate, are you alright?" I called out over all the madness around me.

No answer. "Kate!" I called her again, this time louder, but still no answer. I forced myself to sit up, frantically searching everywhere for her. *Please, God. She was right beside me!*

Then I saw her... on the floor behind the television camera... in a pool of blood. Her red hair was matted against her ashen face. Those beautiful green eyes, now empty.

The entire room was suddenly silent. I was on her front porch again on our first date.

The golden hue in her red hair glistened in the evening sun. She never looked more beautiful.

I was standing with her in front of the church, both of us crying, while Nick said the words I'd waited all my life to hear. *I would like to introduce to you Mr. and Mrs. Daniel Robinson!*

Now I was back in our kitchen. Her warm lips gently kissed my cheek as she whispered in my ear. *I'll never leave your side. Never.*

"KATE!" I screamed. My heart—hot, burning hot—no, now so very cold. It's beating. I can feel it pumping—but God, oh God, I'm dying!

"Kate!" I crawled over the floor. Almost there—

I grabbed her neck and tried to lift her, but she was limp in my arms. "Kate!" I wailed, as I buried my face in hers, mixing my tears with her blood. Oh God, there's so much of it. That horrid smoke was burning my nose. I can't breathe.

"Don't leave me, Kate! Please! Don't leave me!"

CHAPTER 27
SINNERS IN THE HANDS OF AN ANGRY GOD

SALEM HILL, 1985. A light breeze rustled through my hair and the yellow mums dotting the neat little front yard. The fall air so fresh and alive, and I swayed a little, just inhaling it all. I walked slowly up to that door, where everything that gave my life meaning waited for me. But it opened before I could even knock.

"Right on time." said the most beautiful woman in the world. She smiled shyly, tucking some of her red hair behind her ear. Why? What does she have to be shy about? As if on cue, evening sunlight broke through some clouds and decorated a golden strand in her hair. Her green eyes had an emerald sparkle to them.

I opened my mouth to speak—

"Mr. Robinson? Are you listening?"

I blinked. David Henderson's office suddenly pressed in on me. The fluorescent light overhead did little to hide the gloom imbedded in the marrow of these bleached pale walls. Too many broken people sat in this chair before me, desperately trying to make sense of their now shattered lives. Shelves filled with folders detailing all of them lined the wall opposite me, all in alphabetical order, and perfectly in line. Not one thing out of place.

"Mr. Robinson?"

I pinched the bridge of my nose, sighing deeply. "Oh... Sorry. I... ah... I guess I blanked for a minute. What did you say?"

Henderson nodded. After thirty years as Salem Hill's primary funeral director, he was probably well used to this sort of thing by now. "We simply need to know where you want the burial."

I tapped a finger on the arm of the chair. "There are many lovely plots available in the Salem Hill Cemetery." His words drifted past me. I was back at the Oakland Wilderness—where we walked together so many times, where we shared our thoughts and our love. That forest exploded again in a sea of fall colors as we stood there, in silence, just breathing in this sanctuary. Her words echoed in my head. *Our commitment is written in ink. And you can't erase ink.*

It would be beautiful burying her in that special place—our place. But that's too far away now—and I want her near me. And I could never bury her in the Salem Hill Cemetery like Henderson suggested. Never.

Then where? *My God! Who plans a funeral for his 33-year-old wife?* Minutes ticked by. I stared at the blank white plaster wall behind Henderson. He moved a few things around on his desk. More time passed.

"No," I said finally. Henderson raised an eyebrow. The words just flowed now. "I'm not leaving her alone in some cold, lonely cemetery in that god-forsaken part of town. She belongs with *me*. No, I want her cremated, and I want her ashes kept with me—in our house. That was our sanctuary from all that hatred and violence. That's where I want her —in a special urn. Um... something... with... with a rose to match the red of her hair. Red roses were her favorite. And with green leaves and vines that match her eyes." I leaned over the desk now. I had to make him get it. "Those eyes looked right through me on our first date and stole my heart. The green has to be the same color as her eyes. Do you understand?"

Henderson shifted in his seat. "I'll see what our staff can produce. And our artists can consult you on the proper palette that you want," he said carefully.

But I wasn't done yet. "And I want it engraved," I said, my ideas coming clearer with each word. "I want it to say *Together for all eternity,* because someday my ashes will be put in there with hers. And... a locket!" With each word, my voice got louder, more insistent. "A gold locket that will match the hue in her hair that always took my breath when the sun touched it gently. And with the same engraving. I'm going to put some of her ashes in it...so I can wear it around my neck every day..." I took a slow, deep breath. "...until we're finally together again. That's what I want! Do you understand?"

I had to stop to breathe. Mr. Henderson waited for me, then nodded. "Anything you want, Daniel," was all he said. For the first time since that horrid night in the city building, I felt... I felt in control of *something* in my life!

———

"At times like this, we all try to make sense of what happened." Doc Samuels stopped, looked at me, and my three children. I had one arm around Susan and another around Jonathan. Emma was sitting in my lap, her face buried in my chest. She probably felt my new gold locket there, where part of her mother rested forever. It was a solid, reliable anchor around my neck every waking moment. I held my kids—Kate's kids—as tight as I could. It was all any of us could do, just hold onto one another for survival. I was *their* anchor, now more than ever. But I couldn't look at their faces. Not now. I saw Kate in every one of them...and it was too much...

Doc was speaking again. "Where is God now? It's a natural question. One I've asked too many times."

Where is God? I looked all around the chapel. I hadn't been in this room since Mum died more than two years ago. Nothing changed. There was the same book at the entrance where everyone signed their names, the same table with all the pictures of a life that was nothing more than a memory now, the same line of people all looking sad, and saying how sorry they were for me and the kids.

Nick Blanton and his wife Pam sat with us at the service. I called them right after Doc.

Even Maggie was there. "I had to come," she said when she saw me. "I got the two of you together, didn't I?" That diner—and my life—was so gray... until I saw her standing by the kitchen door, waiting anxiously for me to accept her dinner invitation. But now...

I gave Maggie a stiff smile and made some excuse. I didn't want to think about that day. I couldn't.

"All I can say is God *is* with us the most when we can't see Him, when we feel so lost and alone, when we can't go another step. That's the God I believe in. That's the God I think we all need at times like this...the God of broken lives."

Charles was there too, next to Jonathan. Our eyes met a few times, but... I had nothing to say... to him or anyone else. The only times I really spoke to anyone, other than some guttural response, was to my children. I told them something about staying strong and brave for Mama, and that I'm here for them. I know I must have said that. But the words were wooden. To Doc, Charles, Nick, my other friends... I said whatever they needed to hear. They were with us when it counted. That's all that mattered.

"If all of you will stand with me as we say good-bye to Kate," Doc said. My legs wouldn't support me, but I had to stand... I had to be strong for my children. Slowly, I managed it, clutching Emma tight with one arm. On my right, Jonathan had his face tucked against my coat. Susan's face was downcast. Her eyes, when she happened to look at me, were glazed, distant, unseeing. I put my left hand on her shoulder and squeezed. *God, oh God... they're just kids... babies. They don't deserve this!*

I felt a hot tear rolling down my cheek, then another, and a third. I shook, just a little at first, then hard. I couldn't help it. In my ear, I heard Emma sobbing too, almost a sharp wail. Maybe if I wasn't holding her, I would have collapsed from the weight of my pain... and my guilt. I asked Kate to come with me that night. There were plenty of warning signs. She didn't need to be there, but she did it for me. For me!

The room felt so cold now. My tears stung my face.

At the front of the funeral chapel, Mr. Henderson had placed a tall white urn. Green vines and leaves swirled around it in beautiful paint-work. The last time I saw that green... I was bent over Kate's empty face, back in the City Hall. A huge rose sat in the center, blooming as proudly red as her hair.

I stayed with the artist, refusing to move, until he finally had the perfect color. I was *not* having anything less for Kate. Those eyes looked right through me on our first date and stole my heart. Oh God, why didn't I look into them more while I had the chance? Why didn't I...?

Nick started singing. Soon everyone joined in. *Nearer my God to Thee, nearer to thee...* I sung it a hundred times growing up in the Clairton Baptist Church. I even had the people sing it at the couple funerals I held in the Methodist Church in another lifetime. I knew all the words by heart, but for some reason, I couldn't remember any of them. I just stood there, staring at that beautiful urn with the red rose and the green leaves so perfectly detailed. It was exactly what I wanted.

Together for all eternity.

Because we were... and we will be again... when my time comes, and my ashes are mixed in with hers... we *will* be together. Forever.

I blinked back into the present. Around the urn, people had laid pictures of Kate and a life I would never have now. I couldn't make a sound. I just listened to Nick's words, especially that last verse.

Though like a wanderer, the sun goes down, darkness be over me, my rest a stone.

"Oh God, that's me!" I was empty. No more tears, or despair, or anything. All I could feel now was Emma's warmth against me, and closer still, the locket, the safeguard of my love. My legs trembled, but I forced myself to stand firm, holding tight onto Susan and Jonathan. I *had* to be strong—for them.

Nearer my God to thee. Nearer to thee... But I wasn't listening anymore.

Nick and Pam drove us back to our house in silence. I sat in the middle seat with Emma now asleep on my lap. Charles was next to me. Jonathan and Susan were in the back row seat of the van. No one said anything. We all just stared straight ahead. Nick checked the rearview mirror once, raising his eyebrows at me. I nodded and mouthed, "I'm fine," then looked out the window, sighing softly. Maybe tonight we'll get some sleep. But I knew none of us would sleep for a long time.

When we pulled up to the house, Nick and Pam both offered to stay longer with us. I thanked them, but I said we needed to rest. Nick nodded, and Pam promised to call us every week, "to see how you're doing." I watched them drive off, then turned toward the kids waiting on the steps. "There are chips in the pantry, and cokes in the fridge. And watch whatever you want on television," I said toward the kids. "Charles, I'll be upstairs for a while.... to change clothes." I thought Susan wanted to say something, but she just nodded, her eyes studying me.

I dragged my feet up the sixteen steps to my room, but all I saw was Kate's face when I finally installed that Victorian hall rug and matching wallpaper she found in a magazine. "I never thought this creaky old house could look more beautiful than it does right now," she said as she hugged me. But now... it just looked empty.

Walking to our closet, I reached for that soft green dress she wore on our first real date at Machus Red Fox. It hung perfectly on her shoulders and made her emerald eyes glisten. I held it to my face, breathing in her scent. She looked so perfect... that night.

I fell back into my chair, rubbing my eyes. Beyond exhausted. Numb. Today pulled me in a thousand directions, and now I needed to just breathe. This room was the only place I felt safe, in this home we shared together, this broken house no one wanted. We gave it new life together, this... this symbol of our fractured lives that our love redeemed. This room that sheltered us from all the hatred and violence that surrounded us, had been our sanctuary. Now, it was just some dark cave.

I stared at the bed we shared all those nights. We held each other here, safe in our love. This was our healing place. No matter what they said or did, they could never take that from us. But now Kate was gone, my bed was empty, and there was no one here to hold me. Empty bed. Empty room. Empty.

A couple knocks on my door shattered the silence. Ah, Susan. There was a small rhythm to how she knocked. Just like her mother... There was another knock, then she slowly poked her head in. "Dad?" She didn't say anything about me sitting in the dark. "Should I get dinner ready? The kids are hungry."

Ever since Kate was... gone, she'd been calling them 'the kids,' like she had to take care of them now.

"Dad?"

"What? Oh, sorry. Dinner? Already?"

She nodded slowly. "You've been in here for two hours. I... we were... Are you okay?"

"Oh, sorry. I guess I lost track of the time. But I'm fine." I rubbed my eyes, desperate now to block out all those memories. "Maybe... if you can get something started... Then I'll be downstairs in a minute."

I stumbled into the bathroom, staring at a stranger in the mirror. I remembered another mirror in San Francisco, when I was so bloodied and broken. But that pain healed easily. What I feel now will never...

I sighed. *Get hold of yourself! The kids need you.* I splashed cold water on my face, changed my shirt, and walked slowly down those sixteen steps again.

Charles sat with the kids around the dining table. Susan had laid out several bowls of something the neighbors brought to us this morning with their sad faces and bland words of comfort. I couldn't help wondering where those people were before all this happened. Maybe if they had...

But they meant well, I guess.

"Daddyyyy," Emma hopped off her seat and wrapped her arms around my waist. "I miss Mommy."

Oh God, what do I say now? I had to be strong... for the kids... no matter how hard it was. I dropped down on my knee, pulling her close. "I miss her too, baby. I miss her... All. The. Time." My voice broke on that last word. *I don't know if I can do this... if I can be strong enough...*

I stood up slowly, still holding Emma in my arms. "Everyone okay?" It was a stupid question, but I had to say something. Susan looked down, poking at a piece of chicken with her fork. It was clear she had no appetite. Jonathan at least had taken a couple bites. But he kept looking at the chair where Kate... always sat. Emma's plate was empty. There was that, at least.

And Charles nodded quietly toward me, probably trying to read me like he did when we first met in prison. I gave him a small smile. "Well, you guys," I cleared my throat, wincing at how scratchy it felt. "I know it was hard today... but you did well. All of you. I... I am so proud of you. I mean it."

Jonathan and Emma were staring at me. Emma never heard me talk so 'grown-up' to her before, but there had been a lot of that these past few days. Jonathan was never good with his emotions. I know he wanted to say something, anything, but he couldn't. Not yet anyway. Susan wasn't looking at me at all. *What do I tell them? What can I tell them?*

"This has been hard f-for me too..." My voice cracked. "...and... and it's... not going to get any easier... for a long time" My eyes burned as a tear rolled down my cheek. "But... but we need to stick together and just... just help each other right now. Okay?"

They all nodded. "Good." I said, lowering Emma back into her chair. "Hey, I'm gonna talk to all your teachers. I think we need to stay here for a couple days. You know, just be together. I'll pick up your homework. Okay?" It was all I could think to say. But it was what they needed...what we all needed. Jonathan offered a small smile.

"Sounds like fun," Charles announced. "Why don't I help you guys?" He tried to sound excited, but he wasn't very convincing—until he turned toward the kids and winked. "Maybe we can watch TV and do your homework at the same time," he whispered.

"Yeah!" Jonathan chirped. That was the most emotion he had shown all week. Emma clapped, but I doubt she really knew what was happening. Even Susan managed to raise a half-smile. "Thank you," I mouthed at Charles.

"But they have to do ALL their homework, Charles...." I offered an exaggerated frown toward them. "...or I won't order that pizza I planned for tomorrow night." This time both Jonathan and Emma were ecstatic with the idea of pizza, and Charles played along. Thank God for him.

Acting normal like this was exhausting. I looked toward Charles, who took Jonathan and Emma into the living room. Now it was just Susan and me. Sliding back a chair, I sat down next to her. "Dad, you didn't eat your dinner yet," she tapped my plate with her fork.

"Thanks, sweetheart. I'll eat it later. I promise." I gave her a side hug. "Sometimes... you remind me so much of your mother." Then I lowered my voice, just for her to hear. "I'm really, really proud of you. Your mother... would have been..." The words stuck in my throat.

Her lips quivered. Then she started to cry, silently, but harder, and harder, until her whole body shook. "Shhh... shhh..." I pulled her close.

"It's okay, Susan. I..." *Oh, Kate... how could you leave us?* I bit my lip, blinking my own tears away. No, not now. Susan needed me.

From the living room, the TV volume rose a little bit. Charles must have heard her sobbing.

"I just... miss... her..." She choked out between sobs.

Some days, I forgot she had known Kate longer than anyone else... even me. "Shhh... I know, honey." I gently stroked her back again. "Me too, Susan. Me too."

———

Susan cleared the table, just like she did hundreds of times, and Jonathan and Emma watched something on the television with Charles. I sat there alone, watching all of them. *They really are good kids. But how am I going to raise them alone? I can't do this alone. But I don't have a choice. I'm all they have.*

It must have been near bedtime when I finally made it to the living room. Charles had taken the kids upstairs, leaving Susan on the couch, staring at the television. She could barely hold her eyes open, so I carried her to her room, laying her on the bed, where she fell asleep in a few seconds. Then I brought her plate upstairs and set it on her desk. *EAT*, I wrote on a note, in big letters. Then, *Love, Dad.*

Kate would've killed me for giving her a cold dinner.

"Hey." I found Charles at the dining table again, looking nothing like the happy person he had acted at dinner. He seemed as weary as I felt. I fell into my chair, dropping my head onto my chest as I caressed the locket under my shirt. "Thanks for all your help," was all I managed to say.

He shook his head. "You have really amazing kids, Daniel. They make it easy."

I lifted my head and looked at him. "They're the only thing keeping me alive right now."

He leaned over, putting his hand on my shoulder, as both of us fell quiet. Staring at nothing now, a thousand faces flooded past me. Kate... Brookfield... Baintree... Lettie... Charles... Kate... McKenzie... Charles... Doc... Kate... Susan... Daequan... Kate...

Finally, I was the one to break the silence. "What I did tonight, with the kids... I've got to do it again... and again... and again." My voice was just a dull whisper. Charles stared at me. Was he worried? Should he be worried?

"But..." I looked toward him. "...they're all I got... I waited all my life to have these three amazing kids. Kate's kids. My kids."

I reached into my shirt and slipped out the locket. *Together for all eternity*. It weighed nothing... and everything, all at the same time. "I wasn't here for her so much of the time, even when I was here... and I lost sight of the one person that mattered most." I shook my head.

"What I'm trying to say..." I looked him dead in the face. He stared back... and waited. "My three kids..." I breathed in. "...are the most beautiful memories Kate l-left me. And—and I owe it to them... to her... to make sure they get through this. For her memory." My fist clenched around the locket, cool against my skin. "For her memory."

Charles' hand tightened on my shoulder. I heard a sob. Was he crying? Was it me? I don't know. *I don't know anything anymore...*

———

"Kate!" I sat up with a jerk.

Sweat soaked my bed. I threw off the blanket, frantically scanning the darkened room. The clock on the dresser blinked 3:10 am. Without thinking, I checked my hands for blood. When would it end? Every night... just like this. That blinding light in my face. Anthony Turner running toward me. The screams. I always woke to the deafening blast of a gun, and the burning smell of gunpowder. I checked my hands again because I knew they were covered with her blood. I saw it.

I tried to go back to sleep, but without even thinking, I reached across the bed for her, and touched.... Nothing. Staring at the ceiling now, I just laid there, squeezing the locket in my hands.

Together for all eternity.

———

I tried to go back to work, but I was wooden, just going through the motions. My students never complained, but sometimes I saw them staring at me, shaking their heads, like they didn't know what to say. Too many times, I found myself reaching for the phone to call Kate, without even thinking, like I did so many times during the day, to talk about something, or nothing. Just to talk. I would punch in our number, and it would ring. Then I'd realize she wasn't there to answer it, and all those feelings of loss would flood over me again.

At home, it was a different matter. What I really wanted to do was hide in my room—our room—and sleep forever. It would've been so easy to stick the kids in front of the TV all day, every day. But I couldn't. Not when they needed me. I forced myself to go about the business of the living. Like sitting at the dining table making crayon drawings with Jonathan and Emma, or helping Susan with her math homework.

What I wasn't prepared for was something as simple as making breakfast. All I ever needed to start my day was some coffee and a piece of toast, and I was out the door to work. Not Kate. She made breakfast a major presentation, like she did everything in life. And that was something the kids expected me to do now.

"You want what for breakfast?"

"French toast!" all three of them called from the dining room.

"Wait, French toast? I opened the pantry and pulled out a bag of bread. Well... Kate mentioned eggs once... I grabbed a carton from the refrigerator. Now what? I went back to the pantry shelves and searched through all the jars and cans. Were there any special spices in French toast?

"Daddy, I'm hungry," Emma called.

"One minute!" I glanced at the clock. Damn. I scratched my head as I scanned the pantry. Didn't Kate have a recipe book somewhere? I yanked open several drawers.

"You okay, Dad?" Susan asked, sticking her head in the kitchen. She had been asking that a lot lately.

I grunted something about Kate's recipe book, shrugged my shoulders and offered her a sheepish grin.

"I see you found the eggs. That's good," she said, walking past me. "And we'll need milk, and sugar."

Without missing a beat, she cracked four eggs, poured a cup of milk into a glass bowl, added a teaspoon of sugar and a dash of salt, all while whipping it into a rich lather. In another minute she had four pieces of bread soaked and sizzling in the pan on the stove. I just stood there, watching her. *My little girl is so... so grown up now!*

"The kids like the Aunt Jemima syrup." She pointed toward the second shelf. Just then, the sun broke through the morning clouds, and her hair glimmered gold. I blinked. For a minute, Kate was right there, in front of that stove.

Susan turned, handing me a plate, and the moment passed. "Breakfast is ready." It was the best meal we had in a long time.

But I couldn't expect her to do that every day. Sure, she was a copy of her mother, but she was just thirteen. Taking care of the family..., that was *my* job.

But what about dinner? Another crisis. After reheating for a week what I learned was chicken casserole from the neighbors, Charles announced he had a couple recipes to share with us. "Not prison food." He smiled, catching my raised brow. "My Mama had me help her all the time, and I still remember how she used to cook." We all clapped.

That night, staring at the ceiling in the dark for hours again, like most nights, I heard Emma crying.

"Mommy... Mommy..." She was whining when I slipped into her room.

"Shhh, baby, it's okay. Daddy's here." I bundled her in my arms, fell back into the chair by her bed, and gently rocked her. This had become our nightly ritual. Bit by bit, her cries eased, as I tenderly touched the locket that hung from my neck and rested against hers. "I miss her, too, baby." I whispered over and over until we both fell asleep together.

The days passed slowly, one after another. We settled into a routine of sorts. We survived. Charles did his best to help with anything he could—laundry, gardening, dishes. He was becoming more than someone we helped after prison. He was one of us. Family.

Susan found her place in the kitchen teaching me how to cook. She had me practicing how to make French toast. And omelets. And grilled cheese sandwiches. The works. It wasn't easy, but I just knew I had to learn. For them.

For her.

Over time, it seemed the three kids were doing better, but I watched Jonathan closely. His eighth birthday was coming up on Thanksgiving. How would he handle it without his mother? Susan decorated the dining room for a double celebration. We hung pilgrim pictures on the walls, streamers across the ceiling, and set the holiday hats that Kate made for us beside each plate, just like we did last year. Emma even lit all the candles on the cake, just like her mama taught her to do. And Jonathan blew all of them out with one breath, just like he always did. But it wasn't the same. We did everything exactly the way Kate did, but there was no feeling in it now. There was no Kate—and we all knew it.

Maybe that's why I took Jonathan to K Mart the next morning. "What do you think, son? Your first big boy bike. Do you like it?"

He looked at me, then at the bright red 24-inch Schwinn, complete with handlebar brake controls like all the big kids at school had, then back at me again, not sure what to say. But his face said volumes. His smile was the biggest I had seen since...

"Your Mama and I were planning to buy this. And I know she's watching us right now."

He didn't say anything, but his smile disappeared. He looked suddenly serious. I knew he was thinking of his mother, just like I was. I couldn't force a smile, but I slid my arm over his shoulders. "Happy birthday, son. From both of us."

I had thought about getting him a smaller bike, or maybe waiting another year for this one, because those Schwinn models can be a lot to handle. But this year was... harder... and he needed something special. He just needs some clear instructions from me. When we got back to the house with his brand new Schwinn, I tried to show him how to use the handbrakes, and how to stand on one leg when he came to a stop. *Slow down before the intersection. And don't go past it. Just turn around and come back.* I said it three times, clear and slowly.

But he kept reaching for the handlebars, barely listening. "Okay, son. Give it a try," I finally said. Without missing a beat, he kicked up the stand, jumped on the seat, and was peddling down the street as fast as his legs could manage. For a few minutes, I actually thought he was okay. Like Kate always said, "he doesn't say much, but he can figure things out on his own. Like you, Daniel."

So I watched him, smiling as he peddled faster and faster, his hair whipping back in the wind. But when he didn't slow down near the intersection, going past the stop sign at full speed, I caught my breath. Before I could call out, he hit the curb and went flying into the air, crashing down on the sidewalk.

"Jonathan!" I ran down the street as fast as I could, scooping him up in my arms. "Are you okay, son? Do you hurt anywhere?" I asked over and over, frantically scanning his body. Just a large, jagged cut on his knee. It was shallow, but bled a lot. For a second, Kate was lying back in my arms, her face covered in blood. I shook that thought out of my head long enough to see that Jonathan was fine... until he saw all the blood. That's when he bawled out in pain.

I pressed my hand on his cut to stop the bleeding, and to calm him, but he only cried louder as I pulled him into my chest, "Am I going to die too, Daddy?"

What was I supposed to say to an eight-year-old boy who just lost his mother? What could I say? I just held him tight and rocked him. "No, son. You're not going to die... and I'll never leave you. Never."

———

It was some time in December. I'm not sure when, but Susan was gulping down the last bite of French toast I had made. "Tastes great, Dad," she said, grabbing her books off the table. "But I overslept, so I gotta run. I'll make my bed when I get home from school. Promise."

"I'll take care of it," I called to her as she ran out the door toward the school bus.

That's when I found the picture under her pillow. It was the one I took of her with Kate standing on their porch together just before we went to Oakland Wilderness for one of our many hikes there. It was worn and wrinkled, and obvious that she had been holding it close every night while she slept. My little Susan, who introduced me to dolls and tea parties, was thirteen years old and becoming a woman... without her mother. She had been so strong, so much help with the kids since Kate was gone. I never realized how much she missed her mother too—until now. "Where are you, God, when we need you the most?" I muttered. It was more of a demand than a prayer. "Doc said you're with us when we feel so lost and alone, and we can't go another step. Well, God, none of us can go another step. So where are you?"

———

Everything was mostly a blur after that. We did something for Christmas. Nick and Pam got us a tree and decorated it with the kids. They bought them gifts too. I remembered watching them open their presents, but I couldn't remember what they were now. All I knew was we made it through the winter, and when the first warm breezes of April started to blow through Ohio, I was desperate to feel the sun again on my face. I needed to feel something, anything. I thought about going back to Hocking Hills and walking the trails, smelling the fresh buds on the trees, hearing the first birds of spring. That place always reminded me of Oakland Wilderness... and Kate... But it turned cold again on Friday... too cold to tromp up and down a muddy trail with three kids who didn't want to be there anyway.

"Why don't you and the kids come to Detroit this weekend," Pam asked when I called her. They had been coming to our house at least once every month since November, and they made me promise to call them between trips. At the time I complained about all the fuss, but looking back, I don't think we would have made it through the winter without them. "It's Easter. Celebrate it here, with us."

I wasn't sure what to say. I hadn't been in church since... since Kate died.

"For the kids," she said, sensing my hesitation.

"Okay," I mumbled. "For the kids."

I was surprised how much Nick's church had grown. Every pew was nearly full when we found a couple open seats next to Pam. It felt good to be here again, at least until Nick walked to the front, looked toward the congregation, smiled broadly, spread out his arms as a gesture of welcome, and said, "We are gathered together today in the sight of God, and in the presence of friends and loved ones, to celebrate..."

It was frightening how such a simple gesture, something he did at the beginning of every service, could conjure up a memory of Kate that was so clear, so vivid, so real... and so painful... Sweat beaded on my forehead. I couldn't breathe. Loosening my tie, I pulled off my jacket. The room started to spin. I saw her standing beside me in front of this church... Nick was again saying, *Troubles may have surrounded them in the past, sometimes too many to count. And sometimes they couldn't see their way out. But you brought them through it all to be here today, together.* "But we're not together!" I said too loud.

Pam quickly turned toward me, her brow raised as she mouthed, "Are you okay?" Several people in front of me turned and glared, like I had somehow sullied their special time with this God who obviously didn't give a damn about me. I struggled all my life to believe. I tried to live what little faith I had. I really did try to make a difference with other broken people I met. Then why did He let that mad man shoot Kate? What kind of God does that?

I grabbed up Emma into my arms. "Susan, you and Jonathan get your coats. We're going back home!"

———

I laid awake, staring at the ceiling late into the night, long after everyone was asleep. How could I raise my kids like this? How could I even make it through another day without Kate? Maybe I didn't deserve to be happy. I knew I hurt a lot of people. Maybe I deserved to be punished like this. But not my kids! They didn't do anything wrong. Or maybe there was no God after all. Everything Doc said... Everything Nick said... All lies. And I was the biggest liar of all—thinking I could change the twisted minds of an entire bigoted town... All lies!

When I couldn't stand it any longer, I threw off the blanket, turned on the light and grabbed my pants. I walked down the stairs to Charles' apartment.

"Are you okay?" He asked in the dark when I opened the door. He had been asking that a lot lately.

"I just need some fresh air," I said. "I'm going for a walk."

"Okay," he answered, but I knew he wouldn't sleep until I got back.

I walked up one darkened street and down another, not paying any attention to where I was going. Not caring. Just walking. I was surprised when I found myself standing in front of the city building. I hadn't been anywhere near this place since...that night. Suddenly, everything flooded over me.

Larry Miller held up that petition in front of the council.

John Brookfield accused Charles of stalking his little girl again. 'Now I can't let my kids even go out in our own backyard.'

All those ignorant people packed that room, their faces contorted, their eyes wide in anger, all screamed, 'Get that nigger rapist out of town, and Robinson too!'

That madding crowd of bigots ran toward us again. A rock smashed into my forehead. A young cop yelled, 'Follow me, sir!'

A blinding light flashed in front of me now. Cheryl Atkins shoved a microphone in my face. She told me Harold Davenport was arrested for that girl's murder. There was an explosion... and screams! Oh God! There's Kate on the ground! Blood, blood... everywhere I look, there's blood!

"Kate!" I screamed. All the rage, the violence, the unbridled hate, that had been boiling in me since Donaldson printed that first article, exploded now. I shook my fist at that place, at everyone on the council where it all started, all of them who killed Kate. "God damn all of you to hell! I *will* make you pay for what you did to her!" I screamed into the night.

That's when I knew what I had to do. It was so clear now. I was surprised I hadn't thought of it before. *If you won't act, God, then I will!*

"I want to sue everyone responsible for Kate's death," I told Douglas Baintree as soon as I could reach him in the morning. "All the council members, Livingston, Brookfield, and especially Donaldson. He stirred up all this in his newspaper, just so he could get elected to some office. We've got to hold him responsible for what happened!"

Baintree didn't say anything. There was nothing but awkward

silence on the line. I thought he would jump at the chance to stick it to Livingston again. "Well?" I asked.

"I understand how you feel, Daniel, but it's not that simple. There are a lot of legal protections in place regarding government officials. And the press—even rags like Donaldson's paper."

"But we already sued them once and won... and we were going to sue them again for a million dollars. But we never filed that suit after..." That last meeting with the council flashed through my mind again. "Why can't we do that now?"

"That was an entirely different situation. Tortious interference. It was an illegal ordinance that targeted you. That's a suit we can win. But what you're talking about now is suing individuals within the government and the media."

"You mean all those people can say anything, and make any law, no matter how dangerous, even if Kate was killed because of them, and there's nothing we can do?" I screamed into the phone.

He didn't answer. For a second, I thought he hung up, and that made me even more angry.

"That's not what I'm saying," he finally answered, his voice even, without a hint of emotion. I got the impression he had a lot of clients scream at him. "All I'm saying is there are legal protections for those people as long as they are operating reasonably within the requirements of their job. A criminal malfeasance case, like the one you're suggesting, is very hard to prove. But if that's what you want, I'll look into it."

"That's all I'm asking," I said, this time much calmer. "Thanks." I was about to hang up the phone, but I felt he wanted to say something else.

"I do have a question for you... if you don't mind." he said. "I don't normally get into anything personal with my clients, but I was wondering why you want to sue everyone now. I mean, you were always so hesitant to do that before. What changed?" There was something different in his voice. His words seemed warm, even compassionate now.

"Nothing's changed. I just want justice," I answered too quick. We both knew it.

"I understand. I really do. But is it justice you want, or revenge?"

I didn't answer.

"Okay," he finally said, but it was clear there wouldn't be any more personal questions. "I'll get back with you after I've done some research," and the line went dead. I sat there, still holding the phone in my hand.

Is it justice you want, or revenge?

―――――

I called Baintree every day. "Any word on our suit?" I asked again and again. Every time he gave me the same answer. "Like I told you, Daniel, a criminal malfeasance case is almost impossible to prove." I wanted to scream. 'That's what you're getting paid to do!' I wanted to slam down the phone! I wanted the council to pay—and pay. And I wanted it NOW!

And then Baintree's words would seep in. *Justice or revenge?*

Between calls to Baintree, I tried to act normal, but everyone could sense something different. I caught Susan eyeing me with worry too many times. Charles as well. Whenever he looked at me during dinner, his eyes probed, frowning, I avoided their gaze as much as possible. I already had Baintree's annoying question haunting me, I didn't need Charles' searching look joining in.

Jonathan stayed in his room between meals. I asked him a couple times if he wanted to ride his bike, but he just shrugged. *Readers need their space.* Kate and I made him a bookworm early. *At least he'll know how to find the library before he goes to college.*

Now Emma, my sweet sensitive Emma... When she found me sitting alone, in the dark, staring at nothing, she would climb up on my lap, and wrap her arms around my neck. "Let me hug away your hurt, Daddy," she always said.

"Oh, baby. Daddy needed that hug." And every single time, I hugged her back—hard.

I would always breathe easier after that. Somewhere in my chest, a knot would ease. And we would stay like that, holding each other, for hours, a whole night even. Those times were as close to peace as I could feel.

I tried to keep that feeling with me every day, really, I did. Anytime I felt the rage rising up, I rubbed my locket and remembered those hugs.

But whenever I finally fell asleep, the same nightmare came back. I woke up to the same empty bed, and all my anger rushed over me like a wave. Each good thought I tried to have during the day would be gone—just like Kate. Then I would call Baintree again. And he would always say, "I'm working on it," in that same maddingly calm voice.

"Okay," was all I muttered every time, but hearing that same damned response too many times, I wanted to explode.

Two weeks later when he called me, I knew it wasn't good news before he said a word. "We can't even get on a court docket. I'm sorry."

You're Sorry! That's it? I slammed down the phone. Hard.

I couldn't breathe. All I saw was Kate's bloody, lifeless body cradled in my arms, and it was all Brookfield's fault. Brookfield... He instigated all the violence with his lies. He led that mob to attack us. And now there was nothing, absolutely nothing, I could do to avenge her. I threw the phone at the table, knocking the lamp onto the floor with a crash. "I don't care what Baintree says. I *will* make him pay for what he did to Kate—somehow!"

Staring at my bedroom ceiling that night, my only thought was how easy it would be to buy a gun. Show my driver's license, sign some papers, pay five-hundred dollars, and I could have my revenge right in the palm of my hand. I'll kill Brookfield! Just like he killed Kate!

But the kids... I can't leave them... alone—without me.

Damn everything! I hammered the bed with my fists until I was exhausted, drained, empty.

Why did I ever ask her to come with me that night?

God, why did you let this happen? Just this once... please... at least tell me that.

I stared at the clock, as it slowly ticked one empty minute after another, all night long.

At 5:17am, I reached across my bed. My empty bed. "Is that your answer?" Reaching for her locket, I called out toward the ceiling. "I thought so. Thanks for nothing!"

"I need to talk to Charles. At least *he* listens to me," I muttered, grabbing my pants and walking downstairs to fake being strong one more day for what's left of my family.

After the kids were off to school, I found Charles in the yard, sitting under the maple tree. He looked up. His brow furrowed when he saw me. "You okay?" he asked and patted the bench. I dropped down beside him. I was too tired to lie any more.

"Am I okay? You really want to know?"

His eyes locked on mine. "Yeh. I really do."

"Okay, then I'll tell you." All of it came pouring out. "I remind myself every morning that I have to go through one more day that has no purpose, no meaning, because Kate was the missing part of me that I waited all my life to find. I knew that on our first date..., and I'll even tell you the exact moment I knew."

I leaned my head back and stared at the spring leaves in the tree branch that stretched over us. Just then sunlight shone down, warming my face. She was standing right in front of me again...

"It was our first date... when she opened her door, just as the evening sun suddenly broke through the clouds and landed directly on her." I closed my eyes. Every second of this vision counted. "It made her gorgeous red hair glisten in contrast to her emerald green eyes. It was like a sign... and I just knew. From that magical moment, she made everything in my life... perfect."

I looked toward him, then took a deep breath. "Perfect... and everyone in Salem Hill took her away. They killed her. Anthony Turner and all those people on the city council, Donaldson and especially Brookfield. I hate all of them so much that..." I hesitated. The only sound now was the rustling of the leaves, as a gust of wind from the west blew through the yard. "...I was actually thinking about buying a gun..." I turned away, leaving my words to hang in the air between us.

"Don't worry." I said, looking back at him. "I couldn't do it because of my kids."

His face had a thousand questions, but he didn't say anything. "This hate is eating me up inside." I sighed. "So I *have* to know. Did you ever... hate white people... for what they did to you?"

He looked at the clouds moving slowly overhead for a long time. Praying or thinking, I didn't know. Finally, he turned toward me. "For a time... Too long. I hated all you white people. Got into fights almost every week, if not every day." He rubbed his knuckles slowly, as if reliving it all again, then sighed heavily. I could almost see this... this weight of gloom press down on him. Suddenly he seemed smaller, bent under the burden of that memory. "I hated everyone... for a long time. That hate was all that kept me going..." His words drifted off, growing more distant, as if he was back in that cell in Mansfield. He closed his eyes. "...until I met Chaplain Stanton."

"Explain..."

"I still remember his exact words." His body straightened, his eyes wide. "He said, *'hate can't drive out hate. Only love can do that.'*"

I slumped back against the bench, looking up at the sky. "I wish it were that simple. God, I really do. But it's not... and we both know it."

He dropped back beside me. "Sorry. I didn't mean it to sound that way."

"Okay, Charles, then explain it to me. How can I not hate them... for what they did to Kate? To my babies? If you've got an answer—any answer, please, tell me, because I'm listening."

"You can't." Charles laid his arm on my shoulder, just like Doc did so many times. "No one could go through what you did... and not hate."

We were silent for several long minutes, listening to the rustling of the leaves and my labored breathing. Finally, Charles cleared his throat. "I'll tell you what I did with my hate. I had to give it to God. It was killing me, more than anyone in prison ever could. The same way it's killing you now."

The wind calmed, and the leaves were suddenly quiet.

"It took a while. It really did." He offered a slight smile. "And I argued with Chaplain Stanton... a lot."

The thought of him arguing was enough to make me chuckle, briefly, dryly. I shook my head. "I would love to have seen that..."

"I had to learn to forgive in prison. Day in and day out. I kept trying. And all the time they threatened me, beat me." Charles closed his eyes, rubbing the back of his neck. "Listen... I never lost anyone, not like you lost Kate. I know it ain't the same, what we went through. I can't imagine. But you got to try. If you don't, your hate will kill you... and your babies."

"They're the only reason I didn't buy that gun." A large dark cloud passed in front of the sun, casting a shadow over us. "I know you're right... about forgiving people," I said. "I've had to do that all my life. But..."

"But what, Daniel?"

I stared across the yard, seeing nothing but Kate, and sighed again. "But how do you forgive God? For allowing all this..."

"I... ah..." He looked down at his hands and wrung them in his lap. "...everything me and Mama went through. All us black folks... And you and your babies... There's so much cruelty out there. Somedays, Daniel, I just don't know."

The air drained from me. I felt suddenly so tired. So old now. So very old. "He just took and took..."

Charles watched me, his eyes teary. But all I saw was Kate... emerald eyes... her proud red hair striped with gold..." I just miss her," I whispered. "That's all." My eyes misted, and my lip quivered. *Oh, God. Oh, God... Kate...*

CHAPTER 28
REQUIEM

CINCINNATI, 1986: A warm breeze drifted in through the open window. The familiar smell of aged wood and old books tickled my nose as I stared at the picture of St. Francis above the kneeler on the side wall.

I was so nervous the first time I was in this office, especially when he asked about all the jobs I had. *I guess my life took a lot of twists and turns.* It was a stupid answer, but that was all I could think to say. And my explanation only made it worse. Something about heading in the right direction. But that didn't seem to bother him at all. He just said I was learning from what he called 'the way of the negative,' like all my mistakes were actually a good thing.

I closed my eyes for a second and pictured Kate. *I had no idea how hard that learning would be.*

I thought about talking to him several times since Kate... *died.* I could actually say that word now. I cut my work schedule to spend time with my kids, and he was in Columbus meeting with legislators a lot more now. Even when I did see him, it was just a hello here and a passing word there. No real conversations. But I was just going through the motions with my classes, and even with my kids—like I was stumbling down some dark road, lost and alone. I couldn't bear the long nights into dawn anymore, staring at nothing, but remembering everything. I had to talk with Dr. Webber.

"I haven't seen you much this past semester," he said as he walked into the room and dropped a stack of papers on his desk. "I've been very concerned. How are you doing?" My first instinct was to tell him I was fine. That's what I told everyone. Nobody really wanted to know my kids cry themselves to sleep at night. Or that I felt adrift in an ocean, with no compass, no one to guide me back home.

I looked slowly around the room. "Do you remember when I came to you three years ago, when I lost my job at that church? Remember what I said?"

He tilted his head, looking over his thick glasses. "I think you said you had more questions than you had answers. And if I recall, you also said you were going to quit my program."

"I was. But remember what you told me?"

He smiled. "I believe I said some days I wasn't sure what I believed either."

"That was something I never expected to hear. I mean, from a priest. And you even said God wasn't offended by my questions. That my questions would lead me to God. Do you remember that?"

He nodded.

I took a slow breath. "Well, that's not true. Because I've still got a lot of questions, and God hasn't answered one of them. Like why did he allow Kate to be taken from me? From my kids? And those people who killed her, why hasn't He punished them? I'm sorry, Dr. Webber, but God has only been silent for me... all my life."

His face softened as he leaned in. "So how do you feel about that?"

"How do I feel?" My body stiffened, my heart hammering. "I'm angry! That's how I feel. So angry I even thought about buying a gun!"

My words sounded louder, echoing against the plaster walls and bare wood floor. I shouldn't have said that. I waited for some reaction, but he didn't move, or even blink. I expected him to say something, but he just sat there, stroking his chin, just like Doc used to do so many times.

My face flushed, as the silence filled the room. "But I worked through all that. I'm okay now," I said, hoping to change the subject. "I'm not angry anymore."

Dr. Webber still didn't say anything for another awkward minute, maybe longer. Finally, he picked up a pencil on his desk, turning it over in his hand several times. "I don't talk about it a lot..." he said, looking at that pencil, "...but my parents died when I was just twenty years old."

"What...?"

He ignored me and kept staring at that pencil.

"They were young... just forty. It was a car accident. A drunk driver." His words halting, barely more than a whisper, seemed distant, as if he was speaking from another place. "I felt like I walked into a plate glass window that I never saw... until it shattered."

All I could manage was a slight nod. Why was he telling me this?

He laid the pencil on his desk again, then looked up at me. "Do you know what was even harder than the shock of losing my parents? It was picking up all the glass shards in my life afterward. No matter where I went, or what I did, I always seemed to step on some reminder that left me limping in pain. It could be a picture, or a letter, or even a special Christmas ornament we kept in the attic. It didn't matter what it was. It still hurt terribly when I stumbled on that memory."

He reached for that pencil again, hesitated, picked it up, then laid it back down. "I had to drop out of college... to take care of my brother and sister. You know, because they were still in high school... and they both needed me."

He looked up, past me, out the window. "Five years," he said slowly. "That's how long I worked at AK Steel in Middletown... until they were old enough to be on their own." He paused, still looking out the window. "I tried to go back to school, but my scholarship was gone— and with it any hope I had to be a doctor."

Turning toward me, Dr. Webber leaned back in his chair, pulled a handkerchief from his pocket, and wiped his glasses. "So trust me, Daniel," he placed them carefully back on the bridge of his nose, "I understand all too well how you feel about all those unanswered questions. And I'm the last person to ever blame you for being angry."

He cleared his throat, folded his handkerchief, and stuffed it back in his pocket. "So what are you going to do about it? Your anger, I mean."

I offered a long sigh, struggling to grasp what he just told me. "I don't know. Maybe if I had your faith.... maybe that would make it easier now... without her." I slumped back in my chair. "But I don't..."

Dr. Webber pulled his chair close to mine, then took my hand in both of his, something he had never done before. "I understand. I really do. There are some days, even with my faith, when I feel like I'm still picking up glass shards. What has it been, nearly forty years since they died, and there hasn't been a single day when I haven't wanted to see my mother's smile or feel my father's pat on my back and hear him say 'I'm proud of you...'" He hesitated. "...just one more time."

He looked past me again, far beyond the campus. "They were my anchor... and without them, sometimes I still feel like I'm drifting. Not sure what to do."

My mouth dropped open as I stared at the man who was *my* anchor when *I* was drifting. He gave me a second chance, when no one else would. He taught me how to give other people a second chance. Now he seemed so... so much like me.

Dr. Webber looked back toward me again, his eyes moist. "That's why I entered seminary—to help other people pick up all the broken glass in their lives. That's how I learned to live again. And what you're doing for your children, what you're doing for Charles, that's how you'll learn to live again."

I leaned forward in my chair. "Truth is, Charles is helping me more than I'm helping him. Ironic, isn't it?"

"Sometimes that's how God answers our questions." he said, smiling now. "But I believe that is where you will find your faith too."

"Maybe," I said, then stood to leave. Dr. Webber came around his desk and put his hand on my shoulder. "Have you ever wondered why we pray to the saints to watch over us, Daniel?"

He ignored the blank expression on my face. "They're never far from us," he said. "The dead, I mean. And I'm praying that Kate will watch over you." Then he hugged me. Not some prescribed ritual that a priest was required to offer a parishioner. But like a... a brother.

I hugged him back. Hard.

———

As summer passed, a quiet resignation of sorts settled over the house. We all needed to get on with our lives, for everyone's sake. I still wasn't back to full time yet, but I was in Cincinnati more now. I knew Charles would watch the kids when I worked with Dr. Webber, but I still asked. "Not even a question," he said. There were days, when he was always there for us, willing to do whatever needed to be done, without a complaint. I just shook my head in disbelief. I... all of us... would have been nowhere without him.

Susan was still teaching me how to cook. Tuna salad sandwiches for lunch—my latest assignment. And I was getting pretty good at it—once I mastered all the nuances of sandwich making. With or without onions, lettuce or plain, toasted or cold, and wheat or white. Who knew making a sandwich could be so complicated?

I had coaxed Jonathan back on his bike, and now, with Charles' help, he took to it like a champ. No more headers on the sidewalk. In return, he helped Charles with the yard work. And Emma learned her way around the kitchen as my 'First Assistant to the Chef-in-training.' I even gave her an apron with her new title.

I couldn't say everything was okay now, the way it was when Kate filled the house. But we all learned to help each other. We became... better.

I wasn't sure when it was exactly, probably after the fourth of July. "We all need to get out of the house," I announced when I found Charles putting the lawnmower back in the garage. He wiped his brow, and gave me his best what-do you think-I've-been-doing-for-two-hours look. I ignored it.

"Maybe something... like hiking."

Saying that word again, I was back in the Oakland Wilderness walking with Kate down the trails. The smell of pine needles tickled my nose, as the sound of wind rustling through a thousand trees filled the air. I breathed in that sanctuary.

Click—click—click—click. The garage door rattled as Charles pulled it down.

I blinked as that spectral vision faded. "I-I've... talked to the kids about it a couple times... but it never worked out. School starts in a couple weeks...and I think we should do it."

His face was blank, as if I was speaking a foreign language.

"Have you ever been hiking?" I asked.

He feigned a laugh. "I spent half my life in Cleveland and the other half in prison. There weren't a lot of places to go hiking."

I shrugged sheepishly. "Oh, yeah. I forgot." That day I picked him up outside the prison flashed through my mind. It seemed like another lifetime—for both of us. "Anyway, I was thinking about Hocking Hills, south of Columbus. I've been thinking about it for a long time. And I hear there's lots of trails through the woods. Supposed to be beautiful. You game?"

He hesitated, then nodded.

"Good. I'll tell the kids."

Jonathan and Emma were too young to remember Oakland Wilderness. But Susan remembered it well. "I'll make lunch for us. You know, so we can have a picnic, like we did with Mama."

———

Columbus traffic thinned with each passing mile as flat corn fields gave way to the wavy hills of the Appalachian wooded landscape. These slowed our drive and let me absorb the vista opening in front of us.

For a minute I was on that bus again, climbing out of Wheeling and a life I was desperate to leave behind. Without even thinking, I rolled down my car window and filled my lungs with air so wet, so alive, it was all I could do to just breathe it in, just like I did then. "We're going to have a great time today," I said, taking in another slow, deep breath and looking at the kids in the mirror. They were asleep, but it didn't matter. I was talking more to myself anyway.

An hour later, we finally pulled into the park, and I handed Susan the map. "Since you've got some hiking experience, you pick the trails." Her face lit up as she quickly scanned it.

"Here's a good one for you, Dad. *Old Man's Cave!*"

Everyone laughed.

"Very funny, Susan. But if I recall, the last time you went hiking with this old man, I had to carry you down half the trail."

"That doesn't count. I was only three then. Besides, it says the cave is haunted."

"Really?" Emma gasped. "I don't want to go hiking, Daddy. I'm scared."

"Don't listen to your sister. She's just teasing. There are no ghosts here... unless you count Susan, because I'm about to kill her!"

She laughed, and Charles joined in. It felt good to hear her laugh again. It had been a long time. But Emma just looked at Susan, then back toward me, not sure who to believe.

"Pick another trail," I said, opening the car door. "And without the editorializing."

She smirked. "Let's try Ash Cave. It says it's so big that Indians would have their whole tribe live there in winter."

"Will we see any Indians, Daddy? I'm scared." Emma's eyes widened again.

"Susan! Enough teasing! Give me that map."

She stuck out her tongue at Emma, handing the map to me. "No fair!" she mumbled just loud enough for me to hear.

"Teenagers." I rolled my eyes toward Charle and grabbed the map.

Of course, it didn't help when Jonathan asked if he could bring the BB gun Nick got him for Christmas. "I brought it with me, you know, in case we run into any bears today."

"No, you can't take your gun into the park," I muttered, quickly eyeing all the trail descriptions

"Here's an interesting place," I announced. "It's called Conkle's Hollow. Listen to what it says. 'Deepest gorge in Ohio... some of the most stunning scenic overlooks... gorgeous scenery and multiple cascading waterfalls.' The lower trail is just a mile alongside a stream. We can stop for lunch after that, then do the upper trail in the afternoon. That's where there's supposed to be a spectacular waterfall. Sounds good to me."

Emma still wasn't convinced, until I flipped over the map and read to her the Official Children's Disclaimer on the backside, near the bottom. "There are absolutely no ghosts, Indians, bears, or anything dangerous, contrary to what Susan and Jonathan Robinson said, anywhere in the entire park."

"Does it really say that, Daddy?" she asked. The other two howled in protest, but I cut off both of them with my best don't-you-dare-say-a-word-or-else glare that stopped them both cold. "It sure does, baby. See, right here in this official park document."

Thank God she can't read yet.

So off we marched toward the trail head—five pioneers about to conquer the wilderness. Except for Emma, who held my hand in a death grip with each cautious step, looking all around for any bears, ghosts or Indians that might be laying in wait for us.

For the next two hours we followed a stream that wound and weaved through a wooded valley, surrounded on both sides by huge rock palisades that grew taller and steeper as they closed in on us with each turn in the trail. Soon they towered over us protectively, as if welcoming us into this sheltered sanctuary. With only the sound of our footsteps, I walked silently, even reverently. Somehow this seemed a special place, where all of us could leave behind everything that was Salem Hill. But Emma held my hand tight, still looking all around for whatever might be hiding in the woods. *Don't worry, baby. I'll protect you.* I squeezed her hand as we walked together.

Susan was leading us down the trail, like she did hiking in the Oakland Wilderness, when she stepped into a clearing. Suddenly the sun shone through an opening in the gorge and landed on her at just the right angle, making her red hair glisten. She looked more like her mother every day.

Jonathan ignored us and spent his time skipping rocks in the creek. I smiled watching him. He was growing up so fast. Kate would be proud of him.

Sometime around noon, we found a flat rock just off the trail, where Susan served us the tuna fish sandwiches Emma and I made. "Not bad, if I do say so myself," I said, toasting my assistant chef with my water bottle. She giggled, relaxing now for the first time since we started our hike.

Unfortunately, Jonathan discovered that his voice could actually echo back and forth three times off the rock walls, if, and only if, he called out loud enough, and at precisely the right angle.

"Hello! Hello! HELLO!"

That kept him busy for ten minutes—until Susan threatened to throw him into the creek if he didn't shut up! This time I didn't correct her. I thought about doing it myself. Charles laughed—and Kate would have laughed too.

We spent the afternoon hiking the upper trail to the waterfall the brochure described as 'spectacular.' And it was! Here, the only sound now—thank God—was the soothing lullaby of that stream tumbling gently over the sandstone cliffs two hundred feet to the basin below, something it had been doing, undisturbed, for a million years. Wordlessly, Charles took off his shoes and socks, sat down at the edge of the creek, and slipped his feet into the water. He dropped back and spread his arms wide, as if taking in the full warmth of the sun. Eyes closed, he laid there serenely. Jonathan watched him for a few moments, then kicked off his shoes, sat down beside him, put his feet into the water and looked up at the sky too. I nodded at Susan and Emma, and we joined them beside the creek. Reaching for my locket, I held it in my open palm as it glistened in the sunlight. A perfect place to end a perfect day.

Late in the afternoon, everyone was asleep as I slowly meandered Route 33 north back to Columbus. Lulled by the quiet hum of the highway, my thoughts drifted back to another drive home from another wilderness hike.

I reached for Kate's hand and squeezed it. She slid next to me in the seat and put her head gently on my shoulder. "This was a beautiful day with you, Daniel," she whispered.

A horn blared from somewhere! Startled, I looked up at the green light glaring in front of me, then to my side.... Kate was gone—and so was my perfect day.

That damned horn blasted again, and I turned onto Interstate 70 toward Columbus and drove on home... alone.

———

It was after midnight. I was staring up at the ceiling in the dark... and remembering, when I heard Susan's voice. "Mama..."

I'm not the only one who missed her today. I made my way down the hall to Susan's room, and gently opened her door. "Mama," she called again. Sweat covered her forehead as she tossed in her bed. Her face was tight, eyes pinched, in some phantom pain.

I pulled the covers tight around her, gently wiping her forehead, and kissed the top of her head. "I'm here, Susan," I whispered and sat down on the end of the bed, so she could rest her feet against me until her nightmare passed. But it would return again... to all of us. It always did.

———

I got up early and dragged myself to the kitchen. Maybe some black coffee would clear my head. How good it felt to walk those trails. Yesterday—all of yesterday—reminded me of Oakland Wilderness... and Kate...

I poured a cup and took a long drink, feeling the caffeine rush over me, as I stared out the window into the dark sky.

"Dr. Webber said you're watching over us, Kate. Then you know Susan had another nightmare last night. And she's not alone. The other two are still struggling... We all feel so... so empty without you."

The wall clock in the stairway chimed five times.

"It's like I have to remind myself to breathe in and breathe out every day. But...but it's just so hard for me to do that sometimes."

I emptied my cup, then poured another one.

"But when I think of Susan and Jonathan and Emma... I know I can't stop breathing... for their sake."

I sat there for a long time, holding the locket close to my heart.

"I just wish you'd tell me what to do now, Kate. That we'll be okay... But I don't think we will ever be okay... not without you here with us."

———

A cold and dreary October day brought the first anniversary of her death, and with it, the full weight of my loss in the dark of our bedroom.

She stood by the kitchen door of that diner, her eyes downcast, looking so bashful, sneaking nervous glances at me. The dreariness of that city, and my life... all that disappeared on our first date.

447

'You'll do great,' I said, and kissed her goodbye when she went to her first college class. Her eyes were red and swollen. She was so afraid. But she did it! I hugged her tight that day she finally graduated—and with honors! There was that impish grin she always wore whenever she reminded me her grades were better than mine.

Oh God, how could something make me smile, but hurt so much at the same time?

Then we were back in our kitchen, the day all the ghosts in my life rushed over me. *Some things we just carry forever.* Her arms folded around me, so soft and warm, as she tenderly kissed away my pain. *I'll never leave you.*

But she did leave me!

"God, I'm so alone," I cried out to my empty room. "I can't go on for another tormented minute without her. I can't do it. I can't." I dropped my head into my hands. The locket dangled heavily from my neck. "I just need to know I'll get through this. Please, God. Give me a sign. Something. Anything..."

I slumped back into my chair, drained. Seeing nothing, hearing nothing. Just the emptiness of my room.

"Daddy?" came a voice from the hall.

Oh, Emma...

There she stood, shaking at my door, her eyes anxious. Seeing her like that, looking so alone, so scared... My eyes were suddenly wet.

"Hi, baby," I wiped my cheek and held open my arms, as she threw herself on my lap. "Oh Daddy," she buried her head against my cheek. "Are you okay?"

"I was just thinking of Mama. But I'm okay... now that you're here."

Emma wrapped her arms around my neck and squeezed until she 'hugged away my hurt.' That's what she always called it, when she found me sitting here, remembering Kate. *Oh, Emma.* I closed my eyes and hugged her back. The room was quiet. Outside, a light drizzle started to fall.

We stayed like that for a long time as I gently rubbed her back. "Go to sleep, baby," I whispered. "We're all so tired..." Rained pattered my window without end.

Her chest rose and fell against mine as I wiped my eyes again.

The clock chimed in the stairway. One, two, three times. Emma stirred, then looked up at me. "I... I almost forgot, Daddy. I found something in the closet... It's got red ribbon on it, like Mama used to wrap presents. I think Mama left it there for us." Her eyes grew wide. "Can I go get it?"

Kate always planned for Christmas months ahead, ignoring all my complaints. Was this something special she had been planning to give us? Or maybe it was something Susan put there?

One way to find out.

"Sure, Baby. Get Mama's surprise so we can open it."

It was a box, maybe twenty-four inches wide, wrapped in Christmas paper with an ornate red ribbon tied around it... and heavy. *Emma's right. This is Kate's work.*

My hands shook as I loosened the ribbon, then slowly pulled off the tape, careful not to tear the delicate wrapping paper. Emma stood alongside my chair, her arm draped over my shoulder, staring intently at her mama's surprise.

Carefully, I pulled the paper off, folded it, first the right side, then the left. I held the box in my hands, both of us staring at it, holding our breath, as I tenderly opened it.

"Oh, Emma," I murmured. "It's that picture Mama had taken of us at her college graduation." Even Charles was in the picture. Susan had insisted. *You're family now.* "And look how proud Mama is, holding her diploma, surrounded by all of us."

I slowly ran my finger over the picture, gently touching everyone in it. Susan's hair glistened in that evening sun. *Only the prettiest girls have red hair, and I can see gold in your hair, just like your mother.*

Even Jonathan smiled for the picture. *I can feel his heartbeat, Kate. He feels so... so helpless.* Holding him in my arms that first time, I had kissed him over and over, breathing in his sweet aroma of new life—of my son. "I'll always be here for you," I whispered again, just like I did then.

"And look, Emma. You were wearing that special dress Mama made for you." Remember how she said it made your blue eyes shine?"

"It doesn't fit me anymore, Daddy... but I still have it... Sometimes I like to hold it 'cause it reminds me of Mama." Almost from the day she was born, Emma has been a copy of her mother. Every time she walked into the room and looked at me, I saw Kate. The tilt of her head, the gentle look in her eyes, and even the way her lower lip quivered when she was about to cry. Staring at that picture, her lip quivered again. So did mine.

"Oh, Daddy," she breathed out, then kissed the picture. I kissed it too. Both of us just stared at this woman we both loved desperately, missed more than anything, and at the family she helped us all build. We couldn't look away.

"What's this, Daddy?" Emma turned over the frame and slowly pulled loose a piece of paper taped to the back. We both held our breath as I tenderly unfolded it.

My dearest Daniel,

When Susan and I were so alone, you showed us what it really means to be loved by someone. And now we have a real family together that no one can ever take from us. You and our children are my healing balm. You have been, and always will be, the better part of me. My love for you will never die. Merry Christmas, Daniel. I love you with all my heart.

Kate.

Holding that picture to my chest, pressed against my locket, I pulled Emma to me. "We're all going to be okay now, baby. I know that because a very wise man once told me the people we love never really die. Even though we can't see them, they're still watching over us. Like your Mama is watching over all of us right now. This picture proves it. I know that now."

Kate's aroma filled my nose and quickened my heart. Her arms wrapped around me as she kissed the tears streaming down my cheeks. I heard her—so clearly, like she was right here, curled up next to me, her head pressed against my chest. *I'm still with you, Daniel—in Susan and Jonathan and Emma. And I'll never leave you. Never.*

EPILOGUE

SALEM HILL, 2016: It's hard to believe it's been thirty years since that day I first read your note to me, Kate. It seems like only yesterday, and I still miss you as much as I did then. Not a single day goes by that I don't think of you, and especially how much your love healed my broken life. You saved me in every way a person can be saved.

It was so hard at first, sometimes it seemed I couldn't breathe without you. But then I would read your note to me again and again, and I could actually feel you here with me, holding me like you always did. You gave me the strength to go on one more day, then another, and another, all these years.

But I've got to tell you, Susan and Jonathan and Emma have been my healing balm too. They remind me so much of you. I never could have made it without them.

Susan's an attorney now. You'd be so proud of her. She worked every summer during college for Douglas Baintree, and did so well he recommended her for law school. She even helped Mr. Baintree when he took Charles' case all the way to the Ohio Supreme Court. And they won. Can you believe it? They got his conviction overturned! He said she's the best law partner he ever had.

Jonathan surprised me when he said he wanted to be a policeman.

He's a detective in Cincinnati, and he's gotten a lot of awards. I expect he'll probably be the chief someday.

Emma is our sensitive one. She has your heart for people. When I was missing you so much that first year, and she would find me sitting in the bedroom you and I shared, tears running down my cheeks, she always climbed on my lap to "hug away my hurt." That's what she called it. She's a social worker now, and a good one too. So it wasn't really a surprise when she and Charles opened a homeless shelter in Salem Hill. They call it Samaritan House because of all the stories they heard about what you and I did for Lettie and Damien in the beginning. Everyone says she can reach people no one else can help.

There are five grandkids too, all boys until Emma had our first girl this summer. She named her Kate after you. You'd be so proud of every one of them. They're all so smart. But I always knew they got that from you. I still cringe thinking about Sister Monica Ann. But you proved her wrong when you graduated from college. I know, Kate, with honors—something I never did. You always have to remind me of that, don't you?

But what the kids can't give me, and what I miss most since you've been gone, is just talking with you.

Remember what you said when we were dating, and I was so afraid I would hurt you, like all those other people? You said my life was written in pencil, and I would get lots of second chances. That's when I knew I loved you.

And when I thought I failed Lettie and Damien, you reminded me I got them off the street in the middle of winter, and that was what they needed most.

You were the reason I met Dr. Webber, and he introduced me to Charles—and Charles saved me and the kids when I was so lost without you.

All my life I waited for a sign from God to believe. When I got your note, your beautiful note, I realized *you* were my sign. *You* were my reason to believe.

I miss all those times talking with you more than anyone knows. But my heart no longer aches, not like it has all these years. My doctor said I have cancer. He said he's sorry, but there's nothing more he can do. He said I need to prepare. But I'm not afraid at all, because I've been preparing for thirty years. That's why every single day I've worn this locket with your ashes—so I would always have you right by my heart.

And when my time comes, as it will soon, I told the kids to put my ashes with yours, in your beautiful urn with the leaves the emerald color of your eyes, and that magnificent rose on the front that matched your hair. Because you were, and always will be, the rose of my life.

I've kept it in the living room of our house. All these years I never moved from here, because it was our special place. There hasn't been a day when I didn't see you in the kitchen, sit with you in the living room, or lie next to you in our bed. This was the house our love restored, just like your love restored me.

Together for all eternity. That's what I had engraved on your urn. From our first date when we sat at your table and talked all night long, I knew we would be together forever. You have been, and always will be, the better part of me.

Soon, Kate, very soon, we will be talking together again, as we walk hand-in-hand, like we did for those eight glorious years we had together.

ACKNOWLEDGMENTS

I started to write this story fifty years ago when I was twenty-five. I was living in my truck, alone with just my dog, and traveling the country "to find where I fit in." I bought some paper, a notepad and pencil, portable typewriter, and sat down to write my story. I even had a title—*The Trap*. But after too many days staring at a blank page, I realized I had nothing to say. Not yet anyway. I needed to live my life first. I needed to experience a lifetime of love and loss, joy and grief. I needed to develop calloused hands and a tender heart to tell this story. Like wine, a good story needs to mellow over time.

Finally, ten years ago, after six career changes and four thousand pages of journal notes, I sat down at my desk in Texas and started writing, and writing, and writing. That was the easy part. Actually writing the story well—that was very hard to do, and it was a team effort.

On a practical level, I want to thank all those who helped edit, edit again, then edit this story another twenty times over seven years. To Debbie Buckingham, Gayle Butler, Shirley Hendricks, and the members of the San Antonio Writer's Guild who gave me invaluable feedback, I am deeply grateful.

I am especially thankful for all the work that Ian Tan, my development editor, did to help bring this novel to fruition. He took a flat, two-dimensional story and helped me transform it into an intense emotional healing journey.

But actually publishing this story, like everything else in my life, was a never-ending series of rejections by the mainstream agents and publishers. That is, until I realized a story about an outsider struggling to fit in, written by an outsider who struggled all his life to fit in, would only appeal to an outsider publisher. So, like Daniel Robinson, I made my own way and founded Don Quixote Press, because outsiders should be able to tell their story too. *We tilt at windmills passionately.* It's not just a motto, it's a mission. We have started with my book, but it is our hope to help more outsiders tell their stories as we go down another road on our journey.

I also want to thank Candice Jarrett, with ElectraFox, who felt the passion of this story and helped me present it to all the other outsiders who can identify with Daniel Robinson.

On a personal level, I want to thank David Seamands, my college mentor, whose conversations on healing and forgiveness were like a fresh spring in a barren desert. To Bob Westfall, a fellow pastor during a time when I tried to fit into what I called the "normal world," who taught me that people don't care what you know until they know you care.

And especially Bob Webber, my graduate school mentor and spiritual guide on my long, and sometimes frightening journey from a dogmatic faith of the mind, of doctrines and debates, of winners and losers, to a forgiving and compassionate faith of the heart.

Most of all, I want to thank my wife, Kathy, for all she has endured on our forty-six year journey together. She welcomed me in from the outside and walked hand-in-hand with me through all the career changes, financial crises, repeated moves to find a place we could call home, and especially all the legal battles with too many government entities who tried to prevent us from offering a safe place for men and women coming from prison. Her love and support saved me in every way a person can be saved. She healed my shattered life. She is my "Kate," my reason to believe my life has meaning and purpose.

I think the ancient African proverb describes my journey best. "If you want to go fast, go alone. If you want to go far, go together."

I hope you enjoyed reading Daniel Robinson's story as much as I enjoyed writing it.

John David Graham

ABOUT THE AUTHOR

JOHN DAVID GRAHAM is the founder and executive director of Good Samaritan Home, a non-profit social service agency in Ohio, offering ex-offenders reentry housing and mentoring support. He is the author of an academic book, *Citizen Circle: A Mentoring Model for Rehabilitating Ex-offenders in Darke County, Ohio*, that documents the positive impact that mentoring ex-offenders has on the community.

Prior to that he was a door-to-door salesman, a children's home counselor, substitute school teacher, truck driver, fireman, building contractor, minister and a journalist. Sometimes the road home takes many twists and turns.

This novel, although fiction, is the very real story of too many of us who struggle to overcome generations of poverty, neglect or abuse that have left us totally incapable of the life, and love, we desperately want. It is everyone's story because we all deserve a second chance.

John is a member of the San Antonio Writers' Guild and the Writers' League of Texas.

He can be contacted at his website: www.johndavidgraham.com.

Made in the USA
Middletown, DE
18 March 2024

51132383R00276